Fobbit

Fobbit

David Abrams

Harvill Secker
LONDON

Published by Harvill Secker 2013

2 4 6 8 10 9 7 5 3 1

Copyright © David Abrams 2011

Author has asserted his right under the Copyright, Designs and Patents
Act 1988 to be identified as the author of this work

First published in 2012 in the United States of America by
Grove/ Atlantic Inc.

First published in Great Britain in 2013 by
HARVILL SECKER
Random House
20 Vauxhall Bridge Road
London SW1V 2SA

www.vintage-books.co.uk

Addresses for companies within The Random House Group Limited can
be found at: www.randomhouse.co.uk/offices.htm

The Random House Group Limited Reg. No. 954009

A CIP catalogue record for this book is
available from the British Library

ISBN 9781846557217 (hardback)

The Random House Group Limited supports The Forest Stewardship
Council (FSC®), the leading international forest certification organisation.
Our books carrying the FSC label are printed on FSC® certified paper.
FSC is the only forest certification scheme endorsed by the leading
environmental organisations, including Greenpeace.
Our paper procurement policy can be found at:
www.randomhouse.co.uk/environment

Printed and bound by Clays Ltd, St Ives plc

for Jean
for this, for everything, forever

Wars are nothing, in the end, but stories.
—Frederick Busch

In a hole in the ground there lived a hobbit. Not a nasty, dirty, wet hole, filled with the ends of worms and an oozy smell, nor yet a dry, bare, sandy hole with nothing in it to sit down on or to eat: it was a hobbit-hole, and that means comfort.
—J. R. R. Tolkien

Fobbit

1

GOODING

They were Fobbits because, at the core, they were nothing but marshmallow. Crack open their chests and in the space where their hearts should be beating with a warrior's courage and selfless regard, you'd find a pale, gooey center. They cowered like rabbits in their cubicles, busied themselves with PowerPoint briefings to avoid the hazard of Baghdad's bombs, and steadfastly clung white-knuckled to their desks at Forward Operating Base Triumph. If the FOB was a mother's skirt, then these soldiers were pressed hard against the pleats, too scared to venture beyond her grasp.

Like the shy, hairy-footed hobbits of Tolkien's world, they were reluctant to go beyond their shire, bristling with rolls of concertina wire at the borders of the FOB. After all, there were goblins in turbans out there! Or so they convinced themselves.

Supply clerks, motor pool mechanics, cooks, mail sorters, lawyers, trombone players, logisticians: Fobbits, one and all. They didn't give a shit about appearances. They were all about making it out of Iraq in one piece.

Of all the Fobbits in the U.S. military task force headquarters at the western edge of Baghdad, Staff Sergeant Chance Gooding Jr. was the Fobbitiest. With his neat-pressed uniform, his lavender-vanilla body wash, and the dust collected around the barrel of his M16 rifle, he was the poster child for the stay-back-stay-safe soldier. The smell of something sweet radiated off his skin—as if he bathed in gingerbread.

Gooding worked in the public affairs office of the Seventh Armored Division, headquartered in one of Saddam Hussein's marbled palaces. His PAO days were filled with sifting through reports of Significant Activities and then writing press releases about what he had found. His job was to turn the bomb attacks, the sniper kills, the sucking chest wounds, and the dismemberments into something palatable—ideally, something patriotic—that the American public could stomach as they browsed the morning newspaper with their toast and eggs. No one wanted to read: "A soldier was vaporized when his patrol hit an Improvised Explosive Device, his flesh thrown into a nearby tree where it draped like Spanish moss." But the generals and colonels of the Seventh Armored Division all agreed that the folks back home *would* appreciate hearing: "A soldier paid the ultimate sacrifice while carrying out his duties in Operation Iraqi Freedom." Gooding's weapons were words, his sentences were missiles.

As a Fobbit, Chance Gooding Jr. saw the war through a telescope, the bloody snarl of combat remained at a safe, sanitized distance from his air-conditioned cubicle. And yet, here he was on a FOB at the edge of Baghdad, geographically central to gunfire. To paraphrase the New Testament, he was *in* the war but he was not *of* the war.

On the day a soldier was roasted in the fire of an IED in al-Karkh and then, in a separate attack, a suicide bomber rammed into the back of an Abrams tank, Gooding's deployment clock was at 183 days with another 182 days to go (plus or minus 60 days, depending on extension orders, which could come from the Pentagon at any minute, triggering an increase in suicide attempts, raids on the stash of contraband vodka concealed behind the false wall of a certain NCO's wall locker, and furious bouts of masturbation). Halfway there. The tipping point. The downhill slide.

Staff Sergeant Gooding was a career soldier with ten-plus years in Uncle Sam's Army, but this was the first time he'd set foot on the soil of a combat zone. Like the majority of Fobbits, this filled him with equal parts dread and annoyance—fear of being killed at any moment, yes; but also irritation at the fact that he was now on what felt like a yearlong camping trip with all the comforts of home (flush toilets, cable TV, sand-free bedsheets) stripped away. Going to war could be a real pain in the ass.

The infantry grunts—the ones in the wrinkled desert camouflage uniforms, the ones with worry and fear knotting the tight landscape of their foreheads—had nothing but scorn for soldiers like Gooding. To be a "Fobbit" or "Fobber" or "Fob Dog" was the same as calling someone a dickless, lily-livered desk jockey back in the States. In another war, REMF was the preferred term . . . but now, in this modern asymmetric theater of operations, there was no "rear" echelon elite sitting in their motherfucking safe-from-harm shelter.

But, hey, that was okay by them. The Fobbits told themselves, broken-record style, they Just. Did Not. Give. A Shit.

They were all Fobbits, everyone who worked in this palace—with the exception of a few foolhardy officers gunning for promotion who grabbed every opportunity to ride on patrols to water treatment plants, school renovations, and neighborhood council meetings in the Baghdad suburbs. Those officers didn't really count—they maintained a desk at Task Force Baghdad Headquarters, but you could hardly call them Fobbits. They were ghosts, gone outside the wire more often than not (and making damn sure everyone saw them depart, slurping loud from travel mugs of coffee, uniforms clinking and whickering, a patchwork of 550 cord and carabiners and duct tape).

Everyone else? Solid-to-the-core Fobbits who kept a wary distance from the door-kickers when they came into the chow hall smelling of sweat, road dust, and, occasionally, blood.

Let the door-kickers ride around Baghdad in their armor-skinned Humvees getting pelted with rocks from pissed-off hajjis. Let *them* dodge the roadside bombs that ripped limbs from sockets and spread guts like fiery paste across the pavement. As for Fobbits? No thanks! They were just fine with their three hots and a cot. The Fobbit life is the life for me, they'd singsong to each other with sly winks.

"Don't wanna be no bullet sponge," said Private First Class Simon Semple.

"Oh, *hell*, no," agreed Private First Class Allison Andersen. She stuck her forefinger in her mouth and sucked with cheek-collapsing vigor because she was, at the time, eating a Ding Dong cupcake and the broiling Baghdad heat had melted the frosting onto her hand, the corners of her lips, and the tip of her chin. She was back in the cool oasis of the palace now but her skin still throbbed from the 110-degree temperatures outside, which she'd had to endure on the half-mile walk between the dining facility and headquarters. The heat was a bitch and she wondered again why they couldn't just build a tunnel between the two places. For that matter, they should just dig tunnels everywhere, make this whole FOB a network of connected passageways so they could go around like moles and not come up until after the sun went down.

Pfc Semple watched Pfc Andersen suck the Ding Dong off her finger and felt the stirrings of a hard-on. *Damn* that girl!

Semple and Andersen had twice engaged in against-regulation, punishable by Uniform Code of Military Justice sex: once in a Porta-Potty in a remote corner of the FOB, sloshing the toilet to and fro and mashing their lips together to stifle their orgasms; the second time on guard duty shortly after midnight when the moon was waning and no one could see them thumping around the guard shack at the opening in the coils of concertina wire around the motor pool. That time hadn't really counted, though—it was coitus interruptus because insurgents picked that particular night to send four mortars raining down on the FOB and the two horny privates quickly disengaged, clapped their Kevlars back on their heads, grabbed their M16s, and sought shelter in a concrete bunker thinking, oh, sweet Jesus this was the fucking end, not just the end of fucking. But then the mortars stopped, the all-clear siren blew, and the privates stood up, brushed themselves off, and, too embarrassed to look each other in the eye, finished their guard duty in silence.

Semple and Andersen worked in the division's G-1 Casualty Section and were in charge of cataloguing the dead. They sat at their desks in headquarters and waited for e-mails to pop into their in-boxes, announcing the serious injury or death of another soldier who'd been scythed by the Grim Reaper while out on patrol. The reports came to them in capital letters, shouting in military jargon:

SOLDIER ON MOUNTED PATROL TRAVELING IN VICINITY OF AL-KARKH WATER TREATMENT PLANT FLAGGED DOWN BY IRAQI CITIZEN CLAIMING AN IED 200 METERS AHEAD. SSG HARDING AND TWO OTHER MEMBERS OF THE PATROL DISMOUNTED M1114 TO SEARCH FOR IED EVIDENCE. TWO ADDITIONAL SOLDIERS SEARCHED ADJACENT FIELDS FOR WIRES, BAGS OF GARBAGE, ANIMAL CORPSES, ETC. INDICATING LOCATION OF IED. SSG HARDING ALSO WALKED FORWARD, BUT REMAINED ON THE ROAD. IED WAS ONLY 30 METERS AHEAD OF SOLDIERS. AS TEAM MOVED FORWARD, IED EXPLODED, CAUSING IMMEDIATE AMPUTATION OF SSG HARDING'S FOUR LIMBS. FRAGMENTS OF IED ALSO PENETRATED SSG HARDING'S HELMET, RESULTING IN MASSIVE HEAD INJURY AND SUBSEQUENT DEATH. UNIT CONDUCTED IMMEDIATE CORDON AND SEARCH FOLLOWING THE ATTACK TO FIND RESPONSIBLE PARTY OR PARTIES AND DETAINED FOR FURTHER QUESTIONING ONE POSSIBLE WITNESS, THE INDIVIDUAL WHO ORIGINALLY WARNED THEM ABOUT THE IED.

When the e-mails with their wounds and smoldering body parts arrived in their in-boxes, it was up to Semple and

Andersen to place a call to the Medical Treatment Facility that had received the casualty and verify a U.S. military doctor had officially determined the body was indeed dead. Until a doctor put his stethoscope on that blackened, suppurating chest and gave a tight, nauseous nod, it didn't matter who was weeping and wailing over the corpse of Staff Sergeant Harding—not his loyal and sickened soldiers, not his commanding officer, not his mother, not even the Great White Bwana himself briefly pausing in the Oval Office to brush away a simpatico tear. Without the doctor's nod, he wasn't officially dead. And he needed to be officially dead before G-1 Casualty could enter him into the system and begin the transatlantic next-of-kin notification process, which ended with a chaplain and a casualty assistance officer, both of their necks tight and sweating against the collars of their starched dress uniform shirts, standing in the doorway of a home in Hinesville, Georgia, the sun having just swapped places with the moon, a porch swing knocking against the side of the house in the soft evening breeze, the crickets rubbing their legs together and bursting forth in symphonic prelude, the casualty assistance officer clearing his throat and starting his rehearsed speech: "Ma'am, I regret to inform you . . ."

Until then, there was nothing they could do except finish their cupcakes, wipe their fingers, and go back to playing computer solitaire (Semple) and leafing through the pages of an old *People* magazine (Andersen). Tom Cruise was, after all, in the midst of a very passionate, very weird affair with doe-eyed Katie Holmes. And then there was that vegetable girl, Terri Somebody-or-Other, who nobody had thought to ask before she went into a coma whether or not she would want her plug to be pulled. And Jesus, what was *up* with Michael Jackson going to court in pajamas? *Day-um*. America sure was a funny place to look at when you got far enough away, thought Private First Class Andersen.

Hovering unseen at the edge of the G-1 cubicle, Staff Sergeant Chance Gooding watched the two privates toss a cupcake back and forth across the cubicle and thought, *Oh, man, this isn't going to be easy*. He needed a word, a simple little word.

Confirmed.

That's all. Just those two syllables.

His life, at this very moment, depended on it. If, that is, you could call press releases a matter of life and death. Which, at this point in time, he did.

Gooding cleared his throat. "Semple," he said.

The private turned his head, saw the sergeant standing there, and quickly minimized the solitaire screen. "Hello, Public Affairs," he said. "What can Casualty do for you this fine afternoon?"

"Same old, same old, Semple. Need to know if you have doctor's confirmation of the latest one—the guy from Second Brigade. The press release is done and ready to send out to the media. I'm just waiting on you guys to give me the go-ahead."

"Sorry, Sar'nt." Semple shook his head.

"Why? What's wrong?"

"Server's down," Andersen said, riffling the pages of *People* a couple of inches from her throat. As if that would cool her skin. She closed her eyes and tried to concentrate on ice cubes, Antarctica, a guy from Alaska she once dated.

"You've gotta be kidding me," Gooding said.

"Wish we was," Semple said.

"It was fine when I left my cubicle on the other side of the palace."

"Don't know what to tell you, Sar'nt. Sandstorm must have come along in the time it took you to walk from there to here. Maybe a mortar hit. Whatever. We're dead in the water right now."

Gooding gritted his teeth. Dead. Dying. Done for. By now, death was a way of life for him, a prescribed job skill he performed with automatic finger taps and wrist lifts across his keyboard. Death was just one of the commodities he traded on a daily basis.

It hadn't always been this way. He could still remember a time, at the start of this deployment, when he'd been a death virgin, cherry unpopped by all the casualty reports and photos of roadside bombings. Long before the Butcher Shop of Baghdad had dulled him to cynicism.

Once, when he was still down in Kuwait, waiting to deploy north to Iraq and join the rest of the division, which had already been in-country for three weeks, a captain from the G-2 Intelligence Section walked up to him in the makeshift Tactical Operations Center and asked, "You PAO?"

Gooding had looked up from the Dickens novel he was reading, then quickly got to his feet, heart pounding. "Yes, ma'am."

"Thought you should know we just got word from up north. Division took some fatalities earlier this afternoon. A vehicle out on patrol rolled over into a canal in south Baghdad. Two dead on impact. Another one trapped in the wreckage. Two other soldiers jumped in to rescue the vehicle crew but they got swept away. Monsoon season up there is a bitch, apparently. Anyway, last I heard, we've got three dead and two missing."

Gooding had dog-eared a page of *A Tale of Two Cities* with trembling fingers and said in a hoarse voice, "Thanks, ma'am. I appreciate you letting me know."

Back then, he'd slumped against the wall, reeling from his first deaths as a public affairs soldier serving in his first war. He pictured the Humvee tipping, tumbling into the water, the two soldiers on the bank shouting, acting on instinct, jumping into the water, misjudging the current, and getting sucked down into the muddy swirl of the Euphrates (in his mind, the canal had become the mighty Euphrates), their mouths trying to snatch air but filling instead with dirty water. He pictured those two soldiers flailing against the pull of the water, soon losing all strength as their lungs filled with the Euphrates, and their limp bodies floating downstream. He had thought about their personnel files quickly being pulled from the division's records and labeled "Killed In Action," their ghosts quietly falling out of company formations, their names laser-etched on a memorial plaque back in Georgia.

Not many days and three U.S. KIAs later, Gooding had written in his diary:

February 13: *This is how a death is announced. In the midst of the hum and buzz of idle boredom in the Division Tactical Operations Center, you hear one officer, bent over the back pages of* The Stars and Stripes, *ask another, "What did you get for 17 Across?" Two people are arguing about which* Matrix *movie was the best. Another soldier in his early twenties is surfing the Internet looking at engagement rings and wondering aloud what difference a half carat made in the quality and price and—most importantly—a chick's response to the bling.*

Then, like a blade swishing through the air comes a sudden sharp voice from the other side of the room, cutting

through the growl-buzz of the generator and the fist-thump
of wind against the tent walls. You look over and an NCO
is pressing a telephone receiver tighter against his ear and
saying, "Repeat that last transmission. What did you say?" He
waves his hand at another NCO to get him a pen, where-
upon he scribbles on an index card. Two or three others
cluster near him, heads pressed in a tight circle. One head
pops up and catches the eye of the battle captain sitting in his
leather office chair at the front of the room. He rises from the
chair—he'd been watching a NASCAR race on the TV—
and walks over to the growing knot of huddled heads.

At this point, something like cold fear creeps around
your heart like icy vines. The information on the index
card is read back into the phone for confirmation, then the
battle captain grabs the card and strides to the front of the
room, yelling, "ATTENTION IN THE DTOC! ATTEN-
TION IN THE DTOC!"

All sound and motion in the tent stops. Someone
mutes the NASCAR race. The battle captain reads
from the index card: "We have reports of one IED in
the vicinity of Scania along the convoy route. One KIA.
Battle-damage assessment still being made. That is all."
He reads it as carefully and dispassionately as someone
quoting stock market prices, then he turns and writes the
information on a large sheet of paper taped to the wall at
the front of the room where all significant activities—the
loss of an M16, the arrival/departure of a convoy, the
publication of an operations order—are recorded.

As you watch him write with the magic marker, the
conversation-buzz of the room gradually returns to its

former volume. Some drop their heads in sorrow, shaking
them back and forth as if that will counteract the loss and
bring the KIA back to life, or at least change his status to
WIA. But the magic marker ink is permanent, seared there
by the heat of an IED blast. No wounds can be reversed.
The battle captain returns to his leather chair. A couple of
officers return to their crossword puzzle. Someone turns up
the volume on the TV and the NASCAR race resumes.

But now, five months later, death was a matter of course, one more task in a day already filled with a heavy workload. Gooding could type his KIA press releases blindfolded. If, that is, he could get these two cupcake-smeared clerks in G-1 to cooperate and give him the nod.

Gooding ground his teeth. CNN was breathing down his neck, calling every ten minutes to ask about the explosion half the people in al-Karkh saw and nearly everyone heard, the deep thud rippling through the neighborhoods, the smoke pluming like a gray finger. The producers had called an hour ago and said they already had a cameraman on the site who was telling them there were U.S. casualties. The rest of the meat-wagon media were right on CNN's heels. By the time he walked back to his cubicle, Gooding could expect to see three or four e-mails in his in-box from the *New York Times*, NBC, and Reuters. They wanted details. They had deadlines. They needed confirmation of death.

"Not much we can do right now, Sar'nt," said Semple, clicking uselessly at his e-mail in-box. "Dust storm's fucking up the whole computer network from here to Basra."

"CNN just announced this guy's death and they have footage of a body wearing a U.S. uniform being hauled from the blast site on a stretcher."

"You know the drill, Sar'nt," Semple said. "He ain't dead until we get the e-mail from the docs at Camp Bucca saying he's dead."

"And you can't pick up the phone and call?"

"C'mon, Sar'nt. You know it has to be official and in writing. We can't go vocal on casualty confirmation."

Semple looked at Andersen to see if she'd agree with him and get this sergeant off their ass. She had stopped sucking her fingers and was now picking at a piece of dried lunch caught on the ample breast of her DCUs. She scraped her nail back and forth right where the nipple would be beneath the uniform, the brown T-shirt, and the bra. Sweet Jesus have mercy!

When he had the chance, Semple was going to tell her about a new Porta-Potty he'd seen by the chapel where no one went except Wednesday nights and Sunday mornings. He was going to make his invitation smooth as chocolate milk and maybe she'd reconsider her previous reluctance for toilet sex.

For now, he couldn't say anything because the sergeant from PAO was still standing there.

"So," Gooding said, "even though you know he's dead and I know he's dead and by now his momma probably knows he's dead, the dude's not really dead, is that what you're telling me?"

Semple leveled a flat gaze at Gooding and clicked at his equally dead in-box. "He ain't *officially* dead yet."

"What about unofficially?"

"Unofficially, yeah. He's road meat. But if anyone asks, you didn't hear it from me."

Gooding was already gone. He'd spun on his heel and started speedwalking back to his cubicle by the time the word *meat* had fallen off Semple's lips.

"*Day*-um," Andersen said.

"Ole sarge needs to slow hisself down," Semple said. "Guy's gonna have a heart attack if he starts taking this shit too seriously."

"Yeah. He needs to pace himself. We still got another six months to go in this shit hole."

"Ticktock, ticktock."

"Why you always gotta bring up the deployment clock, huh?"

"What else we gonna talk about?" Semple asked. "It's all one big fuckin' Groundhog Day anyway, so what does it matter?"

"It matters. I'm sick of this shit already."

Semple snorted. "Your words: pace yourself."

"Whatever." Andersen brushed off her breast with wide, hard strokes to dislodge the crumbs, then picked up her *People* and moved on to Brad Pitt. Semple watched her, crossing his legs to hide his hardness.

"Hey," he said and Andersen looked up from the magazine. The words *Porta-Potty* were there on the tip of his tongue, but what he said instead was, "Check the server again."

Andersen clicked her in-box. "Well, lookee here. It's back up. Whaddaya think? Should we call him back?"

Semple grinned. "Naw. Let him sweat it out for a little bit longer. Pass me that other cupcake, will ya?"

2

DURET

This was not good.

With Iraqis pressing around him on all sides like circus spectators leaning forward to see the man on the high-wire act slip and tumble, Lieutenant Colonel Vic Duret looked through his field glasses at the man slumped in the driver's seat. The man should be dead by now but he was still breathing and every so often his shoulders gave barely perceptible twitches.

This was *definitely* something to be filed under "Not Good."

This was "Hello, soldier! Welcome to the Land of Lose-Lose!"

This was chopping off his hands, then asking him to conduct a symphony.

This was dangerous and delicate and would not be resolved to anyone's satisfaction.

This was, in fact, the classic tar-baby situation. But what could he do? They were here and here they'd stay until they yanked free of the tar.

Duret fingered the focus ring, pulling the car closer into view across the two hundred yards. The roof was caved in and the steering column had broken loose, pinning the driver against the burgundy upholstery. Half the guy's skull seemed to have been knocked ajar, but the scene was still definitely a problem. The half-dead terrorist was, after all, still half-alive.

The battalion commander lowered the binoculars and wiped the sweat from under his eyes. He kept his fingers to his head for a few seconds, hoping his men wouldn't notice how he rubbed his temples, trying to press away the noise inside. It was just one of many tricks to hide the tremors. Make it look like you're full of ballsy confidence, ready to kick the situation's ass. Never let 'em see you sweat, right?

Not so easy when your skull roared with what sounded like four dozen people trapped on the upper floor of a burning skyscraper, all of them screaming and making last-minute deals with God, Ross's voice the loudest among them. It had been like this for Duret since that twelfth of September— starting with a low pulse but building in volume. Stateside, he'd managed to keep it under control: sitting in the brigade commander's back-briefs, he could keep his head down, doodle in his notebook—words like *high pucker factor, blah blah blah,* and *manifest destination*—while the rest of the room filled with PowerPoint graphics of launching missiles set to a peppy Sousa march, laser pointers, and the ticking buzz of fluorescent lights.

Once here in Baghdad, however, the volume knob had snapped off and he was left with battering-ram headaches. Moments like this brought it all front and center: the muttering Iraqis; the bleating goats; the restless, sideways glances of his own soldiers; the scraps of trash snapping in the wind; the broken and bleeding terrorist in the middle of the marketplace.

Fuck! Here it came again. A tsunami of pain roared up through his spine and crashed against the bottom of his skull.

Ross dead Ross dead Ross dead. Running through the remains of his office, crackling and sizzling, flesh dripping off the tips of his fingers, legs carrying him forward by reflex alone because there was nothing left inside of Ross not already cooked by fuel and flame.

The pounding in Duret's brain vibrated against his sinus cavity. Behind the curtain of his fingers, he broke into a sweat as, inside his head, his brother-in-law bumped against desks and plunged through the blizzard of once-important papers, finding his way by instinct, not sight or touch, to the blown-out window. Once there, he launched into the cool blue space, soaring aflame into the buffeting wind. Ross was already gone—no longer the brother-in-law Vic had fished with, laughed with, clinked beer bottles with, mutually grouched about the wife/sister with—so it wasn't really Ross that morning who arced like an ember out of the tower.

Duret pressed hard but the static in his head didn't diminish.

There were just two things he wanted at this particular moment: his golden retriever, Ginger, snuffling and slobbering against the palm of his hand; and his wife's tit in his mouth. While Ginger licked his hand, he'd suck on his wife like he was a baby and if he was lucky she wouldn't catch him crying over all the bad shit he'd brought home from Baghdad.

He pressed and pressed against his head, trying to snuff out Ross. Begone, begone, begone.

They were watching, they were watching. Pull yourself together. This is *not* how a career officer in the United States Army is supposed to conduct himself.

In times like this, he should call on all his training, the momentum of all the years he humped through field exercises, the assault of PowerPoint, the dance of laser pointers across maps, the chess-piece shuffle of sand-table briefings, the subscription to *Military Tactics Quarterly* for fuck's sake!

He should break this down, compartmentalize the scene into workable pieces. *Arrive. Assess. Act.* Yes, that was the textbook.

But at the moment he couldn't do any of that. His head was shrieking and there were no empty compartments left. He knew it would pass, but until then he had to bear with it, ride the pain.

Nearby, one of the soldiers flicked his M4 selector switch from *safe* to *semi* and back again. The sound magnified like the second hand on a stopwatch. They were waiting.

Vic Duret sucked in a deep breath, gathering into his nose the worst of what Baghdad had to offer: dust, diesel, dog shit. He uncovered his eyes. He'd been behind his fingers ten seconds but it felt like ten minutes.

He set his face into a more traditional lieutenant colonel mode of expression: accomplishment of the mission by whatever tactical means necessary. He looked at his men and nodded. "Okay, let's get on with it."

This asshole in the white Opel was just the latest knot in a long string of rotten luck Duret's battalion had encountered since arriving in Baghdad five months ago.

It started with Jerry, his executive officer, getting his left leg sheared off at the knee while en route to a neighborhood council meeting in Taji. Then the sewage backed up in battalion headquarters and three of his staff officers—the valuable ones who knew the difference between a head and an ass—had come down with dysentery. And last week, the Sunnis had finally gotten lucky with a mortar, lobbing it (bull's-eye!) into the middle of Forward Operating Base Triumph, where it landed in the post exchange food court, killing two of Duret's men as they sat at a picnic table outside Burger King merrily snarfing down Whoppers on their day off.

Now this: a suicide bomber who'd rammed himself up the ass end of an M1 Abrams tank. Fortunately for the men inside the Abrams, the bomber had been mortally injured in the crash and hadn't triggered the explosives. Unfortunately, however, the white Opel was now lodged under the tank treads and everything had come to a standstill forty minutes ago. No one knew if the bomber was still holding the detonator, or if the explosives were still potent, or even if there were actually explosives in the trunk of the car. Maybe this was just another drunk Local National who couldn't drive and the stupid bastard had made the A-Number-One fuckup of getting in a fender bender with a U.S. tank.

This was one of those situations you could not prepare for. The patch of black ice on the highway. The piano falling from the sky. What was it Rumsfeld had said about known unknowns? Duret had written it in his notebook and practically committed it to memory: "There are known knowns; there are things we know we know. We also know there are known unknowns; that

is to say we know there are some things we do not know. But
there are also unknown unknowns—the ones we don't know
we don't know."

If someone had taken immediate action forty minutes
ago, none of this would be an issue, but the commander on the
scene—a pinch-faced captain named Shrinkle, known for his
hems and his haws—had waited too long. He'd been hesitant to
slide a foot out onto that high-wire and now a crowd had gathered,
including a couple of news cameras. Fucking CNN complicated
everything on this battlefield, Duret thought for the hundredth
time in as many days. Fuck them and the cameras they rode in on.

Pretty soon they'd be over here with their microphones.
"Colonel Duret, Colonel Duret—what can you tell us about
what's going on out there?" Except, like everyone else, they'd get
his name wrong. It was pronounced *Dur-ray*, true to its French
roots, but his co-workers persisted in calling him, ignorantly,
Durette. They'd even taken to making a joke about it in Iraq:
"This tour sucks, but I guess we have to en-Durette."

Duret looked away from the news crew on the other side
of the cordon and made another assessment of Intersection
Quillpen, where this particular known unknown had plopped
itself. Everything was the color of dust, including the dust itself.
Low, boxy buildings. Tattered posters advertising mint chewing
gum. The vomit-spill of bricks where a shop's facade had finally
given way. A tangle of power lines reminding him too much of
his wife's hair on her pillow in the morning. The street, the sky,
the air he breathed. The goats, the babbling Iraqis, even the
faces of his own men. All of it dust, dust, dust. Fine-grained as
baby powder. From dust we began, to dust we'll return. It was
fucking biblical here at this Sadr City intersection.

He'd been called out of a staff meeting with the brigade commander when word of the would-be suicide bomber reached headquarters. Duret had ordered his driver to take him to the site, hoping he could fix the situation quickly and with minimal death to innocent Iraqi citizens or his own men (in that order, as per the rules of engagement). But when he arrived at the scene in the north sector of Baghdad, he realized solving this situation would be like trying to stuff eels into a can of grease. It could be done, but you had to know how to hold the eel.

Duret turned to the pale, visibly shaking captain at his side. "What do we know?" he asked. "And don't feed me a line of bullshit—I want this thing fixed *now*."

Captain Abe Shrinkle, clearly a man out of his element who was now paying the price for indecision on the high-wire, blanched and scientifically proved it's possible for fear to involuntarily suck your testicles up into the body cavity. "Sir . . . sir . . ." he sputtered.

Duret looked hard at him, timpanis rumbling in his skull. "No bullshit, Captain Shrinkle. We don't have time for it." He stepped closer and lowered his voice. "Listen to me, Abe. There are men inside that tank depending on us to resolve this situation so they can dislodge from the ticking time bomb and take their happy asses back to FOB Triumph where they can sit in their air-conditioned hooch, drink their limit of near-beer, and beat off while thinking about their wives back home. They don't have time for wiffly-waffly bullshit and neither do I." (Duret talked tough, but oh, how he himself wanted his wife's tit and Ginger's tongue.)

"Sir," the captain began again, his voice stuck in a higher, testicle-less octave. "The problem is, we know nothing of the car's contents. The men still inside the Abrams don't have a vantage point of the Opel's interior. We've kept them inside the tank for their own protection. None of us have been able to get close enough to see what the car was carrying."

"You mean you haven't *wanted* to."

"Sir?"

"The fact of the matter is, Abe, you *could* have gotten closer, you *could* have walked right up to the Opel. You just didn't have the *balls* to do it, right?"

Sergeant Brock Lumley, crouched a few yards away, rifle at the ready, overheard the battalion commander and wanted to tell him, "*Some* of us had the balls, sir. *Some* of us wanted to chance it and creep up on the Opel." That's what he wanted to say aloud but he held his tongue. This was Shrinkle's hanging party; let him put the knot in his own noose.

Lumley put his cheek back on the stock of the M4 and continued scanning the crowd, hajji by hajji. Let just one of them motherfuckers move a single sandal-clad toe in the direction of the car and he'd put a hole the size of a baseball in his chest. Lumley had eleven of his younger soldiers crouched on either side of him, sweat-slick fingertips fondling triggers. They could handle this, if they were allowed. He and his men had the courage, the resolve, and the intestinal fortitude. The balls to git 'er done.

Captain Shrinkle, whose balls were bobbing somewhere around his liver, said, "Sir, we lost the opportunity for recon right from the get-go due to the size of the crowd that formed around the accident site, making it impossible for us to risk collateral damage."

Duret stared at his junior officer, wondering if he should call him on the bullshit. Instead, he grimaced and said, "All right, go ahead."

Shrinkle sucked in a quivery breath and described the afternoon's events.

A platoon from Bravo Company (under the command of one Captain A. Shrinkle) had been escorting Alpha Company as it returned from a mission in Khadhimiya, taking Route Franklin as briefed in last night's update. No issues; everything going swimmingly. Until they got to Intersection Quillpen where, at approximately oh-nine-thirty hours, the convoy of Humvees and tanks was forced to a halt by a herd of goats crossing the road. Like goats everywhere, these animals had no sense of urgency, bleating and blinking and bumping into each other. The soldiers stared at the goats and the goats stared back, some with trash dangling from their jaws. The goatherd didn't look at the Americans but picked his nose and clucked at his goats. "Like I said, sir: *no sense of urgency,*" repeated Shrinkle.

Then came a sound off to the left as the soldiers sat at the goat-clogged intersection. Number Three Tank was the first to spot the suspected insurgent vehicle coming at a high rate of speed toward the formation. As the car accelerated up the frontage road, it quickly changed status from a *possible* Vehicle-Borne Improvised Explosive Device to a *probable* Vehicle-Borne Improvised Explosive Device. Gunners from Tanks Number Two and Three immediately applied Force Protection Measures 1 through 4 and would have implemented Force Protection Measure 5 except by that time the VBIED had already rammed into the left rear of Tank Number Three. Tanks One and Two had moved forward out of the potential blast zone and had established the outer perimeter of security.

"We're labeling it a failed suicide bomb event, sir," Shrinkle concluded.

"Give it time," Duret replied. "We're not out of the woods yet."

"From what we've been able to determine, the insurgent's right leg and right hand are pinned beneath the dashboard, restricting his movement on that side," Shrinkle said, pointing at the distant car. "Our spotters can see what looks like a timing device on the passenger seat but it appears to be beyond his reach at this time, sir."

"How far out is EOD?"

"I put in the call thirty minutes ago, sir, but they—"

"They just arrived, sir," Sergeant Lumley spoke up, pointing his thumb toward the Explosive Ordnance Disposal team working at the rear of a Humvee. They unloaded what looked like the love child of Tinkertoys and a giant Erector set.

"They're sending out the 'bot first," Shrinkle said. "In order to negate human contact with the vee-bid."

"Okay," Duret said. "Let's wait and see what we can see." This was the *assess* which would trigger them to *act*. For the first time since he *arrived*, Vic visibly relaxed. In his head, he started a gradual retreat to the bed where his dog and his wife waited for him.

As an EOD sergeant worked the controls, jiggling a joystick from side to side, the robot—all silver limbs and thick tires—moved up, back, up, back with a *whir* and a *grrr*. He was named Robby and he was loved by his human handlers. Robby paced from side to side, impatient to move out and investigate what looked to be a FUBAR situation. The robot loved hair-trigger scenarios (especially those fucked-up beyond all repair) that required precise, mechanical movements, not the fleshy, heavy-thumbed attempts by the humans. You've got a touch-and-go, blue-wire-red-wire dilemma? Send in the 'bot. He'll get the job done and won't get blown to a million little pieces.

The robot focused on the man slumped in the wedged-under car. His opti-eyes dilated to what humans would call a squint, telescoping on the half-dead half-alive human behind the wheel. The computer chips in his head lit in a surge of green lights as he took in the facts and quickly analyzed a path to the solution. The robot paced and even had a bit of a spring in his step as he waited for the joystick to move him forward.

Behind him, the EOD sergeants held their collective breath. These were the dicey moments. You never knew with the 'bot. Maybe he'd run out of battery juice or have an electrical breakdown halfway through the mission. They liked to complain about the piece-of-shit-lowest-bidder T-271 but, in the end, the sergeants knew they had to depend on the silvery Erector set to keep them and the other soldiers alive when facing up-against-the-wall scenarios like this. And, truth be told, though they wouldn't admit it to each other, they loved the T-271 with a deep and abiding affection. If the robot was a girl, they would have bought it beers and taken it home with them on the first date.

"Here we go, sir," Captain Shrinkle said as the robot rolled forward.

Duret, Shrinkle, Lumley, and the rest of the men stood in a tense knot two hundred yards from the crippled tank as the EOD team maneuvered the robot to within metal-arm reach of the Opel.

On the other side of the cordon, the CNN reporter—the one with the good hair—turned to her cameraman. "You getting this?"

The robot *whirred, grrred,* and swelled with joy. Moments like this made up for all the other shitty days in Baghdad.

The sergeant at the joystick watched the progress as it streamed from a direct-feed camera to the laptop he'd set on the hood of his Humvee. He could see the driver's head smashed against the cracked window, the blood forking down his temple and matting his beard. The robot raised itself on its legs and peered into the backseat.

"Ho-ly shit, sir!" the EOD sergeant exclaimed.

At those words, Abe Shrinkle's testicles pirouetted around his gall bladder, Brock Lumley's index finger tightened against the trigger in a movement that could only have been measured under a microscope, and Vic Duret reluctantly threw back the sheets and pulled himself out of the bed while behind him his wife, breasts dangling like ripe fruit, asked, "What's wrong?"

Duret joined the EOD team at the computer screen. *Everything* was wrong. There, in the backseat, they could see three propane tanks, two 152-millimeter artillery shells, and several anti-tank mines. Suddenly, two hundred yards seemed too close for comfort. This guy could take out Tanks Three, Two, and maybe even One, not to mention the CNN crew and half the crowd of gawkers—a crowd metastasizing as word spread through the neighborhood. Dozens of feet (and hooves) were moving toward the intersection, filling the air with dust, babble, and bleats. A dog appeared in a shop doorway, gave a short yip, then sat on his haunches, nervously licking his balls.

"Okay, now we know," Duret said, not looking at his captain. At Duret's elbow, Shrinkle swallowed with a dry *click*.

The robot swiveled his head to give them a look at the front seat: a creased, dog-eared copy of the Koran, a cell phone, a timing device, and a grenade.

The half-dead man came to life. He coughed and a rope of blood spurted from his lips. The *whir* and *grrr* of the robot had roused him from his stupor and now he was agitated, taking it out on the robot, which stared back at him without blinking despite the curses the terrorist hurled at it. The robot could care less if he burned in hell with the rest of his Yankee infidel lovers or if he had his privates sliced off with a dull, rusty knife and shoved down his throat—and, frankly, whether or not the Great Satan, George W. Bush, ever had relations with his mother doggy-style really didn't register in his circuitry. He was metal and machine, here to do a mission clumsy humans could not accomplish. He would render this bleeding, screaming man inert and do it with a steady calm that would earn him a hero's accolades.

That's when the terrorist, fighting off waves of nausea, pain, and dizziness from a brain gone askew, summoned a reserve of strength and reached for the grenade in the passenger's seat.

It was just beyond his fingertips.

The robot backed away with a growl and, with two flicks of the joystick, was returned to the safety of humans.

"My recommendation, sir, is we try to neutralize the threat with a water charge," the EOD sergeant told Lieutenant Colonel Duret.

"Do it," Duret replied, a snap in his voice. The midday sun was high and burning a hole through his helmet, roiling the screams in his head, but Duret was able to cut through the clamor and clearly see the path ahead: get rid of this Sunni troublemaker and move on with the day, but do it in a way that minimized the appearance of collateral damage on CNN later that night. The rules of engagement made it clear this was tantamount: complete the mission, but make it clean and professional so no Local Nationals were left broken, bleeding, or oozing in the wake. And if there were news cameras in the area, make good goddamn sure the soccer balls and lollipops were distributed. Don't forget to tousle the kids' hair for good measure before moving on.

He turned to the top NCO on the scene. "Sergeant Lumley, while EOD is setting this up, I want you to take six of your men and move the cordon back another two hundred feet. Get those civilians away from the vehicle. And have someone check to make sure we have enough lollipops to go around."

"Roger, sir," Lumley said, and moved out with his squad to push back the civilians.

Lollipops, Lumley thought. *That'll make it all taste better, won't it? How many licks does it take to get to the center of an insurgency?*

As Brock Lumley flapped his hand at the hajjis who'd ventured too close, and used the butt of his M4 to nudge those who looked like they intended to stay put, he felt the returning rise of frustration at his impossible task. And not just this mission here in the bull's-eye of Quillpen, but nearly everything he and his men had been handed since they arrived five months ago. Just like these bastards in their dirty dishdashas who were slow to move back from the ticking time bomb, hajjis in general could give two rat fucks about what the Americans were doing here.

And what *were* they doing here? Lumley had no fucking clue.

When it came right down to it, Lumley and his men were just playing that old carnival game Whac-A-Mole. Smack down one terrorist with the rubber mallet and right away another one pops up over *here* and while you're whacking that guy another one has popped up over *there*.

Like the dickwad in the crumpled Opel shoved up the tank's ass. They could *neutralize* or *exterminate* him, but his brother or cousin or second cousin's best friend would show up with his own backpack of explosives in another neighborhood on another day. Lumley and his men just couldn't move fast enough.

That's why, when he pushed the cordon back to a safer distance, he might have shoved one or two of the stubborn bastards a little too hard and they, in turn, narrowed their eyes and said something in hajji-speak that was filled with a bunch of goat-sounding crap like "laa" and "naa." Lumley didn't really mean anything by the rough shove. He was just tired of this shit, that's all.

Most of the crowd grumbled and shook their fists at the Americans but eventually they complied, shuffling through clouds of dust, backpedaling themselves to a safe distance.

Most, but not all. While Lumley's men were herding the Local Nationals, a small boy slipped through the cordon and dashed out to the crushed Opel. Lumley made a grab for him but missed and let him run into the intersection. He wasn't about to get himself blown halfway to Allah just to save one stupid kid.

The boy approached the driver and held up a bottle of water. The terrorist slowly, painfully turned his head and, for the first time, stopped scowling. He smiled at the boy, tipped his head forward, and opened his mouth. The boy put the bottle to the man's lips and helped him drink, cupping his hand beneath the blood-clotted beard to catch the drips. When the man finished drinking, he leaned close to the boy and spoke a few words before his head rolled back against the headrest and he passed out.

Captain Shrinkle radioed out to Sergeant Lumley: "Have your men grab that boy and bring him back here to us." It was the first decisive thing Duret had heard Shrinkle say since he'd arrived. Even so, his voice had a little seesaw in it.

The pint-sized Samaritan tried to dodge Lumley's team and melt back into the crowd but Private First Class Cassidy Skinner—who'd taken the Pleasant Falls High School football team to the Indiana state finals three years in a row—tackled the kid before he could get far. Pfc Skinner held the boy in a pincer grip around the neck and brought him before Lieutenant Colonel Duret. The battalion commander turned to his translator and said, "Ask him why he did that, why he took water to the enemy."

The translator questioned the boy, then told Duret, "He say Allah commanded him to do it."

"Of *course* he did. All right. Ask him what the guy said when he was out there."

The translator and the boy jabbered back and forth. "He say the man tell him to tell you he is from Syria and his terrorist group has planned to launch many vehicle bomb attacks today and also other attacks will follow. He say he is here to kill Americans and it is his supreme pleasure to follow Allah's will as he sends us to the flames of hell."

Duret stared at the boy, who returned the look without cracking a smile. This was the problem with Iraqis, he thought. They believed everything they heard. Now this asshole is a hero in this kid's mind and he thinks he's earned a place at Allah's right hand just because he gave the fucker a sip of water.

Duret frowned and turned to Pfc Skinner. "Zip-tie the kid and hold him until this is all over. I don't want him anywhere near that car again."

At Duret's elbow, Captain Shrinkle cleared his throat and summoned the courage to speak. "Sir, if I may . . ."

"What is it, Abe?"

"Sir, what if we exploited the opportunity this boy has presented? What if we send him back out there with another bottle of water, one we've poisoned? The terrorist drinks it and then we're done for the day. Everyone can go home happy."

Duret was about to tell his captain he was a well-meaning but ultimately useless officer who couldn't find his asshole with a flashlight and a road map, and he meant it in the kindest way possible, but he was interrupted by the EOD sergeant.

"Sir, we're good to go with the water charge. Robby's ready to roll forward and place it beneath the undercarriage."

Duret looked away from Shrinkle and nodded. This was the preferred course of action; poison would have to wait for another day, another terrorist.

The T-271 moved forward, cradling the water charge in his spindly metal arms. The water and explosives, chambered separately, were contained in a canister shaped like a rocketship to Mars the robot had once seen in a Bugs Bunny cartoon. As directed by the human with the joystick, Robby would carefully set the charge beneath the rear of the Opel, then quickly reverse away from the car.

If all went well, the explosives inside the canister would detonate and, in the space of two seconds—a period Robby was able to compute and witness in time-slowed sequence but which his humans would miss if they took a lingering blink—the pentaerythritol tetranitrate would create shock waves of one million pounds per square inch, cracking open the canister at the bullet-shaped tip, which would then puncture a hole in the car's chassis, and immediately emit a blade-thin geyser of water that would envelope the car, the driver, and the bomb in a sheath of violent, dousing liquid, thus rendering the timers, wires, batteries, and explosives inert through a patented method of "bumping and drowning."

If all went well, the water charge would knock the Opel with a hard punch and defuse the bomb, kill the half-alive Syrian, and preserve the inert IED so analysts back at FOB Triumph could examine the method and dissect the madness of the insurgency.

All did not go well.

Lieutenant Colonel Duret joined his men in a brief, hearty cheer when the charge fountained up and the Opel lifted three feet off the ground, knocking the driver half-asunder; but then Duret's bowels clenched when the dripping water cleared and he saw the driver move first his left arm, then his right arm. The explosion had dislodged the terrorist from where he'd been pinned beneath the dashboard. Apparently the Syrian, his skull still split and leaking at an increasingly rapid rate, was dead-set on triggering his payload. If he could find the cell phone and punch in the code, and if the wires were still attached to the three propane tanks, two 152-millimeter artillery shells, and anti-tank mines, and if the explosives were still dry enough, then Duret would be looking at a fifteen-foot crater where his tank now stood.

Duret blew out a whistle of breath. "Fuckity-fuck!" This was turning into something like those field training exercises where the scenario planners kept throwing up roadblock after roadblock in increasingly far-fetched circumstances to force commanders like Vic Duret to make rash decisions. Like this particular known-unknown situation unraveling here at Quill-pen, those FTXes always made him feel like he was squeezing water between his fingers. Nothing ever stayed in his grasp long enough for him to *assess* and *act*.

Duret turned to the EOD crew. "Get that robot out there with another charge!"

The sergeants scrambled, loaded another cylinder into the robot's outstretched arms, and jiggled the joystick. They didn't get far before Captain Shrinkle yelped, "Sir! He's got the phone!" and dropped to a fetal position behind his Humvee, squirting a tiny stream of urine into his sweat-soaked underwear in the process.

The broken, battered, and now drenched man in the Opel was sitting up like a nightmare Lazarus. He turned his head, smiled at the ring of soldiers, and held up his phone for all to see.

"Fuckity-fuckity-FUCK!" Duret yelled. They were the only words that came to mind as he stood there, firmly but recklessly facing the danger (unlike tinkle-drawers Shrinkle). Duret stood tall, growling at the terrorist punching the code into the keypad of his cell phone.

Lieutenant Colonel Duret was truly the last man standing because everyone else—Shrinkle, the soldiers of his company, the crowd of Iraqis, the EOD team, even the robot—was crouched behind the nearest bit of shelter from the expected blast. That's why Lieutenant Colonel Duret was the only one to see the Syrian shake his phone in frustration and punch the numbers twice, then thrice, but coming up with the same empty results every time. The detonator was no good, there was no signal from the cell phone to ignite a spark under the home-made bomb in the backseat. The terrorist screamed a string of curses at the phone—no doubt calling it a no-good piece-of-shit hunk-of-junk from Japan—before flinging it out the window.

This drained the Syrian's remaining reserve of energy. His head fell forward, hit the bent steering wheel, and then the upper half of his skull appeared to dislodge, sliding an inch to the right. Nothing else moved.

Duret choked on half a "fuckity." The Local Nationals lifted themselves off the ground and began jabbering and pointing fingers at the slumped driver. Captain Shrinkle's men bounced up and resumed their protective security posture, a few of them training weapons on the crowd to keep them at bay. Shrinkle remained curled behind the Humvee, his hands covering his head for a few more seconds before he saw everyone else was already on their feet. He stood, realized the stain at his crotch was visible, and immediately pressed himself against the side of the Humvee, hoping the piss would dry quickly.

Duret looked at the EOD team again. "All right, gentle-men. Let's get another water charge out there. Just to be on the safe side."

"Roger, sir," the sergeant said and finished securing the cylinder in Robby's arms. He nodded at the joystick-sergeant and the robot rolled forward for a second time, moving toward the Opel with a growing reluctance. The robot, like the humans behind him, was tired of this day-in, day-out bullshit. He had nerves of steel, yes, but it was tedious to be carted from one Baghdad street to the other, morning, noon, and night, always expected to go where humans refused, always the same old cautious approach, warily eyeing the suspicious package, the odd swell of fresh concrete, the dog carcass with wires protruding from each nostril, while the humans sat safe and secure behind their armor-skin Humvees, watching his progress via a computer screen. One of these days, he'd show them, he'd just up and—

The robot quit. Stopped dead in its tracks forty feet shy of the Opel.

The sergeant on the joystick jiggled it up, back, right, left. Nothing. He checked his computer screen and tapped several keys. Still no response. He swore, then looked at the other sergeant and shook his head. "Battery."

"You've gotta be kidding."

"Wish I was."

"Godfuckingdammit."

"Plan B?"

"Of *course,* Plan Fucking B." The EOD sergeant would have to examine the car himself to see the extent of damage done to the homemade bomb. If he was honest with himself, he'd seen the inevitability of suiting up from the minute he arrived on the scene. Robby was all well and good but in situations like this where they faced uncertain payloads there really was no substitute for nonmechanical eyes-on. With the crowd of locals growing, simmering, and pressing ever closer to the cordon, and with CNN beaming a live signal to the mothers and fathers of America—quite possibly his own mother and father who were clutching themselves as they gaped at the TV screen back in Portland, Oregon—he had no choice but to go and defuse the situation now that his robot had stopped dead in its tracks.

The sergeant began stepping into his eighty-pound Kevlar-lined suit, zipping and cinching. Before he put on the hood, he said, "I swear, that robot is gonna be the death of me," words he wished he could immediately pull back into his mouth. He wasn't particularly superstitious by nature, but that was like something out of the movies.

Encased in the suit, he started moving toward the white car slowly, as if he were wading through a river of cold molasses. Inside, he had his own personal sauna, raising the morning's 110 degrees another fifteen notches on the thermometer, slow-cooking himself to death within the protective Kevlar coating. Not that the suit would do any good if the Opel suddenly went off. He would never survive the blast of the propane-propelled artillery shells. As he liked to say, the suit just gave them something to bury him in, something to keep the body parts all in one place.

The rest of the soldiers watched the EOD sergeant walk forward, stiff as a zombie. He reached the car in slow motion and leaned forward through the window. The sergeant looked like he was kissing his wife good-bye before she drove off on a school field trip with their fourth-grade son who was bouncing in his seat and making *grrr*ing sounds for a toy dinosaur he held in his hands, the sergeant pecking his wife on the cheek, both of them laughing at how giddy their kid was to go to a museum and see a bunch of skeletons at the Flesh Eaters of the Past exhibit. Inside the Kevlar, he started to smile and drift back to the United States.

But then his eyes widened behind the breath-fogged helmet and he was windmilling away from the Opel, stumbling in panicked retreat. What he'd seen in the backseat meant the end of his world as he knew it. This was it, all aboard for Kaputsville.

A soldier on the perimeter shouted, "Watch out! Watch out!" even though he had no clue what they were supposed to watch out for—he was just reacting to the EOD guy's sudden panic. It seemed like a good idea at the time to start shouting, "Watch out!"

The warning rippled down the line and everyone got into battle-ready position.

That's when this movie went slow motion for Vic Duret. Later, he'd tell his executive officer his brain zoomed out for a wide-angle perspective of the scene and he could see:

- Intersection Quillpen and the three tanks askew in the road, the last of them with a white car up its ass like a half-squeezed turd
- the half-moon of shopkeepers, goatherds, and school-children gathered around the accident site, pressing against the hastily erected cordon and raising a chorus of ululations, tongues flapping at the back of their throats
- the ring of Humvees facing the tanks across an empty expanse of street, a squad of soldiers keeping their M4s trained on the crowd and the Opel, alert for any funny business
- the robot frozen in the center of the tableau, a water charge cradled uselessly in its arms
- an empty plastic water bottle rolling between the robot's legs, skipped along by the wind and moving toward the Opel while at the same time a figure stuffed inside a heavy fire suit tap-danced back as quickly as his cement-weight boots would allow

- a man—thought to be dead on three separate occasions
  —now incredibly, like a movie monster who refused
  to stay down, stirring once again in the front seat of
  the white car, pushing himself off the steering wheel
  with great effort—a sticky string of blood cobwebbing
  him to the dashboard—and turning himself toward
  the passenger side of the car, fumbling, reaching for
  something that might be the Koran or might be the
  hand grenade
- Captain Shrinkle giving himself completely to the
  dread and terror of close-order combat and releasing
  the clench on his bowels
- Duret himself standing tall but paralyzed with indecision, clarity of action unable to cut through the fog of
  headache
- a bullet cutting the day, splitting the air, hurtling from
  the barrel of an M4 and lodging just below the Syrian's
  left ear, the pressure pushing upward, finally knocking
  loose whatever fibrous matter that had been holding
  the cleft halves of the man's head together, painting the
  interior of the Opel with blood-brain-skull
- a tattered copy of the Koran dropping from a limp hand
  and hitting the blood-smeared floor.

Lieutenant Colonel Vic Duret saw all of this but could
not process the events. He was still trying to pull himself away
from his bedroom back in Georgia and walk through the red,
pulsing headache. When his paralysis finally broke, he turned
and saw Sergeant Lumley lowering the M4 from his cheek.

"Good shooting, Sergeant," he croaked. It was hardly the best thing to say in the aftermath of a Bronze Star Medal moment and he would certainly be more poetic in the citation he'd later compose back at his desk in the air-conditioned headquarters, but for now he was just grateful for Lumley's immediate action, which saved a three-million-dollar tank, the crew members inside, the laughing-bleating-jeering hubbub of Iraqis, a few dozen goats, two EOD sergeants and their robot, piss-pants Shrinkle and his men, and Vic himself. "Good shooting," he said again, unable to hide the shake in his voice. The ice water of a headache was already fountaining from the top of his skull and dripping across the rest of his brain. With the death of the Syrian, he'd once again seen Ross ignite: Falling Burning Man.

Lumley said nothing as he flicked the selector switch on his M4 back to *safe*. He looked at his men, all of them staring gape-jawed at him, and snapped, "What the fuck you lookin' at? Get your asses out there and disperse that crowd! And for chrissakes somebody go up there, knock on that tank, and tell them it's all clear!"

His men moved out and when they were safely out of sight Lumley stumbled behind the nearest Humvee, put his hands on his knees, and hurled up that morning's breakfast.

It would be a long time, years and years of therapy, before he could wipe from his mind the sight of that head erupting in a bloody geyser. He'd pulled the trigger without thinking through the consequences. He was not sorry he hadn't hesitated but there was always that nagging, niggling doubt: maybe hajji wasn't going for the grenade; maybe he was reaching to unbuckle the seat belt so he could come out of the car in surrender; or maybe it was just a final muscular twitch of a man who was already dead.

Probably not, but still there was that *maybe*.

Lumley gagged once more, spit a loogey of bile, then wiped his mouth. Oh, well. Didn't matter now, right? What's done is done. What's dead is dead. He took a sour breath. Pull your shit together, Lumley.

Later that night, Brock Lumley would dream he was standing in front of a Whac-A-Mole, sponge-rubber mallet in his hand. Each time the Syrian's head popped up, Lumley smacked it with the mallet. The head would burst like a balloon and drench Lumley's shirt with blood and viscera. Then another head, and another, and another.

The tank crew emerged from the hatch, their beige uniforms dark with sweat. They'd been told what had happened and now they looked over at Lumley, cheered, and gave him a thumbs-up.

He waved weakly and pulled his shit together.

One hour later—after the Abrams had pulled itself free of the Opel with a groan-shriek of metal, the EOD team had gone out to render the explosives completely neutral and retrieve the battery-dead robot, the Iraqi Security Forces had arrived on the scene to disperse the crowd and take charge of the dead terrorist, CNN had packed up their camera and microphone and zipped away in their shiny up-armored SUV, Lieutenant Colonel Duret had ordered Captain Shrinkle to have a preliminary after-action report on his desk no later than 1700 hours, and the infantrymen were allowed to piss and smoke before departure—the platoon was riding back to FOB Triumph and its population of soft-bellied Fobbits.

Lumley was a big guy who had to fold and stuff himself inside the front passenger seat of the Humvee every trip outside the concertina wire, but his eyes were small ("like two pieces of rabbit shit on snow," his granddaddy used to say) and he kept his mouth so tight it was hard to tell what was going on inside. Even so, each time he came back from patrol, driving through the main gate of the FOB, his spleen rose between his teeth at the thought of all the coddled soldiers who never went beyond the wire. Fuck those high-ranking desk jockeys fat, dumb, and happy with their air-conditioning and the illusion they kept things under control in Iraq just by clicking a few icons on the computer screen, moving units around with a tidy drag-and-drop.

Lumley and the rest of the soldiers in his platoon were the ones making a difference in Iraq, not those lazy slugs. He'd be surprised if any of those support soldiers had ever pulled a trigger in their lives, apart from the annual trip to the M16 qualification range. They wouldn't know a mosque from a mosquito.

Lumley's men stared with glazed eyes out the windows of the Humvees, always scanning, scanning, scanning the rooftops, doorways, ditches for suspicious activity. Nobody said anything but a few cracked half-contained smiles when they thought about the way ole hajji's head had popped like a blood-filled balloon when Sergeant Lumley's bullet had done its work.

Soon they would pull into Triumph, clear their weapons at the checkpoint, ratcheting the bolts with a ka-*ching,* and reach down to pick up the ejected rounds. They would park at the motor pool, perform the post-op Preventive Maintenance Checks and Services, then head for showers, chow, and the

soothing calm of an after-dinner cigar. Some would gather for
the ongoing Xbox Halo tournament, some would e-mail their
families, some would open *Maxim* to a wrinkled, dog-eared page
and commence the nightly masturbation session, and some
would lie on their cots in the spreading ink of night, stare at
the ceiling of their hooch, try to push away the burst of a blood
balloon now playing on a loop in their head and know it was no
use—they'd have to deal with this for the rest of the deployment . . . and beyond.

The officers would also sit in the dark, variously watching
Marx Brothers movies on their laptop (Shrinkle) and chewing
Tylenol like candy (Duret).

One by one, they would all give way to the discomfort of
restless sleep.

Just before the sun's yolk broke over the horizon and the
muezzins started singing from the mosques and the Blackhawk
blades took to the sky with pulsing thumps and the morning's
mortars came down with metal shrieks, they would face another
day—Duret, Shrinkle, Lumley, the three thousand soldiers, and
even the Iraqis themselves—all prepared to meet more known
unknowns.

3

GOODING

That morning, he had crept up behind Specialist Cinnamon Carnicle and then, just before a prankster giggle broke out of him, he coughed like a cat with a hair ball.

Cinnamon leaped up and yelped, "Jesus Harvey Christ!"

"Why so jumpy, Carnicle?" Staff Sergeant Gooding looked at her through narrow, amused eyes.

"They don't call it the graveyard shift for nothing, Sar'nt," she said as she scraped herself off the ceiling and settled back into her chair. Carnicle was the other enlisted soldier in the public affairs cell and was responsible for monitoring Significant Activity reports, restocking supplies, fielding phone calls from reporters in other time zones, and editing the Shamrock Division's weekly camp newspaper, *The Lucky Times*. Most nights, it was quiet here in Saddam's old palace, and that's just the way she liked it. Peace and quiet in the middle of a loud war. "What are you doing here now, Sergeant Gooding? Isn't it, like, two hours before shift change?"

"Couldn't sleep." He shrugged off his flak vest and dumped it in the gear pile next to the M16 rack. "I stayed up late watching the *Star Wars* bootleg and ended up eating a whole bag of care-package licorice which, let's just say, didn't sit too well with me."

"You can eat the prunes my grandmother sent me last month, if it'll help."

Gooding ripped a fart, made a face, and said, "Sorry. Licorice is still backing up."

"You couldn't leave it outside, Sar'nt?"

"It comes and goes, Carnicle. Doesn't let me have a say-so." He sat down and logged on to his computer. "Anything interesting pop up on SMOG?"

"Not much. 1-3 was out on some neighborhood-knock mission that started at twenty-two hundred and didn't really wrap up until an hour ago. SMOG was antsy all night long—kept interrupting my sleep to give updates over the loudspeaker every thirty minutes."

"Poor girl. I'll be sure and tell them to keep it down in there so they don't bother you so much."

"Hardy-har-har."

Gooding walked over to the SMOG station. "So, any casualties?"

"One guy got bit in the nuts by a rottweiler but that's about it."

"A rottweiler? Where were they, South Harlem? What kind of Local National keeps a guard dog?"

"Apparently one who's had his door kicked in one too many times. They had to zip-tie this guy and his wife just to get them to calm down. This, of course, after our guys shot the dog."

"Nice."

"Hey, the guy thought his nuts were bit clean off. Turns out he just got a bad bruising, that's all. Didn't even break the skin. He'll probably get bed rest and an ice pack for a day, then he'll be back on the street. Can't keep a good man down, right?"

"This coming from someone who never had to walk around with a sack of nuts."

"I never told you about my sex change, did I?"

"No, but it's pretty obvious to everyone who meets you."

"Ha," Carnicle said, not a trace of laughter in her voice. "So, you're releasing me from prison two hours early?"

"Sure," Gooding said. "Go ahead and treat yourself to an extra course at breakfast."

Carnicle logged off her computer and gathered her gear. When fully bundled into her military uniform and load-bearing equipment, she waddled like a beige penguin. She was short, with bowl-cropped hair and a face compacted with only the sugges- tion of a chin. She forbade anyone to call her "Cinnamon" but asked they keep it at "Carnicle, just Carnicle." She wouldn't even go by "Cindy," as her hippie parents still called her, just as they called her sisters Nutmeg and Allspice by their cutesy nicknames "Meg" and "Allie." On the surface, Specialist Carnicle came as close to a manly man as someone with D-cup boobs could get, but no one knew her little secret: in the privacy of her hooch she spritzed the air with lavender room spray, slept in silk pajamas, and cuddled with a teddy bear (floppy neck, loose button eye, name of Chopin). Lord help the person who discovered this Jekyll to her Hyde because Carnicle stood at just the right height to deliver a crippling punch to the balls. Yes, she had plenty of secrets, but she kept them corralled behind her constricted features; she'd crack a smile every now and then but it was never just a smile; it was a controlled, crescent chink in her armor. After three months of working all-nighters her face had gone pasty and oily and she was still plagued with the coffee jitters but she wouldn't trade the midnight peace of the palace for what she'd heard went on during the day. All that phone-jangling, cubicle-buzzing, KIA-peppering vibe coming from the Sig Act reports made her skin crawl and, if she'd had them, her nuts shrivel. No, thanks, she'd stay right here in the calm of the night shift, if it was all the same.

"So," Gooding said, "besides Luthor-the-Nut-Crunching-Dog, anything big happen?"

"By 'big,' do you mean things like Captain Kilgore in G-6 spilling coffee on his desk and fritzing out half of G-3 Ops computers? Or one of the checkpoint guards coming down with what he thought was food poisoning and ralphing his guts all over the front desk and then for some reason feeling the need to broadcast this news over the loudspeaker? That kind of 'big'?"

"I was thinking more in terms of casualties or captured terrorists."

"Oh, *that*. No, nothing much to report, Sar'nt. All quiet on the western front." This was the same thing Carnicle said every day at changeover and Gooding supposed she thought it was funny.

She handed him the shift report, along with a half dozen Sig Acts (no KIAs, no WIAs, only a few weapons caches discovered during Salman Pak night patrols), and asked, "So, I'm free to go?"

Gooding skimmed through the reports, saw nothing alarming, and nodded at the other public affairs soldier. "See you in fourteen hours."

"I look forward to it like a dog to a fire hydrant." Another daily catchphrase.

And then she was gone, waddling and clunking out of the palace. Gooding listened to the soft click of computer keys and the *hum-buzz* of the overhead lights for a minute, centering himself in the calm of the adagio, before pulling out his desk chair and beginning the day two hours early.

Taking advantage of the lull at the start of his shift, Gooding sat at the computer, cracked his knuckles, swiveled around to make sure no one else was looking, then opened his diary, a document he kept buried in a labyrinth of folders and subfolders on the hard drive. It was here he kept a detailed record of all the sights, smells, and sounds of camp life. This was how he'd be able to remember the war years down the road when it started to fade from his head. If, that is, he ever made it out of here alive.

From the Diary of Chance Gooding Jr.

Forward Operating Base Triumph is an American city unto itself. A small, rustic American city of tents, trailers, Quonset huts, and dust-beige rectangle-houses (leftovers from the regime), but a city nonetheless. Not unlike what you would have seen 150 years ago in Colorado, Nevada, Oregon, or Montana—slapdash communities nailed together by railroads, miners, and lumberjacks, swollen with a flood of prostitutes, grocers, haberdashers, and schoolmarms, then just as quickly deflated as the mines dried up, the railroads moved on, and the forests were depleted. Like frontier America, FOB Triumph has the buzz of newborn excitement, tempered with the understanding that it is, politically speaking, impermanent. Its eventual doom foretold in its name, FOB Triumph will one day wither away when the United States is victorious in Iraq.

That day is still far in the future, however.

For now, soldiers, Local Nationals, American contractors, and Third World Employees (known as "Twees") move through the gravel streets engineers have quickly and roughly laid between the fifteen rows of trailers. Triumph's residents move like ants, orderly and focused, as they go about the business of supporting a war that crackles across Baghdad, well outside the sandbag-fortified entry control points where guards check ID badges, hold mirrors on poles like giant dentist tools to look at the undercarriages of trucks, and German shepherds pull against leashes as they sniff for bombs. Vehicles are forced to navigate a quarter mile of concrete barricades, slowing them to a crawl as they wind their serpentine way onto the base. By the time a suicide bomber cleared the last barrier, he would have been killed five times over by the soldiers at the gate. He'd be riddled with bullets—turned to a bleeding wedge of Swiss cheese—before his lips could even form the words "Allahu Akbar!"

FOB Triumph is located in west Baghdad, caught between the pressure points of the airport and Abu Ghraib prison. Soon after the United States took control of the city in 2003—securing first the airport, then gradually expanding the ring of safe real estate outward—FOB Triumph grew in increments. Hastily dug foxholes next to tanks turned into tents, tents

turned into shipping containers tricked out with cots
and air-conditioning, shipping containers turned
into trailers with windows, doors, and small wooden
porches—the kind of tin-sided mobile home that have
made more than one soldier from Hog Wallow, Tennessee, weep with homesickness.

There are dangers here, too. Lest you forget, you're
smack dab in the middle of a combat zone. While, hori-
zontally speaking, the FOB is well fortified by concrete
barriers and guard towers, this is not to say death cannot
and will not fall from the sky at any given moment. There
is no Kevlar dome over FOB Triumph, no invisible force
field off of which mortars or 107-millimeter Chinese
rockets will rebound. Why, just last week, one Second
Lieutenant Zipperer had a 7.62 round crash down in his
hooch. It punched through his tin roof in the night and
this Zipperer must have been one hell of a heavy sleeper
(or zonked out on Valium) because he didn't flinch, not
even so much as a fluttery pause in his REM. When he
woke, there was the round sitting on the floor of his hooch.
He sat up on the edge of his cot, groggy and cobwebbed,
and stared at the metal shards for the longest time, not
fully comprehending, until finally he uttered the phrase
that he would repeat once every two minutes for the rest
of the day (much to the irritation of his co-workers): "Holy
Mother of Fuck!"

But what Lieutenant Zipperer was really Holy-Mother-
of-Fucking about was the fact that just the day prior he
had done some interior decorating in his hooch, moving his cot from the east wall to the north wall and that

furniture shift had made the difference between a round punching through the roof and landing in the middle of the floor and the same round coming down and sizzle-slamming through his skull, his head bursting into a gory fountain. Thanks to feng shui, he might just make it home alive.

Walk the gravel paths and dirt streets of FOB Triumph and you will come across a post office, a medical clinic, a library, a movie theater, a bowling alley, two churches, five dining facilities, and four fitness centers.

There is a phone center: a single-wide trailer with a loud-banging door that snaps back on a spring getting looser by the day as thousands upon thousands of soldiers and civilian contractors walk in and out of the one place on the FOB offering a tangible link to the comforts of home. The trailer is lined with three rows of wooden-walled cubbyholes where soldiers grip receivers grimed from two hundred thousand sweaty, homesick palms, and murmur into mouthpieces that have by this point heard it all: the sex talk, questions about the dying relative, the soft weeping when the news is not good, the coo-cooing to babies and puppies, the profanity-laced blowhard stories for the drinking buddies left behind, the calculated, casual dismissal of combat zone danger to soothe worried parents. At any given time, a choir of babble fills the phone center, punctuated by the occasional slam down of a receiver. The voices rise and fall, rise and fall. As they ride the waves of sound, some soldiers doodle on the wooden cubbyholes with knives and pens, carving names and anatomies of certain girls left behind. Even today, if you go over there,

you'll find—just below the motto SADDAM SUXX—*an im-
pressive nude study of a Miss Sammie Grafton of Gillette,
Wyoming.*

*The knives whittle, the boots tap on the plywood floor,
the voices swell and ebb, swell and ebb.*

"What's this about a court summons?"

"And then you put it in your mouth while I . . ."

*"No, no, it ain't too bad—we haven't hit an IED in
almost a week."*

*"She took her first steps today? Day-um! . . . I know, I
wish I could have been there, too."*

*"I'm fine, really! . . . No, really, Ma, that ain't neces-
sary . . . Ma, really, I— . . . Okay, put her on . . . Hello,
Jangles. Is you being a good widdle kitty?"*

*Leave the phone center, spring-hinged door bang-
ing like pistol shot behind you, and keep walking, keep
crunching through the gravel until you reach the Morale,
Welfare, and Recreation Quonset hut where, tucked in
one corner, you'll discover a disco club that in 2005 al-
lows soldiers to take off their helmets and weapons and
(males only) strip down to their T-shirts as they boogie up
gallons of sweat each night after work, bathed in the light
from the disco ball whose refracted light moves like bright
moths across their faces. It has been twenty-five years since
disco died but the soldiers at Triumph don't mind. It may
be KC and the Sunshine Band, but fuck it all it's a beat
that grabs their legs and gives them permission to fling
away all the ill will that has built up during the day. Not
to mention it is the only officially sanctioned way boys and
girls can get close enough to touch, an excitement elevated*

whenever a female soldier, daring to flaunt the rules, strips away her Desert Camouflage Uniform top and dances in her T-shirt, shake-shake-shaking the bootie so hard and with such abandon her breasts take on a mind of their own to the delight of every male lucky enough to be in the club that night.

If you exit the club, half-drunk on near-beer and hormone turbulence, take a left turn, and continue down the main thoroughfare for another mile, you'll hit the post exchange. The entrance to the PX is lined with a series of small trailers that house a Burger King, a What-the-Cluck Chicken Shack, and a Starbucks, where you can purchase a venti caramel macchiato and, with the first sip of the froth and sugar, be transported to within an inch of java heaven.

The PX, run by the U.S. military, is the equivalent of the Old West general store. Its aisles are stocked with potato chips, beef jerky, cases of soda, sunglasses, baby oil, panty hose, tennis shoes, magazines (sans the porn, in deference to host nation Islamic sensitivities), video games, tins of sardines, nail clippers, one big-screen TV (which can be yours for only $1,695.99), stationery, music CDs that tilt heavily toward country-western, value-packs of chewing tobacco, T-shirts ("My Daddy Deployed to Iraq and All I Got Was This Lousy T-Shirt"), brooms, fishing poles, cheese-in-a-can, crackers, compasses, canteens, bras, socks, paperbacks that lean heavily toward Louis L'Amour and Nelson DeMille, desk lamps, Frisbees, pillows, and Insta-Gro planters in clear plastic globes whose promise of fresh vegetation in just two weeks makes them *a big seller to soldiers hoping for a little green in this dusty hellhole.*

A fly-by-night bazaar rings the dusty concrete courtyard outside the PX, a hodgepodge flea market of folding tables, open-bed pickup trucks, and outspread blankets full of wares Local Nationals have brought to the FOB for sale, having first gone through a rigorous security scrubbing at the entry checkpoints. This, U.S. military officials believe, serves two purposes: it gives the soldiers a taste of "real life" outside the FOB wire, and pumps good old American dollars into the local economy. It is here that Fobbits can buy the false souvenirs that will later corroborate the equally false stories of their adventures "outside the wire." That same jagged piece of metal that gets slapped down on the bar at the American Legion with the claim that it's from the hull of a Republican Guard tank blown to bits "while out on patrol one day" is actually scrap scavenged from a local auto junkyard by an enterprising merchant by the name of Emad T. Hamad who whaled away at it with a ballpeen hammer in his garage the night before, offering it up for sale to one Specialist Bert Huddleton, a computer specialist in Task Force Headquarters who, after spending 341 days growing pasty-skinned by the light of his workstation monitor, was looking to buy his way into combat authenticity four days before he redeployed to the United States. Bert went away $44 lighter in the wallet but secure in the knowledge he now had something to show and tell for the story he'd been spinning in his head regarding a (nonexistent) patrol that had "gone bad" one terrible day outside the wire; Emad T. Hamad pocketed the forty-four

Yankee infidel dollars with a grin, muttering the Arabic equivalent of "Suckah!"

Walk through the bazaar and you'll find plenty of Fobbits like Bert and plenty of Local Nationals like Emad. In the PX courtyard, the nut-brown vendors chatter like monkeys as they try to pull the pale, blinking American boys and girls to their tables and blankets. "Mister, mister! Here, mister! You like? You buy?" This, then, is where the discriminating shopper can find scarves (gaily patterned with camels and palm trees), musty-smelling Oriental rugs, pirated blockbuster movies, carved wooden camels, elaborate glass-and-metal contraptions that look suspiciously like hookahs, black-velvet paintings of Jesus, Elvis, and Ricky Martin, and silverware once used by Saddam Hussein (authenticated with a computer-generated certificate by a "Dr. Alawi Medrina, History Professor Emeritus, University of New Baghdad").

Did we mention this military city was constructed on the former site of Saddam Hussein's palace and hunting preserve? It's true. FOB Triumph has overtaken the grounds where Insane Hussein once treated his guests to weekend hunting parties. Nervous staff officers would join the dictator when he walked through the fields, knee-high weeds whisking damply against his pants legs as he flushed the stocked pheasants and quail from their nests and killed them in a bloody burst of feathers before their little beaks had a chance to form the words "Allahu Akbar!" On some weekends, when he was feeling especially jaunty, Saddam would place an order to the Baghdad zoo and they would deliver pairs of lions or jackals or foxes for his

*guests to hunt. As the integration handbook given to newly
arriving soldiers will tell you, "Wildlife is abundant on
the compound in the forms of rodents, snakes, deer, fox,
golden jackal, and gazelle to name just a few." It goes on
to advise: "Do NOT, ever, ever, EVER, at any time, feed
wildlife or domesticated animals such as dogs; report sight-
ings of loose dogs on the compound at once, so they can
be disposed of properly. The keeping of pets for personal
pleasure or profit is STRICTLY prohibited."*

*Beyond the realm of menageries, in the midst of the
Humvees rushing to and fro and the helicopters buzzing
through the air like prowling insects, you will come across
a large, shimmering pool of greenish water. Reflected in
that water is a many-tiered building, white as a dozen
new moons. This is the palace, lined with cobalt-blue tiles
and topped with impossibly beautiful minarets, built by
Saddam in the glory days of his reign. Walk inside and
you'll likely gag on the excess of marble, crystal, and gold
leaf. Right down to a kitchen the size of a football field
and the bidets that once cleaned Saddam's asshole, it is
a testament to wealth. Now it serves as headquarters for
the American forces who defeated the dictator and pulled
down his statue with a quick yank. Type A, ass-pucker
lieutenant colonels now scurry through the halls with the
tock-tock-tock of boot steps where Republican Guard
aide-de-camps also once skittered, fearful of the firing
squad's bullet and Uday's beheading sword.*

*The palace is perched on the banks of a shallow,
boggy lake that, decades ago, had been hand-dug by those
disloyal to Hussein or his brothers. The thirty-acre lake,*

built in the shape of a Z, is now prime breeding ground
for disease-laden mosquitoes. In the mornings, bats swoop
overhead, near the end of their night shift. The stillness of
the green water is broken every so often by carp leaping for
breakfast bugs. Mallard bob in the reeds along the shore,
only taking flight when they're disturbed by the muffled
whoompf! *of a car bomb downtown.*

Gooding devoted nearly all his spare moments to capturing what he saw around him. Sometimes he jotted in his little green notebook, sometimes on an index card, sometimes on a cardboard scrap torn off a box of MREs. And sometimes, when he was most daring, he would type the events of the day into the computer at his workstation in the palace, making sure he erased his digital footprint by saving the file to a thumb drive. He was cautious about using his work computer and picked his "diary moments" carefully.

Today had seemed like a good time. When the morning began (before the hot seep of dawn), it had been cloaked in a subdued murmur rising from the cubicles. This was a rare oasis of peace from the typical shout and bark of "Take *that*, hajji-san!" or "Coffee! STAT!" or "Who the fuck fucked with my PowerPoint?" that punctuated the palace work space. Today felt like an intermezzo before a storm of screaming Shostakovich strings (or so Chance Gooding Jr. noted in his journal).

Then, three hours into his shift, there came a sharp rise in the level of voices and an increased frequency of clicks from dozens of computer mice. One minute later, the phone in the PAO cell started ringing.

Chance snatched up the receiver and gave his usual sing-song butter-smooth answer: "Division Public Affairs, Gooding here."

It was Justine Kayser from CNN asking about the explosion in west Baghdad she'd just heard about. Gooding was taken aback, momentarily dislodged from his official veneer of confidence-at-all-costs. He didn't have a Sig Act report of any such incident at that time, which he told CNN in so many words: "Ma'am, right now, I'm not showing any Significant Activity reports regarding this incident. That's not to say it didn't happen, I just don't have anything official sitting in front of me. If you can give me thirty minutes, I'll see what I can dig up." The instant he hung up, he swung around in his chair and started clicking the computer mouse at the SMOG station.

The Secure Military Operations Grid was the heart and soul of the U.S. military command in Baghdad and the rest of Iraq. Using wireless technology, commanders from places as far-flung as Basra, An Najaf, and Mosul linked their computers to the central hub at Task Force Baghdad Headquarters on FOB Triumph and, among other things, participated in a twice-daily conference call with the commanding general and his staff. SMOG allowed a lieutenant colonel in the Lower Mesopotamian Valley to scroll through his PowerPoint while, in Baghdad, the commanding general clipped his toenails into the wastebasket beside his desk, no one the wiser, as he grunted, "Mmm hmm" or "Tell me more" or "Okay, next."

All Sig Acts were filtered through SMOG and recorded in the system's deep, wide database. During the day, G-3 Operations tracked battlefield activities on SMOG in real time so

Fobbits like Staff Sergeant Chance Gooding Jr. could sit in front of the three computer screens at his air-conditioned worksta- tion and watch tiny icons popping up on the map of downtown Baghdad to mark where IEDs had gone off or where patrols had been ambushed in a small-arms attack or where another group of headless bodies had been found in a troubled neighborhood.

After getting the phone call from CNN, alerting him to a possible explosion across the river from the Palestine Hotel, Gooding had been scrupulously checking the Sig Acts on SMOG. It wasn't until an hour after Justine Kayser's call that the KIA Sig Act had popped up on his screen. Chance bolted from his chair and sprinted through the cubicle maze to G-1 Casualty to see what they could confirm, only to be stonewalled by Semple and Andersen. At this point, all he had to go on was the unofficial, "He's road meat."

On top of that, there was the earlier incident when a suicide bomber in Sadr City had rammed into the ass-end of a tank but failed to detonate. After a tense standoff at a place headquarters had dubbed Quillpen, the would-be terrorist had been shot by either the battalion commander or a platoon sergeant—Gooding was still trying to verify all the facts—but then headquarters started getting calls from the Iraqi Ministry of the Interior telling them the Iraqi police who'd recovered the body reportedly found papers indicating the man was from Switzerland not Syria as originally reported, and wouldn't that just be the fuck-a-roo to end all fuck- a-roos if this hajji turned out to be a peace-loving Swiss Muslim who'd gone rotten somewhere along the line and decided to quit yodeling with Heidi and jihad his ass on over to Iraq.

Either way, the whole thing was a mess and Gooding's public affairs cubicle in Task Force Headquarters had turned into Mess Central because, for the last two hours, CNN had been airing footage captured at the scene where someone had put an end to the alleged Swiss terrorist at Intersection Quillpen. The Ministry of the Interior had already called an impromptu press conference in Firdos Square, the Iraqi minister telling reporters that the terrorist was not from Iraq, Syria, or even Iran, but from a European country, yet he refused to confirm which one, sending the press corps off on wild tangents of speculation. Within minutes, Gooding's office was besieged with phone calls from all the wire services and networks wanting a comment, any comment, even a crumb of a tidbit they could print or air—anything he could give them to confirm the MOI statement would be most helpful and most appreciated because, after all, they were on tight deadline and the story was getting more and more stale every time CNN aired its tape, they just needed something to freshen up the earlier reports.

Then, in the midst of dealing with the assassination of the failed bomber who may or may not be from Switzerland, Gooding learned of the IED in al-Karkh and the probability of high U.S. casualties. As it turned out, only one U.S. soldier was killed—a hot chunk of scrap iron finding that two-inch sweet spot between the helmet and the collar of the flak vest and ripping away half of the kid's neck, causing him to stumble and trip into a puddle of ignited gasoline. Three others had been wounded with the usual assortment of burns, partial amputations, and concussions. Gooding needed to throw a bone to the news networks with this release about the soldier killed in action—if nothing else, it would distract them from the earlier incident at Intersection Quillpen—but he could do nothing without the official confirmation from Casualty.

Now, still sweat-slicked from his run through the palace, Gooding's fingers flew across the keyboard like he was playing Mozart's Piano Sonata no. 11 and only had two minutes to finish the damned thing. In fact, he only had one minute. The division's public affairs officer Lieutenant Colonel Eustace Harkleroad hovered at Gooding's elbow, watching every keystroke of the press release unrolling across the computer screen.

Harkleroad was a thick man. Thick in the way a bowl of risen dough is said to be thick. He filled his uniform amply; in truth, there was more flesh than fabric. When he leaned back in his chair, other soldiers flinched, afraid a button would pop off, come flying across the room, and put out an eye.

Furthermore, Eustace Harkleroad—forever shortened by his mother to "Stacie," which had caused him no end of agony over the past forty-odd years—was a spontaneous nosebleeder. Gooding knew if he didn't get this killed-in-action press release done quickly and to the exacting standards of the commanding general, the PAO's nose would start dripping red like a spigot.

Gooding didn't tell his boss he was writing this release based on the barest, unsubstantiated nod from G-1 Casualty. What Harkleroad didn't know wouldn't hurt either him or the rest of the world. Besides, this press release had already been ping-ponging around division headquarters for the past fifty minutes—at least four hours and ten minutes after the charred body had cooled somewhere out there in al-Karkh—and the Task Force Baghdad Public Affairs Office merely needed to tell the media what they thought they already knew. The press release was just another useless, redundant scrap of information in the reporters' e-mail in-boxes and eight times out of ten would be deleted without being read. But to the majors, lieutenant colonels, colonels, and generals running around division headquarters in a constant state of ass-pucker, the press release was as important as an edict from the pope.

In its life cycle, the press release went through several layers of approval and sometimes contradictory editing by the various staff officers along the way. From Staff Sergeant Gooding it went to Lieutenant Colonel Harkleroad, who would red-pen the sentences, give it back to Gooding for corrections, then distribute it to several other staff officers—Intelligence and Security, Plans and Operations, staff judge advocate, provost marshal, sometimes even the chaplain got a say-so—before hand carrying it upstairs to the command group, where Harkleroad would give it to the chief of staff's secretary—fingers trembling, nose already tingling with the threat of blood—and wait outside the chief's office door while the secretary ventured inside to place the press release on the colonel's desk. He would be blasted with either a bark of, "What the fuck is it now?!" or a battle-weary, "All right, let me have it. And for God's sake, tell Harkleroad to stop sniffing out there."

Lieutenant Colonel Harkleroad did his best to suck the beginning drips of blood back into his nostrils and prayed the chief read the press release before he couldn't snuffle it up anymore and he had to walk in there to retrieve the paper with a tissue wad sticking out of his nose.

The chief of staff, a colonel named Belcher, had lost his temper right around the time he lost all of his hair—age thirty. He was known (and feared) on Army staffs as the man whose bald head perpetually glowed like an overheated thermometer.

While he waited, Harkleroad kept the left side of his body angled toward the chief's office door. Stacie's right eardrum had been punctured when he'd stepped too close to a howitzer during artillery training eleven years ago. Then-Captain Harkleroad had been thinking about his mother's church group in Murfreesboro, Tennessee, and how at their Wednesday Bible study meetings Eulalie Constance Harkleroad ("Connie" at her insistence) would announce to the other ladies fanning themselves with *Our Daily Bread* the latest accomplishments of her son Stacie as he made a name for himself in the United States Army. Most of what his mother relayed to the First Church of Redemption ladies were half-truths Stacie Harkleroad kneaded and pulled like Silly Putty for her benefit.

"Well, Mother, today I led my men on a twelve-mile road march in the pouring rain." (He'd stopped to tie his bootlaces at the three-mile mark, telling his first sergeant to continue on with the rest of the company and he'd catch up, then surreptitiously slipped back to headquarters.)

"Next month, I'm taking my company on a joint training exercise to Italy." (The three-day command post exercise had taken place right there at Fort Knox, Kentucky; the staff officers sat at a bank of computers and moved icons around a map of the Italian Alps, while a group of Air Force officers at Warren AFB in Wyoming and Marines at Twenty-Nine Palms in California did the same thing—each of them trying to out-maneuver the other until the exercise observer-controllers called "game over.")

"Yes, Mother, yes, the brigade commander is certain I'll be promoted this year, it's just a matter of checking the right blocks on my annual evaluation form." (The colonel barely knew

Stacie existed—called him *Harrison* every time he saw him, despite the fact *Harkleroad* was embroidered above the breast pocket of his uniform.)

Eustace had gotten so deep into the habit of lying to his mother to fuel her Wednesday evening Bible studies that he wasn't sure how to stop, except to one day actually do something that, if not exactly brave or significant, would at least have the truth as its foundation.

This is what he had been thinking as the gun crew prepared the artillery round for deployment on that day eleven years ago. The idea entered Harkleroad's head that if he was the one to pull the lanyard and fire the howitzer, he could actually give his mother something to bust her buttons over.

He started walking toward the gun crew with his great idea, but he was half an idea too late. He was three paces away and in the midst of saying, "Here, Sergeant, let me—" when the squad leader gave a huge tug on the lanyard, the rest of the crew having already bent over, plugging their ears. There was a belch of smoke, the howitzer recoiled, and Harkleroad's right ear popped like a hot tomato. He was thrown to the ground in inky silence.

Since then, he was forced to cock his head in order to catch the mumbled words that fell off his superiors' lips, hoping he could fake his way through the conversation with a nod or a grimace, as seemed appropriate from his best guess of what had been said.

And so, three-quarters of the way through the life cycle of a typical press release, he would wait outside the division chief of staff's office, straining to catch a meaningful cough, sigh, or an outright "what the fuck is this shit?"

Once the chief had read and initialed the press release, it went one of two places: back into Harkleroad's hands for more corrections and a subsequent review or to the commanding general's desk for his approval. Harkleroad would then have to position himself outside the CG's door and pray *he* was a mercifully fast reader, too. Stacie Harkleroad had, on too many occasions, stood in front of the CG's desk with one nostril plugged and a dried delta of blood on his upper lip, the general trying not to look at his pathetic face because it would only make him scowl and want to kick his PAO's ass from here to Ankara. The majority of Harkleroad's time in Baghdad had been spent anxiously dabbing at his nostrils while waiting for pieces of paper to be initialed and approved.

On every Army division staff there is always at least one officer who is the object of pity and/or ridicule. He is the one who sits stranded around the polished mahogany table before the briefings to the CG while the others from G-1 Personnel, G-2 Intelligence, G-3 Operations, G-4 Logistics, and G-5 Civil Affairs (the Gee-Whiz Gang) scoot their chairs closer together and talk with blustery guffaws and manly winks and conspiratorial nods; he is the one who sits there fiddling with the clicker on his ballpoint pen and pretending to find something of great interest in the sheaf of PowerPoint slides he printed and brought to the meeting; he is the one who begins his daily update to the CG with a choked, squeaky wheeze before clearing his throat and trying again while the commanding general stares hot impatience at him, chewing his spleen and wondering how in the good goddamn he ever ended up with this doofus on his staff.

In Task Force Baghdad, Lieutenant Colonel Eustace Harkleroad was that designated staffer—even the chaplain was held in higher esteem—but there was little Harkleroad could do to penetrate the burly, hairy-chest circle of colonels ringed around the commanding general, except to try harder—flap his wings and hope he flew.

Which is exactly what he'd done earlier that day when news of the al-Karkh explosion crackled over the loudspeakers in division headquarters: he'd flown from his office to Staff Sergeant Gooding's desk, rounding the corner of the cubicle so fast he almost skidded out and landed on his fat ass in front of his PAO staff. He recovered with a half-skip worthy of Fred Astaire, albeit a 250-pound Fred Astaire, and walked up to Gooding, jabbing a fresh-printed copy of the Significant Activity report at his chest. "We need to start drafting a press release, *now*! We need to beat CNN to the punch."

Gooding grabbed the Sig Act and spun around in his chair to his computer, pulling up the already written press release template he used whenever a division soldier died, which lately was at least twice a day.

His fingers stabbed the keyboard, pecking the letters of what would surely be a brilliant six-sentence press release destined for the Press Release Hall of Fame. He punched the PRINT button then put the finished product in Lieutenant Colonel Harkleroad's hands.

FOR IMMEDIATE RELEASE   **June 6, 2005**

RELEASE 20050606-04a

Soldier killed in al-Karkh suicide car bomb blast

BAGHDAD — A Task Force Baghdad soldier was killed when a suicide car bomber detonated his payload in an al-Karkh neighborhood around 11 a.m. on June 6.

Three Iraqi bystanders were also killed in the blast, which ripped through a shopping district, destroying a tea shop and fruit seller's stall.

The soldier's unit was assisting Iraqi security forces on a patrol of the area when it came under attack from terrorists. The soldier was evacuated to the 86th Combat Support Hospital where he later died of his injuries.

The name of the soldier is being held pending notification of next of kin. The incident is under investigation.

Harkleroad hunched over the press release. The tiny hairs in his ears were bristling where they sprouted around the hearing aid he claimed cost him—or, rather, cost the Army—$6,000. Gooding wasn't sure how well the government's money was spent since the man still had selective hearing.

"Hm. Okay. Uh. Do we know for a fact it was a suicide car bomber?"

"It was on the Sig Act, sir."

"But confirmed by anyone on the ground?"

"No, not that I'm aware, sir. I don't think any of our men actually saw a crazed, wild-eyed terrorist sitting behind the steering wheel, if that's what you mean." Normally, Gooding wasn't this sarcastic with his boss but sleep deprivation, the idiocy of those dingleberries in G-1, and last night's licorice had put him on edge.

"Okay, then," Harkleroad said. "Let's take out '*when a suicide car bomber detonated his payload*' and replace it with '*when a car bomb exploded.*' Make that change, then print it out again for me to see."

Gooding's fingers went back to work. Peck-peck-peckity-peck. Save. Print.

Harkleroad bent over the edited release, his lips moving as he silently read Gooding's work.

"Hm. Okay. Uh-oh. Look, you've got 'suicide' in the headline.

"Aw, shit."

"That's okay because I've got another change. Let's take out the part about the shopping district and the fruit and tea. It tends toward humanization of the Local Nationals—you know, blurs the line of our neutrality here. Looks like we're sensationalizing the deaths of these three poor Iraqis."

"Okay, sir."

Harkleroad continued to stare at the press release, his index finger curled beneath his nose as he pondered the significance of each and every word, weighing the verbs against the nouns before he had to make the long walk upstairs to the chief's office.

"On second thought . . ."

"Yes, sir?"

"Let's take out all reference to the dead Iraqis. We'll let the Ministry of Interior make that announcement. Besides, I'm a little reluctant to play up the fact that only one of our guys was killed, versus the three on the home team. Collateral deaths are always a tricky thing, Sergeant Gooding."

"Yes, sir, they are." The licorice rumbled in Gooding's gut.

"It sort of plays into the 'if you weren't here, this would never have happened' mentality," Harkleroad said. "Let's not draw attention to the Local National deaths if we don't have to."

"Roger, sir."

"Good. Go ahead and make those changes, then print that draft."

Gooding pivoted and returned to his desk. His fingers were like Liberace in his finest moment.

Back into Harkleroad's hands. Another ponderous finger perched beneath the imminently bloody nose. "Hm. Okay. But . . . ehhh . . . I don't know. I think we need to put the reference to multinational forces *after* the Iraqi security forces. Right now, it looks like we're trying to hog the spotlight from our Iraqi friends."

"Ooo-kay, sir."

Gooding glanced at the clock. More than forty-five minutes had elapsed. By now, the tow truck was already hauling the wrecked Humvee from the scene and the CNN reporter was calling in a report on her cell phone.

"Go ahead and do the flip-flop, then let me see another draft before we send it up to corps PAO for approval. I'll be in my office."

Gooding bent over his keyboard. He could hear his Timex ticking like a stopwatch at the Olympic trials. His fingers were like Bruce Jenner's feet, running around the keys until they got blisters and started to bleed.

Gooding sprinted to the PAO's office, a room no bigger than a closet (in fact, it had been a janitor's closet when Saddam ran the place) just off the main cubicle area. The boss, Gooding noted, had been hunched over his desk lining up paper clips when he arrived panting in the doorway.

Harkleroad gave a startled flinch, then held out his hand. "All right, let me see it." He read the release, tapped his chin, caressed his upper lip, and thought like a chess player trying to anticipate the chief of staff's first move. "What do you think about calling the ISF *heroic*?"

"I think that's a great idea, sir."

Peckity-peck-peck, tappity-tap-tap. Zing! Back to Harkleroad's desk, front and center.

"Okay, let's see what you got."

FOR IMMEDIATE RELEASE   **June 6, 2005**

RELEASE 20050606-04e

Iraqi Security Forces attacked in al-Karkh

BAGHDAD — Heroic Iraqi security forces, with minimal assistance from Task Force Baghdad soldiers, were patrolling al-Karkh around 11 a.m. on June 6 when they came under attack from terrorists.

One U.S. soldier was killed when a car bomb exploded in the neighborhood.

The soldier was evacuated to the 86th Combat Support Hospital where he later died of his injuries.

The name of the soldier is being held pending notification of next of kin. The incident is under investigation.

Harkleroad read the gutted-and-thrashed release twice, thrice, then once more, holding a hand over one eye for a slightly different perspective. "Okay. Looks good. I'll take it to the chief."

Staff Sergeant Gooding collapsed against the door frame of the PAO's office, his fingers throbbing, but sweet relief coursing his veins.

Lieutenant Colonel Stacie Harkleroad thanked him again then drew a deep breath and climbed the stairs to the second floor of division headquarters. They were as steep and long as a path up Everest. At the top, the chief waited, a growing scowl on his face.

He was a tall man, his bald head adding to his menacing height. His face seemed carved from granite with a pair of eyes sharp as laser beams. When he looked at his staff, their souls withered. Even picturing him in his underwear didn't help reduce the intimidation factor.

"What the fuck do you want now, PAO?"

"Release on the Second Brigade casualty, sir."

"Oh, yeah? Lemme have it." He thrust out his hand like he was asking Harkleroad for a roll of toilet paper.

The chief gripped the press release, his large thumbs crinkling the edges as he read it aloud in a growl-mumble: "Heroic-*grrrgrrr*minimal assistance from*grrrgrrr*Karkh*grrrgrrr*attack from terrorists…One U.S. soldier was killed*grrrgrrrgrrrgrrr*evacuated to the*grrrgrrr*later died of his injuries*grrrgrrrgrrrgrrrgrrrgrrrgrrr*under investigation."

Harkleroad simultaneously felt his bowels loosen and his nose go soft and fluid. He sniffed deeply and blinked twice when the chief raised his head from the press release. "All right. It'll do, I guess. Fuckin' liberal news whores'll fuck it all up anyway no matter what we say, right, Harkleroad?"

"Right, sir." A bit of blood peeked out from one nostril. Harkleroad silently urged the chief to hurry with the pen scribbling his initial in the left-hand corner.

The chief gave the half-crumpled paper back to his PAO. "There you go."

"Thanks, chief. We'll get this out pronto."

"Right, right, whatever. And hey—" the chief raised a brow over a twinkling eye "—next time you talk to Fox News, ask 'em when I get my exclusive one-on-one interview with Lana Thompson."

"Roger, chief."

"Tell 'em I'm ready for my close-up."

"Roger."

Harkleroad about-faced and quickly marched from the second-floor command group area back down to the Public Affairs cubicles, sucking up the blood as he went. He rounded the corner with a yip and a hoot. "Staff Sergeant Gooding! Send it!"

Harkleroad was a cigar-chomping city editor and Gooding was the copyboy in a green eyeshade, racing through the room of clacking typewriters and cynical reporters on his way to the pressroom where, above the clang of bells and *whirring-clanking* presses, he'd scream in the half-deaf pressman's ear, "Okay, Pops! Print it!"

Gooding composed the e-mail, inserted the corps PAO addresses, attached the brilliantly written Press Release Number 20050606-04, then prepared to send it zigging and zagging along the highways of cyberspace.

"Stop! Sergeant Gooding! Don't send it!"

Gooding's finger froze above the ENTER button. He looked back over his shoulder. Harkleroad was staring at the TV. His face was white and, as predicted, his nose had started to bleed. "It's all over," he croak-whispered. "CNN beat us to the punch. They're running a report about the attack."

Well, what the hell did you expect, Mr. Longfellow Rewrite? Gooding thought.

He closed the e-mail without sending it.

"What now, sir?"

"Oh, good gravy, I don't know." Eustace Harkleroad stuffed a tissue up one bloody nostril. "Now I guess we start over with a new angle. Give me a minute. And give me a pen."

"Here you go, sir." Gooding whipped a ballpoint out of his pocket. Harkleroad took the last version of the press release and

began extensive surgery with the pen. Blood soaked through the
end of the tissue wad but thankfully dried before it could bead
and drip onto Gooding's beautiful press release, now splayed
open before Harkleroad on the desk. *Scritch-scratch* went his pen,
crossing out whole sentences and moving entire paragraphs with
an elaborate series of arrows and *Insert this here* and *Change to*.

Ten minutes after CNN broadcast its first report from
the scene of the attack, he handed an ink-muddied paper to
Gooding. "See what you can do with this."

"Roger, sir."

"I'm guessing this will probably have to go through several
more drafts before we're through with it."

Somewhere in Oregon, a tree whimpered.

Gooding returned to his computer screen. He cracked his
knuckles. He started anew, decoding the colonel's scribbles and
adding extra flourishes of his own.

FOR IMMEDIATE RELEASE   **June 6, 2005**
RELEASE 20050606-04f

Iraqi Security Forces respond to al-Karkh attack

BAGHDAD —Iraqi security forces put months of coalition-backed training to the test today as they quickly responded to a terrorist attack in an
al-Karkh neighborhood around 11 a.m.

Iraqi police and Baghdad emergency response teams were first on the
scene after an explosion went off near an Iraqi Army patrol combing houses
in the area and looking for caches of weapons and insurgent propaganda
material. The Iraqi security forces immediately cordoned off the area to
ensure no Iraqi citizens were killed or injured by potential subsequent blasts.

One U.S. soldier was killed in the attack. The name of the soldier is being
held pending notification of next of kin. The incident is under investigation.

"Hm. Okay. Uh. Good . . ." Harkleroad turned and walked out of the room, the press release in his hand and a thoughtful look on his face. His gaze was fixed at a spot far ahead, as if he was trying to see the chief's next reaction.

That should have been Gooding's first clue they weren't completely through.

Three minutes later, Harkleroad rounded the corner, a pen clicking against his teeth and that ponder-heavy expression wrinkling his face. "You know, I've been thinking . . ."

"Yes, sir?" Gooding's voice was a croak.

"We need to punch this up with a few adjectives here and there. What about *as they responded with lightning-like speed and efficiency* and *The daring Iraqi security forces immediately cordoned off the area?*"

Gooding tried to swallow the dry knot in his throat. "Sir, isn't there some agency in the Iraqi government that's already putting out a press release on this?"

"No," Harkleroad said. "I've talked to corps and apparently MOI is taking no action on this one. We need to produce something about the attack and get it out there for the rest of the media."

Chance Gooding stared at his nosebleeding colonel and tamped down his dark thoughts. You mean, even though the smoke has cleared, the ambulances have picked up the meat and taken it to the morgue, and all the bystanders and terrorists have already gone back home to their families—the old men eating rice and lamb and boasting about how they'd show those Sunni bastards a thing or two about democratic government; in other houses, the young, politically zealous husbands lifting the veils off their wives' faces as foreplay to an evening of sex;

even the insurgents packing away their rocket launchers and grenades and calling it a night—you mean even though the news is now as cold and dead as the soldier himself, we should still put out a press release?

Okay.

FOR IMMEDIATE RELEASE   **June 6, 2005**
RELEASE 20050606-04g
Brave Iraqi Security Forces repel heinous al-Karkh attack
BAGHDAD —Dozens of brave Iraqi security forces put months of coalition-backed training to the test today as they responded with lightning-like speed and efficiency to an unwarranted terrorist attack in an al-Karkh neighborhood around 11 a.m.

Iraqi police and Baghdad emergency response teams were first on the scene after an explosion went off near an Iraqi Army patrol combing houses in the area and looking for caches of weapons and insurgent propaganda material in an ongoing effort to defeat the enemies of democracy in the region. The daring Iraqi security forces immediately cordoned off the area to ensure no Iraqi citizens were killed or injured by potential subsequent blasts.

One U.S. soldier was killed in the attack. The name of the soldier is being held pending notification of next of kin. The incident is under investigation.

Harkleroad pushed the tissue plug tighter in his nostril and winked at his NCO as he finally hit the SEND button. "Good job, Sergeant Gooding. Score another minor victory for the name of truth and democracy."

"Right, sir." If Harkleroad held his hand up for a high five, Gooding swore he'd puke. He turned back to his computer screen as a new message pinged into his in-box. It was from the

Associated Press Baghdad Bureau; the subject line was "Stale News—better luck next time."

On the TV at his elbow, Justine Kayser had one hand cupped over an ear as she gave her report back to Wolf at the war desk, her voice at hurricane pitch: "What we're seeing here, Wolf, is another attempt by Ba'athist extremists, a splinter group that reportedly has ties to members of the former regime. Three Iraqi bystanders were killed in the blast, which tore through a shopping district, totally destroying a tea shop, a nail salon, and a fruit seller's stall. You can see the charred fruit rinds littering the street behind me. The people we talked to here at the scene tell us today's car bombing would never have happened if it weren't for the lax security measures in this neighborhood. One shopkeeper told us it took Iraqi police nearly an hour to respond to the attack. Their excuse? They were in the middle of a training session with their U.S. counterparts at a base on the other side of Baghdad and couldn't get away. As you can imagine, this only adds more fuel to the fire of anti-coalition resentment building here in the streets. Back to you, Wolf."

Lieutenant Colonel Harkleroad moaned. "Oh, good gravy! Where the heck did they get *that* information?"

"They were there, sir," Gooding said, silently adding, *And we were not*.

4

SHRINKLE

Men," Captain Shrinkle's voice rang across the courtyard of the palace. "These are the times that try our souls."

The rows of soldiers standing in formation rustled, exchanging sidelong glances without moving their heads.

"I know some of you have had difficulty sleeping since that unfortunate incident at Quillpen last week. Maybe you've been tossing and turning in your beds at night. Instead of counting sheep, all you can see is that Sunni's head exploding—going *ka-blooey!*"

There came a short, suppressed groan from the general direction of where Sergeant Lumley stood in formation.

"But I want you to know, I'm here for you." The formation of men shifted from foot to foot. "My door is always open, any time you want to talk it out." Abe liked the way his voice bounced off the walls of the palace and into the ears of his men. It filled him with a good, affirmative feeling of authority. If he spoke a little louder, he wondered if maybe he might draw a couple of colonels to their windows, pull them away from their Fobbit duties to see him out here addressing his men who stood in a neat block of helmets with M4s at right-shoulder arms. Most commanders dispensed with the practice of company formations while here in Iraq, preferring instead to stand in the center of a loose, raggedy circle of at-ease soldiers. But not Captain Abe Shrinkle. He believed tight discipline would be the key to getting them through this year.

As the company first sergeant, a barrel-chested black man with a voice like raspy thunder, was fond of saying, "This is a ding-dang war, gentlemen, and don't you ding-dang forget it." (First Sergeant was a semi-devout Baptist who avoided profanity whenever possible.) "The ding-dang hajjis out there don't give a hoot whether you want to be here or not. They'll still be here when we're packed up and gone home. But for the year you here, you just better suck it up and drive on and listen to the ding-dang commander and myself. We the ones gonna get you through it. We the ones gonna make sure you go home with all you arms, legs, and dick still attached. You listen to us. We the ones gonna show you the way to win."

Whether or not First Sergeant believed everything that came out of his mouth with his ding-dang bellow, Captain Shrinkle backed him one hundred percent. He even let loose a couple of *Amen*s after some of First Sergeant's speeches.

Abe wanted them to succeed at all costs. He loved America, he really did—purple mountains majesty and the whole nine yards. He believed there were no finer bedrock principles of any government than the ones founded by those powder-wigged Philadelphia fathers all those centuries ago.

Abe was *born* patriotic, a squalling baby striped red, white, and blue. By the fourth grade, he'd memorized the preamble to the Constitution; before he'd graduated high school, he had five ribbons hanging in his bedroom for the speech meets where he'd recited the entire Declaration of Independence (including the signatures) with a dramatic flourish that none of the other debate teams could equal. He mowed his neighbors' yards—for *free*—because it was the right thing to do, the American way of democratic community. He pulled the chair out for his mother at the dinner table and called his father *Sir* without the smallest crumb of condescension.

There was never any question he would enter the military. His grandfather had served, two of his uncles had served, and his father would have served if it hadn't been for the lupus. When the time came and Abe, a high school senior, stood on that cusp of decision, the choice was already mapped and plotted. There followed a brisk four years at Northwestern, eager participation in the Young Republicans Club, application and acceptance into West Point, and a steady rise through the Army ranks. Abe Shrinkle was on his way toward something big, something great, something magnanimous that would benefit his family and America at large.

The train of ambition had been barreling down the tracks so fast Abe hadn't seen the washed-out bridge ahead.

Things had not always gone as he'd hoped, no. There had been setbacks, letdowns, and reversals of fortune.

There was that kerfuffle over his paper on Ethan Allen ("Beyond Furniture: Tactics and Techniques of the Green Mountain Boys"), which his West Point instructor had handed back to him pinched between two fingers, saying, "It's dry when it needs to be wet, and moist when it should be practical. Altogether, a lackluster attempt, Cadet Shrinkle." Undaunted, Abe had gone back and rewritten the red-inked, slashed, and arrowed sections and emerged with a C for the course.

Then there was his initial field problem at his first duty station in Alaska, where he'd been placed in charge of range safety for three days as soldiers rotated through the foxholes to qualify on the M16. It had been Abe's job to scan the firing lanes, then raise his wooden paddle, signaling to the control tower that the downrange area was all clear. He hadn't seen the mother moose and her calf browsing the willows at the 150-meter interval . . . but soldiers on the line had, and they took great sport in pumping rounds downrange right into the animals, even after Abe started waving his white paddle like a semaphore. The incident had blotched Abe's record and slowed the acceleration on his chances for promotion but he had tried to shrug it off, knowing he would move on to better things at his next duty station.

And it *was* better at Fort Bliss, Texas . . . until three of his soldiers (two of them overweight, and the other a known alcoholic) had collapsed during the annual division "fun run." The battalion commander looked at Abe with his lemon-juice lips and wanted to know whether or not he had read the forecast for that day and, if so, had he willfully and maliciously chosen to ignore the heat index, which topped 110 degrees, a clear indicator he should keep his men hydrated? Abe tried to explain that canteens were on back-order with battalion supply (when really he'd forgotten to order them in the first place), but that excuse didn't hold water with the commander.

Still, these were molehills, not mountains, and Abe persevered, believing in the absolute moral superiority of his Army, his country, and his role in both.

When the towers collapsed and evil tried to gain a foothold in America, Abe had dug in his heels and vowed to be an immovable brick in the wall of security that they must now put up around his country. He was gung ho for war as a way to kick evil's ass and he lustily cheered for the president during each Oval Office broadcast.

Since his arrival in the Cradle of Islam, Abe tried not to read the headlines in the newspapers left on the tables in the dining facility. He wouldn't let the "gloom and doom" prognosticators dampen his mood with their implied doubts about the success of the missions in Iraq and Afghanistan. He would hold fast to the belief that a united America was behind them when he and his men went on patrol to help improve this impoverished nation of power outages and fractious sheikhs.

That's why encouraging his company to work through their complicated feelings about killing the suicide bomber at Quillpen was a good idea. If they could scrub the sight of that Sunni's red-misted head from their nightmares by getting in touch with their feelings, then they'd be more effective killing machines the next time something like this came up. At least that's what he remembered the clinic psychologist saying during that predeployment briefing back at Fort Stewart: "The Killer Inside Me: No Shame in That."

And yet . . .

And yet Abe himself *did* feel shame over what had happened at Intersection Quillpen. He'd been too slow to react, too hesitant to commit to the bullet. Why was that?

He didn't know and he'd been kicking himself from here to Sunday ever since, agonizing over the indecision. Had it been an urge to protect the soldiers inside that Abrams tank and the gathering Iraqi onlookers? Was it a question of wringing his hands for one minute too long as the moment of opportunity peaked and other factors came into the picture to clutter the situation? Or maybe he was just afraid of picking the wrong door in this "Let's Make an Iraqi Deal." Abe was pretty sure his grandfather never had one stuttering moment of waffle-waffle before sticking his bayonet in a Jap's throat. So what the hell was his problem?

He made a mental note to go to the clinic and find that psychologist when they got back to Fort Stewart.

Captain Shrinkle turned the formation over to First Sergeant, who looked out at the soldiers and gave a slow shake of his head and purse of his lips before telling them they better listen to what the commander had to say about "talking it out" otherwise they'd end up going back to the States with a ding-dang case of PTSD and that was no joke, not like a ding-dang case of the clap that you'd get rid of with a shot of "penis-cillin." (A few snickers at that and a cautious glance toward the commander at the back of the formation who shrugged to let the joke fly this time.) Then First Sergeant reminded them about weapons check at 1630 hours and said he needed to see the platoon sergeants right after formation. He dismissed them with a loud "Hoo-ah!" which was echoed by the men of Company B.

The way it rang off the side of the palace like a deep, throaty bell made Abe Shrinkle's blood run even redder. Quillpen or no Quillpen, he thought, this war was going pretty good so far.

5

GOODING

Chance Gooding juggled IED reports like they were flaming tenpins. The IED and vehicle-borne IED rate was on the rise, spiking within the past week. They were now coming at Gooding at such an alarming rate he was unable to keep track of them. With each Significant Activity report, he opened another press release template and started typing, trying all the time not to get events confused.

Only the body count kept the Sig Acts straight in his mind—that and the many typos peppering the Sig Acts. A squad patrolling along Route Vulcan was said to be on "Route Vulva." A staff sergeant rounding up suspected bomb makers grabbed them by their "shits." And, Gooding's favorite, a private first class injured by the concussion from an IED blast was said to have suffered "a loss of conscience."

Another time, as his glazed eyes were skimming through all the IED, VBIED, and small-arms-fire attacks, he stumbled across this in a description of a platoon coming under an RPG attack: "Unit also observed peanut-butter colored Mercedes,

which left scene right after attack." *Peanut-butter colored*. Who
says Sig Acts can't make for interesting reading?

Quirky details of IED attacks usually helped make Gooding's job easier. On an otherwise quiet night two weeks ago, three
VBIEDs were detonated within the space of a few minutes in
a west Baghdad district filled with small, Mom and Pop busi-
nesses. The terrorists set off one bomb, then sat back and waited
for the Iraqi police and firefighters to respond before they set
off the other two. *Complex multistaged ambush,* G-3 called it.
Several IPs were killed, dozens of civilians wounded. One car
was blown into the air and, like a flaming metal meteor, landed
on top of the row of shops, destroying an electronics store, a
barbershop, and, ironically, an auto parts store.

Reporters routinely called Gooding on the phone, wanting
more information about, for instance, "the explosion on Airport
Road," and he would ask them for more information—time of
explosion, number of killed and injured, any unusual body parts,
et cetera—to pinpoint the event. His press release headlines
all sounded the same with vanilla-oatmeal predictability: "Iraqi
police, Army secure bomb blast site" or "Baghdad explosion
kills eight, wounds twelve" or "Iraqi security forces, U.S. Army
mop up blast site."

At one point, Gooding got so frustrated that, in his confusion, he turned to Major Filipovich in the next cubicle and
said, "Sir, can't we start naming these attacks, just like we name
hurricanes? I mean, I could keep them all straight if we could
call them IED Martha or VBIED Larry."

Major Philip "Flip" Filipovich, never one to crack a smile,
even at his weakest moments, leaned back in his chair, yawned,
rubbed his black billiard-ball head, and said, "Fan-fucking-tastic

idea, Sarge. Why don't I propose it to our Most Esteemed Leader at the next staff meeting? I'm sure Harkleroad will treat it like every other brilliant idea I've brought his way: he'll drop it straight into the toilet and give it a good flush."

Filipovich was the deputy public affairs officer, a lazy-ass midlevel field grade officer who hated Lieutenant Colonel Harkleroad with a vein-throbbing passion. He often dreamed of "Harklefuck" meeting his death in any number of abrupt, violent ways: choking on a fish bone during the dining facility's weekly Bounty of the Sea dinner; seeing a snake on the ground while running to board a Blackhawk, which scared him so much he untucked from his hunched run and shot straight up into the chopping blades; or riding in the lead Humvee of a convoy that strikes an IED, sending 245 pounds of PAO skyward in a geyser of blood, bone, and government-subsidized hearing aid.

"Now, if you don't mind, some of us have work to do—important, global-level, earth-shattering work." Filipovich chair-scooted back into his cubicle to finish the local media assessment that Harkleroad, the fat fuck, would be wanting on his desk precisely two hours from now.

Gooding gritted his teeth and turned back to his headline. "Al-Dora blast kills eight, injures three." No, wait, it was supposed to be "Al-Dora blast kills three, injures eight." Now he was confused and he pawed through the pile of Sig Acts on his desk to get everything straight in his head again. He was near the end of his shift and it hadn't been a good one.

The morning had started with a terrorist sabotaging water lines at a water treatment plant outside Baghdad at 4:40 a.m. The bomb burst the pipes at a crucial joint and sewer water had flooded the control room. Iraqi Department of Water officials rushed to the scene and shut off water for everyone in Baghdad west of the Tigris River. The government reported it could take up to three or four days of round-the-clock work to repair this latest sabotage. Citizens were riled and started venting on *Al-Jazeera,* mouths chewing the microphones and spittle misting the camera lens.

Then, shortly after one p.m., a VBIED detonated behind an Iraqi police patrol, killing two Iraqi Army soldiers and two IPs and wounding twenty-seven others. Gooding named that one IED Vaporized Cop.

The worst was yet to come. There was still plenty of daylight left on the clock.

Before three p.m., a man wearing a suicide vest packed with explosives walked into a restaurant. He killed five Iraqi soldiers and thirteen civilians and wounded at least thirty-four civilians. These were just the initial reports Gooding received over the SMOG's Sig Acts. The Associated Press later tallied it at twenty-three dead, thirty-six wounded.

Nobody on the scene saw the bomber carrying anything into the café. According to a group of Iraqi soldiers inside the restaurant at the time of the explosion, they had just ordered their lunch when the suicide bomber entered and detonated the device. Survivors at the scene said the majority of the patrons were soldiers who were fond of the special goat gyros served there for lunch every day, guaranteeing there would always be a large group of Iraqi military at the restaurant at any given mealtime. Area residents knew the café would be targeted for this reason and most of them tried to avoid it whenever possible, taking a wide detour around the block during the noon hour.

Gooding's e-mail dinged. It was a series of photos from the brigade public affairs team that had rushed to the scene in the smoky aftermath.

Gooding clicked on the attachments.

The first photos showed the hole-in-the-wall (now literally) restaurant gutted by swift, lethal fire. Part of the ceiling was gone and sunshine flooded the charred interior. Viscera was smeared across the floor. Tables and chairs, inextricably married in a tangle of chrome legs and plastic cushions, rested against a back wall where they'd been propelled by the blast. Bright packages of crackers, tins of tea, and cellophane-wrapped candy were still neatly arranged on a shelf next to a register, waiting for someone to come along and make a purchase. A man, presumably the owner, stood in a still-smoking door frame—the door was gone, thrown halfway down the block. His eyes were glassed with shock as he stared at what remained of his café.

Gooding clicked into the next e-mail, subject line: "The remains of the suicide bomber."

A head. Two legs that appeared to be sprouting from his neck. A hand, fingers twisted and broken, in the region where normally the right hip bone is located.

That was it. Nothing more. Everything else—skin, bone, muscle, organ—had vaporized in a red splash through the dust and rubble of the restaurant.

In the blackened head, the eyes were squeezed shut, as if in the final reflex before the bomber pulled the det cord. His feet on the end of those neatly severed legs were turned in opposite directions—one forward, one backward. If you didn't know better, you might mistake his legs for arms, his feet for hands. He looked like a meaty jigsaw puzzle of parts—with those feet-hands, he looked like a child's drawing of a traffic cop, one hand saying "Stop!" the other beckoning "Go!"

Gooding decided to zoom in on the ragged end of the shoulder. His cursor changed to a magnifying glass. The closer he got to the sheared-off torso, the less his stomach churned. Soon it started to look less like meat, less like the abrupt ripping away of life, and more like strawberry jam. That was okay, right? Strawberry jam was delicious under the right circumstances.

He zoomed back out and—*damn!*—started gagging again. Saliva flooded his mouth and he prayed he didn't ralph all over his keyboard.

Gooding closed the photos and rubbed his eyes.

When Specialist Carnicle showed up for shift change, Gooding handed her the day's stats—the death tolls tallied and compartmentalized into means and manner—reminded her to sweep out the entire cubicle area when she had nothing else to do, then started to leave the office without saying another word to Carnicle or Major Filipovich.

"Hey, Sar'nt."

Gooding turned. "Yeah?"

Carnicle pointed to the weapons rack in their cubicle. "Forget something?"

Gooding felt the odd absence of weight around his neck. "Damn." He grabbed his M16 from the rack. "Thanks, Carnicle. Fine NCO I am, walking around the FOB without a weapon, huh?" He left the palace and stepped out into the brassy moonlight.

All soldiers, including Fobbits, were required to carry their M16s with them wherever they went: back and forth to work, when they took a shit, even if they were just stepping out onto their porch for a smoke.

Gooding cradled his rifle like a newborn. If he set it down, he kept a watchful eye on it, worried someone might come along and snatch it. When he walked around the FOB, he hung it from his neck, muzzle pointing at the ground, one arm and shoulder through the sling so his hand could rest on the stock or trigger housing. You never knew when you might be called to action.

Yes, the handgrips were starting to get sticky from all his palm dirt and sweat. And the tip of the barrel was scratched from all the times he banged it against a doorway. And, okay, once a week he had to take the rounds out of the magazine and clean off the accumulated dust, but what of it? This was war, after all, and he was in the hot middle of it.

Walking home through the dark Life Support Area dotted with pale puddles cast by porch lights on the gravel, Gooding passed three soldiers sitting around a plastic table outside their hooch. They laughed and slapped dominoes on the table with triumphant *Boo-yah*s. The smell of cigars hung thick in the sludgy air.

A few trailers down, a young black man, blending with the night, leaned over a young black girl sitting on her porch. He crooned persuasive words to her, working his charms while she put up a noncommittal wall. Her posture all but said, "Talk to the hand, playah!"

Three trailers down on the right, a mother sat on her porch, talking on a cell phone to her kids. "Heather, sweetie, I *know* the Cookie Monster shampoo is your favorite, but I don't think your little sister spilled it on *pur*pose . . . No, she didn't . . . Heather, honey, listen to me— . . . Listen— . . . Okay, okay, sweetie . . . I know, I *know* she is . . . Listen, can you put your daddy on the phone?"

Two buff white guys passed Gooding in their PT uniforms, neon-yellow safety belts glowing in the dark, reeking of sweat and talking about how nothing compares to the kind of muscle failure you get at the gym.

Gooding grabbed a towel at his hooch, then headed to the shower trailer, hoping he would have the place to himself. Light spilled from the frosted window in the door, barely illuminating the NO DEFICATION IN THE SHOWER sign. A puff of humid steam hit Gooding as he opened the door and stepped in.

Sergeant First Class Browning from G-5 stood at one of the sinks, scraping a razor across the stubble on his throat. "Evening, Sar'nt," Gooding said.

Browning, one hand still pulling his skin taut, looked over at Gooding. "Just coming off shift?"

"Yep. Just going on?"

"Yep. Same shit, different day." Browning had a voice like the scratchy end of a phonograph record.

"I hear you." Gooding found a place on the bench in front of his favorite shower stall.

Browning finished shaving and walked over to the bench, sat down, and started untying his boots. "So, how was your day, honey?"

"You better be meeting me at the door wearing an apron and holding a martini when you ask me that, Sar'nt. Oh, and you better have a decent pair of boobs, too."

Browning laughed as he stripped naked. "No, really," he rasped. "Any exciting shit rock your world today?"

"Oh . . ." Gooding thought about telling him it was all sunshine and furry kittens. Instead, he said, "Rough one today. Suicide bomber. They say they're not sure if he was wearing a vest or not, but I know for a fact he was. I saw the pictures."

"Damn," Browning said, shaking his head and testing his stall's water in the palm of his hand.

"Guy walks into a restaurant full of soldiers."

"Sounds like the start of a bad joke."

"Except no one was laughing at this one."

Gooding squeezed past him—always a very delicate choreography in order to avoid the dreaded penis graze—and got into his own shower stall.

"He fuck it up pretty bad?"

"Bad enough," Gooding said over the hiss of water. "Twenty-three dead. Lots wounded. So, yeah, it was a pretty rotten day for a lot of folks."

Browning hawked a loogey and spat it into his shower stall, watched it wash down the drain. "I dunno…These guys sure are getting . . . what's the word? . . . *ambitious*."

"Yeah, that's one way of putting it, I guess." What were the words he used in his press release? *An isolated, desperate attack*. Which was bullshit, of course. Gooding wasn't allowed to use the words *cunning and calculated*.

He poured a tablespoon of body wash into the palm of his hand, sniffed it in a private moment of aromatherapy, then rubbed it across his chest, his shoulders, his legs. He scrubbed and scrubbed. But it was no use. Nothing could mask the smell of melancholy.

From the Diary of Chance Gooding Jr.

Early morning. Another Groundhog Day in Iraq.

I run. I take up a light jog, traveling down the dirt service road passing in front of the chow hall (where I can smell them baking the cream pies for today's lunch), onto the paved road that follows the shore of Z Lake. Bats swoop overhead.

My brain unravels as my legs reach forward along the road. I think about how my ex-wife, Yolanda, had shown up at my door two nights before I shipped out, driving to Georgia all the way from Reno in what she later said was a sentimental weakness, and invited herself in. I think about how she stood there and said she couldn't fucking believe I was actually going to war and how, even though we'd been broken up for nearly ten years now and she'd had two husbands in the meantime, she would worry about me every day. I think about how one thing led to another. I think about how I unbuttoned her shirt and buried myself in the familiar valley between her breasts, hiccupping with sobs. The tears came because I was afraid of dying from al-Qaeda bullets, and because I was shocked with joy at Yo's generosity, and because I hadn't had sex with anyone but myself for more than three years.

The dawn air hangs like a miasma over the FOB, carrying with it something that smells like deep-fried tires, dog shit, and month-old bananas. If I take too much of it into my throat and lungs, I'll start gagging.

I run. There is a scarf of gray smoke, at least three miles in length, hanging low over the city. The lake laps softly against the reeds on my right. I think about Saddam and his cronies crouched here on the banks, rifles cocked, waiting for the servants to start beating the brush a half mile away, scaring the wild boars in their direction. Were the bats also under his dictatorial sway? Did they nip the insects from the air around his face, clearing a sting-free zone for his imperial visage? My mouth open and panting, I pass through small clouds of those same bugs and I start choking and spitting.

The sun isn't even over the horizon and it's already scorching the earth.

I decide to press on, waste as much time as possible circling Saddam's alphabetical lake. I'm due at the palace in an hour but I try to push it off as long as possible. Just more of the same crap waiting for me at the cubicle: churning out more tree-killing reams of press releases for jolly ol' Lieutenant Colonel Harkleroad.

The division task force is now heavily engaged in an offensive against the terrorists, called Operation Squeeze Play. Over here, a tactical operation is not a tactical operation until it has been christened with a code word. There are entire offices in the Pentagon and here in Iraq whose job it is to sit around and come up with clever names like Operation Righteous Fury or Operation Coffin Nail. Once, during cold and flu season, one of our brigade commanders came up with Operation Influenza and Operation Barking Cough.

Just this week, the task force commander decreed: "Every time a platoon-sized element or larger rolls out the gate, it's to be a named operation."

Roger that, sir. Pretty soon, we'll have "Operation Go to the Bathroom" or "Operation I Just Need to Gas Up the Humvee."

No, but really, the dweeby guys in the planning cell come up with the cutest names for these daylong or weeklong combat operations where Iraqi and U.S. soldiers go into the neighborhoods to flush out terrorists. Yesterday, it was Drake, Pintail, and Mallard; today, it was Chicken Little.

I can just hear them now on one of their door-kicking searches of the neighborhoods:

"Shamrock X-ray, this is Clover 3-2, over."

"Go ahead, Clover."

"Uh, Roger . . . we're here at the objective, but don't have any reports of skies falling, over."

"Affirmative, Clover. Go ahead and return to rally point, over."

"Roger, Shamrock X-ray."

And don't forget to make way for ducklings.

Now it's summer and so the operation namers in Task Force Baghdad Headquarters are commemorating it with baseball-themed titles (Operation Babe Ruth, Operation Khadhimiya Shortstop, Operation Home Plate). At last count, we'd rounded up more than four hundred bad guys in two days thanks to Operation Squeeze Play. Of course, not all of them are guilty of crimes—there is a *certain amount of collateral damage when we make these raids and trap insurgents in our net, sometimes we pick up a few innocents along the way . . . to whom we later apologize and send on their merry way. Yesterday alone, I put out three press releases on Squeeze Play and the media started calling when they heard one raid on a house in Mansour turned up $6 million in cash—stacks and stacks and stacks of U.S. $100 bills. I have pictures—unreleasable and stored on my hard drive—of American soldiers grinning and pointing at the loot. By the end of the day, I was exhausted, having spent the entire time going back and forth from my computer, answering media queries via e-mail, and being interviewed on the phone. It's like running on a treadmill. And every day is the same thing. Groundhog Day redux.*

6

DURET

Lieutenant Colonel Vic Duret had come to the point where he hated Fobbits: self-preservationists who never admitted to the fear inside, and instead found ways to stay busy within the boundaries of the triple-rolled concertina wire and walls crenellated with shards of glass. Duret knew of an entire platoon's worth of officers who clung to the security of headquarters, their asses gradually molding into the shape of a chair. Their aftershave reeked of self-importance and at any given moment of the workday, you could find them standing at a SMOG workstation, arms akimbo, grim-faced and intent as they stared at the unit icons on the Area of Operations maps. Periodically, they'd point and redirect one of the icons with the tip of a finger—just like that, flicking a company from Mahmudiyah to Diyala. These were the idiots shat out by West Point, turds in starched uniforms and glistening high-and-tight haircuts, shiny-foreheaded future corporate executives who used words like *envisionment* instead of *vision*. These officers never came right out and said it (in fact, it was much better for the conscience if it was never verbally expressed), but they were content to spend their entire thirteen-month tour inside the womb of fluorescent lights, air-conditioning, and three hot meals a day.

These dicks never had to face the nut-shriveling terror of careening through traffic, never certain whether or not the car pulling up behind them was trunk-loaded with explosives or just carrying a beheaded corpse to be dumped in the Tigris; never had to paste a forced smile to their lips while having tea and sautéed camel entrails with the province's sheikh, all while trying to unlock the enigmas of the sheikh's labyrinthine way of speaking—not approaching a subject head-on but entering the true heart of the matter through a series of side doors and secret passageways known only to Local Nationals; never felt the despair of visiting an electric substation one day and congratulating the mayor on his remarkable progress in the last three months, only to revisit that same substation a week later to inspect the damage from the bombing, which set the project back eighteen months and forced the mayor to impose a daily quota of two hours of electricity. What was that saying the Local Nationals had? "We're blowing into a punctured bag."

No, Duret thought as he dug his pen into his notebook, tracing the words "Continuous Process Improvement." *Fobbits would never know any of this.*

Not like Vic Duret, who was knee-deep in the shit day after day.

And when he wasn't out there in it—when he was trapped in air-cooled, fluorescent-lit briefings like this one—he got itchy and drifty. Influence Targeting Meetings, Casualty Evaluation Briefings, Effects Assessments Huddles, International Engagement

Team Planning Sessions. Ass-numbing hours and hours of Power-Point and laser pointers and the complacent drone of midcareer staff officers. Duret never let himself get comfortable, for fear he would morph into a Fobbit. He could already feel his ass spreading—and that scared the shit out of him.

The brigade commander, Colonel Quinner, was on a roll this morning with a new program the Pentagon was trying to integrate at the lower-echelon level. "Continuous Process Improvement, gentlemen, is a strategic approach for developing a culture of upticking positives—particularly, I'm told, in the areas of reliability and process cycle times. CPI will ultimately eventuate in less total resource consumption. Deployed effectively, it increases quality and productivity, while reducing waste and cycle time. So what do you think about that?" Quinner's face always reminded Duret of an owl who'd run into an electric fence. Now when Quinner glanced around the room at his slack-jawed battalion commanders he looked like he understood the Pentagon directive even less than they did. "I, for one, am excited by the potential possibilities in this new program. We overlay it on current ops here in theater and I fully believe it will eventuate into something tangible, something for which the Iraqi people will praise us for years to come."

Duret should have been listening to Quinner but he couldn't stop staring at what he'd written in his notebook three minutes earlier.

Tanks for the mammaries.

As Quinner talked about the timely need for SitReps to populate the daily BUB slides, due no later than oh-five-forty-five hours to the adjutant in the SMOG room, Duret couldn't stop thinking about his father. Tanks for the mammaries.

The word *mammaries* naturally took Duret back to his wife and the recurring fantasy with which he consoled himself while an ocean sloshed between them. Her breasts were waiting for him at the finish line so, head down, arms pumping, Duret ran the marathon toward the end of the deployment.

Duret thought of his wife straddled atop his torso, negligee pulled off her shoulders and puddled around her hips as she leaned forward, breasts swaying like wind chimes, left nipple dropping into his mouth, his tongue rolling the little button against his teeth until it hardened like candy . . .

He stopped himself with a sharp intake of breath, which caused some of the other battalion officers to shoot a glance in his direction. Duret stared straight ahead at Quinner, as if he hadn't made a sound. He really shouldn't be doing this to himself during the brigade briefing. He crossed, uncrossed, and recrossed his legs. He traced the words in his notebook and put his mind back on his father.

His old man had been Armor, too. Like Vic, he was built like a Bradley: all neck, swollen-red head, a fierce way of leaning forward from the chest when he walked. The old man took no shit from pansies and organized his family along the battalion structure, from dinnertime to Yellowstone vacations. He could be a hard man, but he also loved a good story. God*damn*, he could spin a yarn. And that's what Vic Duret was thinking about now instead of the morning Battlefield Update Briefing to the commanding general: the time his father leaned close, man-to-man, and poked fourteen-year-old Vic's chest with the two fingers that held his ever-unlit cigar. "I ever tell ya about the time Bob Hope came to Fort Knox?" (Yes, he had. Many times) "This was, oh, sixty-five, sixty-six, somewhere around there. Armor school was tough back then, son. It'd eat you for breakfast and shit you back out at lunchtime then grind you to mayonnaise by dinner. Anyway, it was tough, *tough,* I tell ya. Like John Wayne toilet paper: tough as nails and don't take shit off nobody. Ha!" (A weak, agreeing *ha* from Vic.) "Anyway, we needed a little comic relief. So here comes Hope on a USO tour and he brings with him a bevy of Playmate bunnies. That's not the only thing we called 'em—a 'bevy'—but I don't think your mother would appreciate me repeating what we really said. So there they are, these bunnies with their tits onstage, shimmy-shaking to some Ike and Tina song and we're hootin' and hollerin' like all get-out cuz by that time we'd had nothin' but weeks and weeks of classes and turret exercises and getting up at four fucking o'clock for rifle drills in the rain. Then one or two of us try to climb on the stage, but the MPs hold us back, the fuckers. Man, those girls were something! You could have put us facedown on the ground and twirled us around on our boners—that's how bad off we were for women by that point in Armor school." The old man put the cigar in his mouth and sucked on it, ruminating about decades-old hard-ons. "Then Mr. Bob Hope walks on stage, swinging his golf club and he grins at the bunnies doing their thing. When the song was over and they were bouncing off the stage, he looked at all us Armor students sprawled on the grass in front of him and then he leans into the microphone and calls out, *Tanks for the mammaries!*"

Each time he'd told it, and those times were too many to count, his father laughed until his eyes squeezed shut and a single tear tracked down his face.

Sitting in the briefing, Vic traced the words in his notebook again, etching the ink deeper. Bob Hope was dead, his father was dead, and there sure as shit weren't gonna be any Playboy bunnies coming over here to Iraq anytime soon. Nervous politicians and moral majority do-gooders had drained the Army of all that blood a long time ago. No, the most his men could hope for was a visit from a NASCAR driver and some guy in a black hat who was climbing the country charts back in the States.

Bob Hope, dead. Pops, dead. Ross, dead.

Fuck! Here it came again. He held his breath as the hot red tidal wave swept upward from his neck.

Ross dead Ross dead Ross dead. Vic's wife, Dawnmarie, unable to bear up under the weight of the news and screaming, crashing down in a heap of hair and robe, their dog Ginger anxiously sniffing the bottoms of her feet, Vic simply standing there numb before the onset of pain, staring at the cell phone dropped on the floor just beyond Dawnmarie's curled hand, a howl of empathy coming from his mother-in-law through the phone's speaker grille, the tinny sound of grief filling the whole of their family housing unit at Fort Bliss. And then his own cell phone buzzing, his sergeant major telling him in a fear-struck voice that he needed to get to the office quick because it looked like some bad shit was going down in New York.

Sitting in Colonel Quinner's briefing, there now came a pounding in Duret's head that drained him of all thought except for that image of his brother-in-law's body launched in an arc away from the tower, a parabola of pain, blackened skin crackling, disintegrating to ash in the buffeting wind.

Falling Burning Man. Duret's pen traced the words again and again.

Every week, he added a new phrase to his notebook dur-ing Quinner's meetings: *It's a marathon, not a sprint* or *Drinking from the fire hose* or *The voice of the bullets*. He also wrote words that he just as quickly scratched out with hard strokes of his pen: *Quagmire* and *A kluge of contradictions* and *Nonpartisan binding irresolution*. *Falling Burning Man* was not the latest addition but it was the most traced. He outlined the words in little licking flames. He flipped the page and tried to turn his attention back to Quinner and his blinking owl eyes.

He started the relaxation breathing—in through the nose, out through the mouth—that his wife had urged him to give a try after she'd read about it in one of her magazines. It only dulled the headache, didn't erase it. But dull was better than nothing and, at this particular moment, Vic Duret was surrounded on all sides by Dull.

As the Baghdad sunlight bore through the fly-specked windows and you could hear the crinkle of men sucking the water dry from plastic bottles, Quinner told his commanders about the congressional delegation scheduled to arrive next week. "You can expect the pucker factor to be very high around here, gentlemen. Very high indeed. Word from above is that the area around the palace is to be in a state of spit-and-polish unlike any seen before. We will whisk these four members of Congress in, and we will whisk them back out again. Whisk in, whisk out—got that? But while they are touring the brigade headquarters, they will be stunned into silence by the sparkle coming off the brass doorknobs. They should be forced to wear their sunglasses indoors. Do I make myself clear, gentlemen?"

There were grumbled assents from around the room of "yessir, right sir, got it sir."

Quinner was a man who talked tough to his staff but, Duret suspected, deep down inside he was irresolute as a child given two choices for dinner: pepperoni pizza or chicken nuggets with barbecue dipping sauce. When faced with a fork in the road, Quinner probably wrestled with himself for hours on end, wondering if he should take the high road, the road less traveled, or if he should just stop by the woods on a snowy evening. This didn't mean Quinner was necessarily a cautious, prudent man; no, just a dumb one who couldn't tell a fart from a turd.

Was he a quitter? No. Was he a winner? No. He was Quinner!

To his men, though, he bully-bluffed his way through his leadership, betraying not the slightest iota of namby *or* pamby. He made a particular point of ending each briefing with a Thought for the Day, certain he was sending his officers out into the world armed with inspiration and fortitude.

The drone stopped. Quinner really was wrapping up this time. "All right then! Any alibis?"

No one had anything else for the group that hadn't already been brought up.

"All right then. We reconvene at sixteen-thirty for the BUB prep . . . Oh! And gentlemen?"

The ones not lucky or smart enough to have already escaped the room stopped and looked back at their commander.

"The Thought for the Day." He pulled an index card from his pocket. "*War is not polite. It is not fought on 'pleases' and 'thank yous.'* Remember that when you're out there, men. And good luck!"

Duret lingered behind, adding that phrase to his notebook as something to be mocked later at the O Club back on Fort Stewart.

As the rest of the men streamed out of the room, a captain from brigade operations pushed his way against the tide, walked over to Quinner, and cupped his hand to his ear. With a sidelong glance at Duret, the captain gave a terse, whispered report then left. Duret didn't like the way Quinner's owl eyes snapped open like window shades. He especially didn't like it when Quinner held a finger in the air, then pointed it at Duret.

"Hold on," he said. "We have a situation that I think you need to be aware of, Vic."

Two minutes later, Duret was speedwalking the polished hallways of the palace en route to the SMOG room.

Situation. *Another* fucking situation.

There were reports of a Local National disturbing the peace at a gas station in Quadrant 7 of Duret's area of responsibility. G-2 in SMOG was pretty certain the guy was packing a ball-bearing vest and was ready to pull the det cord when a big enough crowd had gathered.

Duret ground his teeth, molars squeaking, when he thought of the ridiculous redundancy of his time here in Iraq. Another Day, Another Bomb. Maybe it's a Swiss-Syrian halfway up the ass of an Abrams tank . . . or maybe it's a pair of Sunni teenagers crouched behind a berm waiting for a U.S. convoy to roll past . . . or maybe it's a disgruntled Republican Guard holdout pedaling into a crowd of police recruits on his bike, the frame packed with nails, the explosives triggered by a bell on the handle that the hajji fucker thumbed with a pleasant jingle at the police candidates one second before taking himself and nineteen others skyward to Allah. Only the locations and body parts changed. No, scratch that—there was *always* an arm. A charred, blood-ooze stump, sometimes in a knot-hard rigor mortis fist, sometimes splayed in a five-finger starfish hand releasing all responsibility for the act just performed.

These martyrs were speed-bumping the brigade's *real* work in and around Baghdad: the nation rebuilding that was, in itself, a constant struggle, suicide bombers or no suicide bombers. There were sewer lines to patch, electric substations to rewire, schools to build, backpacks to distribute to solemn-faced boys and girls, local sheikhs to convince that what America brought to the table really *was* better than anything Saddam had offered during his decades of tyranny. *That* was the mission that was supposed to consume the larger percentage of his time, according to the Division's Tactical Ops Blueprint, which had been so dearly cherished before they left Fort Stewart and headed into the Great Unknown.

But no, Duret and his men spent their days running from one molehill to the other, whacking anything that moved with their amusement-park mallets. He'd picked that up from his soldiers—Whac-A-Mole—and soon was letting it slip into his daily reports, much to the grunting, frowning consternation of Colonel Quinner. But Quinner could go choke himself with all his esprit de corps Thoughts for the Day, as far as Duret was concerned. Quinner wasn't out here running around with a hammer, was he? No, that would mean leaving the security of air-conditioning and neatly patterned workdays. And Colonel Quentin P. Quinner was, despite all his bluster and blather to the contrary, nothing but another card-carrying member of the Fobbit Club.

Vic Duret stopped himself outside the door to SMOG, took a yoga breath through his nostrils, and tried to dissolve the throb hugging the base of his skull. He couldn't afford to get worked up over the clowns in the command group.

Vic breathed in, breathed out . . . in, out, in. His head continued to turmoil. God*damn*, how he wanted his wife's milky tit in his mouth right now!

He yanked open the door with the force of a man determined to kick the situation's ass from here to the Tigris.

The Command Operations Center (informally known as "The Cock") can be overwhelming to the unsuspecting visitor. It is a place of calculated chaos—like walking into NASA Control seconds before a launch. Against one wall are three TV screens, each ten feet by fifteen feet, which are the eyes to the COC's brain. The main screen displays a battle map of Baghdad, red diamonds marking Items of Interest (IIs or "Eyes") such as IEDs, small-arms fire, ambushes, enemy forces, friendly forces, and "neverminds" (mistakes on the part of the computer operators that flash green for two minutes before blinking off the screen). The screen on the right cycles through PowerPoint slides for the upcoming Battlefield Update Briefs and reminds viewers to "Get your agenda input to the battle captain no later than 1600 hours, thank you kindly." On the left-hand TV screen are fuzzy-gray images of a live video feed from one of the many blimp-cams floating over Baghdad, panning and zooming around the streets to keep an eye on shoppers, schoolchildren, and little knots of terrorists digging holes for their IEDs along the highway. These floating cameras are known as Triple Bs ("Big Brother Blimps"). Facing the screen are four steep tiers of desks stretching across the entire room. Each staff section and unit has a seat in this gallery. It's like the United Nations or Congress or the control room in that 1980s movie *WarGames*. Most of the desks have computers, phones, and headsets with which to communicate with the rest of the room. The men press their TALK buttons and chatter in milspeak to their neighbors, who are often only a few desks away: a self-contained language full of words like OPSUM, BDA, LSR, MSR, and AIF.

The battle captain sits in the midst of it all, at a desk larger than anyone else's—perched near the top of the amphitheater and built on a wooden platform that juts out like the prow of a ship. Any given day might find him waving his arms left and right like a symphony conductor, or—on the grimmest days—using those same hands to rub the muscles on his neck.

Vic Duret climbed the stairs to the battle captain's station. "Okay, what've we got?"

Major Zimmerman straightened in his chair at Duret's arrival. "Hard to tell at this point, sir. About ten minutes ago, we saw something over the blimp feed we didn't like. We were able to zoom in on this Loco Nat ranting and raving and generally making a nuisance of himself around ten thousand pounds of fuel. Take a look."

Duret watched the silent blimp feed on the big-screen monitors at the front of the room. A thickset man windmilled his arms above his head and moved his mouth like he was singing. He played hopscotch in and out of the gas tanks. Though it was easily 110 in the shade, the man was dressed in a heavy parka and what looked like snowpants. *Who the fuck sells snowpants in Iraq?* Duret thought.

"You're sure he's packing a vest?"

"Not *sure,* sir. But as close to it as we can be. Why else would he be wearing a parka on a day like today? And honestly, sir, those snowpants? Where the hell do you get snowpants in Baghdad?"

"Exactly what I was thinking, Major Zimmerman."

"G-2 thinks this guy is consistent with anti–Iraqi Forces behavior. They say he fits the profile."

"Who do we have on-site?"

Zimmerman pointed at the screen. "They just showed up. Let me zoom in." He toggled his joystick.

And there, coming into focus and looming large, was a face Duret immediately recognized.

Fuck me, he groaned to himself. *It's Shrinkle.*

7

SHRINKLE

Captain Abe Shrinkle was working at the desk in his no-bigger-than-a-breadbox office just off the company orderly room when word came in of another Something Bad going down in his area of responsibility. Word didn't actually come to him directly—he overheard the chatter between First Sergeant and the platoon sergeants. The NCOs were finishing their weekly training meeting and First Sergeant was in full-bore preaching mode, wound tight with another cocklebur up his ass.

"Tell your soldiers that every time they go outside the ding-dang gate, they need to be carrying they full load of ammunition. Believe it or not, we had soldiers outside the wire without all the ammo they was issued. Just last week, three soldiers went and got theyselves kilt in a firefight because they ran out of ammo and hadn't brought they ding-dang full load with them."

Around the table, the platoon sergeants murmured in disbelief.

"All y'all think I'm joking. I tell you what, I've gone around during guard duty myself and checked on your soldiers—*your* soldiers, sergeants—and I've found some of them walkin' around a little light. Sure they had all they magazines, but guess what? Some of them magazines only had three rounds in 'em. Soldiers be tryin' to lighten the load they gotta carry around they necks, but guess what, ladies—we at war and you damn well better be sure you got all your ding-dang bullets with you."

The orderly room phone rang and Sergeant Lumley picked it up quickly, hoping to cut off First Sergeant before he popped one of those wormy veins throbbing on the side of his shaved head. "Lumley here . . . Yeah?" Shrinkle could hear Lumley snapping his fingers for somebody to bring him a pen. "Okay, go ahead . . . Mm hmm . . . Got it, thanks." Lumley hung up the phone. "Looks like another one, Top."

"Oh, yeah? What you got?"

"Suicide bomber near Checkpoint eight-nine-seven."

First Sergeant sighed. "Another ding-dang day, another ding-dang dumbass out to make something of himself."

"How bad izzit?" one of the other platoon sergeants asked. "They have a casualty count yet?"

"That's the thing," Lumley said. "He hasn't detonated yet. Some hajji fool walking around a gas station making like he's gonna do something. They want us to go out and monitor."

"Another Quillpen," someone said.

"Fuck yeah."

"And fuck that."

"Awright, ladies. That's enough," First Sergeant cautioned, most likely with a glance back at the commander's door. "We got the mission, now we gotta go."

Shrinkle's ears had pricked up at the word *bomber*. He stopped in the midst of signing a form to requisition socket wrenches for the motor pool. A four-inch stack of paper rose on the right side of his desk, a slightly smaller stack of forms occupied the left corner of the desk. All morning, he'd been working through the paperwork, moving it from right to left. With every signature, he felt like his veins were filling with more and more Fobbit blood. He had to get out of here before he was trapped in a life inside the wire. After the disaster at Quillpen, he needed to prove himself worthy of the infantry tab on his collar. He stepped to the door, clutching a half dozen forms in his hand. "I've got this one, Top."

First Sergeant wheeled around to look at him, his gray-flecked eyebrows rising up over his dark face. "Oh now, sir. I—"

"Really, Top. I'll do the ride-along on this one."

"Sir, I don't think that's a good idea, considering—"

Abe stopped him before the word *Quillpen* could leave his lips. "Besides, you haven't finished that paperwork you owe me, have you?"

"What paperwork?"

"This paperwork." Abe held up the half-ream of forms he'd been holding. "Perfect opportunity for you to get caught up, don't you think?"

Abe could see one of those veins coming to life at First Sergeant's temple and he was certain a long string of *ding-dang*s was about to fly from his mouth but Top just set his lips tight and nodded at his commander. "That's right, sir. This is the perfect opportunity for me to get somethin' done."

"Very good," Abe said. He looked at the rest of the NCOs watching him with hard, closed faces. "Anyone need to use the potty before we head out?"

*   *   *

When they arrived on the scene, there was already a barren ring around the gas station, as if the suicide bomber had already pulled the det cord and cleared his own radius.

A nearby school had been evacuated and meat sellers had retreated deeper into the shadows of their stalls; the gas station owner had long since fled to a safe spot a block away, leaving his customers to decide their own fates (to a man, each one of them drove off without paying for the gas).

The moaning man at the center of it all flapped his arms like a pair of flags. He wore a jester's hat, one of those brightly colored floppy things with little bells on the ends of three petals. From their perimeter across the street, Shrinkle's men could hear the jingle-jangle of the head bobs. Every now and then, hajji would lift one of the gas nozzles and sing into it like a microphone.

"What do you make of that hat?" Shrinkle asked.

"Could be some sort of signaling device, sir," Specialist Zeildorf said. "I bet you dollars to donuts his Sunni buddies are lying in wait a few hundred meters away ready to remote-det him if he loses his nerve."

They watched the man spin around the tanks, doing his *la-la-laaa* thing. He was toying with them. He knew he had an audience and he was trying to draw them within range of his ball-bearings and nails. It's a wonder he hadn't already passed out from the heat, wearing a getup like that.

"EOD been dispatched yet?"

"They're on their way," Lumley said. "About ten minutes out, last we heard."

Shrinkle swallowed a thick clog of phlegm in his throat. This was déjà vu all over again. He took a chest-puffing breath. This time he would redeem himself, show them he was a man of decisive action.

Nevertheless, his balls still bobbed untethered somewhere between his underwear and his stomach.

Now the man in the parka was moving his fingers in front of him, playing a piano in midair. He sounded like he was singing "Goo-goo-goo."

"Can we get a clean shot, do you think?" Shrinkle asked Lumley.

"Not yet we can't. We need him to dance away from the gas pumps."

Abe grew short of breath as he pictured himself six months ago at the firing range at Fort Stewart, his legs spread, his arms raised, elbows locked, front sight on the 9 mm going in and out of focus. Then the neat hole through the head of the black silhouette on the paper target.

His mouth was dry as he asked Corporal Boordy, "What about it? Do we have authorization for a kill here?"

Boordy was on the horn with the SMOG battle captain. "Not yet, sir. The Head Shed says the situation hasn't reached critical mass yet."

"And just when do they expect critical mass to arrive?"

Boordy spoke into the headset and waited for an answer. "They're still working on that, sir."

"Meanwhile . . ."

"Meanwhile, we *wait,* sir," Lumley said from where he stood a few feet away. Shrinkle resented Lumley's tone of voice. It carried a load of unnecessary caution and he wondered why he'd even left First Sergeant back at Triumph only to have another ding-dang mother hen like Lumley watch his every move.

Who was in charge here anyway? He was. And was he about to let an NCO tell him what to do? No ding-dang way.

He was out here on the ground and he would get the job done. The *real* job he'd been sent here to do—not sitting behind a desk moving papers from right to left.

"Sir?" Lumley said. "Sir? You okay?"

Even the bells on the hajji's hat were mocking him, singing a cruel song about his failures, his indecisiveness, his wiffle-waffle.

"Sir, you look like you need a drink of water. You got anything left in your canteen?"

But Abe Shrinkle was far from here. He pictured himself years in the future, holding a little girl he hadn't yet sired with the wife he hadn't yet married, and the daughter-to-be looked up at him with her big brown fawn eyes and asked, "Did you kill anyone in the war, Daddy?" And he thought about what his response would be.

He also thought about stepping off the plane onto American soil. He thought about ticker-tape parades, about John Philip Sousa marches, about buying a round of drinks for everyone down at the VFW. He thought about how his chest would inflate because he'd done his part in the war. He'd killed the enemy.

He reached for his pistol. Sounds magnified as if he was in an empty room with himself: the unsnap of the strap, the grainy rub of the barrel against the fabric of the holster as it whistled free from his hip, the click as he took the pistol off *safe,* the tick of the trigger, the thunder roar of powder and bullet.

The heavy man crumpled to the ground, arms spread in a Y above his head, the jester's cap giving one last surge of bell music when it hit the ground.

Shrinkle's men stared at him; all mouths dropped open. Everything was silent. There wasn't even a "Ho-ly fuck!" (which would have been fully justified and a bit of a relief, actually).

Abe lowered his pistol, put it back on *safe,* slid it back into the holster.

It was done.

The man started to groan, arch his back, and kick his legs, heels digging into the dirt.

Okay, Abe thought, it was *almost* done.

Two black-robed women came running around the corner of the pharmacy at the end of the block, wails rising from their throats like sirens. They alternately clapped their hands to their heads and pointed at the man writhing on the ground. Their tongues ululated and strings of saliva dripped from their chins. They rushed up and bent over the body. They seemed to know the dying man. There was an intimacy in the way they bathed him with tears and saliva.

Abe's stomach clenched as he realized this might not turn out as hunky-dory as he had hoped.

*   *   *

SIG ACT 18 AFTER VISUAL REPORT FROM BLIMP FEED 3, HQ DISPATCHED SQUAD FROM 3-2 QRF TO SOUTHERN SERVICE ROAD, SOUTH OF CP 897. LOCAL NATIONAL WAS SIGHTED ACTING IN SUSPICIOUS, ERRATIC MANNER. LN ATTIRED

IN HEAVY PARKA, SNOWPANTS, AND JESTER HAT.
LN WAS ALSO BELIEVED TO BE WEARING A SUI-
CIDE VEST. 3-2 QRF ARRIVED ON SCENE AND
FORWARDED THE REPORT VERIFYING LN BE-
HAVIOR. G-2 IN SMOG CONFIRMED LN ACTIONS
CONSISTENT WITH AIF INDICATORS. SMOG WAS
IN PROCESS OF AUTHORIZING USE OF DEADLY
FORCE WHEN ON-SITE COMMANDER NEUTRAL-
IZED THE SITUATION BY FIRING ON SUSPECTED
AIF. THE LN'S FAMILY THEN ARRIVED ON SCENE
AND STATED HE IS NOT AIF, BUT HE IS MENTALLY
RETARDED. ON-SITE CMDR STILL BELIEVED IN-
DIVIDUAL WAS A SUICIDE BOMBER. THE FAMILY
MEMBERS THEN ROLLED LN OVER, OPENING
PARKA AND EXPOSING HIS ABDOMEN. LN HAD
NO SUICIDE VEST. 3-2 MEDICS MOVED FORWARD
TO PROVIDE FIRST AID, HOWEVER THE LN HAD
SUBSEQUENTLY EXPIRED FROM WOUNDS IN-
CONSISTENT WITH LIFE. THE FAMILY RECOV-
ERED THE REMAINS. AS BLIMP FEED SHOWED
CROWD GROWING AND INDIVIDUALS PICKING
UP ROCKS, SMOG ADVISED 3-2 QRF TO VACATE
LOCATION AT EARLIEST OPPORTUNITY. SUM-
MARY: 1X LN KILLED. REPORT CLOSED.

8

HARKLEROAD

From: eustace.harkleroad@us.army.mil
To: eulalie1935@gmail.com
Subject: Dispatch from a War Zone, Day 193

Mother,

First of all, THANKS for the care package! The mixed nuts,
foot powder, dried apricots, and church bulletins were most
appreciated. Unfortunately, the GooGoo Clusters did not
make it through the Iraqi heat so well. But I put them to
good use anyway! I gave them to our translator Hussein (no,
he's no relation to Saddam!) who had never tasted GooGoo
Clusters before. Hussein's family is quite poor even though
they are considered middle class here in Baghdad. How poor
are they, you ask? Do you remember the Borsippies who
used to live up the road from the Macklins before the mill
shut down and they (the Borsippies) had to move all the way
up to Pittsburgh? Well, Hussein and his wife and their five

children (and Hussein's wife's father, two cousins, and their
wives and children—all crammed into one three-bedroom
apartment) are worse off than the Borsippies. For instance,
they (the Husseins, not the Borsippies) did not even own a
TV until last year and when at last they got one you would
have thought it was a national holiday—or so Hussein tells
me. Now, I cannot get him to shut up about *Two and a Half
Men*.

Speaking of which, I hope you are still taping *Survivor* for
me. And DO NOT under ANY CIRCUMSTANCES tell me
who gets voted off! I want to be surprised when I come home
on my R&R leave next month.

Speaking of which, are you as excited as I am? I cannot wait
to get back to Murfreesboro and out of this combat zone,
even if it is only for two weeks. Two weeks of clean sheets,
driving on the right side of the road, and your Corn Flake–
crusted meatloaf will do me worlds of good, I believe. I am
thoroughly bushed these days.

Which brings to mind something else I keep forgetting to mention to you, whether or not you'll like it, I do not know. When
the men around headquarters here say they're "bushed," what
they really mean is that they are sick and tired of our president
keeping us (the U.S.) in this country where—secretly—those
men think we don't belong. I know, Mother, I know. I don't
particularly appreciate their Democrat-tainted humor, either.
But that's just how it is with some of my colleagues. These,
I might add, are the lower-class officers. Men who will never

amount to much, will never get promoted beyond the limits of
their nearsightedness—men like Jeb Standish down at the mill
who let the loss of three fingers keep him from advancing any
higher than bobbin tender (of course, his wife doing all that
drinking and nagging didn't help matters). Yours truly, of course,
has ambitions, goals, and the drive to get there. So, when I say
I'm "bushed," I certainly don't mean it in the same way those
other men do.

But the truth is, I am wrung dry inside and out with the daily
cycle of activities over here. I do not want to burden you
with too much in the way of worry, but you've heard that old
expression "War is hell"? Well, hell has nothing on this place,
let me tell you! I am kept awake each night by the scream of
mortars streaking across the sky. It is worse than the semis
on I-24. Last week, the enemy finally got lucky and one of
the rockets landed on FOB Triumph. You may not have heard
about it on the five o'clock news on WSMV because we try
to keep a lid on those kind of tragic incidents over here—my
boss is a big one on "good news" and besides, there's only so
much tragedy we should burden the American public with,
right? But, yes, a rocket did fall—smack dab in the middle
of the post exchange courtyard in the smack-dab middle of
the day. And guess who happened to be there at the time,
patronizing one of the little shops run by the local Iraqi
vendors who sell rugs and jewelry and discount copies of
the latest DVD movies? Yes, yours truly. DO NOT WORRY,
MOTHER—I am not writing this to you from the hospital—I
was not at the site of impact, but was on the other side of the
courtyard paying for my purchase from a friendly little rug

merchant named Benzir (by the way, I will be shipping back
a nice surprise to you—and just to confirm, the dimensions
of the living room floor are such that they will accommodate
something that is, oh, say, 18 by 24 feet?). The explosion
knocked me forward into the arms of Benzir and after we
had dusted each other off and he had given me my change,
I rushed directly over to the smoking crater to see what I
could do to help. Would you believe no one else was running
toward the impact zone? That's right, not a single blankety-
blank person. Everyone else was running *away* and it turned
out your son was the only one to move forward to give comfort and aid to the wounded. I could hear other folks yelling
at me to take cover and save myself, but I put my hearing
loss to good use and just continued to walk toward what I
could immediately tell was a very bad scene. I will spare you
all the horrific details but do you remember that movie we
once watched, the one with Brad Pitt and the serial killer and
you had to cover your eyes during that one scene until I told
you it was okay to look again? Well, what I saw there in that
PX courtyard was ten times worse. Maybe even eleven times
worse! I could right away see at least two, maybe even three,
of the soldiers who had been sitting at the picnic table eating their Burger King sandwiches were goners—and not just
goners, but completely gone—disintegrated, if you will. (No,
thank goodness, I did not know any of the victims in this vi-
cious & brutal enemy attack!) I knelt and said a brief prayer
for their departed souls and then I brushed aside whatever
feelings were welling up in me and hurried to do what I could
for the rest of the wounded. I felt a little like Clara Barton
on the battlefield (or was that Molly Pitcher?) As I said, no

one else was coming out from behind the protective concrete
barriers to help, so I had to do the best I could all by myself.
I will spare you the burden of knowing what all the specific
wounds I treated were like, but many of those poor soldiers
turned out to be so bad off they had to be shipped out of
Iraq, back to Germany, and then all the way to Walter Reed
Army Medical Center in our nation's capital, where they
will have to undergo months of recovery and rehabilitation
—that's how bad their injuries were! So, there I was, moving from victim to victim, dressing wounds and stopping
the bleeding with tourniquets and, in one case, performing
CPR to bring one young girl with especially plump lips back
to life! It was a real mess and suffice to say, the uniform I was
wearing that day is no good anymore and I had to toss it away.
I'm not going to lie to you, Mother—I was quite sickened
that day by the horrors of what I saw, but I take comfort in
knowing I saved some lives and those soldiers will go on to
fight another day.

In anticipation of what I know you will ask, no, I do not know
if I will get a commendation or medal of some kind for my
actions that day. I *do* know the chief of staff, Colonel Belcher,
is quite proud of me and even the commanding general himself interrupted yesterday's staff meeting to make mention of
what he called my "unselfish act of courage." I tend to think I
won't receive any specific award for what I did—not because
they think I don't deserve it but because, like so much of
what we do here, we're trying to keep all this on the hush-
hush and down low. It would only give comfort and aid to the
enemy if they knew they succeeded in a bull's-eye hit on our

PX at FOB Triumph. So that is why you won't see me on the evening news or in the *Daily Tennessean*. In fact, there was a *Stars and Stripes* reporter who happened to be on the scene when the rocket hit, but I ordered her to delete the photos on her digital camera and hold the story until given approval by the proper authorities in division headquarters (which—ha ha, joke's on her—is me, the PAO).

As I said, I don't want to burden you with all my horror stories but I thought you should know what your son is doing over here in the name of democracy and freedom. Because this is TOP SECRET information I am telling you, I beg you not to contact Jim Powers down at the *Murfreesboro Free Press* and blab about all your son's accomplishments and heroism over here in Iraq, though I understand how you must be longing to do so—as you would say, you're "fairly bursting the buttons with pride and joy." No, Mother, we must keep this between ourselves.

I suppose if you want to share it with the other ladies in your Sunday circle, then I would understand, but those First Redemption ladies must UNDER NO CIRCUMSTANCES tell their husbands!

Shifting gears, did I ever tell you about the swimming pool? If I already did, then bear with me (being in such close, intense combat has made me a little scatterbrained of late); if not, then here goes: Some of the men here like to venture over to the other side of FOB Triumph on hot days, to where there is a pool. The pool is "owned" by the Australians—whose

illicit drinking I think you'll remember me writing about in
my previous e-mail—and until recently there was a sort of
international agreement between the division's staff and the
Aussies regarding use of the pool. I myself have never been
there but I have heard the stories—some of them were pretty
salacious, let me tell you! Liquor! Half-clothed women! Taking an unauthorized break from combat duties in the middle
of the day! Still, a man must do what a man must do to blow
off steam in such a hostile combat environment, that's what
I believe. Though I could never afford to allow myself such
a luxury, I understand why some of the lesser class of officer
would want to explore the sinful delights of the Aussie pool.
Anyway, all was well with the pool arrangement until last
week. Something happened—I am not exactly clear but I
believe it had to do with a female private from our Army
fraternizing with a lieutenant from the Australian Army—and
whatever it was, the commanding general (ours, not theirs)
got hopping mad. Little puffs of steam actually coming out of
his ears. And now he has expressly forbidden us to use the
pool. If you'll remember, the Old Man does not think partially
unclothed female soldiers properly represent the United
States, especially in mixed-nation company. And so he has
issued a new general order that we were ordered to publish in
The Lucky Times, but I tell everybody, don't shoot the mes-
senger, all right? Now morale has plummeted to a new low—
lots of men are moping around the headquarters with long
faces and sullen mouths, all because they can't go swimming
with females from another nation anymore. Not yours truly,
though. I'm sure I don't have to tell you, Mother, that I have
better things to do with my time than to commingle with girls

in bikinis. I'll leave that to officers who are not serious about their careers.

Well, Mother, I have rambled on long enough and you are probably tired of staring at the computer screen, so I will sign off now.

By the way, if you could see fit to slip a couple pairs of black socks, the over-the-calf variety, into your next care package, they would not go unappreciated. Also, some more dried apricots.

Your loving son,
Stacie

9

DURET

Lieutenant Colonel Vic Duret liked to come to his office in the palace early on Sunday mornings, well before the fan cranked up and shit started hitting it.

He'd been given a small room off the once ornate reception area and, because of his rank, he'd been privileged with a door. The office had belonged to Saddam's chief gamekeeper and Duret had left everything on the walls just as he'd found them when he moved in six months ago. The head of an ibex, spiral horns stabbing upward, stared glassily at him while he worked, as did a warthog, a zebra, and, most unnervingly, an Afghan hound. The opposite wall held a stone mask, which the division's cultural liaison said dated to 3000 BC, and a portrait of the old goat himself, beret jauntily cocked and His Dictatorshipness, smiling like a loon beneath his thick, black porn mustache. Duret had tried to remove the portrait from the wall but the frame was securely screwed into the concrete and, in the end, it had been more trouble than it was worth, so he left Saddam alone. Even with the leering presence of Hussein and his animals, Duret's office space was a refuge from the clatter of keyboards, men's voices, and echoing footsteps just outside the door.

The subdued, religious hush of Sunday mornings was his favorite time of the week: a cool oasis in the otherwise hot, clanging chaos of the nonstop war. Sure, bad shit still went down on Sunday mornings, but Duret's head was able to handle it because there weren't so many American voices ringing off the palace walls, barking self-important directives, arguing the merits of PowerPoint, and speaking in alphanumeric code—the kind of Fobbity chatter that drove him right out of his skull with madness.

God knows, Duret didn't want to end up like them, like the lieutenant colonel he knew from another battalion, a decent guy who had somehow gotten sucked into working out of the palace more than he'd wanted to. This guy had been fast-tracking—he was only thirty-nine but he already had a battalion (and a damned good one at that). But then someone somewhere had a visit from the Good Idea Fairy and came up with the brilliant notion of moving this guy off the line and into SMOG central where he could bring valuable "real world" expertise to the decisions made there in the nerve center.

"It's driving me crazy," the other officer had told Duret. "I spend three-quarters of my day going from meeting to meeting. Then, when I get done with those and go back to my office, people are stacked up outside my door."

This particular officer, Duret joked, had once been "hale and hearty," but now he was just "pale and farty," holed up in the palace and subsisting on the cabbage and beans and yogurt from the dining facility. The two of them had laughed about it but Duret saw something he didn't like in the other guy's eyes:

a vacant, bottomless insanity that now placed the edicts of SMOG above anything else, including the welfare of the men he'd once commanded in the battalion.

Duret vowed he'd self-ventilate with a 9mm before he ever let something like that happen to him. He made it a point to spend as little time in the palace as possible, sacrificing the air-conditioning and the security of four walls for the intolerable heat and the intolerance of the sheikhs—both of which only served to turn up the volume of his headaches.

But Vic Duret *did* like Sunday mornings at the palace.

The commanding general, a devout man, had told the division he wanted minimal staffing—key-and-essentials only—until 1300 hours each Sunday in order to allow each soldier to practice his or her faith in whatever manner they saw fit. Most saw fit to get gorged on near-beer and beef jerky on Saturday night and play Xbox or watch the bootleg porno DVDs they bought from Local Nationals at the vendor stalls just outside the Triumph checkpoint; most saw fit to catch up on their laundry and hooch dusting; most saw fit to honor their Sunday mornings by sleeping until noon.

Not Lieutenant Colonel Duret. Sunday mornings were the only time he could get some peace and quiet in his office, a little pool of silence broken only by the occasional lazy squawk from the SMOG computers giving a weather report or an update on a suspicious vehicle the unmanned reconnaissance planes were tracking. Vic Duret could even sit in his padded leather chair behind his desk, have a casual conversation with the ibex, and leave the door open without fear that another pucker-assed do-gooder would come bouncing in on the balls of his feet with another situation report gripped tight in his hand.

Monday through Saturday, Duret could rest assured he'd be besieged with complaints about ammunition shortages, petty rivalries between company commanders, or, God forbid, impetuous officers like Abe Shrinkle shooting innocent, mentally handicapped Local Nationals who went around wearing snowpants in the middle of June. This particular captain was starting to feel like a popcorn husk caught between Vic's molars.

Duret closed his eyes and forced Shrinkle from his mind. When Abe was replaced by Ross with his flaming arm torches running through the halls of the North Tower, Vic opened his eyes and stared at Saddam's moth-eaten zebra until his head simmered down to a low boil.

He liked to keep his door wide open on Sunday mornings and listen to the low, unhurried hum of the large outer room, which was filled with a cubicle maze of staffers from personnel, intel, ops, logistics, and civil affairs, as well as the chaplain, the lawyers, and the computer network gearheads. If they knew the CG was at church and wouldn't walk in unexpectedly, someone might even have a football game tuned in on satellite TV, keeping the volume low but just loud enough for the cheers of the crowd to rise and fall like fuzzy waves. Duret always took surreal comfort in the sound of the thousands of people back home roaring open-throated at a couple dozen men who moved a ball back and forth. He liked to think those cheers were also for the work he and his men were doing over here in Baghdad where, it was true, they were also, in a sense, moving a ball back and forth across a limited field of play.

The reality was, of course, that of those thousands packed into the stadium, only a couple hundred knew what was happening over here in Iraq; and of those two hundred, only a dozen actually gave a shit—and those twelve were probably the wives of the men who were over here listening to the game on a Sunday morning. America, the beautiful ostrich—Oh, beautiful, for heads buried in the sand, for amber waves of ignorant bliss. There were times when, given the choice, Vic thought he'd disown his country, chuck it all and live the life of an expat in some neutral European country. If it weren't for his wife and his dog, he might give serious consideration to the thought of spending the rest of his days snacking on Swiss cheese.

Today, as Duret walked along the gilt-edged passageway that led to his brigade's area of operations in the east wing of the palace, he saw two men playing Frisbee. They were tossing the disk back and forth—rather sloppily—and it banged against the walls and the thick marble columns, then landed in the goldfish pond Saddam had built in the middle of the foyer. The two officers laughed as they scooped the Frisbee out of the water and kept tossing it, sprayed droplets catching the sunbeams that knifed through the overhead windows. There must not have been any deaths last night, Duret thought. The Frisbee tossing was a good sign the war was in a temporary overnight lull.

This happy, airy mood lasted only long enough for Duret to reach his office, settle back into his leather chair, boot up his computer, and pick up the packet of Early Bird news stories public affairs had compiled overnight. Then the voice of SMOG broke through his Sunday sunshine.

"The following staff representatives need to report to the battle major in the Ops Center immediately: G-5, IO, JAG, and PAO. That is all, thank you."

Duret closed his eyes and leaned his head back against the leather. He started to count and, sure enough, had not quite reached twenty before another pucker-ass poked his head into the office.

"Sir?" It was Major Leon Fisher, his executive officer, knocking softly against the door frame. "Sir?"

"Yes, Leon." Duret kept his eyes clamped shut, gripping the last few evaporating seconds of peace. He braced himself against the oncoming knife stabs that would attack his brain without mercy. In just a few moments they would come, yes, they would come, blades sharpened and ready to cripple him.

"Sir, I don't know if you just heard the SMOG—"

"I did."

"From what I gather, sir, you might want to head to the Ops Center, too."

"One of ours?"

"I believe so, sir."

Duret opened his eyes and allowed the day to come back into his head. "Bad?"

"Don't know yet, sir. But I believe so."

"Fuckity-fuck."

"Just thought you should know, sir." Fisher hesitated. "If you'd like me to go and assess the situation, I—"

"No, Leon, no. Go back to what you were doing. I'll take this one. But be ready for whatever might be coming our way."

"Roger, sir."

Fisher vanished and Duret rubbed his temples. *Please, Lord,* he prayed on this Sunday morning, *don't let the shit be bad.* He tried to shove aside everything but the images of his wife's naked breast, the aureole tip glowing in a sunbeam, and his dog running through the yard to crash into an autumnal leaf pile with a series of throaty yelps, begging Vic to rerake and repile so they could do this all over again.

Then he rose and walked to SMOG.

On this particular Sunday morning, Major Cletus Monkle was at the helm. He stood at his station, patiently waiting as all who'd been summoned flowed to him from their workstations in the palace.

Lieutenant Colonel Duret, little green notebook gripped in his left hand, slowly made his way up the steps to the battle captain's desk, passing soldiers in various stages of activity: some clicking cards on computer solitaire, some reading battered Tom Clancy novels, some speaking into phones while repeating phrases like, "I know that already . . . Yes, I'm fully aware . . . But what you don't understand is . . . ," some graveyard shifters just sitting there glaze-eyed and waiting for the morning shift to come relieve them from this drudgery. A female soldier from G-1 sat in the middle of her empty section of the amphitheater, filing her nails. The sound buzzed across the room like a small hacksaw. Two Iraqi officers, liaisons on loan to the division, huddled together at the back of the room, rolling what looked like a cigarette.

"Sir, glad you could make it," Major Monkle said, breaking off in midsentence as Duret joined the huddle. "I was just telling the rest of the group here—" he gestured to the civil affairs, information operations, judge advocate general, and public affairs pucker-asses who were already standing there, pens poised over notebooks "—about what went down earlier this morning."

"Give it to me," Duret said.

"Roger. Uh, as I was just saying, this is a hot one. I wanted to give all of you a heads-up because this situation has the potential to be really spun against us with some negative public perception. IO, PAO, I'm looking at you."

The IO officer nodded and kept chewing his gum. The PAO rep—a staff sergeant with dark circles under his eyes—went pale and noticeably gulped.

Lieutenant Colonel Duret disliked people like this battle captain using the words *spun* and *negative* in the same sentence. He braced himself and wondered if it was a little Shiite girl raped by some GIs in a back alley or if one of his units had tossed a case of pork rib MREs to some hungry Muslims during a humanitarian mission. Whatever the "situation," he really hated that word *spin*. He thought of the CNN camera crew back at Quillpen last month, then—without warning or prelude—he was back in the moment, once again seeing that terrorist's head burst open. He could smell the blood carried on the dust particles swirling through Intersection Quillpen. It was musty and coppery and made his nostrils flare. There was also the tang of piss from Abe Shrinkle's undies, which hung beneath all other smells.

Duret had to forcibly bring himself back to SMOG and listen to what the battle captain was saying.

"At approximately twenty-fifteen hours last night," Monkle droned, "we got a call from the 442nd Transportation Company, which was on a convoy from Taji to Adhamiya when they were involved in a traffic accident with a vehicle carrying some Local Nationals. One of our fuel trucks swerved to avoid a herd of goats and slammed into a city bus. We have three injured Local Nationals and two injured U.S.—nothing serious, a broken arm, lacerations to the face. They're all being treated at the nearest aid station. Nothing a little Motrin and a splint won't cure.

But—and here comes the fun part, gentlemen—back on the scene, the convoy commander, a lieutenant, decided to call for backup. Even though Iraqi police were already on the scene, the looey calls for a U.S. QRF to come help him out. I guess he felt like he couldn't handle a half dozen angry goatherds by himself. At this time, we don't have any reports of the Local Nationals on the scene getting unruly or out of hand. I guess this lieutenant just panicked. So he brings in backup." Here, Monkle looked at Duret.

"My guys, huh?"

"Roger, sir. As you know, ever since the incident at Quillpen—"

Why, when the battle captain said it like that, did it sound like "Incident at My Lai"?

"—Company B has been on QRF duty—"

"Sir? Excuse me, sir, but could you define QRF?" It was the PAO staff sergeant.

Monkle leveled a gaze at this pale noncom as if he were the class dunce who had just interrupted his lecture on atomic principles. "Quick Reaction Force."

"Got it. Thanks, sir. Just wanted to make sure I had everything squared away for the press release."

Lieutenant Colonel Duret looked at the staff sergeant's name tag: *Gooding*. He opened his little green notebook and wrote "Gooding Two Shoes."

"*As I was saying*, gentlemen," Major Monkle continued. "A platoon from Company B out of Lieutenant Colonel Duret's battalion was rolling through the area, led by Captain, uh—" Monkle shuffled through his notes.

"Shrinkle," Duret said.

"Right, sir. Captain Abe Shrinkle. He arrived with his men on scene at approximately twenty-one-thirty hours—full dark and getting a little rough in that part of Adhamiya. The natives were restless, as they say. I don't know if there were any pitchforks and torches at this point, but the Transpo guys were sure getting nervous. They would have pulled out but they were waiting on the Iraqi police to finish their report and there was the issue of the disabled fuel truck, which I'll get to in a minute. So, Captain Shrinkle arrives and stands around with his thumb up his ass. The 442nd lieutenant had already put his men in a defensive perimeter—which totally confused the IPs, by the way—they thought they were under attack and they scrambled for their vehicles and got the hell out of there before finishing their report."

"Typical hajji bullshit," muttered Civil Affairs.

"So, Captain Shrinkle takes charge and, for whatever reason, he determines the banged-up 442nd's fuel truck wasn't recoverable. So he decides to throw a thermite grenade in the cab of a perfectly good Heavy Expanded Mobility Tactical Truck in order to completely disable it and render it useless to the enemy. Yes, you heard me right: one of our illustrious, school-trained captains threw a grenade at a U.S. fuel truck. *Whoosh-kaBOOM.*"

Eyebrows raised and note taking paused. Jungle drums beat inside Vic Duret's skull.

"Wait—it gets better," Monkle said. "The fuel truck doesn't blow up. No *Whoosh-kaBOOM.* More like sizzle and fizzle. The grenades just burn the cab of the truck and so Company B and the Transpo team decide to carry on with their missions. They figure the truck is out of service, everyone's been treated, no goats were killed, and everything's hunky-dory. They leave the scene. At which point, the flames start to get bigger."

Duret closed his eyes. *Abe, Abe, what the fuck are you trying to do to me?*

"Pretty soon, another patrol comes along—a military police unit from Tenth Mountain Division who's not up on our sheriff net and who just happen to be passing through the sector— which, right there, presents a problem in and of itself. We're still trying to figure out how these guys got on your turf, sir."

Duret nodded, swallowing this additional headache, and allowed the battle captain to finish his back brief.

"Anyway, when they see the fire, they stop to investigate. By this time, the Iraqi police have gotten over what frightened them and they're back on the scene. Local firefighters are there, too, unrolling their hoses. The MPs help cordon the area and keep the pitchforks at bay. When they finally get the flames doused, they discover the body of a dead Local National under the truck."

"What the *fuck*?"

Monkle grinned like the Cheshire cat. "Now you know why I called you all for this little Sunday morning prayer meeting. Anyway, how hajji got there is anybody's guess, but you can imagine how *Al Jazeera* will spin this if they get their hands on it."

The lawyer from JAG shook his head. "Of all the lameass, cockamamied things for that captain to do. Somebody must've sprinkled stupid dust on his Cheerios that morning—" He stopped when he saw the look on Duret's face. "Sorry, sir. Didn't mean to—"

"Don't worry, gentlemen," Duret said. "By this time tomorrow, Abe Shrinkle will be shitting out of two assholes. I'll be ripping him a new one today as soon as I get done here."

"Aw, sir, go easy on him," Monkle grinned. "It *is* Sunday morning, after all."

"Sir, if I might—"

Major Monkle's grin faded and he turned to Staff Sergeant Gooding. "What now, PAO?"

"Sir, I just have a couple of clarifying questions. Do you know the status of the Local National's body?"

"How the fuck do I know? What the fuck do I care? Put down *dead as doornails* in your report." Monkle had little patience or respect for pale, quivering types like this PAO puke (and by the looks of it, this was the staff sergeant's first deployment—no combat patch on his right shoulder). "Probably already buried the guy—you know how these Muslims are about getting the body in the ground before sunset."

"And, uh, second: what is Captain Shrinkle's status? Are there plans to relieve him or put him on R&R until this blows over?"

Monkle shrugged and turned to Duret. "You'd have to ask the colonel here."

Duret tightened his lips. "No comment."

Gooding nodded and scribbled several words in his notebook, then retracted his pen with a click.

"Anything else, PAO?"

Gooding shook his head and Monkle looked at the rest of the group. "Gentlemen?"

No comments, no alibis.

"All righty then. I'll keep you updated as I learn anything new. PAO, I'm sure the CG will want to see some sort of press release as soon as he gets out of church, so be prepared." Gooding reclicked his pen and wrote in his notebook. "Okay, that's all, gentlemen."

The group broke up.

"Sir, if I could have a private word with you?" Major Monkle pulled Lieutenant Colonel Duret to a close huddle.

"Sir, if I could be frank?"

"Go ahead," Duret said.

"Sir, is your captain a complete and utter idiot prone to eating Stupid Sandwiches at every meal?"

Duret couldn't meet the battle captain's eyes. "Something like that, I guess."

10

LUMLEY

Sergeant Brock Lumley and his men lived in metal shipping containers on the hot edge of FOB Triumph, ovenlike boxes that sat in the middle of a windswept field next to an Army Reserve unit's motor pool, which had once, a long regime ago, been the site of a sewage collection pool. The Connex shipping containers were packed together side by side, each of them generating their own solar heat and reflecting it onto the neighboring container. On the hottest of days, Lumley and his men were buffeted by the stink of shit ghosts—all that waste and effluvia that had once fudged out from the assholes of assholes like Saddam and Uday and Qusay.

The Connexes were just another example of the sharp division between grunts and Fobbits. While Headquarters staff soldiers who worked in the palace were given air-conditioned trailers to call home, the infantry took its lumps with living in something akin to a Dumpster. The softies got cushy quarters, but the ones doing the *real* work of Operation Iraqi Freedom suffered the indignity of cleaning out the packing material—the wooden crates, the metal straps, the bubble wrap—and making a nest in what had once held tents, cots, MREs, field desks, office supplies, and a certain sergeant major's stash of soft-core porn DVDs, very cleverly concealed in a false bottom of his foot-locker (beneath an equally healthy supply of *Our Daily Breads*).

How had this happened? How had the haves once again triumphed over the have-nots? Sergeant Lumley could only imagine a scene in the Pentagon once upon a short time ago: a logistics general, his mind warped in equal measure by Army regulations and a lifetime subscription to *Psychology Today*, must have been talking to his attentive staff of majors and lieutenant colonels—men who, yes, were themselves softened around the middle, bellies spilling over belts—telling them, "This is how war functions, gentlemen. Keep the infantry uncomfortable, miserable, numb to hope. Fill their lives with sharp angles, rough surfaces. Bring to bear the most extreme of stresses and be relentless in your cruelty. When they are fully engaged in combat, allow them no relief, no downy pillow. Make them *want* to go home and, I guaran-damn-tee it, gentlemen, you will soon have a fighting force of insatiable men bent on the art of killing. Their desire to fight will be in direct proportion to their desire to end combat and return to the arms of their wives, their girlfriends, their mistresses, their hookers. Pillows and pussies will be their lights at the end of the tunnel.

"Support staff, on the other hand, needs to be coddled on a daily basis while in a combat zone. If you make their lives miserable, they'll become distracted. They'll drop a stitch as they knit one, purl two. Make them sleep on the hard ground in a frozen rain and they'll sure as shit fuck up a battle order or relay an eight-digit grid coordinate when what we really need

is a sixteen-digit coordinate. Yes, men, if we ever fail to tuck
the REMFs good night with a kiss and a teddy bear, we'll have
only ourselves to blame when someone gets killed thanks to a
distracted desk jockey in G-3 Ops. And we wouldn't want that,
would we?"

(Murmurs of "No, sir, wouldn't want that," and the collective hitching up of pants among the Pentagon staffers.)

And so, this unofficial dispensation of sleeping quarters
spread throughout the Army with the end result of Bravo Company at the edge of FOB Triumph sweating themselves to sleep
every night, lullabied by the echoing clang of a loose door on a
Connex somewhere down the line blowing in the wind, a wind
that carried Saddam Hussein's turds right up their nostrils.

The official story handed to Bravo Company: the Connexes
were all the Army could afford to give them at this point in time.
The surplus deluxe air-conditioned trailers were on order but
had been delayed due to scheduling conflicts with the Kellogg,
Brown and Root contractors. Something about a golf course in
Dubai, but Captain Shrinkle said he couldn't be entirely sure.

"Buck up, men," he told his company during morning formation soon after their arrival in Baghdad. "We'll get through
this as best we can. Before you know it, we'll be living in style."
When Shrinkle said *we*, he meant *you* because *his* address, of
course, was 232 Lap of Luxury Lane. *He* had a trailer with the
aforementioned air-conditioning and a floor that didn't sound
like a hollow metal drum every time you put your boot down.
Still, he had the nerve to stand there and tell them, "Buck up,
men."

Shrinkle's men stared back at him with the eyes of prison-
ers watching the warden's every move, waiting for the merest

slip, the smallest lapse in concentration, for the moment they could rush in and devour him with homemade knives and forks. Some of the men in the company still clung to a few threads of respect for Captain Shrinkle but, for the rest of them, respect had stepped across the line to resentment a long time ago. Now they were resigned to patiently biding their time until things were different. And they *would* be different. If there was one thing the men of Bravo Company had learned in the last half year in Iraq, it was this: change was always on its way, in shapes large and small. All they had to do was watch Shrinkle, obey his commands, no matter how brutal or boneheaded . . . and wait.

There was the matter of Bravo pride, of course. They weren't about to let any of the other companies in the battalion, or any of the other units on Triumph—especially those dickheads from Tenth Mountain—think they were anything but kick-ass Warriors with a capital *W*. They had a legacy stretching back to doughboys that needed to be preserved and upheld—their military ancestors had been at the fucking *Rhine* for God's sake and kicked Kraut ass all the way from hell to Hamburg. You couldn't just let bravery like that get tarnished by one indecisive officer who didn't know shit from Shinola. If it was up to them, the enlisted soldiers, the cogs, to keep this machine running, then so be it. No matter how ill-conceived Captain Shrinkle's plans might be, the men of Bravo were determined, for the sake of appearances, to carry them out to the fullest extent allowed by law and common sense.

Who were they to bitch (publicly, at least) about living in oven boxes?

Shrinkle was already a ghost, a nothing man on his way out, and not soon enough if you asked Brock Lumley. The company commander had reached a new level of useless on this last Quick Reaction Force mission to rescue the 442nd fuel truck in Adhamiya. Sergeant Lumley was finding it harder and harder each day to mask his contempt for Shrinkle. He tried to put on a loyal face in front of his men—good order and discipline and all that crap—but Shrinkle made it too easy to sneer and jeer. Practically gave it a red-carpet invitation.

It was maddening the way he stuttered when he stood in front of the company formation, his hands clasped behind his back where, Lumley suspected, he was wringing his fingers like they were little damp sponges. The way he started most of his sentences with "So, uh . . ." The way he kept all those care packages to himself and never shared with the rest of the company—pretended, in fact, he wasn't even receiving any care packages at all. The way he never let anyone, not even the first sergeant, inside his trailer. The way he stared you up and down if you bumped into him in the shower trailer. The way he'd so typically cowered at the Quillpen standoff with the half-dead terrorist, not even bothering to hide his fear from the battalion commander. The way he just whipped out his pistol and capped that short-bus hajji at the gas station without so much as a blink of common sense. The way he walked with little mincing steps as if he were following a dotted line on the ground. The way he kept nervously sucking in his breath on the Humvee ride to Adhamiya eight hours ago.

Lumley had been crammed behind Captain Shrinkle's seat, face pressed against the window to avoid getting knocked around by Zeildorf's ass as he swiveled in the gunner's seat, scanning the building-slant shadows for terrorists.

As they rode through the streets, Lumley could hear—even above the roar of the Humvee engine—the *tsip . . . tsip . . . tsip* of Shrinkle's nervous breathing. Every pile of roadside trash, every broken chunk of concrete, every dead dog they passed, Shrinkle would flinch from the potential IED and emit a louder *TSIP* before settling back. Lumley almost felt sorry for the guy. Almost.

When they pulled up to the accident site in Adhamiya, Shrinkle was the last to emerge from the Humvee. When the captain finally unfolded himself from the vehicle, you could practically hear his teeth rattling in his head.

"Stand fast, Sergeant Lumley, while I go assess the situation."

"Roger, sir." Brock looked at his men and said, "You heard the man."

Someone lit a cigarette and kept it cupped in the dark hollow of his hand. Someone else softly tapped the beat of a song on the butt of his M4. Noise and light discipline.

They stared at the two crumpled vehicles and the injured who stumbled around or were curled into balls on the ground.

"Somebody should go help those fuckers," Zeildorf said.

"Yeah, somebody should," Rodriguez agreed.

They stared and smoked.

There was a quick slam of car doors and a vehicle pulled away roughly from the site.

"There go our good buds, the IPs," Boordy said.

"Weenie cops."

"Damn straight."

The men watched their captain half-walk, half-crouch across the street to talk with the 442nd lieutenant. The young Transportation officer—another member of the Ass-Pucker Club—had put his men in a defensive perimeter around the site and they were swiveling the barrels of their M4s in careless swings, which made Lumley and his men even more nervous.

It was an hour past twilight and the dark had snuffed the neighborhood, save for a lone bare bulb that spilled a yellow cone of light above the doorway of an auto parts store, struggling to hold back the shadows by itself. There was no wind and it smelled like one of them had picked up dog shit in the waffles of his boots.

"Someone's gonna get killed here tonight and it ain't gonna be hajji," Zeildorf muttered.

Zeildorf, Rodriguez, and Boordy quietly snicked their selector switches from *safe* to *semi*. "What the fuck you doing?" Lumley said.

"Nothing," Boordy said. But all three of them went back on *safe*. No way were they gonna piss off Lumley on a night like this.

"Jesus, let's not get carried away," Lumley said. "This is a traffic accident, nothing more than that."

"So far," Boordy said.

Ever since Quillpen, and then that thing with Hajji Snowpants, everyone was a little twitchy around crowds. Too many bodies, too many sullen stares to keep track of. Now, ants to sugar, Local Nationals were gathering at this accident site, dark blobs bobbing their heads in the shadows. A weak moon spread thin light across the scene. Three men in their early twenties watched the Americans sullenly, hands in their pockets as they leaned against a corrugated steel curtain pulled across the front of a butcher's shop. They didn't speak, just stared from beneath black locks of hair. Another hajji, a teenager in a Nike T-shirt, pedaled his bike back and forth along the edge of the street. Other knots of men, muttering and smoking cigarettes, watched the American soldiers from the corners of their eyes.

"Shouldn't these fuckers be home in bed with their wives? What the hell are they doing here this time of the night?"

"Easy now, Rodriguez," Lumley said.

"Yeah, I thought there was a curfew," Boordy said.

"Apparently not in Adhamiya. At least not tonight."

"I don't like the look of this," Zeildorf said quietly as he started to pace. "This is nucking futs." He came from New England stock and usually released his words with reluctance. Tonight, they came in short bursts, flying into the night like bullets. He was starting to make all of them uneasy.

"None of us like the looks of it, Zeildorf."

"Hey," said Boordy, "I heard a good one the other day."

"Oh, yeah?" said Rodriguez.

"Yeah. Mickey Mouse may be nuts, but Minnie is fucking goofy."

None of them laughed. They'd already heard that one. From Rodriguez last week.

Zeildorf had not stopped pacing. "I say let's show 'em some good old infantry ingenuity."

"And *I* say," Lumley shot back, "we just wait and see what the commander wants to do."

Shrinkle was still conferring with the 442nd lieutenant, pointing to the crumpled bus and the dozen passengers who were standing off to one side, two of them lying on the ground moaning and a kid, his nose bloodied, who was walking around holding his arm and screaming something that sounded like "*Dick Rabbit! Dick Rabbit!*" The bus driver trailed after him, trying unsuccessfully to calm him down and get him to take a seat on the curb until the medics arrived. Shrinkle and the lieutenant flinched every time the kid with the broken arm came near them.

At that point, Lumley knew this night would probably not turn out the way any of them were expecting.

Shrinkle and the lieutenant had finally reached a decision after walking slowly, cautiously up to the front of the truck, pointing here and there at the busted engine, nodding once or twice, then playing two rounds of "Rock, Paper, Scissors." Shrinkle mince-stepped back across to Lumley and the team.

"Give me a grenade, Sergeant Lumley."

"Say again, sir?"

"A grenade." Shrinkle snapped his fingers impatiently. "You got any thermites on you?"

"Back in the Humvee, but—"

"Well then, go grab 'em, Sergeant."

"Roger, sir." Lumley looked back at his men but they glanced away as if they weren't privy to the conversation, and that's the story they'd stick to if they were ever called to the witness stand. *Yeah, well, fuck them. And fuck Captain Shrinkle. Fuck everybody.*

Lumley returned to the Humvee, went around to the back, and unlocked the ammo box that held the red canisters. Later, Lumley would replay how his hand reached for the thermite grenades and he'd think about how he should have paid better attention to the color. Red for fucking danger.

But no, he grabbed one and carried it back to Captain Shrinkle. "Sir, I really don't think this is a good—"

"I appreciate your input, Sergeant Lumley, but in this instance, I'm going to override you. Lieutenant Middlecamp and

I determined their truck was inop and it would take too long to get someone out here to tow it away. So we're gonna take care of it, then get the heck out of here and call it a night. I don't like the look of that crowd."

"I don't either, sir. But—"

But Shrinkle was already walking back toward the truck with the grenade in his hands. Lumley looked at his men.

"Awwww shit," someone said.

"*Dick Rabbit! Dick Rabbit!*" from the kid with the flapping arm.

Shrinkle was no longer mince-stepping but moving forward with determined purpose, not caring what he crunched beneath his boots. He'd reached the tipping point and was on the other side now. With a one-two flick of his hand and arm it was done. The grenade sailed through the air. The crowd of Iraqis collectively flinched. Then came the blooming explosion and the truck cab was briefly filled with white light, a cloud of smoke, and a small lick of flame, which Lumley and his men could see climb the seats and spread to the dashboard. The driver's window burst in a tinkle of glass and flames erupted outward, crawling down the doors to the undercarriage. Someone screamed and everything fell silent until one of Lumley's men said "Awwww *shit*" again.

Then the fire sputtered and dwindled to a chemical hiss.

Shrinkle stood facing what he'd done, arms akimbo, the bluish flames silhouetting him in the night. Then he backpedaled several feet and, regaining his old decomposure, walked back to the rest of the American soldiers. After shaking hands with the 442nd Transpo lieutenant, Shrinkle rejoined his dumbfounded soldiers and said, "Okay, let's call it mission complete, men." He climbed back into his Humvee and sat there as if waiting for his chauffeur to whisk him away.

Lumley and his squad had no choice but to follow, after stubbing out their cigarettes on the sides of their boots and saying "Shitfuckdamn" several times.

On the ride back to Triumph, Lumley stared out the window, eyes scanning the pools of darkness, the alleys, the silhouette of rooftops, looking for the outline of a grenade launcher, two men hunched over a spool of wire, anything out of the ordinary. Zeildorf swung his ass back and forth like a nervous tic. Captain Shrinkle continued *tsip-tsip-tsipp*ing all the way to Triumph.

11

SHRINKLE

Six months before that ill-conceived grenade toss, when they were in Kuwait waiting to move north into Baghdad, they tested Captain Abe Shrinkle's mettle by shitting in his helmet. At least *some*one did. Maybe it wasn't an entire company of "theys," maybe it was just one rogue hater who had it out for him. No one ever confessed and the CID investigation, launched by an irritated Lieutenant Colonel Duret who had better things to do at the time, never found the Culprit of Shit.

Nonetheless, the incident altered the character of Bravo Company.

Sure, Abe was rattled. Who *wouldn't* be, coming back to the tent from the shower trailer to find your helmet upside down, front-and-center on your cot with a fresh coil of human waste on the padding inside and a crudely written note ("Have a Nice Day, Shithead")? Abe stood there, towel around his neck, staring with slowly seeping comprehension at the gauze of steam rising from his helmet.

Sunlight from the early dawn filtered into the sleeping quarters, burning off the night chill. Behind him, the tent—large as a circus big top and filled with more than a hundred cots, footlockers, duffel bags, and sleeping soldiers, mouths agape—was quiet, *too* quiet. It was their fourth day in Kuwait, nearly a week out of the States, ten days until they ventured north into Iraq, and Abe knew his men were feeling a stew of homesickness and fear of what lay ahead across the border. The soldiers were loud with braggadocio, quick to punch and wrestle each other to the ground, and stony with their silences when they stopped to think they were now "men at war." Abe cut them some slack because they were all feeling the threat of snipers and mortars that came to them in invisible, pulsing waves from the restless land to their immediate north. They read the headlines in *Stars and Stripes*; they knew what waited for them.

So yes, for the time being Abe would grant them their little moments of indiscipline—the day-growth of beard stubble, the smuggled-in issue of *Playboy* to which he'd temporarily turn a blind eye, the unauthorized stash of pogey bait (the Cheetos, the Oreos, the Slim Jims), the sloppy way they stood in his formations. Yes, he'd give them an inch for the next ten days they were here in the waiting room of Kuwait because, he truly believed, he was a kind and generous commander, a leader who looked out for his men.

But *this*, the steaming stink of shit in his helmet, *this* was something else entirely. It was a personal, "fuck you" message direct from the heart of those he'd trusted and loved (and whom he thought felt the same about him). What was he to do with this?

Without turning around, he strained to hear the muffled snicker, the unsuppressed chuckle, but heard nothing except the even more meaningful silence filling the tent.

Not once did he look at his men, who pretended to sleep in their cots. Not once did he try to ferret out the conspiratorial glance, the wink, the suddenly averted eyes. No, Abe simply picked up the helmet with both hands and carried it to the nearest latrine where he dumped the turds into the gaping hole. Then he scrubbed the inside of his helmet with hot water and an old toothbrush. He went about his business, never once saying anything that would give the shitter the pleasure of seeing his commander rattled.

But when, three days later, someone from another company reported the graffiti in the Porta-Potty—"I can hardly wait until I get to Iraq and get me some live ammo so I can kill Capt. S."—well then, there was no getting around it. Abe Shrinkle was frightened of his own men.

Lieutenant Colonel Duret took the only reasonable course of action available to him: he forbade Abe to go on the convoy to Baghdad that was scheduled to leave in a week for fear his stalker would take him out during the trip north. Instead, Abe was forced to catch a ride with a later convoy from another unit.

So, because some crazy sonofabitch (or sonsofbitches) scrawled death threats, Abe's company moved through enemy territory without a commander.

Worst of all, his men seemed to be okay with that.

12

DURET

Vic Duret agonized over the Shrinkle problem. This was the fuck-a-roo to end all fuck-a-roos, he told himself. The indecision at Quillpen, then shooting that kid—an innocent Local National—and now the impetuous toss of a grenade (when indecision would have been a *good* thing) in Adhamiya. This particular company commander was starting to feel like a hot poker rammed up Duret's pecker.

The battalion commander didn't need any more trouble than he would normally attract in the course of business in a combat zone. There would always be the regrettable decisions, the logistical shortages, the unplanned deaths, but they were something he could handle—or, at the very least, delegate to someone else to handle.

Abe Shrinkle, on the other hand, was not some hot potato he could pass to another battalion to resolve. Duret wasn't like one of those grease-fingered Fobbits who let bad things fall slick out of their hands for someone else to catch before they hit the floor. He'd always been a do-unto-others-as-you'd-have-them-do-unto-you

kind of guy, and he went to work every day in this war zone trying to put that into effect, despite the challenges of confronting
a faceless enemy who couldn't give a gnat's fuck about karmic
Good Samaritans.

No, he wasn't going to toss Shrinkle away like a snot-
soaked Kleenex. That just wouldn't be right in the whole scheme
of the universe.

Besides, Duret owed it to the men of Abe's company to
get things squared away. He'd seen the look on the faces of
the soldiers in that company when they were crouched there
eyeballing that sedan embedded in the back of the Abrams
tank. Those guys had been scared to death he wouldn't step
in and save them from their commander. As it turned out, that
NCO—what's his name, Bromley? Brumley?—had taken matters into his own hands with that one clean shot.

No, he needed to mop up this latest mess quickly and
quietly. He also owed it to Abe to do it in a manner that was
honorable and subtle. As much as he couldn't stand the guy's
jellied spine, Duret had a hard time just kicking him to the curb
without so much as a how-dee-doo.

Relief-for-cause was inevitable—Shrinkle's and, if Duret
wasn't fast and wily enough, his own. That particular shitball was
already headed his way from the brigade commander, gathering
sticks and stones as it rolled downhill. Relieved, investigated,
arrested. It was coming, unless—

Unless he could pull a fast one to make it look like he, Vic
Duret, was the one to make the first move—fire Shrinkle's ass,
publicly and loudly avow he was a worthless piece of shit, and
make a big show of cleaning house. Beat the brigade commander
to his own punch, grab the wind from the commanding general's

sails. It could be done, but only if he was a Houdini—and a quick one at that, since that battle captain in SMOG had already filed his report and sent it up the chain. The CG was probably already grinding his molars.

Then again, maybe the CG would see it his way and stifle the noise of this incident before it leaked out and grew to Abu Ghraib proportions. He was, after all, in line for a third star. Yes, indeed, there would be a lot of gamesmanship and hush-hush huddles going down in the next few days.

Duret sure hoped that PAO weenie—Sergeant Goody-Two-Shoes—knew how to string together words in order to spin them all out of this steaming pile of fucked-upedness.

Duret sat at his desk, under the watchful gaze of Saddam Hussein's taxidermied animals, working himself into a bone-cracker of a headache until finally, temples throbbing, he thought of something that would buy him a little time to sort it all out. One magic word: Qatar. Which rhymed with "R&R."

The Good Idea Fairy had landed on Vic's shoulder with a stop-gap solution: send Shrinkle off on a four-day jaunt to Qatar, the sun-washed country on the Persian Gulf, for a little rest and relaxation. Brilliant. Brill-fucking-yant.

He left the palace and went in search of Captain Fuck-a-Roo.

13

GOODING

At the same time Lieutenant Colonel Duret was on the warpath for his nincompoop commander, Staff Sergeant Chance Gooding Jr. sat in his cubicle trying to figure out the best way to tell the American public about how a member of the U.S. Army pulled the pin on a grenade, Nolan Ryan'ed it into the cab of a fuel truck, and destroyed $250,000 worth of government property. Not to mention the life of an anonymous Iraqi.

Gooding pulled up a fresh document template on his computer. Even though his fingers typed phrases like "full cooperation of Iraqi police and local firefighters" and "minor injuries" and "unavoidable accident," he couldn't help thinking about that charred body under the truck and how it got there.

Was he hit by the truck and nobody noticed? Did he have a heart attack and fall to the ground, unnoticed by the gathering crowd of Local Nationals? Did he drop his car keys and crawl under the truck to look for them just when the grenade went off over his head? And how do we even know it was a *he*? Maybe it was a woman who was raped by the GIs after the accident and the GIs had then tried to burn the evidence. These were the dark alleys his imagination wandered, especially after sticky lingering situations like Abu Ghraib.

It was still too early to speculate on this one, though. Gooding punctuated the last sentence—"An investigation is ongoing and statements are being taken"—then printed the release for Lieutenant Colonel Harkleroad to review while eating his breakfast of a bran muffin and Diet Coke (with a side order of jelly donut).

A few minutes later, Major Filipovich arrived for work, trudging into the cubicle maze with carabiners, mini flashlights, compass, and earplugs case dangling off his flak vest like Christmas ornaments. "Morning, Gooding."

Chance stood next to the printer, waiting for the press release to spit out into his hand. "Morning, sir."

"How goes it today?"

Chance hesitated, knowing if he broke the news to Major Filipovich before Harkleroad could read the release, Filipovich would go all bat shit and try to take matters into his own hands. Chance decided to play it cool. "Oh, you know, sir. Another damn day."

"Ain't that right. Just another Monday on a shelf of Mondays."

"Way I look at it, sir, every day is a Monday when you're over here."

"Groundhog Day."

"Word up."

The one-page release landed in Gooding's hand and he quickly concealed it behind his back as he walked toward Harkleroad's office. He needn't have been so stealth, however: Flip

Filipovich was already clicking through another hand of solitaire on his computer.

Harkleroad sat at his desk, head tilted back, a wad of tissue jammed up one nostril. There was a bloodstain the shape of Australia in the center of the PAO's chest.

"Guh muhwig, Sergeant Goodwig."

Gooding edged cautiously into the room. As always, he kept a close eye on the fit-to-burst buttons straining against the PAO's belly. "You okay, sir?"

"Nose bleed," he said, the hanging-down part of the tissue fluttering like a skirt from his breath. Harkleroad's thin hair was sweat-plastered across his scalp, his meaty shoulders hunched around his neck. He pointed apologetically at his nose. "Came ober me all ub a sudden."

"Cheer up, sir. Maybe you'll get a Purple Heart for this."

Harkleroad stared at Gooding until the NCO cleared his throat and waved the release in the air. "This just a needs a once-over, sir. As soon as I get your initials, I can press the *send* button."

As Gooding waited for Harkleroad to copyedit the press release about that grenade-pitching Captain Shrinkle, he tried not to pinpoint the location of cities like Sydney and Melbourne on the PAO's chest.

When he returned to his cubicle, Gooding was pinching the press release between two fingers as if it were wet and dripping.

"More red ink?" Filipovich asked.

"That and a little bit of Harkleroad's hemorrhage." Gooding held up the story.

Flip whistled. "Looks like *Friday the Thirteenth, Part Twenty*. Well," he stood and yawned, "good luck with that."

As Major Filipovich donned his battle rattle, Gooding asked, "Off to the gym, sir?"

"Yep. Gotta get in the daily workout." They both knew this was code for "forty winks back at the hooch."

"We'll see you later, sir."

"Yep, okay. Have fun scrubbing those words until they're all shiny and pretty," Filipovich said, pointing at the story about the grenade incident. "Meanwhile, do what I do: think dark thoughts about Harklefuck. It's the only way I get through this shit."

Staff Sergeant Gooding had his own miniature subversions (though they were less violent and more respectful of his military superiors).

Take his list of Forbidden Words, for instance. Halfway through this deployment, Gooding had started to keep a running tally of catchphrases that popped up in conversations around the palace, the evening BUBs, and from the talking heads on TV. He kept a yellow legal pad at his desk, jotting down the latest inane verbal turd that dropped out of the mouths around division headquarters—words like:

Iraqi Face (as in "we have to put an Iraqi Face on this news story to take the emphasis off of U.S. involvement")
Global Cosmopolitan Media
Information Dominance (favored by Corps PAO)
Iraqidocious (favored by Major Filipovich)
Pretzel logic (practiced by Lieutenant Colonel Harkleroad)

Metric assload (as in "I've got a metric assload of ammuni-
tion to deliver to the battalion tomorrow")
Iraqinization
Baghdad Ladies (as in "I know a dude over in Logistics
who goes up to the chief's office every day, begging like a
Baghdad Lady")
Pole-vaulting over mouse turds (i.e., worrying about the
inconsequential and insignificant)
Nexterday

The next candidate for his list would almost certainly have
something to do with the latest "terrorist versus insurgent" brou-
haha. He just needed a clever, pithy expression to write on his
notepad.

Gooding pulled up his e-mail and read, from the bottom
up, for the eleventh time in as many hours, the message trail
that had come down from higher headquarters.

From: reginald_t_lesser@multicorpsiraq.mil

To: eustace.harkleroad@us.army.mil, jack.birch@us.army.mil, frances
.finkle@us.army.mil, jeff.jefferson@us.af.mil, edward_m_lesser@
multicorpsiraq.mil, david_p_adams@multicorpsiraq.mil, rtp@yahoo.com,
milreporter@gmail.com

29 JUNE 2005 0849hrs

Subject: Informal Public Affairs Guidance Regarding Current Use of Terms

All:

This is a friendly reminder that we need to cease and desist our habitual
use of the term "insurgent." Remember, we now have a democratic country
with an elected transitional government that we so wonderfully helped

install. This is no longer a provincial puppet gov't ruled by an evil puppeteer. The Iraqis are fast approaching something that resembles Philadelphia, circa 1776. Anyway, bottom lining it: Sunnis and other extremists are targeting and killing civilians along with Iraqi Security Forces. There is no discriminate use of force on the part of the attackers—it's a free country and violence is a free-for-all, just like it is in any democracy.

Our intel reports indicate that at least a significant portion of the violence is imported from outside the borders of Iraq, so one can't reliably call them rebels.

Thus, we here at STRATCOM consider your prolonged use of labels not only to be politically incorrect but grammatically improper. "Insurgent" lends a dignity the thugs and murderers opposing us don't deserve. The word is too palatable for our audiences.

Therefore, we are asking you to cease and desist with "insurgent" and use "terrorist" instead.

Again, just a friendly reminder.

V/R,

MAJ Reginald Lesser

Deputy Chief, Strategic Communications

MCI, Baghdad Branch

From: eustace.harkleroad@us.army.mil

To: philip.filipovich@us.army.mil, jack.birch@us.army.mil, frances.finkle@us.army.mil, chance.gooding@us.army.mil, cinnamon.carnicle@us.army.mil

29 JUNE 2005 1325hrs

Subject: Fw: Informal Public Affairs Guidance Regarding Current Use of Terms

I queried higher HQ on the guidance about changing our term for Anti-Iraq Forces from "insurgents" to "terrorist" per STRATCOM's query/concern. I was told the guidance was premature. The folks at Multi-Corps

Iraq are only *considering* a change at this time. Don't jump the gun. We'll still use INSURGENTS for now.

V/R,

LTC Harkleroad

From: reginald_t_lesser@multicorpsiraq.mil

To: eustace.harkleroad@us.army.mil, jack.birch@us.army.mil, frances. finkle@us.army.mil, jeff.jefferson@us.af.mil, edward_m_lesser@ multicorpsiraq.mil, david_p_adams@multicorpsiraq.mil, rtp@yahoo.com, milreporter@gmail.com

29 JUNE 2005 2043hrs

Subject: Fw: Re: Fw: Informal Public Affairs Guidance Regarding Current Use of Terms

All,

At the present time, there is no OFFICIAL guidance to change use of terminology. I may have miscommunicated when I said earlier that there is a move. There is no move, only a suggestion on our part. SUGGESTION does not mean DIRECTIVE.

My suggestion was prompted by some low-level discussion here at MCI but has not been vetted with senior leadership or higher headquarters. For now, we need to stay the course with "Insurgent" while continuing to review our choice of words. Words are important. Words can wound, maim, and kill.

There's more background we can discuss when we next get together, privileged information that I'm not at liberty to divulge at this time.

Perhaps a few poolside drinks over here in the Green Zone are in order? Look forward to seeing you!

Cheers,

MAJ Reginald Lesser

Deputy Chief, Strategic Communications

MCI, Baghdad Branch

From: hgunderson@mafiraq.mil

To: MCI Staff_All, STRATCOM_PA_Group, reginald_t_lesser@ multicorpsiraq.mil, edward_m_lesser@multicorpsiraq.mil, david_p_ adams@multicorpsiraq.mil, eustace.harkleroad@us.army.mil, jack.birch@ us.army.mil, frances.finkle@us.army.mil, chance.gooding@us.army.mil, jeff. jefferson@us.af.mil, rtp@yahoo.com, milreporter@gmail.com

Cc: paolovrs@listserv.com

30 JUNE 2005 1431hrs

Subject: AIF Semantics

Gentlemen,

Word has reached our office about increased confusion regarding the use of "terrorist," "insurgent," and all associated terms. After much discussion behind closed doors and numerous consultations with our cultural liaison staffers, we have come to a decision point regarding the bomb planters.

Multi-Corps-Iraq has decided to get away from the term "insurgent" because of its formal definition: *a person who revolts against civil authorities or an established government.* In other words, a rebel but not necessarily a belligerent. He could merely be one who acts contrary to the policies and decisions of one's own political party. Indeed, our very nation was founded on the principles of rebellion and it would not be out of line to call great men like Alexander Hamilton, Henry Clay, and Paul Revere "insurgents." So, to link what's going on here in Iraq at the street level to the glorious cause of our nation is, in my opinion, a travesty and, frankly, something that turns my stomach.

Bearing that in mind, the term "insurgent" is thus not entirely correct for this particular time or phase of the newly reborn Iraqi government.

Whereas the term "terrorist," whereby a deranged individual employs a systematic use of terror as a means of coercion, is a more appropriate and acceptable term to use in our briefings, press releases, and everyday conversation. "Criminal" can also be used as a substitute in some cases, by its definition: one who has committed a crime against a lawful government.

So we will no longer dignify these horrible, despicable creatures with the title of "insurgent." I am directing all subordinate staff members to immediately start calling them what they are: **TERRORISTS.** We are, I need not remind you, currently waging the Global War on *Terrorism*.

Please train your minds and tongues accordingly.

Regards,

Harold Gunderson, Brigadier General, U.S. Army

Chief, Public Affairs Division

Multi-Allied-Forces Iraq

14

SHRINKLE

Shrinkle had earned a reputation around the FOB as the Care Package King.

It started with a trickle of boxes from his mother, her friends at work, and a few of his online friends (those who posted regularly to the American Civil War reenactors group at northVsouth. net). Then Shrinkle had learned there was a multitude of organizations back in the United States—mothers of deployed soldiers, mothers of dead soldiers, prayer circles at churches, Girl Scout troops, Harley-Davidson Vietnam Vet clubs, the Vermont Republican Purple Ladies, you name it—who had made a nonprofit cottage industry of collecting items that would "bring the comfort of home" to "our men and women who have placed themselves in harm's way."

Most Americans had no concept of what it meant to live in a world of car bombs and mortar threats and severed arms cocked in the grass beside the road. But, Abe was certain, most of them *wanted* to know. They wanted to empathize with him and his soldiers and they felt slack and helpless sitting back there in the land of cheeseburgers and Paris Hilton perfume. They wanted to say or do something, so they reached out a hand in the airport or they mailed a package of chocolate chip cookies to a person they would never meet, and still they knew it wasn't enough, but at least it was *some*thing.

And so, across America—but especially in the central belt of the Heartland—men and women, boys and girls, young and old, armed with plastic baggies and black markers, formed assembly lines and packed boxes full of donations that had flooded into the collection center. They spent hours upon hours each week carefully nesting baked goods and toiletries into boxes bound for soldiers they didn't know from Adam (or Eve). They pulled the names off the Web sites they'd built, which allowed soldiers to sign up to be on the receiving end. It gave these mothers and fathers, these teachers and students, these pastors and their flocks, hot butterflies of happiness inside their chests and though they didn't truly understand what was going on over in Iraq and really had no idea what it was like to wear eighty pounds of body armor in the 120-degree heat, it helped salve their collective guilt over the way America had treated the boys returning from Vietnam. Along with the yellow-ribbon stickers on the backs of their cars, it was a way for them to show the rest of the world—Democrats especially—they really knew how to Support the Troops. It was incredible how the screech of pulling tape across the flaps of just one box could bring spiritual harmony to a person, make her feel like she was doing Something that Mattered.

Once Captain Shrinkle stumbled across this network of do-gooders, there was no stopping him. In truth, he was supposed to share what he got with the rest of his company but he'd always been a hoarder and this just fed his hunger—like grabbing an addict by the hair, tipping back his head, and pouring baggies of cocaine into his nostrils. It wasn't until much later (long after his bad death) that the rest of the battalion realized the extent of Shrinkle's greed. Each day he received anywhere from two to ten boxes of items carefully packaged by happy-hearted patriots in Omaha and upstate New York. Many days, he made multiple trips between the company mail room and his trailer, wading through the ankle-deep gravel with a load of boxes.

Here he is now, moving earnestly across the rocks for another armful. His boot steps, rough and determined, sound like someone punching a box of Corn Flakes. Other soldiers give way, parting on either side of him; they know he is a man on a mission. He has that look in his eye.

On this day, despite all that has happened to him recently (the piss-pants embarrassment of Quillpen, the oh-crap-what-did-I-just-do grenade toss at Adhamiya), Abe whistles a peppy Glenn Miller tune (something he's picked up from a big band CD that came in a recent care package). At this particular moment, he loves this war and all its bennies, he loves the time of day with its slow-boiling sunset, and he loves the way the rocks sound beneath his boots.

He even loves the corrugated-steel shack that serves as a battalion post office. Truth be told, he has a bit of a crush on the mail clerk, despite her thick glasses and the oily patches of acne high on her forehead. If time and circumstances were any different, Abe wouldn't give her a second glance on the street. Here, however, he wants to sweep her off her feet and waltz around the gravel path with her in his arms as he hums "In the Mood" (or maybe "Signed, Sealed, Delivered").

Here she comes now, glasses askew, staggering out of the back room beneath the weight of five boxes. One of them is almost certainly full of books—a set of encyclopedias from the feel of it. She hoists the boxes onto the counter, then steps back and wipes her forehead with the back of her hand, further enraging the pimples to an angry red. She is breathing heavy and, of course, this stirs Abe's lust.

"Sir, I gotta ask: has there been a day when you *didn't* get any mail?"

Abe puts a finger to his chin and ponders. "Yes, I believe there was that Monday about two months ago when I went package-less."

She laughs. "We figure you've gotten more than three hundred boxes so far. You're the King of Care Packages!"

There it is. His title endorsed by a U.S. government postal clerk.

To her, he is just an oddity—charming, but deserving of muttered curses because of all the backaches from lifting and toting those boxes every single blankety-blank day.

To Abe, however, Little Miss Mail Clerk is an angel, delivering fresh supplies of hand-packed home goodies every afternoon, starting at 1600 hours.

See how he skips back to his hooch, pondering the mystery of the boxes in his arms. See that candy-store gleam in his eyes. At this point, he's not even thinking about a terrorist's brains splattered across the interior of an Opel sedan or a Local National enflamed against the undercarriage of a truck or the dying jingle of a jester's hat. No siree Bob.

Abe's dwelling, called a CHU (Containerized Housing Unit), is the deluxe long-term abode for the most privileged infantry soldiers on Triumph (and the standard housing for all regular Fobbits). If a realtor was showing off a CHU, she would be bragging about the linoleum floor, electrical outlets, and fluorescent lighting—"Just look at how the light opens up the space! Perfect for the first-time deployer looking to get a gentle start to his war!"

Each night, the tranquillity of CHU sleep is disturbed by low-flying Chinook helicopters whose dual rotors hammer the air without mercy. The force of the downdraft beats against the roofs of the CHUs and, lying there with their unsleeping eyes popped open, the Fobbits can actually see their ceilings flex. Each grips his or her mattress with both hands and wonders if they will be sucked into the sky, carried in this particular Chinook wind over the landscape of Baghdad, spinning like a carnival ride, the vomit of fear gagging the back of their throats.

Sleep easy, Fobbits! You're going nowhere. Your CHUs rest on foundations sunk deep into the tough Iraqi soil. There's no way you're going to Wizard of Oz yourselves out of this war.

The CHU comes in three basic colors: white, beige, and the gold-brown of your average bowel movement. If they weren't air conditioned, they would melt straight away into tin puddles, so most Fobbits fall to their knees each and every night, praising the foresight of the engineer who provided enough extra space in the corner for the large, boxy AC unit that rattles and drips without cessation. CHUs are large enough for two people to live in comfortably; four can be squeezed into one, but then it is very crowded, with much stepping on toes and groaning about the humid stink rising from just-removed boots.

Abe Shrinkle, for reasons completely unbeknownst to him, has been grinned upon by the gods. Whether by luck or (more likely) oversight by the billeting authorities, he dwells alone in his CHU.

It bothers Abe, pricks at his conscience, but what can he do? He's been ordered by the battalion commander to remain with the rest of the officers and to avoid mingling with the enlisteds as much as he can. So there you have it: his happy solitude is in keeping with good order and discipline. Who is he to buck the system? To share his private space would be a violation punishable by UCMJ. At least, that's how he figures it.

Abe keeps to himself, spending most of his time in the trailer, arranging the various contents of his care packages and whiling away the remainder of his time reading the W. E. B. Griffin paperbacks that arrive with predictable regularity.

On this day—two days after Abe accidentally killed a Local National by roasting the body beneath a truck—most of the boxes contain the usual assortment of granola bars, mixed nuts, hand sanitizer, and magazines (*Muscle & Fitness, Vermont Life, GQ,* et cetera). The encyclopedia-weight package turns out to be a year's supply of shampoo and conditioner, along with three oily fruitcakes in Ziploc baggies.

One thick envelope, however, is from a woman in Laramie, Wyoming—an oilman's wife who fancies herself something of a poet. She has written to Abe several times and he has answered promptly and enthusiastically, their correspondence revolving around Wyoming geology and literature and the joys and frustrations of being an unpublished poet trapped in a loveless marriage. In this day's envelope, Mrs. Norma Tingledecker has included two packages of jerky "made from genuine Cheyenne beef" along with another epistle (handwritten in lavender ink)

about her "bluebird-soundtracked life on the High Plains." Abe
sits there and snacks on the Wyoming cows as he reads the
two-page letter she's enclosed.

> Wyoming got its typical Father's Day snow last week—in
> the north. But down here (in Laramie), it's all burning
> blue skies and the golden tumble of leaves from the aspen
> and cottonwoods when the wind shakes the boughs. I saw
> a tiny warbler in the juniper bush outside my window
> two days ago; she's on her way south—confused by the
> unseasonal snow, perhaps . . . The fishing, too, is magnifi-
> cent . . . mostly because of what you can see and smell and
> hear when you're standing in the middle of the warmish,
> slow-moving Platte River. Mint. Dew-frosted sage. The
> trilly scoldings of kingfishers and ravens. The careful sip of
> a rainbow trout . . . And in the fall, the farewell serenade
> of Canada geese, which breaks one's heart with the re-
> minder of seasons . . . I feel blessed every day to live in a
> place where nature still has the upper hand. Ah, if only I
> felt the same glorious surge of love for my husband, Ray.
> He's a stinking, no-good bastard who always finds it nec-
> essary to stop at the Rockin' R before he sloppy-stumbles
> his way home to an ice-cold dinner . . . But don't get me
> started. No doubt you already have too much to fret away
> at your nerves and occupy your mind over there for me to
> be going on about Ray.

Abe clutches at her words. He doesn't want to leave this
letter and the sensory images it conjures. "A place where nature
still has the upper hand." Yes, yes, yes. He wants to go there so

desperately—right now—it nearly doubles him over in pain. He rolls the jerky on his tongue, savoring it as long as he can.

He sighs. *No, I must remain here in a land where* evil *has the upper hand. It is my duty and proud obligation.*

He carefully refolds Norma Tingledecker's letter, tucks it back into its lavender-scented envelope, and turns to the next box, ripping away the tape, which resists with an angry squeal. More socks. Abe doesn't have enough feet for all the socks he's received since February.

Luckily for the Care Package King, he lives alone with this accumulated goodwill in his trailer, a single room which is—he'd paced it out—eleven by thirteen, wood paneled, tile floored, with one window, an air-conditioning unit, a metal wall locker, a two-drawer night stand, a small lamp, and a bed that came with a pillow, a comforter, and one sheet. He got lucky with the sheets—his were beige with an ivy pattern running along the borders; the KBR contractors had issued some of his fellow officers sheets with cartoon characters like Strawberry Shortcake and Care Bears.

The entire single-wide mobile home was lined with Hesco-barrier blast walls. The Hescoes were seven-foot-tall canvas sacks with wire mesh on the outside and they had been filled with dirt by backhoes, then stacked like bricks around the FOB's tin-skinned trailers. They were like sandbags on steroids and protected soldiers from shrapnel, bullets, and the relentless wind. From where Abe sat, he was enclosed in something resembling a womb. Nothing—except for the most determined, manic-eyed terrorist or the most randomly lucky mortar—would be able to penetrate.

Within the trailer, he was nestled inside an extra padding of baby wipes, travel-size Kleenex, and enough Louis L'Amour paperbacks to choke a horse. Thanks to Abe's care package hoarding, wall space was getting squeezed to a minimum. After the first few weeks, he'd custom-built a large shelving unit along one side of the trailer and shoved his bed into the corner as tightly as he could just to accommodate his care package booty.

Over the months, he'd received dried fruit, microwave popcorn, paperback books, packets of ketchup and mustard swiped from fast-food restaurants, comic books, DVDs, a bar of blackberry soap, four boxes of envelopes, three cans of apple juice, two kitchen scrubber sponges, gel insoles for combat boots, nail clippers, chocolate chip cookies, lemon bars, eye drops, bookmarks, pencils advertising local insurance companies, powdered drink mixes, tampons (from a site where he'd registered as "A. Shrinkle"), months-old copies of *Car & Driver*, *Cosmopolitan*, *Newsweek*, and *Organic Gardening*, combs, toothbrushes, butterscotch candies, rosary beads, photos from the 18th Annual Fireman's Pig Roast in Eau Claire, breath mints, cheese crackers, raisins, Band-Aids, a tuft of pubic hair tenderly sealed in a Ziploc baggie by a Ms. Wanda Showalter (recently divorced) in Boise, cocoa mix with mini marshmallows, boxes upon boxes of Kleenex, a calendar with Norman Rockwell paintings, foot powder, jock itch cream, twenty-one bottles of Tylenol, crossword puzzles, fifteen copies of *The Da Vinci Code*, miniature American flags (made in China), antibiotic ointment, a studio "boudoir" portrait of Ms. Wanda Showalter (still divorced), a CD of Irish jig music, original cast soundtracks of *South Pacific* and *Cats*, thirty-six decks of playing cards, Christmas decorations that arrived in February, Hershey's Kisses that came in one glob of melted chocolate and tinfoil, kazoos, a pair of slippers, stationery, Post-it notes ("From the Desk of Jack Cramer"), powdered laundry soap, saltwater taffy, sunscreen, and baby wipes. Oh, Lord, the baby wipes!

Somewhere along the line, some soldier at the beginning of the war must have mentioned to his mother that he and his buddies had no way to wash their hands after eating T-rats out in the middle of the desert, where running water was hard to come by (at least in the early days of Operation Iraqi Freedom, this was very true), so if she could manage to send a box or two of baby wipes to him and the rest of the guys, that would be totally awesome. Word must have spread. Since then, baby wipes had been appearing on the "Much Needed" lists at the care package Web sites, and now Abe Shrinkle's west wall was completely bricked with plastic tubs of baby wipes. They numbered in the hundreds, floor to ceiling, and provided a noise buffer against the Blackhawks chopping low overhead.

They also served a more immediate, economic purpose for Abe Shrinkle. He hadn't known what to do with them until Second Lieutenant Pepperhill came to Bravo Company in March. Pepperhill's wife had given birth one month before he shipped out. It was their first child and Pepperhill wasn't taking being away from his new family very well. So every five days, like clockwork, he paid Shrinkle $4 for a tub then took it back to the privacy of his hooch, pulled out a baby wipe, sniffed the antiseptic powdery perfume, and remembered what his baby's butt smelled like back in Lafayette, Louisiana. There were nights when his soldiers came back from patrol and found their lieutenant sitting there on his cot rubbing a baby wipe all over his face and crying deep, heavy homesick sobs.

Sometimes Shrinkle received large envelopes full of letters written by entire classrooms of students at the behest of their teachers.

Dear Hero,
Thank you for your hard work on keeping me and my family safe. I know that you have been their for a long time. It's been hard for everyone.
Sinserily your friend,
Fernando M.
P.S. Stay safe. Oh by the way, even if you die you will still be my hero.

and,

To Abe: Yore in my famly's prayers evry nite at dinner. Be verey verey verey verey verey verey verey verey verey verey verey verey carful. My name is Kirsten age 7. Yore friend, Kirsten.

and,

Dear Soljer,
Mrs. Parker is makeing me write this. I don't like Mrs. Parker. Did you like your teechers? Teechers are the worst. They're worser than splinters. My dad agrees with me and says Mrs. Parker is a dried-up ole bitch whose cooch fell out a long time ago. I don't know what a cooch is, but if Mrs. Parker ever had one, I'm sure she lost it a long time ago like my dad says. Well, I hope you are well over there. Stay cool!
Darius K. Abernathy

Shrinkle was sitting on the edge of his cot reading through some of his favorite letters and trying to forget what had happened at Adhamiya when a knock rattled the door of his trailer.

Shrinkle's heart seized up.

This was it! They were coming for him!

Despite the comfort of his care packages and the solace of Norma Tingledecker's Wyoming poetry, Abe still had not been able to completely exorcise the guilt of that night when, it was alleged, he'd barbecued an Iraqi to death. He'd been listlessly combing through boxes and rereading letters, all the time trying to stifle his sobs. He figured it was early onset of PTSD but he felt powerless to stop it.

BAM! BOOM! BAM! The fist continued to thunder on his trailer door.

Abe sat quiet as a mouse on anesthesia.

Another explosion of knocks and, "Captain Shrinkle? You in there?"

It was the battalion commander. *Curses!* No way he could get around this now. He'd been ferreted out (though, he realized too late, if he really wanted to hide from his fate, he could have picked a better spot than his own trailer).

"Abe! I know you're there. I can hear you sniffing."

"C-coming, sir." Abe's voice was still rough from all those tears, that crying jag he'd been on for the last hour. "Just give me one minute, sir."

Muffled through the door came the words: "I'll wait. We've got all day." The wooden steps creaked as Lieutenant Colonel Duret settled back for the coming pounce.

Shrinkle stuffed the third graders' letters back in the envelope, his hands not just trembling but visibly shaking with a palsy now. First Quillpen, then Mr. Snowpants, and now this mess with the grenade. Adhamiya, he had to admit, might have been the worst. It roared back into his head, unbidden.

The night, the street, the Iraqis. The crumpled hood of the truck, the engine rendered useless. The caved-in side of the bus. The teenager holding his broken arm and screaming Arabic curses. The growing mob of Local Nationals. The way they always hemmed him in. Always pressing, pressing, pressing closer. *If they'd just give him some room to think, some time to sort this into compartments!* The night, the street, the mob, his hasty decision to toss the grenade. The quick-blooming flower of fire. His self-satisfaction—what a joke!—of mission complete. The long drive back to Triumph, his gunner swiveling in the roof of the Humvee, complaining aloud about how the sling cut into his ass. All of them ducking their heads to avoid a face full of gunner ass. Abe thinking about how his own ass was now in a sling (and he didn't even know about the dead Local National at that point). The wary looks his soldiers gave him the whole ride home. The way Sergeant Lumley's eyes slid away from him. The rapid, slot-machine cha-*ching* of his soldiers clearing their weapons at Triumph's entry control point. The look on the staff duty officer's face as he asked Abe if he was Bravo Company's commander. The way he said, we've got a problem—*you've* got a problem. There was a body. There was a body under the truck. The way Abe's heart had plummeted. The way it was still plummeting.

Abe knew he was in the stickiest of wickets. He was thinking UCMJ, relief for cause, court-martial, execution by firing squad (for which he would request a cigarette, even though he didn't smoke).

BAM BAM BAM!

Captain Abe Shrinkle rose from his bed, praying he wouldn't piss his pants when the final moment arrived.

15

GOODING

The morning Battlefield Update Briefing puckered assholes from Taji to Triumph, each satellite station joining the SMOG conference call with a remote anxiety that couldn't be concealed from fellow listeners. Tremulous baritone voices had their say, broadcasting from their various SMOG locations: the commanding general had his usual responsive grunts of approval (or was it disapproval? Sometimes the two types of his grunts were indistinguishable); the chief of staff had his requisite chime ins, reinforcing what the general had grunted, adding his own strenuous giddy-up-and-go admonitions. The overall tone of the briefing was one of, "Okay, hold on, keep it together, we're almost through with this, just pray he doesn't single me out." (*He* being the Old Man himself, General Bright, whose raspy commanding-general voice could reach right through the SMOG speakers and choke even the most hardened artillery officer into incoherent stutters.) Now, deep inside the Desert Camouflage Uniform pants of the most nervous staff officers crowded around SMOG stations in the palace, assholes were

starting to unpucker—if not quite all the way, then there was
certainly a little more sphincter breathability in the wedged-up
cotton Hanes; or, in the case of those who went commando, the
sandy folds of DCU'ed butts. A couple of pent-up farts were
allowed to escape.

Now the Intel officer was briefing from his SMOG station. "Ensure all soldiers understand there is a very high probability we will have increased security measures as an interior
guard of some sort is stood up. Ensure they are ready to assume
what would be a typical combat operational manning posture
of eight-eight-eight [eight hours performing primary function,
eight hours performing maintenance or guard, and eight hours
for sleep/physical fitness/personal hygiene]. Interior guard may
be required as the terrorists become more desperate to achieve
success."

"You have reason to believe these attacks are imminent,
G-2?" the general rasped.

"Yes, sir. We have credible sources that pinpoint time and
location to within a probability factor of plus/minus three-point-
five, at a minimum."

"Very good, G-2. Proceed."

But it was *not* "very good" for all those Fobbits sitting at
their desks listening to the report. Their spines were chilled,
their veins were icy. Their imaginations buzzed with the idea of
dark figures slipping over the concrete walls, slinking through
the concertina wire, hundreds of them trying to overrun FOB
Triumph en masse. Fobbits clung to the hope that most, if
not all, of the attacking terrorists would be cut down by the
machine-gun fire from the gate guards and perhaps the helicopters that would be airborne at a moment's notice. But what if four

or five or fifteen of the more determined and more devout terrorists slipped past the defense, moving deeper into the camp with
their AK-47s? What then? Were the Fobbits prepared for that?

At his desk, Staff Sergeant Gooding stopped typing that
day's media report and thought about the loaded magazine he
carried around in his cargo pocket. He wondered how fast he
could unbutton the pocket, unzip the Ziploc baggie he used to
keep the ammo dry and lint-free, shove the magazine into his
M16, bring it up to fire, and move the selector switch from *safe*
to *semi*. What then? How many more seconds would he waste
trying to decide whether or not he should pull the trigger at
the man advancing toward him with *his* gun raised to fire? Yes,
Gooding had had semiannual training at the rifle range, but the
targets there only popped up on springs, they never got to their
feet and walked toward him.

"I'm screwed," he groaned to himself. "We're all screwed."
He prayed G-2 was not-so-intelligent in at least this one instance.

Now the Civil Affairs officer was reporting on yesterday's
successful Beanie Baby mission to al-Khadhimiya: "The indig-
enous population was so receptive to our cultural handouts
they had to be restrained with a hasty perimeter we quickly
established using force protection measures one through
three."

"Okay!" General Bright barked through the SMOG speakers. "Let's continue with today's update. PAO! You're up next."

At his workstation, head clamped between the earphones,
Lieutenant Colonel Harkleroad blanched. With his microphone
on mute, he turned to the G-5 major sitting next to him. "Did
he say *me*?"

"He said you."

"He can't have meant *me*. I'm always second-to-last to brief." Harkleroad's voice elevated to schoolgirl pitch.

The G-5 major pointed to the TALK button on the keyboard. "You'd better say something, he's waiting."

"PAO!" the general crackled through the headset. "I'm waiting on you, PAO."

Harkleroad pushed TALK. "Y-yes, sir."

"You got a major malfunction this morning, PAO?"

Scattered, subdued laughter rose from cubicles throughout the division's area of operations.

"No, sir. No malfunction, sir. Just getting my notes together."

"Well, hurry up, PAO. The war can't wait on you to get your act together." Now it sounded like he was laughing conspiratorially to those sitting around him in his office.

Harkleroad dropped his binder and the metal rings broke open, spilling papers everywhere. All across the division, staff officers could distinctly hear him say, "Oh, fiddlesticks!" Most of the officers were unable to punch the MUTE button before their laughter bubbled out across the SMOG speakers.

General Bright's irritated rasp interrupted the proceedings. "Time waits for no man, PAO! We'll come back to you later. G-6! Let's have your report!"

At his desk, Staff Sergeant Gooding sank lower into his seat. He was already used to cringing every time Lieutenant Colonel Harkleroad opened his mouth but this was a new low. He predicted he'd be met with the sympathetic wink and snicker when he entered the dining facility at lunchtime today. Thank God he had the relief of R&R coming up in three days. He would bake his brain in the sun of Qatar and, for a brief blessed span of time, erase Harkleroad and his continental bloodstains from his mind.

General Bright barked for the chaplain to take his turn. Each day's BUB was brought to a close with the daily homily —by order of the CG, a semireligious man himself—and these ninety-second sermonettes could sometimes get out of control, stretching to three or four minutes, which the CG allowed without interruption. The chaplain's voice over the SMOG loudspeaker would continue to chirp away unabated while all around the division's Area of Operations—from Baqubah to Mahmudiyah—staff officers at remote computer stations shifted on their chairs, many of them rolling their eyes or silently mouthing things like "waste-o-time" or "Yea, though I walk through the valley of knee-deep shit," all of them eager to get on with the day's business. The CG had just issued a fuckload of marching orders during the BUB and now the staff officers' minds were racing ahead to PowerPoint briefings, Op Orders, crisis management plans, and—in one specific case—ensuring enough lobster was procured in time for Friday night's Bounty of the Sea dinner menu at the chow hall.

The chaplain nattered on, unleashed. His too-kind, too-melodious voice washed out from the SMOG speakers, winding its way hither and yon across Baghdad and the surrounding vicinity, wherever men's souls were tattered and in need of spiritual mending. Today, it went something like this: "Do you often lie awake at night worrying about the burden of responsibility you're carrying around? We have all felt the weight of grief, the anguish of frustration, the gut twist of impatience. Maybe it's a language barrier between you and the local sheikh . . . perhaps it's that young sergeant who insists on doing things *his way* and tries to buck the system . . . or maybe you're knotted up with problems from back home—the wife who let the car run low on oil and now your beloved '75 Mustang has thrown a rod, the son who is *acting up* during kindergarten recess, the high school daughter who adds a new body piercing every month. Whatever your burden, please know we all carry them around with us in our knapsacks. Talk about your Load-Bearing Equipment, eh?" The chaplain laughed and paused, expecting his unseen listeners would also be having a little chuckle at his joke, forgetting the Army had phased out the LBE while Clinton was still in office. "But seriously, folks . . . Too many times, we hold everything inside rather than following the simple rule of *Let go, let God*. I'm sure you've all heard that one. Now, let's put it into practice. Tonight, instead of trying to count sheep, maybe you should lie there and talk to the Shepherd instead."

The division staff scattered across central Iraq listened to the static crackle across SMOG, most of their ass cheeks now squirming with frustration and impatience.

The chaplain clicked his microphone again. "Today's Scripture reading is taken from First Corinthians, Chapter Fifteen. You may follow along in your pocket-sized King James." (Save for a devout supply clerk at FOB Eagle and three die-hard Catholics over in Legal Affairs, none of them carried around the miniature Bibles handed to them during their "Welcome to Iraq" in-briefing.)

"'Now this I say, brethren, that flesh and blood cannot inherit the kingdom of God; neither doth corruption inherit incorruption. Behold, I show you a mystery; we shall not all sleep, but we shall all be changed, in a moment, in the twinkling of an eye, at the last trump: for the trumpet shall sound, and the dead shall be raised incorruptible, and we shall be changed.'"

The chaplain droned on, burrowing like an insect into his listeners' ears. Alone in his office on the top floor of the palace, the commanding general clipped his toenails, aiming (not always successfully) for the wastebasket. Three doors down, the chief of staff sifted through reports, sorting them into piles according to brigade. On the ground floor of the palace, Lieutenant Colonel Harkleroad leaned closer to the computer screen of his SMOG workstation, hanging on the chaplain's every word because, he feared, he might be quizzed later on the sermonette by the CG and he wanted to get all the answers right this time. Two cubicles away, Major Flip Filipovich napped lightly, depending on the sudden absence of sound from the SMOG loudspeakers to wake him when it was all over. And, two miles across FOB Triumph, Lieutenant Colonel Duret sat with the rest of the brigade staff in front of the SMOG screen, thinking not about First Corinthians, but about his wife and his dog—though not necessarily in that order.

At last, the chaplain reached his crescendo. "'Then shall be brought to pass the saying that is written, Death is swallowed up in victory. O death, where is thy sting? O grave, where is thy victory?'"

The chaplain left that word, *victory,* hanging in the air like the echo of a trumpet blast.

When the hissing SMOG silence had stretched to an un-comfortable length, the CG cleared his throat and said, "Thank you, chaplain. As always your words of inspiration are . . . are *inspirational*. Now—"

"Sir, if I might—?"

"Yes, chaplain, what is it?"

Groans of agony throughout the SMOG network.

"Sir, I almost forgot to put in a plug for this Sunday's service at Lakeside Chapel—eight a.m., Protestant; noon mass for our Catholic brethren. I'm calling this week's sermon 'Good Grief.' You know—" his voice shifted into melody mode again "—we have all experienced sorrow during our time here in Iraq, but we each handle it in different ways. How one deals with 'small grief' from challenges and disappointments relates to how one handles 'big grief,' such as the loss of a loved one or a particularly good soldier. Be sure to come out this Sunday to hear the full prescription for Good Grief."

Another extended pause, during which could be heard what sounded like the soft *snick* of a nail clipper.

"Okay, thanks again, chaplain. Is that all?"

"Yes, sir. Thanks for allowing me to jump back in with that."

"Okay. Well, if there's nothing else, and no alibis . . . ?" Several staff officers clasped their hands in supplication, silently willing no one to utter a peep that would prolong the BUB with a bit of forgotten business. "In that case, go forth and do great things. Keep your chin straps tight. Nothing further. Luck of the Seventh!"

From a hundred SMOG stations came the echo of the division motto, "Luck of the Seventh!" They all clicked off and set about the day's business.

A groggy Major Filipovich lifted his head from his desk, then muttered, "And don't let death sting you out there, motherfuckers."

16

SHRINKLE

One week after "Adhamiya-gate," Shrinkle was exiled to the tiny kingdom of Qatar. At least that's how he saw it: exile. The Army called it R&R, a quaint term that came out of the mouth like a pirate growl and carried a strong whiff of nostalgia for the Vietnam War—stunned days of sitting on Hawaiian beaches, ears still ringing from NVA grenades.

Abe was joined by thirty others from FOB Triumph who rode in the ass-crunching seats of the C-130. They were leaving the bullet-peppered combat zone, headed for four days of freedom, sun, and endless hours of sleep at As Saliyah, an Army base none of them had ever heard of before but which now sounded better than Disneyland. In Qatar, the soldiers walked around with swollen chests and unlimbered tongues that liked to belt out, "Oh, *hell* yeah!" at the way their cottony civilian clothes felt against their skin or whenever a girl in a bikini jiggled by, showing off her rubbery, sweat-glistened flesh under God's oven-bake sun just as natural as you please. They were all giddy with joy.

Coming out of Baghdad, the plane had risen and banked sharply. The men inside the C-130's hot, metal belly were thrown side-to-side—rib cages crushed beneath the shell of flak vests, bowels flattened into laps by the G-forces, teeth rattled in clenched jaws, and sweat slicked the foreheads of thirty otherwise jubilant soldiers on their way to rest and relaxation in a place few of them could pronounce.

"Qatar, here weeee coooommmme!" cried a freckle-faced finance clerk who sat, thick as a piece of fudge, between Abe and a blunt-faced sergeant who looked like he'd come on R&R straight off a patrol in al-Dura.

"It's *cutter*, you dumbfuck," the sergeant said.

"Say what?" the clerk said, turning his still-beaming face to his neighbor.

"You said it like *guitar*, but it's pronounced *cutter*."

"Yeah, well fuck you, motherfucker."

"All I'm saying, asswipe, is you better get it right if you're gonna mingle with the locals down there."

The freckled finance clerk sneered, "Who said anything about mingling? I'm gonna lay around the pool, kicking back with my four-beer quota and admiring the tits on the girls smart enough to pack their bikinis on this deployment."

"It's only three, dumbfuck."

"Huh?"

"We only get three beers a day on R&R. Jesus, don't you Fobbits know anything?"

"Yeah? Well, where'd you hear that it was only three per?" The grin evaporated from the clerk's face.

"I heard it from a guy in my battalion who heard it from another guy who'd just come off R&R. Besides, everyone knows it—everyone except Fobbits who go around with their heads lodged in their asses, apparently."

"Yeah? Well, who the fuck cares anyway? The girls will still be bringing their tits with them and that's all I really care about."

"Look around you. You see anything worth nailing on this plane?"

The clerk scanned the dim belly of the C-130, but it was nearly impossible to determine the sex of the bodies encased in Kevlar and DCUs. "What*ever*, dude."

"I'm just warning you that you better keep the bar low cuz I guaran-damn-tee you it'll be Dogs on Parade."

"Yeah? Well, maybe they let locals *mingle* with us by the pool. You ever think of that, asshole? I'll bet those Qatar chicks are some hot babes underneath the black robes."

"You're fuckin' delusional," the sergeant said. "You Fobbits must sit around Triumph getting high on Freon from your air conditioners. Your brains have gone to rot."

"Fuck you, asshole." The clerk tried to turn away but the constrictions of his seat harness and flak vest didn't get him very far so he turned back to the sergeant. "What about you? What are your plans once we get to *Quitar*?"

"I've heard they've got some world-class dive spots there." The sneer dissolved from the sergeant's face as he thought of coral and neon-colored fish flashing through the water. "I'm gonna find me a place that rents scuba gear by the hour and see what I can see."

"Oh, yeah? You think any of the local girls will be there swimming around? Maybe doing a little topless diving?"

"Who knows? Who cares? I just wanna get in the water and wash off all the Baghdad."

"I hear you," the clerk said. "By the way, my name's War-nicke." He reached his right hand around the bulk of his body and the sergeant shook it.

"Hanson."

"Nice to meet you, asshole."

"Same here, motherfucker."

Sitting beside them, Abe Shrinkle couldn't help but think he was now straddling their worlds. Once an armore officer, he figured he'd soon be a Fobbit, the crème-center pussies his men constantly despised. Either that or he'd be dead within the month, courtesy of a reluctant but obedient firing squad.

The C-130 shuddered and started to descend. The soldiers at the front of the cargo bay were crushed by the weight of the others smart enough to pick seats near the back of the plane. The plane rolled left, rolled right, then they heard the scrape-scream of wheels grazing the runway. With little ceremony, the plane jolted to a stop, the rear door dropped, and they were on their feet, pushing toward the exit, anxious to start their four days (three beers per) without delay.

Abe spilled out of the plane and stood blinking in the tanning-bed sunshine, which already seemed more comfort-able than what he'd been suffering up in Iraq (though if he had checked a thermometer at that very minute, he would have been surprised to find Qatar was ten degrees hotter than Baghdad). He looked around and thought he'd been dropped in someone's joke of a suburban America mallscape. Outside the plane, the land was a flat monochrome of beige sand, beige sky, beige ve-hicles, beige buildings. He was at once disoriented and soothed by the seamless, flat color of Qatar.

Abe and the others were herded into a loose formation by permanent-party soldiers who spent their entire deployment in Qatar, the lucky bastards. They crowded onto a bus, belly-dancing music blaring distorted from tiny speakers, and were whisked along a highway. They rode for an hour, passing first through the outskirts, and then the inskirts, of Doha, whose streets were filled with men and women in white robes that flapped like flags as they walked. Outside the bus windows, the country flickered like a movie that was going too fast: mile after mile of half-finished buildings and dusty BMWs and sputtering bongo trucks carrying workers to downtown construction sites where it seemed like every other building was new and thrusting from the ground, cinder block by cinder block, and the sky was filled with the arms of cranes moving back and forth, carrying buckets and winches to the coveralled workers on the scaffolding fifteen stories up in the air. Also flashing past the bus were shops with signs in both English and Arabic: "Hyper Super Market," "Al Jazeera Electronicals," "Your Best Good Buy," and a billboard for a veterinary clinic which, along with a dog and cat, had the silhouette of a camel.

The bus made a sudden swing onto a barren highway, which it followed for three miles before making a left through a pair of tall gates, then snaking painfully through a serpentine maze of side-scraping concrete security barriers until they pulled up in front of a two-story vanilla-white building with a flapping banner that waved like a hand and read "Welcome to Qatar!"

They off-loaded—a couple of the jokers in the group making cattle sounds—then were ushered into a series of rooms where their bags were checked by customs agents looking for contraband (porn, ammo, dildos, 9mm pistols, blades over six inches in length, souvenir teeth from those they'd killed). They sat through a briefing about do's and don'ts around the base and out in Doha, they were told about the various MWR excursions (shopping trips, cruises, a tour of the local zoo, and—*yes!*— scuba diving), they were handed linen, assigned rooms in a building the size of an airplane hangar, then turned loose for the next four days, with the admonition that if they didn't report back to the recall formation ("Tuesday, oh-five-thirty sharp, full battle rattle"), they faced punishment under Article 87 of the Uniform Code of Military Justice.

A stack of sheets and a pillow cradled in his arms, Abe briefly toyed with the idea of going AWOL. He forgot the exact contents of Article 87, but surely it couldn't be worse than Certain Death. Then someone bumped into him, whooping like a siren and running full-bore in the direction of the base's swimming pool. It was the freckle-face clerk and he had lust blazing in his eyes. "Last one in the pool is a lazy, limp-dick son of a bitch!" he screamed.

And just like that, Captain Abe Shrinkle was jostled back into his role as a commanding officer. "Hey, there, soldier, watch your language!"

The Fobbit slowed and looked over his shoulder with a scowl, which melted into an O-mouthed expression of surprise when he saw the rank on Abe's collar. Soon, they would all be clad in the anonymity of civilian clothes but for now Abe played his role for all it was worth. It might be his swan song as a commander. "And stop running! You're supposed to be resting and relaxing down here."

"Ye-yes, sir. Sorry, sir."

"Okay, that's better." Abe allowed a grin to break his "commander's face" and said, "Carry on, soldier."

"Yes, sir." The clerk snapped off an embarrassed salute, then turned and started speed-walking toward the pool.

Abe was still smiling as he fluffed the sheets across his bed and changed into the one set of civvies he'd been smart enough to pack in his duffel bag. He might be stripped of his command when he returned to Triumph but he wasn't there yet, was he? He damn sure intended to make the most of his remaining four days as an officer and a gentleman.

Abe Shrinkle sat in the Qatar base's Top-Off Club, nursing the second beer of his three-per. He'd ordered a ribeye and was going at it with knife and fork and all the concentrated ambition of an Olympic athlete when another soldier entered and sat down on the stool next to him. He whistled for the bartender, ordered a beer, and, when it came, tossed his head back. It went down like water.

"Easy there," Abe said. "Pace yourself, buddy."

The other soldier cocked his lean, black face at Abe. "This *is* my pace, man. Friend of mine said to slam 'em back, fast as you can. Said the buzz'll last longer that way." He whistled and twirled his finger for another beer.

The Top-Off Club neighbored the swimming pool and so it smelled of chlorine. Done up in 1970's tiki refugee decor, with a bar that curved like a half-smile, it was also pathetic and scummy in the corners. The waitresses brought food to the soldiers from the Chili's next door and by the time the plates were put on the bar, they were already cooling. Nothing about this place bespoke "fun, Fun, FUN!" as promised by the article in the *Lucky Times*—a puff piece if Abe ever saw one. No doubt the CG pressed his thumb on some junior officer's soft skull and that officer then stabbed his sharp-nailed index finger into some NCO's chest and that NCO then pounded his jelly fist on the desk of some low-level private who then went to his computer and wrote about how the division's rest-and-relaxation program was fun-tastic—the next best thing to going home.

Abe forked another piece of steak into his mouth. It was starting to taste like liver. He hated liver. He washed it down with the last of his second beer then he, too, twirled his finger for another.

The other soldier pointed at Abe's plate. "How's the steak? Good?"

"All I can say is, there's a definite shortage of dogs here in Qatar."

"Shit, man. I was gonna order me one of those. Guess I'll stick to nachos."

"Probably safer."

"Ain't dat right. You permanent party here?"

"No, R&R. I'm from FOB Triumph. Baghdad. You?"

"Mosul. What's it like down there in Bag City?"

"A car bomb every day. Sometimes three on religious holidays. It never ends." The vision of a man clinging to the undercarriage of a truck, screaming as his skin barbecued in great black chunks, came roaring uninvited into Abe's head. He tried slamming back his last beer but it leaked into his sinus cavity and he sputtered.

"Yeah, we get vee-bids every now and then," the other soldier was saying. "Not as bad now as it used to be. Mostly we get mortared. And snipers on the roofs taking potshots at us whenever we go out."

"Whole different world down here in Qatar," Abe said, stifling his coughing fit.

"Ain't dat right." The other soldier nodded. "Man, when we came in on the bus, the guards at the gate wasn't wearing no body armor or nothing. Not even carrying a rifle, just a 9mm. These people down here don't know how good they got it."

"True," Abe said.

The other guy ordered, then slammed, his third beer. "I was gonna spend my R&R up at Mosul in my room just chillin' but then a buddy of mine says, 'Man, you gotta get you down to Qatar—you wouldn't believe the women down there.'" He cocked an eyebrow. "Well I been here for a day now and I don't know what he's talking about. The dude-to-chick ratio sucks!"

They laughed and Abe sawed off some more of his meat.

The other soldier swayed a little closer and murmured, "Now, over there in the black top, she kinda cute." He nodded toward one of the Top-Off Club waitresses, a Filipino like the rest of the staff. She leaned on the end of the bar and stared vacantly out at the room watching the other GIs clustered at their tables.

Abe gave a noncommittal "Hmm," then tried to chew another piece of steak. Now it was like jawing liver-flavored bubble gum.

"Watch this," the other guy said to Abe. He whistled and called out, "Hey, Mama-san! Over here!"

The waitress peeled her eyes away from the other tables, then slowly made her way over to them.

"Can I get me some nachos, sweet thang?"

"Yeah, yeah," the waitress said in a voice that drooped on either end. "Anything else, mister?"

"Oh, I dunno. Lemme think." He cocked his head and pretended to study the tattered palm-frond ceiling. "Maybe later, out back, huh?" He winked and lifted one corner of his mouth.

"I get nachos first, then we see." She moved away with that slow seen-it-all, heard-it-all slouch.

"Not as cute close-up, though. All those acne pits." The other soldier shook his head ruefully. "She'll do in a pinch, I guess."

Abe had been in Qatar just two days but he already had guys like this figured out. They came down here, all juiced-and-creamy at the thought of finally getting to see girls in civilian clothes—halter tops, tight T-shirts, bikinis at the pool. They had dreamed about a parade of Breasts on Display. But then they're pissed off to find pasty-faced girls, chunky around the waist and making little effort to hide the volcanic pimples on their foreheads.

Abe was thankful he hadn't set the bar of his expectations too high. If he didn't hope, he wouldn't be disappointed.

He left the Top-Off Club, his liver-flavored steak half-finished. The other soldier was still vainly snapping his fingers at the bored waitress, who didn't even bother to lift her elbows from the bar when she said, "Yeah, yeah, yeah. I be there okay soon."

In the eye-searing heat outside, Abe fluffed his Hawaiian shirt, then headed for the pool—just to torture himself with the lousy chick-to-dude ratio.

It was late afternoon and the thermometers showed no signs of releasing their grip on 104 degrees. He strolled toward the oasis of water.

There were only half a dozen people lounging around the pool. Four dudes, two chicks.

Abe picked out a lounge chair next to one of the men, who was reading a book, the glare bouncing from the pages onto his face. Even at this hour, there was no shade on the concrete apron surrounding the pool. The lounge chair was hot as a skillet. Abe had started to settle himself onto the plastic webbing but with a "Yee-owch!" he leapt to his feet.

"Careful there," the other soldier said from behind his book.

Abe batted at his thighs as if to put out flames.

"Most everyone else here spreads a towel on the seat first," the other guy said.

Abe grimaced. "I was just getting to that," he said as he unfolded his towel over the lounge chair. He settled himself back down gingerly, careful to avoid the metal arms of the chair, which looked anxious to brand his elbows. "Hot day today."

The soldier put down his book. "Is that a joke?"

Abe pointed at the book. "No, but *that* is."

"What's wrong with *Catch-22*?" Abe's pool companion said. "It's a classic."

"Yeah, classic antiwar rhetoric." Abe had never read the novel but he remembered how, during office hours, one of his West Point professors had gone on a vein-throbbing rant against "that ass-clown Yossarian," who spent the entire book trying to weasel his way out of his patriotic duty. On the basis of that alone, Cadet Shrinkle vowed he would never touch *Catch-22*.

"Why in the world," he asked the other soldier, "would you want to read *that* book at a time like *this*?"

The soldier grinned. "I can't think of a better time to read it, can you? It's helped me get my perspective skewed in the right direction. Sort of like an owner's manual for this war."

Abe would have continued to argue against the book he'd never read, but—he had to remind himself—he was down here for rest and *relaxation*. He was damned if he'd spend his last hours as a company commander all knotted with patriotic fury. So he swallowed his bile and asked, "All that aside, how do you like Qatar so far?"

The soldier shrugged. "So far, it's not much different than life on Triumph. I just get more time to read and less time to deal with dickhead officers."

Abe cringed but continued to smile. "I'm from FOB Triumph, too—Second Armor. What about you?"

"I'm in division public affairs."

"Oh, so you're one of those Fob—" Abe caught himself "—uh, people who work at the palace."

"You can go ahead and say it: yes, I'm a Fobbit."

"You act like it's a bad thing."

"To most people it is. But not to me."

"Oh, why's that?"

The soldier leveled a flat gaze at Abe. "I'm still here, aren't I? Lot of door kickers can't say the same."

"I guess. If you're playing the odds."

"But this is all one big crapshoot, right?"

"And so far you're winning?"

"So far."

Abe reached out a hand to the sunbathing soldier. "I'm Abe Shrinkle, by the way."

At the name, the other man visibly flinched, and hesitated to take the outstretched hand. When he did, Abe could feel the moist slick of fresh sweat. "Chance Gooding Jr."

"Wow," Abe said, "that sounds like something out of Dickens."

"Trust me, sir, I get that—or something like it—all the time."

Sir? How did this other guy know he was an officer? Did he really wear it on his sleeve even when he wasn't wearing a uniform?

There came a shout and both Shrinkle and Gooding looked over at the pool. Two other men were in the water, vigorously swimming laps past the two girls who were now bobbing in the shallow end. From beneath their crawl-stroke arms, the men barked at each other in voices husky from bomb smoke: "I got you, motherfucker!" "Like hell you do, dick breath!" They churned the water in one final burst to the finish line, both of them touching the side of the pool to end the race in a tie. They glared at each other, first one, then the other, spitting with a *pwut!* to one side and waiting for a concession of defeat to come from the other swimmer. Without a word, one of the men climbed from the pool with a great wet outsuck like a breeching whale, then, still dripping, dropped to the ground and started knocking out push-ups, pumping up and down just long enough for the two girls to notice the hard ropes of his muscles. Then he bounded to his feet and swaggered over to his lounge chair for a bottle of ice water, which he chugged without taking a breath. The other male spit water between his teeth, growl-muttered, "Asshole," then stroked back and forth from one end of the pool to the other.

Abe stood and stripped off his T-shirt. "Well, Chance Gooding Jr., now that there's a little less testosterone polluting the water, I think I'll go for a dip."

Gooding nodded. "Have at it, sir," he said, then went back to his novel. The little red man on the cover of the book danced across a sea of blue as Gooding hid his face behind *Catch-22*.

Abe hoped he would never become so callous, so unpatri-otic, so . . . so *Fobbity*. No matter what happened, he reminded himself, he was still an officer and a gentleman. They couldn't take that away from him, could they?

He eased into the water. It was just this side of lukewarm but to his throbbing skin it felt like crystal-blue water pouring from a glacier.

The lap swimmer took one look at Abe, decided he was done with the pool (besides, his skin was starting to get as wrinkled as a nut sack), and hoisted himself from the water. He, too, dropped to the deck and piston-pumped a set of push-ups —going his buddy ten more just to prove he could—the eagle tattoo between his shoulder blades taking flight as he did so.

The girls bobbed and whispered in the shallows, pointedly not looking at the muscle-bound show-offs.

On the far side of the pool, Chance Gooding Jr. looked like he was deeply engrossed in his book but his eyes peeped over the top of the pages as he watched the disgraced company commander float in the water.

Abe dog-paddled to the deep end, then stopped there, treading water as he listened to the music from the CD the MWR staff had been piping across the pool through speakers concealed behind tiki statues. Abe recognized the CD, *Boston's Greatest Hits*. "More Than a Feeling" started pouring out of the tiki men's mouths. Abe bobbed up and down in Qatar, the pool water lapping at his skin, and tried to put everything in perspective. Despite the war to the north, this felt good.

Closing his eyes, he was in another place, another time. The music rippling over the pool time-traveled him. As he floated, the water turned warm as blood, hot as memory.

1987. Mid-May. A Friday night. The ballroom of the Ramada Inn in Colorado Springs.

At that precise moment, Abe was in love with Cathy Kessel but he was consigned to a date with her best friend, Mona (whose last name has been lost over time). Cathy had a face like a hatchet blade, dark circles under piercing blue eyes. Her brown hair was curled and teased and feathered into a Farrah 'do (changes in hair fashion for Coloradans were at least a decade behind the rest of the country). Cathy hung with a tough crowd but Abe sensed a tenderness at her core, which gave him hope she'd at least notice him, a ghostly nobody in the halls of their high school.

Summoning every shred of courage, he'd asked her to the Spring Jamboree dance in a stuttering phone call so horrific it was blotted from his memory within a month's time.

Unfortunately, by the time he'd screwed his determination to the sticking point, he was too late. She'd already been asked by another eighth grader—Scott DiSoto (who, it turned out, would steal two other girls from Abe later in high school).

But Cathy's girlfriend Mona was available. Would Abe like to go with her?

Sure, he said, supposing he should be happy with leftovers.

Mona was tall and blonde and her hair was cut short, flaring at the ends like a little skirt around her neck. She'd pasted on too much mascara the night of their date and her breath smelled funny—harsh and decadent. She stood tall and stiff beside Abe at the dance and kept looking around the room like he wasn't there. She was probably feeling like she got leftovers, too.

"You want some punch?" she asked after five songs had gone by with the two of them standing there, pinned against the wall.

"Sure," he said, then watched her walk away to the refreshment table. All these years later, he still remembered the dress

she was wearing—it was made of thin cotton and was tied in a
neat little bow at the back of her neck, just under the skirt of
her blonde hair. The dress was backless and, yes, it filled him
with a hot pulse to know she wasn't wearing a bra and, oh, how
that tempting little bow at her neck called to his fingers, begging
to be untied. He closed his eyes and leaned against the wall of
the Ramada Inn ballroom for support.

"Here's your punch." Mona was back in front of him, holding out a glass of syrupy red liquid.

"Thanks." Abe swallowed and suppressed a gag.

"I heard some kids were going to spike it with Everclear.
I don't think they did."

"Chickens," Abe said.

"Pussies," Mona said.

Abe didn't know what to say to that. They both looked out
at the crowded, wriggling dance floor. He could see Cathy with
Scott DiSoto across the room. Cathy was all fluid arms and
elbows and hips; Scott was doing a sweaty finger-point dance
move (which, until this moment, Abe thought he himself had
patented). The air of the ballroom was humid with teenage
perfume and the sad smear of thick makeup. Abe didn't know
what to do with his hands. The drink felt slippery between his
fingers.

"You want to dance?" he blurted.

Mona gave him a sideways glance from between her slits
of mascara. "Ummm . . ." She looked out on the dance floor.
Cathy and Scott came closer, moving to the outer edge of the
dance floor. Cathy's hips swirled like a cobra coming out of a
basket; Scott seemed intent on pointing at a spot on the carpet
while at his neck a gold chain lifted and fell, lifted and fell. They

circled and boogied ever closer. Cathy winked at Mona, who then turned to Abe and said, "Ummm, how about we dance later? Okay?"

"Sure," he said. "Okay." He pretended not to see the wink.

Cathy and Scott moved toward the side door of the ballroom, which led out to the forest at the base of the mountain where the Ramada Inn had been built.

"I'm gonna go out and smoke," Mona said. "You wanna come?"

As those words washed over his face, Abe knew what that wickedness on her breath had been. It had been mystery and desire and danger—most of all danger. Play-it-safe alarms went off in his head. Bad, adult-level things would happen in the forest. His parents would never approve. He told himself he'd better stay in the ballroom with the non-Everclear punch.

"No, that's all right. I'll just wait here for you."

Mona laughed. At the time, Abe thought it was a harmless laugh; two hours later, he realized it was a cruel, harsh, mocking laugh of dismissal. Mona never returned to the ballroom. She slipped out the door after her friends and together they went into the darkening woods to smoke their cigarettes and mock authority and, most of all, to mock Abe, still standing there at the edge of the humid dance floor, holding up the wall and wondering what Scott DiSoto had that he didn't—though he knew all the while it was Scott's willingness to not play it safe, to plunge into danger and sin.

The fast song ended and another record dropped onto the turntable. "More Than a Feeling" filled the air of the ballroom. Abe closed his eyes and let Boston carry him away from the dance floor on this, the most miserable night of his teenage life so far.

How was he to know, eighteen years later, that that precise moment would be cupped in his mind as a golden memory? How was he to know he'd be drifting in a pool in a hot land three hundred miles south of a combat zone, listening to that same song and regretting all the chances that had slipped away from him?

17

GOODING

When Staff Sergeant Gooding returned from Qatar, his tan was the envy of all the cubicle rats whose skin was the color of paper. With his beige glow, Gooding strolled into the palace, feeling radiant and refreshed (the *real* R&R, he thought). He felt like an actor in a toothpaste commercial who shows up with new breath and all his female coworkers swoon when he passes them in the hall.

The palace was filled with an odd buzz when Chance came on shift his first day back—and it wasn't just because he was bright with Persian Gulf sunshine. It turned out that most of the staff was distracted by a preseason NFL game.

By the time he walked through the marbled hallways and entered the work area, it was the fourth quarter. As he passed the cubicles, everyone—officer and enlisted alike—was clustered around the satellite TVs or the computers with streaming live video feeds, all eyes focused on the little men in helmets bashing each other. Sitting at his desk, he could hear voices like rising sirens: "go, go, gogogoGO—aaawwww!"

Even later, during General Bright's morning brief, the officers had their chairs swiveled away from the SMOG station and turned toward the TV screen in the Information Ops section, only half-listening to the G-staff drone on with their reports: "Sir, we expect AIF activity to resume at April levels within the next twenty-four to forty-eight hours. The majority of attacks are expected to be comprised of harassing small-arms fire and IEDs. Targets are likely to be—"

There was a blast from the referee's whistle and a cry of "What the fuck was that? Did you just see what happened? What the fuck was that?" from one of the officers throwing up his hands in dismissal at the quarterback on the screen.

Even the CG seemed abnormally distracted while he sat in his third-floor office, SMOG earphones clapped to his head. Gooding figured he probably listened to the G-staff reports with one eye on his TV. At one point, he grunted his approval for G-4 to retrofit a fleet of uparmored Humvees with sheepskin seat covers because the soldiers in one unit had been complaining of hemorrhoids—and when was the last time you heard the CG give a tinker's damn for the luxuries of life when soldiers should be focusing their attention on the immediate mission at hand ("cleaning up the streets by eradicating Sunni ruffians and foreign troublemakers")? That the CG seemed to care about the inflamed rectums of infantry soldiers showed he definitely had something else on his mind at the time.

By midmorning, the football game was over and everyone had returned to their normal routine of plotting future operations and cataloging the results of current ops.

In his cubicle, Gooding sat holding his forehead in one hand. The glow of his Qatar tan was already starting to fade.

He was depressed because he'd just hung up the phone after
learning one of their moneymakers had been hit with an IED,
which had sheared off the lower half of his left leg. This meant
Staff Sergeant Gooding would have to reschedule all the media
opportunities he'd lined up for the guy, a specialist named Kyle
Pilley. The specialist's moneymaker days were over.

That was Lieutenant Colonel Harkleroad's term for them:
moneymakers. These were the soldiers caught at the crossroads
of luck and bravery, the door kickers who rose to the occasion
and did something true and honorable in the eyes of the U.S.
Army, who participated in moments of selfless action that could
then be packaged into a heart-stirring story and delivered to
the media.

Maybe it was shielding a little schoolgirl from the blast
of a suicide bomber, taking the brunt of the shrapnel, which
embeds in your flak vest but doesn't kill you, just leaving a nasty
set of green-brown bruises.

Maybe it was befriending a Local National, a down-on-
his-luck restaurant owner plagued with vandalism and robbery,
someone in whom you take a personal interest and so you bring
your squad back to the restaurant and spend your week's one
half-day off scrubbing away the graffiti. Still on your own time,
maybe you set up a guard shift at night to catch the Sunni bastards who are doing this to the poor guy, and forever earn the
Local National's gratitude, *winning his heart and mind*.

Or maybe, like Specialist Kyle Pilley, you are shot at close
range by a sniper's bullet and you bounce right back up onto your
feet and, still sucking at oxygen you just thought was lost to you
forever, you give chase to the would-be assassins, tackle them
in a back alley, zip-cuff the bastards, and bring them to justice.

If, as in Kyle Pilley's case, the entire episode is filmed by the insurgents from their hiding place in the back of a van—the resulting footage intended for a propaganda "victory music video" loaded onto the jihadists' Web site that afternoon but instead played and replayed by CNN in the ensuing days—well then that's just icing on the gravy as far as Lieutenant Colonel Harkleroad was concerned.

Kyle Pilley was one of the best moneymakers the division had seen in the past six months and Harkleroad was practically piddling his pants with glee at the thought of all the goodwill his story would buy them in the mainstream media. He was already laying plans for Pilley to be interviewed, via remote satellite, by the Big Three morning-breakfast news shows (*Good Morning America* was on board, *Today* and *CBS This Morning* were teetering on the brink of a *yes*), not to mention features in the *New York Times, Los Angeles Times,* and, if Harkleroad was really, really lucky, *Time* and/or *Newsweek.* Yes, Kyle Pilley was the best thing to happen to Lieutenant Colonel Eustace Harkleroad and the rest of the Shamrock Division since they'd entered Iraq.

First, however, Specialist Pilley needed the short course in Media Interview Tips 101, the preparatory briefing the Public Affairs Office liked to give to all soldiers, from colonel to private, before they spoke to major news outlets. A week before Gooding's Qatar vacation, Harkleroad had given him this task because, he reasoned, the specialist might be more receptive to a lecture coming from an NCO than he would from a lieutenant colonel.

"The first thing you have to remember," Gooding told the twenty-year-old infantryman after he'd brought him into his cubicle and sat him down, "is that *you* are in control of the interview, not the reporter. This is *your* story and you're going to tell it in the way that feels most comfortable to you—with a little coaching from us, of course. We're here to help you smooth it out and make it sound more dramatic for the folks back home."

Pilley, a nervous kid with hair the color of bread crusts, wiped his hands on his pants, licked his lips, and croaked, "Sure."

"Take your time and don't just blurt out the first thing that comes into your head."

"Okay." Pilley tried to loosen something in his throat with an abrupt cough.

"So . . . just a few questions to start off with." Gooding went down the list on his clipboard. "Have you ever been convicted of a misdemeanor?"

"Nope."

"Have you ever been involved in a bitter divorce or a nasty child custody dispute?"

"Nuh-uh."

"Any paternity suits pending?"

"None that I know of."

"Were you ever sent to the principal's office?"

"Once, but it was totally not my fault, what they said I did."

"Have you ever touched a member of the opposite sex in an inappropriate way so they would have cause to file charges against you?"

"Hey, what is this, anyway?" Pilley's eyes flicked around the cubicle, expecting McKnight from his squad to jump out any minute and yell, "Ha! You've been punk'd!"

Gooding waved a not-to-worry hand through the air. "Just trying to shine a light on any shadowy areas of your life. We like to get there before the media does. So, what about it—any inappropriate sexual touching?"

"No. No way."

"Okay, fine. Now, to the matter at hand. Have you ever been interviewed by a member of the mainstream media?"

"Does my high school newspaper count?"

"Not exactly."

"Then I guess the answer is *no*. Never talked to no media person before."

"Here are some of the things you need to know." Gooding handed Pilley a card, laminated to slip smoothly into and out of his wallet, with a bulleted list of do's and don'ts.

Pilley stared at the card like it had the answers to the algebra final exam. He licked his white lips and coughed multiple times.

- **Do** sit up straight in the chair
- **Do** wear glasses if you can't see without them
- **Do** use frequent but natural hand gestures
- **Do** smile (when appropriate)
- **Do** look concerned and sincere (when appropriate)
- **Do** take every opportunity to "tell the Army story"
- **Don't** speculate about things you don't know ("Stay in your lane!!")
- **Don't** tap dance around difficult questions
- **Don't** roll or shift your eyes
- **Don't** let the reporter put words in your mouth
- **Don't** conduct the interview on an empty stomach
- **Don't** consume flatulence-producing foods (beans, raw vegetables, et cetera) twelve hours prior

- **Don't** give vivid descriptions of "kills" that may be shocking to nonmilitary individuals
- **Don't** ever forget: "We are WINNING the Global War on Terrorism"

"You need to avoid acronyms and military jargon at all costs," Gooding continued when Pilley finished reading the card. "Mr. and Mrs. America will have no idea what you're talking about if they start hearing alphabet soup coming out of your mouth—even the things we in the Army take for granted, like APC, RPG, BCT, TOC. To Joe Six-Pack, it's all gibberish."

"No alphabet soup, got it," Pilley affirmed.

"Stay positive, to the degree that you can. We want you to convey the impression we're ahead of the power curve over here, that we're making progress in restoring hope to the Iraqi people, that nothing's gonna slow us down from achieving our goals—the nation's goals."

"Which nation?"

"The United States, of course. We can't speak for the Iraqis themselves. Remember that. One of the tips you'll find on that little card—one of our cardinal rules—is 'Stay in your lane.' Don't go outside the boundaries of what you know for a fact. Our rule of thumb is: if you work on it, own it, drive it, or fire it, then you can talk about it. Otherwise, don't let the reporter trap you into saying something you're gonna regret."

"Uh-huh."

"Believe me, we've had more than one soldier—officers, especially—who didn't stay in their lanes over here and we've had to clean up after them."

Pilley looked like the kind of soldier—earnest, honest, puppy doggish—who wouldn't wander out of his lane even if his life depended on it. He seemed to be hanging on Gooding's every word. *Oh, man,* Gooding thought, *Harkleroad is gonna love this guy like a son.*

"So, let's get down to it," Gooding said. "Tell me about the incident."

"This is the part where I tell my story?"

"Right. Just imagine I'm a reporter asking the questions. But remember, try not to squint under the lights. And don't look directly into the camera."

Pilley gave a dubious glance at the invisible camera over Staff Sergeant Gooding's left shoulder and nodded.

"Well, for starters, I wasn't supposed to live. That's why they were filming me. For training purposes, to show other hajjis—"

"Uh, careful," Gooding said. "We'd prefer you avoided the term *hajji.* Try *terrorist* instead."

"What about *bloodthirsty, heartless ragheads*? Couldn't I just say that?"

Pilley was starting to loosen up—that was good . . . but Gooding couldn't let him get too far ahead of himself. "For now, we need to stick with *terrorists.*"

"So, anyway," Pilley giving the noncamera another sidelong glance, "the *terrorists* were recording the whole thing for training purposes. I was supposed to die. No doubt about it. And I would have, if they'd aimed a little higher, gone for the head shot. I guess I ruined things when I got back up on my feet."

"Let's say *popped back up* or *bounced back up.* The more vivid, the better."

"Who's telling this story, anyway?" (Uh-oh, signs of strong personality emerging. Mental note: check on this guy's medical history.)

"You are, of course," Gooding said, "but we're encouraging you to use as many colorful details as possible. If you want to get a sound bite on TV, it needs to be vivid. Now, let's start at the beginning. It was a hot day—"

"Hot as hell. Am I allowed to say *hell* on TV?"

"We wouldn't encourage it. Try something like, 'It was so hot you could fry eggs on the hood of our Humvee.'"

"That doesn't sound like me."

"Then say it however you like. I'm only here to offer suggestions. In the end, the words are your own."

"Okay." Whatever had flared up in Pilley seemed to be fading. He was back to licking his white lips.

"So," Gooding continued, "it was hot as all get-out and your unit was working a security checkpoint and you were just going about your job, minding your own business, when this happened, right?"

"Yep, minding my own business. Thinking about how my mom used to cook me flapjacks every Saturday morning—"

"Let's not mention that—the fact that your mind was wandering. We want to convey the impression our soldiers over here are totally focused on the mission. Anyway, go on. Sorry to interrupt."

"So, yeah, we'd been working this checkpoint just outside the wire for most of the afternoon. Me, Corporal Allen, and Private McKnight. Our mission was to slow traffic as it approached the West Entry Control Point. We weren't stopping any of the cars, just standing out there, making sure they saw us in full battle rattle with our M4s. It was one of those random checkpoints we set up and tear down in different places around our AO—"

Gooding held up a finger. "Careful with the acronyms."

"Right, sorry. Around our area of operations."

"That's better."

"Anyway, we'd been out there for about three hours already and we were almost at the point of packing it up. Corporal Allen was just waiting for the word to come over the radio. He was sitting inside the Humvee where it was cooler—we were taking turns rotating in and out of the Humvee—and McKnight was standing on the other side across from me. All of a sudden, it's like I get punched in the chest and I'm knocked flat on my ass—on my butt, I mean. I lay there on the ground for about two seconds, trying to catch my breath, and all of a sudden I realize, Holy crap! I've been shot! I've been hit in the freaking chest! *Freaking*'s okay, right?"

"Perfectly. Not sure about *crap*, though."

"No *crap*. Ten-four. So, at that point, the only thing going through my mind was to take cover and try to locate the sniper's position. So right away I'm back up on my feet—I *bounce back up* to my feet—and I'm yelling at McKnight to take cover, take cover! He and Corporal Allen didn't even have a fu—*freaking* clue at that point. They hadn't seen me get hit, that's how fast it all happened. So we all hunker down in a protective posture and it didn't take me long to figure out the shot came from my twelve o'clock. We look across the intersection and there's a white van parked about seventy-five meters away. I'm having a hard time breathing at this point and there's a little bit of blood on my vest. McKnight points at my hand and says, *They got you, Pilley, they got you.* That's when the pain kicks in, when McKnight says something. I look down and there's half my thumb gone. From what the doctors tell me, my thumb saved my life. Never thought I'd say that, but it's true."

Pilley held up his thickly bandaged hand for the invisible camera. Gooding could smell old blood and iodine rolling in fumes off the bandage.

"My freaking thumb saved my life. Evidently, I had been raising my hand to scratch at something on my face when they fired. The bullet hit my thumb at just the right angle so it just ricocheted off my flak vest. I got bruised and lost half my thumb, but nothing else. I got a picture here, if they want to use it." He awkwardly reached with his left hand into a shirt pocket, pulled out a creased photo, and handed it to Gooding. There was Pilley, bare-chested, his sparse chest hairs swirled by his sweat, and just above his left nipple was a bruise the size and shape of a teacup. He was holding up his bandaged hand and grinning like the lucky freaking fool he was.

"We'll want to scan a copy of this photo, if that's all right."

"No problem. That's why I brought it."

"So, back to the story. According to reports I read, the terrorists were hiding in the van, which they'd lined with bed mattresses in order to muffle the sound of their sniper rifle—"

"A Dragunov," Pilley said.

"They'd drilled a hole in the side of the van just big enough for the shooter to get you in his sights."

"Right. And the other guy was filming the whole thing from the driver's seat. You can hear them on the tape praying to Allah the whole time they're lining me up in the sights. Then, when

I get hit and fall down, they're singing and high-fiving each other. But all that stops when I *bounce* back up on my feet and run around to the other side of the Humvee. Then it's almost like you can hear them say, *Uh-oh*. I don't know what the Iraqi word for *Oops* is, but I'm sure they were saying it." Pilley's grin turned into a chuckle.

"Then you start pointing at the van and they really start to panic, right?"

"Right. That's about the time they drop the camera and all you see is the roof of the van, and then the camera's rolling around on the floor as they punch the accelerator and try to get out of there. But they don't get very far because traffic is backed up at the intersection. Everyone had slowed down to watch when I got shot and then right away *popped* back up on my feet."

"And so they're stuck in traffic and your team does what?"

"Since we now have confirmed eyes on the target, we decide to pursue and engage."

"Just as you've been taught by the Army to do."

"Right. Anyway, Corporal Allen radios back to headquarters to make them aware of what's happened and all three of us pile into the Humvee and start to go after ole hajji. The *terrorists*, I mean."

"Good, good. You're catching on." Gooding could hear the *ka-ching!* of this new moneymaker.

"We go about half a block and McKnight tells us he's got a clear line of sight, so we tell him to go for it, and he tries to shoot out one of the van's tires but, instead, he hits one of the terrorists. Turns out it was the sniper himself. By that time, they've run up into the traffic jam and can't go anywhere—forward or back, since we're right on their ass—*tail,* I mean. So then, right there in the middle of the intersection, we see them pile out of the van—there's two of them—and start to run up a nearby alley. We all go after them and Corporal Allen gets one guy pretty quick—a classic linebacker tackle—but the other guy, the wounded one, is a little faster. We chase him all the way down the alley, then he ducks inside this house—I guess it was an apartment building—and runs up this long flight of stairs. We're following him pretty close and it's not too hard because he's leaving a blood trail the whole way. As he climbs, he starts to get a little slower. McKnight winged him right under the armpit and hit a pretty big vein, so he's losing a lot of blood. Me, I'm just getting faster and faster, all that adrenaline, I guess, and pretty soon I'm right up behind him and he knows it's all over because he just stops and sits down on the stairs, puts his hands on his head. But then the blood starts really pumping out of his wound and he passes out and rolls down the stairs, right at me, and I have to jump out of the way. He ends up on the landing one flight down and now the blood's coming pretty fast out of this guy. So I grab my dressing kit out of my cargo pocket, rip it open, and slap it on this guy."

"Let me get this straight," Gooding said. "You took your own bandage—the one other soldiers are supposed to use on *you* when *you* get hit—and you put it on the very guy who had tried to kill you ten minutes earlier?"

"Yeah, I guess I wasn't even thinking about any of that. I just saw a guy with a hole in his armpit and I knew I needed to help him, no matter who he was."

"Dude, this is a *great* story," Gooding said in a half-shout that carried across three cubicles. His heart was pounding hard and he could only imagine the moist state of Lieutenant Colonel Harkleroad's underwear when he heard about this moneymaker. "I can't see anything but good news coverage coming from it. It's all about *love thy enemy* and so on."

"Yeah, whatever," Pilley said. "I wasn't even thinking about any of that. I was just all reflex—*bam, bam, bam*—it all happened so fast. And then there was my thumb to think about, of course."

"Of course," Gooding agreed. "I tell you, the media is gonna eat you up with a spoon. You need to be ready for that."

"Sure," Pilley said. He, too, was now jazzed with adrenaline from the retelling. He was already starting to wonder if he would get one of those babes from CNN to do the interview and what she would think of him. Eating him up with a spoon sounded like a *good* thing. He grinned, but then caught himself and tried to look all patriotic and shit for this staff sergeant sitting across from him. "It's no problem, really. My company commander said I should go around telling the story as much as I could. If nothing else, to give hajji a kick in the nuts, right?"

Gooding looked up from his clipboard, unamused. Pilley wiped the grin off his face. "Sorry, guess you don't want to hear it."

"Hey," Gooding said, "it's not me who doesn't want to hear. Just remember about Mr. and Mrs. America—heck, your own parents—sitting in their living room watching you over their morning toast and eggs. What you say needs to reflect proudly on the Army. I don't think *nuts* is exactly what we're looking for."

"Okay, got it. No *nuts*. I'll even try to keep *balls* out of it." Specialist Pilley started gathering his things to go.

Gooding clapped Pilley on the shoulder before he left the cubicle. "Like I said, America's gonna love you."

Pilley laughed and there was a gleam in his eye that was one part eagerness to sniff a CNN babe's hair and one part bemusement at all the fuss everyone was making over him, Kyle Pilley, war hero.

When he'd gone, Gooding started typing up his notes for Lieutenant Colonel Harkleroad.

Now, two short weeks later, it had all gone bad in an instant and Gooding was feeling the roots of depression take hold.

The Delta Company commander had just called the PAO cell to let them know there was bad news concerning Specialist Pilley. While out on patrol yesterday, Pilley's Humvee had run over an IED. The force of the blast split the Humvee into two pieces. The engine block landed a hundred yards away in someone's backyard. One soldier was killed, two others injured. One of the injured was Pilley: leg blown clean off below the knee. He was on his way to a hospital in Germany and wouldn't be returning to the combat theater of operations. The whole company was devastated by the news because they all loved the guy who'd been killed, but they were especially upset about Pilley. He'd seemed—what was the word? impervious?—to whatever the enemy tried to throw at them. Bounce-Back Man, they'd called him. The captain thought PAO should know about Pilley because of all the interviews they'd been lining up for the boy.

Gooding wanted to ask why in the world the company had sent their most valuable moneymaker out on patrol before he'd even started doing his obligated rounds on the media circuit. But what was the use? Dead was dead, injured was injured. There was no bringing back Specialist Kyle Pilley.

Gooding thanked the half-sobbing captain and hung up. He was holding his head in his hands when Lieutenant Colonel Harkleroad arrived to begin the day's work. Harkleroad bounced into Gooding's cubicle on the tips of his feet and chortled, "A great day to be in the Yoo-nited States Army, eh, Staff Sergeant Gooding?"

Gooding looked up and, with a once tan but now pale face, said, "Not so great, as it turns out."

The curl went out of Harkleroad's smile. "Oh? What is it now?"

"Bad news, sir. Real bad news."

18

SHRINKLE

Towels. Now his life was nothing but towels: morning, noon, and night. No UCMJ, no court-martial, no execution by firing squad. Three weeks after that unfortunate night in Ad-hamiya, his life had been reduced to towels.

Abe Shrinkle pulled another one from the pile and, with a one-two-three rhythm, gave it an Army regulation fold, then added it to the stack on the counter. It was a genuine waste of motion and effort, this folding. When the soldiers smelling of sweat, dust, and musk came through the door of the gym, they snatched his fresh towels off the stack and wrapped them around their necks with nary a care about his precisely mea-sured, eyeball-calibrated folds.

Abe didn't let this deflate him. He was just happy to be alive. For now.

He knew what this gym duty really was: a prelude to his execution. First Qatar, now this. Lieutenant Colonel Duret had all but said the words when he stood outside Abe's trailer three weeks ago. Abe could see the final outcome swimming behind his commander's eyes. Duret didn't have to say it but Abe knew that when he returned to the States there would be a court-martial, ending with him standing in front of a firing squad, one of his (*former!*) soldiers offering him a cigarette.

A series of too many bad events had been piling up and now he'd come to the end, either of his life or of his command (or *both!*). He'd seen too many of his fellow officers administratively replaced or transferred to new assignments when their units performed poorly not to think it wouldn't happen to him. He saw it in his men's faces, heard it in his commander's voice. The trust was gone, replaced by doubt and fear he would get someone (or many someones) killed before they left Iraq. No, he thought as he folded another towel, he was done for. He was Defunct City.

Lieutenant Colonel Duret thought he'd been doing Captain Shrinkle a favor by quietly relieving him of duty and demoting him to gym manager ("lifestyle coordinator," in Army terms) instead of sending him up for trial but Duret hadn't known about the towels and the rough manner in which perspiring men immediately broke the pristine folds upon entering the gym, had he?

Abe didn't know how he'd done it, but the battalion commander had circumvented the system with all the stealth of a white snake gliding across snow. No explanation was ever given for what must have been some extraordinary under-the-table deals cut between colonels (and at what personal cost to Duret?). One day Abe was looking down the barrel of a firing-squad rifle, the next he was staring at a Quonset hut full of squeaking, clanking metal machines. If he was a man with less self-control, he would have shit his pants.

Each morning, Shrinkle unlocked the front door of the gym ("lifestyle fitness center") precisely at seven a.m. and each evening he doused the lights and relocked the door at ten p.m. or when the last patron had climbed off the stationary bike, rubbed the sweat off the back of his neck and top of his crew cut, and thrown the crumpled towel into the bin. It was an easy life, *too* easy. But it was one that Abe Shrinkle accepted with a matter-of-fact resignation, with only a trace of regret and resentment simmering below the surface.

He had no one to blame but himself. As he superfluously folded the white towels, he replayed the film in his mind on an endless loop: the coiled-spring strength of his legs moving toward the truck in Adhamiya, the determined pull of the pin, the hard pitch of the grenade, the slow bloom of flame inside the cab, the way he'd said "mission complete" to his men—*break*—the coiled-spring of his legs, the pin pull, the flames, "mission complete"—*break*—legs, pin, fire, complete—and so on, ad infinitum, until someone would come in and ask him if the treadmill had been fixed yet and he'd snap back to the job at hand: *one-two-three*, fold, stack . . . *one-two-three*, fold, stack.

The FOB Triumph Lifestyle Fitness Center sat among a cluster of hastily constructed buildings on Perimeter Road, which housed the rest of the Morale, Welfare, and Recreation facilities: the Internet café, the library, the game room with its Ping-Pong tables, and the "movie theater" with its VCR and big-screen TV. MWR had built the little complex quickly and inefficiently shortly after the United States had taken control of Baghdad in 2003 (and when President Bush's own lips were still warm with the words *mission complete*). The gym and the other MWR programs were housed in Quonset huts with plywood floors that kept them six inches off the sandy soil. The doors had springs that pulled shut with a clattering slap each time someone entered. The Quonsets reminded Shrinkle of something out of *Gomer Pyle, U.S.M.C.* and he could hardly resist drawling at least once each day as he walked to work, "Goll-ly, sarge!"

Shrinkle worked in a small, low-ceilinged room with a front desk, a small stereo system that tinnily blasted the stack of donated CDs (*Power Rock Ballads, Disco Fever Hits,* and—surely someone's idea of a joke—*The Best of Barry Manilow*), one weight bench, a pyramid of barbells, four stationary bikes, two treadmills (one broken), three jump ropes, and one Nautilus machine (circa 1995). A soldier had to have a fertile imagination and plenty of ambition in order to get a "workout" hard enough to break a sweat with this equipment. Total muscle failure was just a fantasy at this particular gym; most soldiers came to the Quonset hut to sham an hour away from their desks in the palace. Nobody was too serious about bulking up or toning physique or losing dining facility flab here at the FOB Triumph Lifestyle Fitness Center. It was all about the momentary distraction of pedaling fifteen miles per hour on a bike going nowhere while listening to Bell Biv DeVoe and, whatever they did, *not thinking* about the PowerPoint slides due to the battle captain by 1630 hours and by all means *not thinking* about the slow tick of the Deployment Clock; better to contemplate why Donna Summer's career as a disco queen ended so suddenly, or—even better—what that first bite of home-cooked lasagna would taste like six months from now, or—best of all—what it would be like to have their lips fully fastened around the dome of their wife's breast. Happy homecoming thoughts, rather than the real possibility of a mortar shell crashing through the roof of the Quonset hut.

And then the bike would beep, signaling the end of the session, and the soldier would climb off to go wait in line for the one and only treadmill in this goddamned sorry excuse for a gym.

The Quonset huts had been assembled so quickly there were still gaps where corrugated metal met plywood, gaps that allowed a healthy amount of sand and star sparkles of sunlight to stream inside. In addition to folding towels, Abe's other main duty was to keep the floor swept clean of the drifts of sand that worked their way inside. It had been nearly two years and still no one had come to fill the cracks in the Quonset huts. Abe thought about stuffing towels to block the windblown sand, but that would never do because the towel-to-sweaty-patron ratio was heavily favored on the sweaty-patron end of the scale. Abe sent complaints up through the chain, via corps headquarters, and MWR headquarters back in the States had repeatedly claimed more towels were on order and would arrive in due time, but in the three weeks Abe Shrinkle had been on the job, he'd yet to see evidence of fresh terry cloth making its way to the FOB Triumph Lifestyle Fitness Center. So, for now, each afternoon he carried a sack of soiled towels to the laundry center run by the unnaturally happy Filipino contractors who chattered like parakeets, and each morning he picked up the load of fresh washed towels on his way to unlocking the gym.

Fold. Stack. Sweep. Repeat. Fold, stack, sweep, repeat. Step-pin-flames-mission-complete.

To conserve on towels, he kept a tub of baby wipes on the counter for anyone who needed to properly cleanse the sweat from their brow after a workout on the bikes or the weight bench or the jump-rope station. Abe himself used the baby wipes to clean the equipment during lulls in the clanking-huffing-puffing activity, which always seemed to peak in the hour just after the evening brief to the commanding general.

Captain Shrinkle rarely saw any of the men from his company—his *former* company, that is. He had to keep reminding himself he no longer had a company—just a small platoon of towels that needed to constantly be filed in rank and precise order. He would never again have the honor of standing in front of four perfectly rowed blocks of men hanging on his every word. He was no longer worthy of a uniform—just a pair of khaki shorts and an MWR polo. He stood at the counter inside the slapping-clapping front door, folded his towels, monitored the stationary bikes with their twenty-minute time limits, and tried not to think of (accidentally) burning an Iraqi civilian to death with his incompetence. That's what Lieutenant Colonel Duret had called it, *incompetence*. More precisely, he'd clarified, "The last link in the chain of his overwhelming incompetence, which led to what could be an international disaster if it ever hit the press—which, lucky for you, Captain Shrinkle, it has so far avoided doing, against all prediction."

Lieutenant Colonel Duret had been right, Abe thought. Sweeping the floor of a leaky Quonset hut was *not* the worst thing that could have resulted from his (accidental) murder of a Local National. Death by firing squad was definitely worse.

But now he was dying a slow death here at the gym, withering from shame each time the door creaked open, blasting him with a brief faceful of sunlight. Though he knew only a few of the men who came in for their daily dose of sweat and Donna Summer, he was sure they all knew *him*. He was the impetuous captain who'd done the unthinkable: destroying government property, with the unforeseen bonus of killing an innocent

Local National. He was the poster child for the National Klutz Foundation and they all knew it, those men who snuck glances at him while sitting on the weight bench doing barbell curls.

Furthermore, now that he was stuck on FOB Triumph all day long, Abe Shrinkle had become the very thing his men despised: a Fobbit. If his soldiers ever came into the gym, he would have a hard time looking them in the eye. But, except for one time when Suarez and Zeildorf came in to run the treadmill and then left after only fifteen minutes, none of his company—his *former* company—had stopped by the Quonset hut. Shrinkle didn't blame them for wanting to cut their ties. He himself didn't even want to be associated with the killer klutz called Shrinkle.

One day in the dining facility he'd seen Sergeant Lumley but had looked away before their eyes met. Lumley had just come in from patrol and his uniform hung on his body like a dirty potato sack. There was a dark smear—dirt? grease? blood?—on one cheek. Captain Shrinkle could practically smell Lumley from where he sat on the opposite side of the room. Shrinkle's own uniform (khaki and polo) was freshly laundered and he now carried the unblemished glow of someone who led a coddled life inside the wire. He finished his lobster au gratin and left the DFAC before Lumley saw him and was forced to make the moral decision about whether or not to sit down with his—*former*—company commander.

Save for the times he was working at the fitness center— fold, sweep, wipe, stack—Abe avoided other soldiers as much as possible. He spent the days hiding in his hooch, rereading care package letters from good, decent Americans who had no idea of his current status or that he was the perpetrator of

Crimes of Atrocity, and who still kept sending him gum and jerky and lavender-scented stationery. Eventually, however, he got a little stir crazy in his hooch and set out to walk the roads that angled around Z Lake, fully unprotected in his civilian attire.

That's how he discovered the pool in the Australian sector of FOB Triumph. Now at night, and on every second Wednesday (his one day off), he walked to the other side of Z Lake to swim laps.

The pool offered the only relief from the temperatures that climbed to the triple digits by noon and stayed there until evening chow. The heat was a Thing to be endured while walking between oases of air-conditioning. It pressed on his skin, scorched the lining of his nose, and withered his lungs. It was a mile between his hooch and the swimming pool. Around about the half-mile mark, his tongue would swell and he'd think of those words Jesus croaked on the cross: "Father, I am thirsty!" In his heat delirium, he started chanting a mantra: "Cold water, air-conditioning, cold water, air-conditioning, cold water, air-conditioning." Once he passed a group of female soldiers and heard one say to the others, "It's so hot even my sunburn is getting sunburned!" He started thinking about when he'd been stationed in Alaska and the times he'd take out the trash wearing nothing but flannel pajama bottoms, a pair of slippers, and a T-shirt when it was twenty below zero. He thought of bitter Decembers in Fairbanks, when he would drive out near Ester, along a desolate side road, into a deserted forest in search of that year's Christmas tree. When he stepped out of his truck and into the subzero icebox, the air was so still, so frozen he could hear pine needles tinkling to the ground two miles away. A raven crying overhead was like a sonic boom. Walking across Triumph,

Abe started thinking of how his hands, even inside the cocoon of gloves, started freezing after five minutes of hacking away at the trunk of a tree frozen hard as concrete. He thought of how, when your hands are truly cold, the skin of your fingers starts pulling away from the fingernails and you think you're being tortured by Viet Cong soldiers. He thought of how miniature icicles used to form on the tips of his nose hairs, and then—at last, at last—there he was, he'd arrived at the pool. He could hear the cheers and minty splash of water inside the security fence and he nearly wept with joy.

Though patronizing the pool was a violation of General Order Number Five, Abe felt he had nothing to lose at this point (he had already faced the execution squad in his mind) and, besides, he liked the companionship of the soldiers from Down Under. So, Wednesdays and evenings found Abe floating in the Aussie pool, draped on an inflated inner tube, sipping a Foster's through a straw (in violation of General Order Number Two) while holding court with the tanned, muscled sergeants from Sydney and Adelaide. None of them knew Abe was an American because he spoke with a British accent (a slippery British accent but he hoped the Aussies would be drunk enough not to notice or care).

As he had walked to the pool for the first time a week ago, he'd decided to adopt a new identity—start over with a clean slate, as it were. Walking the dusty road with his swim suit rolled up on one hand, he practiced with a few phrases like "blimey!" and "pip-pip cheerio!"

He told them his name was Richard Belmouth and that he was a London contractor who was there to advise the United States on historical preservation. Oh, how he could drone for hours on end about the horrors the Iraqi museums and libraries had suffered during the 2003 invasion at the hands of those barbarous Yanks.

"Save any statues today, mate?" they would ask, rubbing oil on their torsos and pulling the sunglasses off their heads and over their eyes. They were cheeky and seemed to be of the opinion that the war was one big winky joke, and soon enough the Americans would realize they had become the actor who flubbed his lines on the world's stage. They were just waiting for the day when GWB ("Great White Bwana," they called him) admitted defeat, packed up his billion-dollar toys and went home. Then they could all call it quits and let the hajjis resume their centuries-old holy war. In the meantime, it was all a big nudge in the ribs, eh, mate?

"That bloody Great White Bwana has no regard for the treasures of civilization," Abe would yell across the pool, work-ing his face to a beet-red fluster—to the great amusement of his new mates. "Why, just look at how he allowed the Iraqis to mindlessly loot the National Museum back in 2003. Bush's jackanapes just stood back and did nothing, saying they didn't want to get involved. Well, it was a bloody rape, is what it was. A rape of history!"

"Calm down there, Dickie old man. You're likely to burst a blood vessel, you are." They'd toss him another beer and he'd catch it effortlessly, floating there in his rubber ring in the middle of the pool. The can was frosty in his hand and it felt so good to snatch it out of the air. When he opened it, the hissing *snick* was like a miniature blast of arctic air.

Abe was not himself at the Aussie pool. It wasn't just a matter of the British accent and the anti-American bluster;

Abe Shrinkle had never been a man given to drink or deca-
dence. When, during Friday afternoon safety briefings back at
Fort Stewart, he'd preached to his company about the punitive
consequences of DUIs, he'd sounded like a man in the pulpit.
His soldiers had known him as someone who held himself far
above the grime of liquor, sexual deviancy, and profanity. Apart
from hoarding a few care packages, Abe Shrinkle had never
thought of himself as a man of habitual sin.

Now look at him, floating lobster-red in the pool and wax-
ing sarcastic about the U.S. administration with a Liverpool
tongue.

The Australians called their Friday afternoon happy hour
"prayers." In fact, this is what had brought Captain Shrinkle to
the pool in the first place. He'd overheard two Seventh Cav staff
officers talking about the Australians while they lifted weights
at the fitness center two weeks ago.

"You know, the Aussies have got it made, man."

"How so?"

"They're so loose over there on the other side of Z Lake
even their bootlaces are untied."

"Oh, yeah?"

"You ever hear of the Friday prayer meetings?"

"Can't say that I have."

The first staff officer laughed, looked around, then leaned
in close to the other weight lifter, whispering in his sweat-
crusted ear. Then they both laughed.

"Man, I gotta get me some of that," said the second officer.
"'Prayers,' you called it?"

"Prayers," confirmed the first officer.

"Good cover."

"Yeah, that's what I thought."

"Every Friday at the pool, you say?"

"Every Friday starting at nineteen-hundred hours on the dot. Don't be late or they won't have any Bloody Hail Marys left when you get there."

Then they both laughed so hard they couldn't lift the weights anymore.

Standing at the counter, folding towels, Abe Shrinkle also thought the prayer meetings sounded like a good idea. He'd always been a good churchgoing boy, partly to reassure his grandmother, but partly because organized religion had pulled Abe to its sweet bosom and made him feel like he was part of something bigger and greater than them all—a club of huggers and forgivers. And Lord knows, he could use the bosomy comfort of a prayer service now that he was the worst of sinners: a murderer and waster of government property.

When he reached the Australians' pool that Friday at nineteen-hundred-on-the-dot, however, Abe realized he'd walked into an orgy of drinking, cursing, and unnaturally good spirits for people who were in the bull's-eye of a war zone. Abe gripped his towel in his left hand and realized the pocket-sized New Testament he'd rolled inside his extra pair of underwear would be superfluous here. He was about to turn and leave when a bikini-clad girl walked up to him and asked, "What's your pleasure, mate?" She held out a Foster's in one hand and a Budweiser in the other.

Abe's tongue was momentarily strangled in his mouth. Not only could he not choose between two beers (or, better yet, no beers at all), but he couldn't stop staring at the two breasts slung so tightly in the beige bikini.

"Oy, mate! Up here," the girl said, giving the beers a slight shake. "You joining our prayer service or are you giving us the nudge-off?"

Abe brought his eyes up to the girl's face and gave her a wan smile. He still couldn't untangle his tongue so he pointed meekly at the Foster's and nodded like a mute idiot when she slapped the cold can in his hand. "That's the spirit, mate. Welcome to Prayers."

Then she spun around and bounced away, her breasts moving in a synchronized dance. A whoop from the pool caught his attention and he looked over in time to see a red, beefy man take a leap off the diving board and cannonball into the water. He drenched the girl and three others lounging poolside, including another girl who had her top pulled down and was tanning her smallish breasts. The cannonballer received a smattering of applause as he climbed dripping out of the pool and several beers were raised in his honor. He took a bow and, catching sight of Abe standing there with his unopened Foster's in one hand and his towel (with concealed Bible) in the other, walked over to the pale, agape American officer.

"Greetings, mate."

Abe nodded and grinned.

"Why the hesitation? Grab yourself a spot of concrete and join in the fun, eh?"

Others were looking at him now. The topless girl raised herself on one elbow and shielded her eyes with one hand. For a moment, it seemed to Abe she was giving him a salute. That's when he firmly decided that yes, indeed, he *would* change his identity and leave the old Abe Shrinkle behind.

It was as simple as entering an elevator and watching the doors close in front of him. At once, he was lifted up and away and, with the giddiness of a cold beer, bare breasts (the two eyes of nipples staring at him), and all these new eager friends, he felt that for at least the duration of a false prayer service, he could leave behind the death, stink, and shame of his failure at war.

That's when his tongue untied and allowed these words to run its length: "Jolly good show you've got 'ere, guv'nor." He raised his beer in a salute to the rest of the swimmers. "I'm Richard Belmouth, by the by. Assistant curator of Babylonian antiquities at the British Museum. I've been sent here to unfuck all the damage the Yanks have done to the treasures of history."

The red-faced Australian leaned in close and let loose a blast of beer breath. "No formal introductions necessary here, Dick."

"Right-o." Baffled, Abe wasn't quite sure how far he should extend his lie, at least at this first encounter with the Australians. "I just—I just wanted to let you blokes know where I stood so there'd be no, uh, misunderstandings."

"Well, whatever your cause, I'm sure it's a good one. Now, come along and meet me mates."

And so the newborn Richard Belmouth walked to the edge of the blue water winking in the sunlight and joined the laughter already in progress.

19

HARKLEROAD

From: eustace.harkleroad@us.army.mil
To: eulalie1935@gmail.com
Subject: Dispatch from a War Zone, Day 223

Mother,

I write to you at the end of another long and difficult day, sitting on my cot in near total exhaustion. I still have the stench of blood in my nostrils, and my mood has been elevated only temporarily by tonight's meal at the Dining Facility (it's Thursday, so that means it's Mexican Fiesta Night; the cheese enchiladas were almost as good as yours—but only "almost").

Our day here at FOB Triumph began with the news of a planned attack on the northwest perimeter of the FOB. I need not remind you that everything I tell you is of a CLASSIFIED nature and is completely and utterly HUSH-HUSH until I give further notice. Only when I get home in December will I be able to give you a full declassified briefing; only then will you be able to hear the full tale of Stacie Harkleroad's exploits over here in Saddam's Sandbox. I know you likely have already contacted Jim Powers down at the *Murfreesboro Free Press,* and I suppose there is no talking you out of arranging for me to give an interview to Jim and his paper. While it's not something I'm chomping at the bit to do, if I must be in the local spotlight, then I'll go along with whatever you've arranged. I've learned long ago there's no arguing with Mrs. Eulalie Harkleroad when she gets her mind set on a thing.

—but back to the supposed attack today on one of our entry checkpoints. We first learned something like this might be brewing in the terrorist network around Baghdad last night during our daily Intel briefing. General Bright was in fine fettle. It must have been something he ate at the DFAC (it was Wednesday—Polynesian Night—and perhaps the pit-roasted pig with mango-pineapple sauce did a number on him). All I know is, you did NOT want to be in his path last night—his WARpath. If you were, heaven help you! Heaven help that poor Intel officer, in particular. From where I sat at the back of the room, I could hear his knees knocking together as he gave his daily report, which, as I have mentioned before, is mainly conjecture and rumor and hearsay picked up on the street and off Al-Jazeera, all of it cobbled together with safety pins, bubble gum, and string. Believe me, I have nothing against my brethren in G-2, but sometimes they do make life harder for the rest of us. Many is the day when they've briefed the Old Man (General Bright) on Red Level Forecasts in the morning and he, General Bright, has made us scramble to pull miracles out of our ass (sorry, Mother, that's just the way the rest of them talk over here and I can't help slipping into it sometimes), only to stand there at the evening briefings and say, "Whoops! Our bad. Sorry about that, guys." By that time, General Bright is too tired to lift an objection—or else maybe he's just distracted because Polynesian Night is banging a gong in his bowels. But it's maddening to think about all that work we scrambled to get done during the day, based on their Red Level Forecast—all the contingency planning, the dispensing of extra ammunition at the checkpoints, the drafts of press releases Staff Sergeant Gooding and I prepare for the Old Man's approval, all the ad hoc meetings to discuss the whyfores and wherehows—all for naught. All for "Whoops!"

Sorry, Mother, I know I'm getting a little tight under the collar, but I've been chafed one time too many by Intel and, I'm sure you can understand, it's enough to wear a man down after a while.

So . . . back to last night . . . Intel tells the Old Man they've heard rumors and rumblings about Sunni reprisals against the United States. (Remember, Sunnis are the bad guys, Shi'ites are the good guys—I know, it's hard for me to remember, too, because the bad guys sound "Sunny" and the good guys sound "Shitty"—oops, language again). Intel tells us the Sunny Sunnis will be trying to infiltrate our FOB sometime in the next twenty-four to forty-eight hours and, allegedly, they've gotten their hands on a stockpile of U.S. uniforms. This will make it even harder for our guards to recognize them— assuming they shave their beards and ditch the AK-47s in favor of M4s, of course. General Bright asks if the source is credible, to which Intel says something along the lines of "credible as the guys who told us about the WMDs," which immediately throws the whole meeting into an uproar. The Intel officer tries to backpedal, saying he meant that in a *good* way, but it's no use at that point, General Bright has already moved on to the next briefer, has given him the old hand-flick of dismissal, and Intel can do nothing at that point but clamp his lips and sit the heck down.

It all came back to bite us this morning, right around dawn, when the SMOG system started sputtering with radio reports from Gate Two. The guards there were tak- ing fire from a band of terrorists they'd let slip through the checkpoint . . . they thought it was a truck full of U.S. soldiers . . . didn't even see the ones who forgot to shave their beards . . . a U.S. soldier shot in the leg . . . a grenade thrown . . . a Quick Reaction Force on its way . . . and so forth. All of us were crowding around the SMOG station, holding our breath. Well, everyone else was holding their breath. Me? I was already suiting up with my flak vest and Kevlar, telling the rest of them I was heading out to Gate Two to assess the situation and see what I could do to help. I was raring to go, Mother, and would show those Sunnis some what-for (especially after what they did during the PX attack last month). Unfortunately, I didn't make it any farther than the palace courtyard, because there came the chief of staff, Colonel Belcher, yelling in my direction. "Harkleroad! The Old Man wants to see you, *pronto!*" I tried to pull the old deaf-in-one-ear trick and keep moving through the palace courtyard—that's how determined I was to join the fight at Gate Two, I would actually dare to turn a literal deaf ear to Colonel Belcher—but in the end, discretion won out over valor and I stopped in my tracks and came trotting back to the chief of staff, who insisted I take off my flak vest, put away my M16, and go up to see General Bright. It turns out he wanted me to hang around the palace all day just to shepherd the press releases from start to finish. Oh, I tried to protest. I told him Staff Sergeant Gooding is quite capable of the task with supervision from Major Filipovich, but General Bright would hear nothing of it and gave me a direct order to "man my post," as he put it.

So there you have it, Mother—my bravery has once again been thwarted by my duty as a Public Affairs Officer. Oh, I know you are infinitely proud of the work I am doing in this "battle for control of the media" as we "take the fight to the enemy," but I'm sure you can appreciate the disappointment I felt at not being able to go lend a hand for our men who were under attack. Oh, the damage I could have inflicted on those blasted Sunnis!

As it turns out, nine of the thirteen attackers were killed by the Quick Reaction Force, the other four are in deep lock-down at Abu Ghraib. Two of our soldiers were injured—flesh wounds, really—and one Iraqi bystander, a four-year-old boy, was killed by a ricocheting bullet (the official story is that it came from the barrel of an enemy gun, but I can tell you, *completely* HUSH-HUSH, there is some doubt to that story).

So, that pretty much sums up my day. How are things back there with you and Pap-Pap? Is he still giving you a fuss about taking his diabetes medicine? Tell him I said to behave or I will sic some Sunnis on him. Ha ha, that was a joke.

Write back when you're able.

Your ever-loving son,
Stacie

He was standing outside Colonel Belcher's office—*again!*— waiting to hear the scratch of the pen: just those two little letters, the chief's initials, followed by a rough, defiant circle corralling the scrawl, and he'd have the official blessing to launch the press release out to the world. This was a no-brainer press release: a weapons cache uncovered by a patrol in Salman Pak earlier this morning. Three simple paragraphs, fourteen simple sentences, three hundred and twenty-four simple words. So why was he, Eustace L. Harkleroad, quaking so violently? Was it fear of the chief's bark? Was it paralysis while standing at the edge of the precipice? Was it knowledge of his complete and utter failure as a valiant officer in the United States Army, coupled with the understanding that he was a total success as a weenie? Was it a potassium deficiency?

He made a mental note to eat more bananas in the future. But still he quivered.

"Harkleroad!"

"Sir, yes, sir?"

"Move away from my doorway. I can't hear myself think over your knocking knees." The chief seemed to have a grin in his voice; he was enjoying himself at Stacie's expense.

"Moving, sir."

"Thank you." The chief resumed his humming as he read the press release. How long did it take one man to decide whether or not three hundred and twenty-four words passed muster?

Stacie Harkleroad took up a new position on the other side of the division commander's reception area, pretending to study the photographs on the wall, just as he'd pretended to study those same photographs twenty-eight times before. Fire arced from the barrel of an Abrams tank, streaking the night sky. A female medic, a tear pooling in the corner of one eye, helped a deformed Iraqi boy put on a pair of shoes. Three infantrymen kicked down a door in a dusty back alley in Mosul. The photos had all been taken by Combat Camera soldiers, the roughshod and ill-tempered sergeants Harkleroad watched come and go from the neighboring Information Operations section each day. There he'd sit, sometimes stuffing a powdered donut in his mouth, as the Combat Camera guys rushed in and out in their full battle rattle, downloading images from their cameras, re-charging batteries, cleaning dried blood from the backs of their hands with baby wipes, and talking among themselves about whether or not they got "the money shot" of the suicide bomber's head, which had rolled thirty feet away from the body—"right into the gutter, where it belongs," said one. Harkleroad listened to the murmur of their conversations and (no matter what he

told his mother) gave thanks for the hundred thousandth time
he wasn't out there on patrol in the heat, dust, and blood.

Other staff officers were coming up the marble stairs of the
palace and gathering in the reception area outside the chief's
door for the morning briefing. Harkleroad stayed where he was
on the other side of the room, staring at the fiery round erupting
from the tank while the others clustered in tight knots behind
his back and, he assumed, talked about him. He surreptitiously
glanced down to see if he had any donut powder on the front
of his uniform, then went back to straining his one good ear for
the *scritch-scratch* of the chief's pen.

His stomach gurgled and his mind wandered, as it was
wont to do in these moments, to the dining facility. He wondered
what was on the menu for tonight's meal and hoped it would be
a gravy-smothered veal patty and pie, oh, yes, *pie*, and please,
Lord, let it be coconut cream pie. Stacie pulled the excess saliva
back into his mouth with a hissing sip. A couple of the officers
on the other side of the room glanced his way, then put their
heads closer together, mumbling and chuckling.

Thoughts of food continued to tumble through Harkleroad's mind. He thought back to that morning when he had stood
halfway through a line snaking around the dining facility. Sizzling
meat and yeasty breads perfumed the air, driving Harkleroad insane with desire. He kept trying to silently urge the soldiers ahead
of him to move faster, go forward, don't dawdle, for goodness
sake! They seemed impervious to the kitchen smells, the billows
of steam rising from the serving line. Instead, they were gabbing
on and on about sights they'd allegedly seen outside the wire.

"Didjoo hear about 3-25 out in Diyala yesterday?"

"No, what happened?"

"They was on foot patrol, going door-to-door—"

"Hello, Avon calling!"

"Exactly. And they was, like, near this town square when all of a sudden bullets started falling out of the sky."

"Huh?"

"Yeah, no shit. Falling straight out of the sky like some freaky rainstorm, man. One guy's arm got grazed and he, like, fell to the ground, screaming like a pussy while all the other guys fanned out and tried to find out what the fuck was going on. All the while, the shit is bouncing off their Kevlars."

"Like that old song, 'Bulletdrops Keep Fallin' on My Head.'"

"Egg-zactly. Anyway, turns out it was just a wedding party up in the town square. The patrol gets up there and finds a bunch of drunk locals firing guns straight into the air and whooping it up. They didn't know about that old rule, what goes up must come down. Man, I tell you, hajji can be dumb as a sack of rocks sometimes."

"Yeah, no shit."

Harkleroad endured all this with the impatience of a dying man who sees his salvation—food—in front of him but it stays just an inch beyond his grasp. He kept sucking the saliva back into his mouth with loud, obvious hisses but the two soldiers were, apparently, oblivious to anyone but themselves.

Now, standing outside the chief's office and staring at photos of "soldiers in action," just thinking about the dining facility made Harkleroad's stomach turn somersaults of delirium. He closed his eyes and basked in the memory of meals past.

For many soldiers—not just Eustace Harkleroad—daydreaming about food was an effective way to mentally take themselves out of Iraq. Say you're walking to dinner and the hot evening air is thick with the dust-fog and, like Eustace, you're wondering what's on the menu tonight, all the while thinking about those fresh shrimp your wife in her last e-mail said she'd prepared for her own dinner three thousand miles away, the night before, and your mouth is watering simultaneously for those shrimp and the fresh skin of your wife, and you're walking through the gravel-crunch of the path you've worn between your hooch and the dining facility, and all around you soldiers are gathered in groups, some joking about something some guy thought some girl said about another guy, some of them sharing cigarettes, some tossing a baseball down the lane between trailers, and you're starting to think this isn't a combat zone after all, it's just another summer Sunday night back in Des Moines where the livin' is easy and the beer is cool—that's about the time a VBIED explodes in the distance beyond the dust haze, beyond the laughing soldiers, beyond the concertina wire of your camp. It makes the sound of a heavy door slamming, like a thick metal door in a dungeon that echoes through the bowels of the earth. Nobody seems to notice. The laughter doesn't dip, the baseball doesn't waver in its trajectory between glove and glove. Life goes on, same as always. And sometimes, if you're lucky, life tastes like coconut cream pie.

20

GOODING

Chance Gooding had never seen anyone smoke a cigarette with as much intensity as Major Flip Filipovich. He went through one cigarette after another with no pause between pinching off the smoked-to-the-filter Marlboro and the lighter-flick ignition of a fresh one. If he could have shoved cigarettes in both nostrils and smoked from there, he probably would.

Chance stifled a cough and fanned his hand in front of his face. "Jesus, sir." The deputy public affairs officer was putting out so much smoke, enveloping them in a cloud, that even some of the Headquarters' most veteran smokers were getting edgy watching his chimney act as they all squeezed into the designated smoking hut (a regulatory fifty feet from the outer wall of the palace). Once a concrete bunker—complete with machine-gun slits—during the Golden Age of Saddam, the hut was the only place the truly stressed and/or addicted could go for relief during their ten-hour shifts. It was also the best place to vent and rage against "the Man" or "the System" or, most commonly, "the Fuckwads at the Pentagon." On any given day at any given hour, the hut was filled with noxious smoke and even worse attitudes.

Gooding was out here only because Major Filipovich had promised to tell the story about the time he left a CNN reporter stranded in Bosnia because she was taking too long to primp her hair and makeup for the camera. Now that Filipovich was finished with that tale, which had been embellished with plenty of asides about "goddamn prima donnas," Gooding was trapped in the smoking hut.

He fanned away the major's exhaled breath again and said, "Sir, you're killing me here."

"I'll tell you what's killing us," Flip snapped back, stabbing the air between them with Mr. Marlboro. "What's killing us is the fact that Corps PAO can't hear anything anymore because their ears are clogged with shit—"

"—because their heads are so far up their asses," Gooding finished. "I know, sir, I know. You've mentioned it once or twice already in the last half hour."

"*Fuck!*" Filipovich spat a shred of tobacco off the tip of his tongue. "They have no clue what it's like out there. But *I* know. *I've* been outside the wire every week. *I* could tell them a thing or three, the clueless fucks." His eyes were moving back and forth in a stutter, unsure where to land.

It's true, Major Filipovich had nothing but contempt for the system for which he worked and he took advantage of every opportunity to play the nonconformist, grumbling through clenched teeth in a nonstop patter of "fuckthisshit" or "goddamnticketpunchers" or "justyouwaitandsee, justyou-fuckingwaitandsee," though on the exterior he did his best to maintain his military demeanor around superior officers who were responsible for his annual evaluations (occasionally, he'd even manage to plaster a team-player look on his face for Harkleroad, the fat fuck). Life for him was a constant balancing act between disrespect and career preservation.

Harkleroad wasn't the only object of Filipovich's contempt; there were plenty of other candidates populating this palace at any given time, most of them near the top of the food chain. The closer one got to the top of the funnel, the more befuddled, out of touch, and certifiably insane one became. Senior officers lived and worked in the highest reaches of the exosphere where the lack of oxygen clearly strangled their brains, leading to the kind of tunnel vision that turned whole armies left when they should have gone right, made them flounder in the Waterloo mud and underestimate the forces of Wellington and Blücher. These oxygen-starved officers running the show from the palace had no fucking clue about what was unraveling outside the FOB checkpoints, Filipovich grumbled to Gooding.

"Case in point: the latest turd to drop from Corps' ass, the infamous 'How to Suck the Egg' e-mail."

Staff Sergeant Gooding groaned. *Here we go again.*

"You know, Harkleroad made sure I read the e-mail before shift change last night," Filipovich said. "He even printed out a hard copy and literally made me sign off on it. I wanted to write my name in blood—you know, kind of a take-this-e-mail-and-shove-it gesture—but I couldn't find anything sharper than a paper clip on my desk."

"Tell me about it, sir," Gooding said. "I talked to Butch over in Second Brigade Public Affairs and he was pretty jacked up about it, too. They had to practically tie him in a chair after he got done reading it. Total freak-out on his part. He said they made *him* sign a copy, too—like it was, as he put it, 'the fucking Mayflower Compact.' Butch would have signed it with quote one finger dipped in feces unquote if the brigade commander hadn't been hanging around his cubicle at the time."

The e-mail in question had pinged into the in-boxes of all Division PAOs operating in the Iraqi Theater of Operations two days ago and had filtered downward in no time. To wit:

From: hgunderson@mafiraq.mil

To: eustace.harkleroad@us.army.mil, jack.birch@us.army.mil, frances.finkle@ us.army.mil, jeff.jefferson@us.af.mil, edward_m_lesser@multicorpsiraq.mil, david_p_adams@multicorpsiraq.mil

23 JULY 2005 1923hrs

Subject: Increased Emphasis on Joint Operational Successes

Gentlemen,

All wars, but this war in particular, are carried out on ever-shifting ground. Here in Iraq, we have a very visible reminder of this axiom with the sand that crumbles beneath our very boots. A metaphor of granular consequences, if you will. As the battle progresses, our forces must adapt to changes in operational focus, upticks and downticks in OPTEMPO, new battle strategies, and unpredictable shifts in the mood of the local population. Each Local National is a grain of sand beneath our boots—we never know which way he'll **SHIFT** away from us.

To date, U.S. forces and our allies have done a remarkable job in keeping up with this undulating landscape. When first we came to this theater of operations, we were conquerors—the hammer striking the anvil of evil, beating the Ba'athist swords into ploughshares. We toppled a despicable regime and secured the country's borders. Over time, our emphasis **SHIFTED** to the role of humanitarian peacekeeping as we strived to rebuild what had been torn down by three decades of unquestionable tyranny. We became the pillar of Iraqi society and the People looked to us with trust and hope. In time, a criminal element started filtering into the country and wreaked havoc with roadside bombs and assassinations, and our mission once again **SHIFTED** to being Protectors and Shields, Iraq's first line of defense against the infidels who glory in the quick, showy slaughter of dozens at one time. This is the role we have been playing—and quite efficiently, I might add—but as you know it is time once again to **SHIFT** the focus. Recognizing that, like a weak-legged infant taking his first steps, Iraq must begin to stand on its own and defend itself against foreign-based terror, we must now start to step back and let the Iraqi people walk across the floor. Heretofore, we have been focused only in part on training these raw fledgling recruits, and only occasionally accompanying the IA and ISF on *their* patrols through *their* neighborhoods so *their* families can witness firsthand how Iraq protects its own. Word has filtered down from on high that this must now be our primary focus. Though we will still conduct our own patrols and will remain ever-vigilant to guard against domestic and foreign terror, if a few bombs go off and a few lives are regrettably sacrificed while we're at the firing range showing a toothless forty-five-year-old man how to shoot an M16 ... well then, so be it. This is coming from on high, you understand, and not just from me (though I share in the firm belief that, yes, we must begin the slow, messy, painful process of withdrawal while ensuring we leave behind a nation that can protect itself against intruders).

All this is preamble to what I really want to say to you today. As we **SHIFT** our operational focus, so must we **SHIFT** the tone of our press releases and statements to the media.

I have been increasingly concerned about the number of stories coming across my desk that focus primarily on U.S. forces while all but ignoring the tremendous work our Iraqi brethren have been carrying out in the name of New Democracy. The ratio of soft feature stories has begun to greatly outbalance the hard news stories coming from our Divisions and their Brigades. We here at Corps Headquarters call them "Day in the Life" fluff stories: "A Day in the Life of a Motor Pool Mechanic," "A Day in the Life of a Computer Technician," "A Day in the Life of a Tuba Player in the Combat Zone." You get the idea.

The most troubling aspect of the U.S.-centric stories I'm seeing is the tone of negativity and pessimism that is starting to creep in around the edges. Your young soldier-journalists are NOT exercising discretion in their choice of words. I will give you a typical example, one that was brought to my attention earlier this week in a story written by an enterprising young scribe from a certain Brigade that will remain nameless. He opened his story thusly:

> One thing every U.S. soldier assigned to Iraq wants to hear is "The Iraqi Security Forces are sufficiently trained and tested to take control of the future of Iraq." Any soldier who hears this knows the next order will be a redeployment order, one sending him home until his country calls for him again.

> Well, I've got good news and bad news. The bad news is that our Army will still be here until the mission is complete. The good news is that every day the ISF gets closer to being able to take over.

Gentlemen, I've said it before, I'll say it again: there is "sad news," there is "tragic news," but there is NO "bad news" coming out of Iraq. This negative slant is uncalled for and has no place in what is being released from our office. Furthermore, there shall be no mention of timetables or any indication of U.S. soldiers impatient to leave this country before they've fully erected the pillars of freedom.

A trend I've noticed: these stories rarely if ever touch on the most important components of the current mission: Recruit, Rebuild, Restore. That is the standard we at Corps have set and, frankly, your stories are, for the most part, not meeting that standard.

Now, I am not going to tell you How to Suck the Egg—I have never been one who gives instructions on Egg Sucking—BUT it needs to be a very lopsided ratio on the hard news side, emphasizing the triumphant moments of our work over here (and, more to the point, Triumphant Iraqi Moments).

Remember, the focus is now on joint operational success. Multi-Corps Iraq wants to raise the level of Iraqi trust in **THEIR** Army and ISF. Seek the successes, ferret out the positive, corral the optimistic. Your focus must now be on the current mission—Operation National Unity—and you must highlight our success in finding IEDs before they go off, ferreting out weapons caches, and detaining terrorists. Our Army journalists should always be showing how terrorists have failed in their efforts to derail the democratic process. *That's* the sort of thing I want to see coming across my desk, effective immediately. Recruit, Rebuild, Restore, gentlemen.

As we like to say around Corps Headquarters here: **Put an Iraqi face on it!**

Regards,

Harold Gunderson, Brigadier General, U.S. Army

Chief, Public Affairs Division

Multi-Allied-Forces-Iraq

As e-mails go, it was pretty long-winded, filled with as many multiple orgasms as a whore in her first day on the job.

Major Filipovich snorted smoke. "My first instinct was tear that e-mail into little pieces and eat it. But I turned it into a dartboard instead."

Gooding nodded. "I folded mine into a paper airplane."

"Doesn't change the fact that it's complete and utter bullshit." Flip popped another cigarette between his lips. "What they're essentially saying is, they don't want us to report what's really happening out there if it doesn't lend itself to a 'happy' story."

"Operation Smiley Face."

"Fuck, yeah." Filipovich flicked his lighter several times before the cigarette caught fire. "Get this: one of my buddies in Third Brigade was telling me about how his men discovered a weapons cache in Al-Qadisiyyah. They also found some Beanie Babies with hand grenades stuffed inside them. Can you believe that? Fucking grenades in fucking stuffed animals that some kid's gonna cuddle up with in bed at night. Well, word filters upstream and what does the I Fucking A do? They issue a plea for Corps to cease and desist the Beanie Baby program—which, as you and I know, is our most successful PR campaign, putting happiness in the hands of deprived children. Operation Smiley Face to the max. Then, what's more, IA orders their soldiers to confiscate all stuffed animals and soccer balls. It hasn't happened yet, but I can just see the IA going door to door and, at gunpoint, forcing Hajji Jr. to give up his Mr. Cuddles."

Gooding shook his head. "IA couldn't find its own asshole with a flashlight and a map."

At that moment, Lieutenant Colonel Harkleroad came be-bopping down the sidewalk.

"Speaking of . . ." said Filipovich.

"Play nice, sir."

Filipovich spat another shred of tobacco. "The fat fuck."

Harkleroad's Kevlar was askew and his pistol belt all but disappeared beneath the overlapping folds of fat at his waist. As he got nearer, Gooding could see a gravy stain slopped in the shape of Italy on the front of his uniform.

"Lord, just kill me now," he muttered, then raised his voice and gave the Division motto, "Luck of the Seventh, sir!"

"Luck of the Seventh, Sergeant Gooding," Harkleroad returned as he neared. He nodded at Flip. "Major Filipovich."

"Sir." Filipovich was rapidly smoking down his last ciga-rette without reaching for another—a sure sign he was about to bolt on Gooding.

"Looks like Salisbury steak for lunch again, sir." Gooding said.

"It is indeed," Harkleroad said. "How did you know?"

"Just a guess, sir. Never mind."

Beside him, Flip broke into a laugh-concealing cough.

"I've got the daily news clips on your desk—printed, sta-pled, and front-and-center," Gooding said.

"Very good, very good." Harkleroad was still panting and red-faced from his walk back from the dining facility. He was practically spritzing sweat just standing there. Gooding could see he was anxious to get inside the cool bath of the air-conditioned palace.

"Well, I won't hold you up, sir."

"That's all right. By the way, I've got something I need to talk with you about. Er—" He looked at Filipovich. "Inside, whenever you're done here."

"Will do, sir."

Harkleroad resumed his trot along the sidewalk to the guard shack at the palace entrance.

Filipovich waved his cigarette at Gooding. "All right, then. Off you go to suck some eggs."

"Yeah, the soft-boiled kind," Gooding said, then hurried after Harkleroad.

Three minutes later, standing at ease in front of Harkle-road's desk, Gooding asked, "What's up, sir?"

"I need to let you know about one thing that came up at the staff meeting this morning."

"All right." Inside: *Here we go again. Another tale of woe-is-me-nobody-loves-me. I never get to sit at the Big Boys Table and they always pick me last for dodgeball.*

"From what I could hear from my seat along the wall—because the CG's aide is *still* forgetting to put my name card anywhere on the table, and he knows how difficult it is for me with the bum ear—I guess PAO will never get the respect it deserves, huh?"

"Be that as it may, sir . . . You were saying?"

"Right, yes. Well, anyway, from what I gather, the CG is getting pretty torqued about what he perceives is a lack of discipline among the lower-enlisted troops."

"Sloppy soldiers? Really?"

"Well, not the soldiers, per se. It's more a problem with the allowances we're giving them here at FOB Triumph."

"Such as?"

"He's targeting Morale, Welfare, and Recreation in particular. He has nothing against soldiers relaxing and having a good time, per se. But it's the level of activity that has him concerned."

"Yeah, let's make this a no-fun zone," Gooding grumbled under his breath.

"What was that?"

"I said, 'He's right, this *is* a combat zone.'"

"Right. Well, it seems he's got MWR in his sights these days. Things like the Hispanic Heritage Month salsa-dance competition, and the All-Brigade Pinewood Derby, and the talent show, and the women's basketball tournament. By the way, I had no idea there were organized leagues here—when do these people find the time?"

Some people like to do things on their downtime other than grazing at the pastry table, Colonel Lardass.

"Anyway," the PAO said, leaning back and straining the threads on his buttons. The gravy Italy shifted and expanded to the size of Africa. "All this extracurricular activity is a thorn in the CG's craw because, as he puts it, these kind of sanctioned MWR events distract soldiers from their combat mission and lead to potential cases of misconduct and violations of General Orders Numbers One and Two."

"But, sir, they allow soldiers to dance up at Camp Taji, so why not down here at Triumph? It's like they're American Baptists and we're Southern Baptists."

"No, no, that's not it," Harkleroad interjected. "It's a matter of perception. And that's where we come in. The CG wants us to put a tight lid on our coverage of noncombat-related activities in the *Lucky Times*. And I can see his point."

Of course you can. Try not to choke on the lint in the CG's pocket, you old ass kisser.

Harkleroad continued: "For instance, let's say you're a spouse sitting at home back in Hinesville and you turn on the NBC Nightly News and there's your husband doing the John Travolta with some other female on Disco Night, how will that look?"

"It'll look like they're blowing off steam. I say they're entitled to that."

"And *I* say it's a battle we're going to lose, Sergeant Gooding. And frankly, it's a battle where I'm willing to raise the white flag. I'm not about to go toe-to-toe with the CG over something like this."

"But—"

"But *nothing*. This is not something I'm going to back down on. We need to keep a tight rein on what our journalists are covering, and, *especially,* what we're allowing external media to see. Remember, we control the agenda and it's up to us to steer them in the right direction."

Chance said nothing, just stared straight ahead at the continental gravy stain on Harkleroad's belly.

"So, are we singing on the same sheet of music here, Staff Sergeant Gooding?"

Gooding sighed. "Roger that, sir. I'll tell the brigade journalists to steer away from anything that looks like soldiers are having the least little bit of fun."

"No need to get sarcastic with me, Sergeant."

"Sorry, sir." *You fat fuck, you.* "I meant no disrespect."

"None taken."

"If there's nothing more, sir . . . ?"

"No, nothing more. That's all. Just wanted to give you a heads-up about which way the CG's wind was blowing." He paused. "Wait a minute, that didn't sound right, did it? But you know what I mean."

"Loud and clear, sir." Gooding all but clicked his heels and gave a snappy salute before he walked out.

Harkleroad opened his e-mail. It was from one of the brigade PAOs who'd submitted a batch of photos to Specialist Carnicle for the *Lucky Times*. Eustace had been cc'ed in the e-mail; what's worse, so had Corps PAO. The e-mail's subject line: MWR Fun Events.

Even before he opened the attachments, Harkleroad knew he'd be calling down to brigade to give the PAO a what-for and advising him not to be wasting his journalists' time like that in the future, then calling up to Corps to apologize for letting one slip through that didn't adhere to Recruit, Rebuild, Restore.

He clicked on the first photo. The photographer had caught a male and female, both dressed in PT uniforms, doing the salsa, standing at intimate proximity. Their fingers were curled, so it was hard to tell if they were wearing wedding rings. Harkleroad clicked the magnifying glass icon several times to bring the hands in closer. Sure enough, there was the wink of gold coming off the male's hand.

Eustace Harkleroad leaned back in his chair, knowing that by deleting this photo he was probably saving a soldier's marriage. And that's when the last thread on the middle button gave up the fight and flung itself off his uniform, clicking twice against the floor before coming to rest in the dust beneath his desk. Eustace looked down and saw—for the first time—the gravy stain, which now had a cleft running across the northern half of Italy.

21

DURET

With the demotion of Abe Shrinkle, life in Bravo Company had taken a left turn onto a downhill street. They'd been pulling longer days and more Quick Reaction Force missions. No more "ghost patrols" off the brigade's books, no more biding their time until the plane ride home, no more delivering lollipops and soccer balls to Shiite schools. It was the real deal now and, as Zeildorf had said on more than one occasion, "It sucked the dust off my granddaddy's balls."

The new commander assigned to fill Shrinkle's vacancy was a West Point grad called First Lieutenant (Promotable) Matthew Fledger who came to them from Echo Company. Lieutenant Colonel Duret knew he was scraping the bottom of the barrel but this was the best G-1 could find for him. His only other option, the major in Personnel told him, was a Presbyterian chaplain who, due to an overstaffing bungle back at Fort Stewart, was temporarily working as a motor pool officer in Third Brigade.

At Echo Company, Lieutenant Fledger had been the executive officer whose primary duties involved operations at the dining facility and the mail room, tasks that tapped into his natural inclination toward logic, order, and Microsoft Excel spreadsheets. This is what he told Duret when the colonel paid a scouting visit to Echo.

"I'm big on organization, sir," Fledger said. "I'm what you might call married to my day planner." He held up his leather-bound binder, neatly zippered and sheened with an oil that could only be palm sweat, Duret guessed.

Fledger was horribly disproportioned—skull too big for the stalk of his neck, arms foreshortened like a dinosaur. You took one look at that lightbulb-shaped head of his and one word came to mind: thalidomide.

That bulbous, knotty head, however, seemed to be filled with all the tactics, techniques, and procedures his professors had stuffed into it back at West Point. Fledger looked like a man who vigorously highlighted his textbooks.

"It's not like the men are undisciplined," Duret told Fledger as they stood outside the Echo Company ops tent. "It's just that Captain Shrinkle had his own unique way of taking charge. Not one that fit into Brigade standards of conduct."

"I see, sir."

"You would be inheriting a morale mess, but otherwise things are okay with the men."

"That sounds like a pretty big *otherwise,* if you don't mind my saying, sir."

Duret realized his assessment of Bravo Company must have sounded like a weak endorsement, so he tried to get back on course. "I'm just trying to undersell the job so you won't be surprised when you show up on your first day of work."

"Roger that, sir."

But when First Lieutenant (Promotable) Matthew Fledger, accompanied by Lieutenant Colonel Duret, *did* arrive at Bravo Company on the very afternoon Captain Shrinkle was banished to Towel Land, he seemed to be overselling himself as the savior of the unit. Fledger radiated a ballsy confidence that only came from someone working really hard at it. The young officer thought a lot of himself and his untested ability to lead a company of men into battle. If there had been some water handy, he would have walked on it.

Sergeant Lumley and the other platoon sergeants watched with wary, cautious looks as Fledger and Duret threaded their way through the coils of concertina wire surrounding the company headquarters trailer. A heavy backpack strapped across Fledger's shoulders bent him nearly double. The straps and buckles on the backpack jingled as he mounted the steps of the wooden porch and looked up at the NCO welcoming party. Fledger tried to smile but it came across as a trembling mess on his lips.

The lieutenant shook hands with his NCOs and said, "You can call me Fledge." Lumley and the others nodded and said, "Okay, sir," but Duret knew they would never ever call him that, not even if someone held the muzzle of an M4 to their heads and rotated the selector switch from *safe* to *semi*. It would always be "Sir," the one syllable drawn out and dripping with thinly disguised contempt. He himself had been on the receiving end of this kind of acceptable disrespect back when he was a young, striving lieutenant—a time in his life that now seemed like something seen at the wrong end of a telescope.

As Duret led Fledger inside his new company headquarters, he could see the NCOs giving each other wordless looks.

Fledge walked into the orderly room and shrugged off the burden of his backpack (filled with Army regulations, field manuals, a stapler, two dozen choco-chip energy bars, and, yes, a box of yellow highlighter pens). The backpack hit the floor with a sound like a harness of bells on a horse-drawn sleigh traveling through snowy woods.

Duret cleared his throat. "Well, lieutenant," he said. "Now that I've delivered you into the capable hands of your NCOs, I'll be making my exit so you can settle in without me looking over your shoulder."

"Thank you, sir. As I think I've already expressed to you numerous times, I appreciate this opportunity."

"That's all right," Duret said. "I'll leave you with just four words of advice."

"Yes, sir?"

"Don't. Fuck. It. Up."

Fledger reddened to the tip of his lightbulb head and Duret, in the corner of his eye, caught Sergeant Lumley smirking.

"I-I'll try not to, sir. I *won't,* sir. You can depend on that."

"Okay," Duret said. "But, just to let you know, I heard the same thing from Captain Shrinkle's own lips on more than one occasion." He nodded at the group. "Good day, men."

"Good day, sir," the NCOs echoed.

Duret strode out the door of the headquarters and loudly crunched through the gravel. When he'd gone twenty paces, he stopped and then silently made his way back to the side of the building where he stopped beneath an open window. This was always the best part of orienting a new commander to his unit, the secret eavesdrop.

As he cocked an ear to the window, Duret could hear Fledger already in midsermon: "Men, I know you've gone through some hard times with your former commander, times that may have tried your very souls—" (who *was* this guy? Ralph Waldo Emerson?) "—but I can assure you I will do everything in my power to turn things around for Bravo Company. Standing here today I make a pledge to you—call it the Fledge Pledge, if you want—" (they didn't and they wouldn't) "—to reverse the negative energy generated by the moral turpitude of one individual—an individual we will no longer discuss, unless of course you *want* to discuss him—and to instill a sense of pride in Bravo Company, using Army Ethics as our very foundation." He paused to let his words ring through the orderly room. A couple of the NCOs coughed lightly. "I would like to begin with a company formation tonight at seventeen-thirty hours, at which time I will present my commander's philosophy to all the soldiers and I will have them fill out an Excel spreadsheet with all their vital information. This is the way I like to operate as a company commander." (A work ethic developed during his eleven minutes of job experience.) "We will get through this together, gentlemen. And when we emerge on the other side, we will all be the better for it."

As he tiptoed away through the gravel, Duret found himself wondering if that Presbyterian chaplain wouldn't have been such a bad idea after all.

22

GOODING

Staff Sergeant Chance Gooding Jr. sat at his desk, clicking through e-mails at the start of another brain-blurring fourteen-hour shift. A few cubicles away, laughter bubbled up and floated near the ceiling for a few seconds. An officer in an adjoining cubicle started grinding coffee beans and it brought them all one sniff closer to their local Starbucks.

This particular officer had gone online and ordered an espresso machine at the beginning of the deployment and he began every day with this same ritual. Soon, they would hear the whistling officer getting his foam to peak at just the right consistency. Just the very sound of java slurp and hiss could make some Fobbits get all misty with homesickness.

Gooding clicked his mouse, someone made another joke that provoked louder and longer laughter, a voice came over the SMOG loudspeaker—"Test, test," as the Ops staff prepped for the CG's morning briefing—a female clerk walked past Gooding's cubicle bitching about a paper cut, and then
ka-WHAM!!

All voices in the palace stopped midsyllable.

Later, Chance would write about it in his diary: *You could feel the explosion more than you could hear it. It was like a great in-suck, out-suck of air that made the walls creak as nails shifted in their holes a quarter inch. Then you felt it under your feet—a tremendous jarring of the earth. Then, finally, it reached your ears: a dozen simultaneous thunder booms. I swear I could also hear china teacups rattling on a shelf somewhere in Headquarters but I know that's impossible.*

The fillings in Gooding's teeth buzzed and he dove under his desk. The words "Duck and cover! Duck and cover!" rebounded through his head. Then came another explosion and this wasn't fun anymore, dammit. Gooding wedged himself under the desk, computer wires slapping his forehead and getting tangled around his ears. He would curl into a tight, fetal ball and stay out of sight from the Sunni terrorists when they burst into the palace with their AK-47s blazing fire. Surely the explosions had punched a hole in the palace roof and bearded men were already rappelling from the ceiling on hissing ropes. Gooding thought he felt smoke watering his eyes. It was like he was in a movie where soldiers are screaming and running on a battlefield as great clods of dirt go skyward like fireworks behind them. He expected to see a severed arm come cartwheeling past his head any minute now.

Gooding gave a tiny whimper and thought about wills and powers of attorney and he regretted not designating Yolanda as his beneficiary after their divorce. He thought of her tear-streaked face and realized he still loved her and wished he could see her one more time before another rocket crashed into the palace and he was killed in action. He vowed he would die a

noble death, Fobbit or no Fobbit. He would not beg for mercy
or cry like a weenie, no matter how many swords the bearded
men pressed against his throat.

Silence spread across the cubicles as the officers and
NCOs held their collective breath, listening for the next shoe
to drop. Or, in this case, missile. For a full thirty seconds, the
only sounds were the airy hiss of the ventilating system and the
sputter of an unattended espresso machine.

Then the SMOG speakers crackled and a voice, still a little
crinkly around the edges, announced: "Attention! Attention
in Headquarters! All personnel are advised to continue with
the morning's business. We've just received reports that the
preceding explosions were caused by Division howitzers going
off near the Life Support Area. Artillery was draining water in
that vicinity to dry up the mud and improve living conditions.
Headquarters is not under attack. I repeat, we are *not* under
attack. That is all. Carry on."

Someone yelled, "I knew it, motherfucker! Didn't I tell
you it was our own goddamned engineers giving us a wake-up
call?!" The regular stream of chatter flooded back through the
room, peppered with relieved laughter.

Gooding remained where he was, huddled under the desk.
Fear kept him curled among the wires and cords. When Major
Filipovich arrived to begin his shift five minutes later, Gooding didn't move, hoping Filipovich wouldn't see him cowering
behind the chair. He had nothing to worry about. Apparently,
Filipovich couldn't see around the sleepy scowl on his face and
he went immediately to his cubicle, crossed his arms on the
desk, and tried to grab a power nap before the morning briefing began and Harkleroad showed up with his nervous chatter.

When the coast was clear, Gooding silently unfolded himself from under his desk and resumed browsing through his e-mails. When he gave a muffled cough, Major Filipovich poked his head out of his cubicle. "Gooding? That you?"

"Yes, sir, it's me."

"When the fuck did you get here?"

"Been here all along, sir. You didn't see me when you came in?"

"Nope." Filipovich gaped his mouth in a face-consuming yawn. "Can't see past the cobwebs. Fucking sleep deprivation."

"You missed all the excitement, sir."

"Oh yeah? Whazzat?"

"Engineers tried to scare the shit out of us this morning. They blew off a couple of howitzers so they could drain the swamp over at Trailer City."

"I *thought* I heard something when I was walking over here from the chow hall. Engineers, huh?" He laughed. "I'll bet you guys thought it was Al-Fucking-Qaeda, huh?"

Gooding kept his eyes on his computer screen. "Actually, sir, we barely noticed. I guess we were all too busy getting ready for another day at the war factory."

"Another day, another dollar," Filipovich said. "Another hundred and ninety-five million dollars, to be precise." He yawned again, molar fillings winking in the fluorescent light, and retreated to the nest of his cubicle. "Wake me when the war's over."

That afternoon, division headquarters experienced its second fake attack of the day as the staff conducted a previously scheduled "training exercise" (though Gooding still opined the word *training* was a misnomer on the battlefield). For weeks, the

Operations sergeant major had been planning for a simulated attack that would result in multiple simulated casualties. The exercise stemmed from the CG's concern that—in his words, spoken privately to his staff—"the pussies here at Camp Cupcake are not prepared for an all-out, balls-to-the-walls disaster." No one wanted to be the one caught with his pants down by the CG, so the pucker factor started ramping up and eventually they came up with the plan for a simulated attack, the brainchild of G-3 Operations. To pull it off required five bottles of Karo syrup, three letters requesting coordination with security forces, eight smoke grenades, and soldiers willing to resurrect thespian talents not seen since *Our Town* in high school. Staffers in the palace were randomly selected to participate and, just before the attack began, were handed index cards that outlined their roles in the scenario, complete with cues and lines of dialogue.

And so, at precisely 1415 hours, the Logistics sergeant major (chosen for his voice, which was equal parts Darth Vader and earthquake) officially began the exercise by bellowing "BOOM!" This was followed by a specialist in Cultural Affairs reading her part in the script, "OH, MY GOD! OH, MY GOD! WE'RE UNDER ATTACK! HELP ME! HELP ME!" That was the cue for other players, stationed at various locations within the cubicle jungle, to begin screaming and crying and, in one case, calling for their mommy.

The rest of the staff, those not handpicked for roles in the unfolding drama, kept working at their cubicles, clicking their computer mice, and trying not to grin when a master sergeant over in Ops read his lines in a monotone, "Medic. Medic. I can't feel my legs."

Emergency personnel (who'd been conveniently waiting in one of the palace's antechambers) scurried through the slick polished hallways, loading victims onto stretchers and hustling them outside to the ambulance collection point. Each time they opened the back doors of the palace, Baghdad heat puffed inside. Within minutes, everyone was bitching about the temperature and wondering when the exercise would be over. The entire proceedings were timed with a stopwatch as the Division Surgeon watched with a critical eye to make sure the assigned combat lifesavers were performing their tasks correctly—ripping open the dressings and applying firm, hard pressure to plastic wounds oozing red-dyed corn syrup, splinting legs with pallet wood, and, in the particular case of Private First Class Semple and Private First Class Andersen, practicing mouth-to-mouth resuscitation with the tongue-tangle method (a French kiss that later developed into something else altogether).

When Staff Sergeant Gooding—still a little flinchy and shaking from what he'd thought was the real thing earlier that morning—got up to go to the bathroom, he was forced to step around simulated casualties sprawled in the hallway, each clutching a card indicating the type and severity of his or her wounds. A sergeant from Gooding's platoon was flat on his back, staring at the ceiling and drumming his fingers on his chest.

Gooding pretended to almost step on the sergeant's face. "Oops, didn't see you there, Sar'nt."

"Very funny, Gooding. Come stand a little closer and I can see right up your dress."

"Touché. So how's it going?"

The sergeant grimaced. "This fucking sucks. I got a shitload of work to do, waiting for me on my desk, and they pick *this* afternoon, out of all the afternoons they could have picked, to blow the whistle for the exercise."

"You know, there's never a convenient time to schedule mayhem and disaster."

"Fuck you, Gooding. At least you can go take a piss if you want to. Me, I'm stuck here until they finally get around to me."

"What've you got?"

The sergeant looked down at his card. "Sucking chest wound."

"Wow. Serious stuff."

"I know, right? They've got another two minutes to get me on a stretcher or I'm a bleedout."

"Well," Gooding said as he started to move off, "good luck with that."

"Fuck you very much."

An hour later, it was all over and the wounded soldiers were back at their cubicles, sweating from the exertion of having to temporarily trade the air-conditioned headquarters for the 110-degree heat outside. Despite the events of the day, they were still able to joke about their injuries.

"Yeah, they gave me 'deep lacerations to the thigh.'"

"Dude, I got you beat—I didn't even *have* a thigh anymore —leg was completely gone."

"Gross."

"Yeah. At least I didn't have an open head wound."

"Shrapnel on the brain, motherfucker. Too bad it wasn't the real thing and then I wouldn't have to finish this spreadsheet analysis of IED frequencies. Colonel Pain-in-the-Ass wants it *yesterday*."

"Of course he does. Aren't those senior staffers always one step ahead of you?"

"They think they are, but they don't know jack shit."

23

SHRINKLE

A change had come over Abe Shrinkle in the last three weeks, one with which he was not entirely comfortable. For one thing, he had become lax in his duties at the fitness center. Towels, sloppy in their folds, were piled haphazardly at the front desk like pancakes on a plate at Denny's. Sticky grime on the handlebars of the stationary bikes went unwiped and presented a germy situation for the unsuspecting fitness patrons. Someone swiped the Barry Manilow CD and Abe let it go unreported. And, perhaps worst of all, he was late in unlocking the front doors most mornings. Ignoring the line of grumbling and bitter-spitting lieutenant colonels and sergeants major and captains who'd been standing in the morning chill for more than half an hour, Abe kept his head down and fumbled the key into the lock. Without a word, he'd open the door, step into the stale, humid stink of last night's sweat and dirty socks, flick on the lights, and glumly put a fresh sign-in sheet on the counter.

Shrinkle was angry—not an emotion with which he was all that familiar. He was angry at the fat Fobbits who had nothing better to do in this war than waste a half hour standing around waiting for a rinky-dink little fitness center to open. He was angry at the air of self-righteous self-entitlement these men, guts straining against the waistband of their shorts, gave off as they scowled at him and pressed too hard with the pen while signing in for their session, at the way they elbowed each other aside in order to be the first on the treadmill, at the way they shouted at him from across the room to change the CD because their ears were bleeding from all that disco crap—enough already!

Shrinkle was angry at Lieutenant Colonel Duret for taking away his company and demoting him to this low station of life on FOB Triumph—though this anger was tempered by the indisputable fact that Duret's decision was completely justified by Abe's actions. Captain Shrinkle knew his commanding officer had had two choices and he'd taken the one that would leave the least amount of poo sticking to their boots. He supposed he should be grateful he wasn't right now on his way to Fort Leavenworth (and, frankly, he was surprised he wasn't); but still, he couldn't think of Duret's bad-news face as he'd stood in the doorway of his trailer without having to suppress a chest-tightening surge of rage. "It's not fair, it's not fair, it's not fair." Those were the words that looped through his head when he thought of Vic Duret.

He was just as angry at that Iraqi—whoever he was—who'd crawled underneath that fuel truck and started this whole chain of events. This also played like a broken, spliced film through Abe's head: the brown-faced man in his white dishdasha dropping to all fours on the street, peering at the truck's undercarriage, then flattening to his belly and slithering forward. Drop, peer, slither. Drop, peer, slither. If anyone was to be blamed for how it had all turned out, it was this little man who had lacked the brains to know when his life was about to end. "Fucking hajji." There, he'd said it. And he'd say it again. "Fucking hajji." He'd say it any dang time he felt like it.

Swearing was also a relatively new sensation for Captain Abe Shrinkle. Though he'd long been surrounded by potty-mouths in the Army, he had resisted the pull of his tongue, save for a few random moments of excruciating pain or well-run-dry exhaustion. But now he felt the time had come to start letting loose with all the *goddamns* and *shits* and *fucks* and *cocksuckers* that had been too-long pent up inside his throat. If ever there was a time for cursing, this was it.

"Fucking A!" he agreed with himself.

All this anger and profanity was a remarkable change for Abe Shrinkle. It was nothing less than a glacial shift, as distinct as the time when, in Alaska, he had taken a cruise on Portage Lake and as the boat bobbed in the water fifty yards from the base of the turquoise glacier, he had watched a column of ice creak and snap and pull away and then slide into the lake with a plunge, spewing a dozen fountains of water and finally breaking up into several car-sized chunks of ice that rolled once, twice, then started bobbing along with the cruise boat. Now there was something inside him that was just as surely pulling away and breaking into smaller pieces. It was something big, something important, something he'd held on to his entire life: a headstrong loyalty to his fellow citizens and the country at large. It was a fealty that, he was now starting to think, was misplaced.

He felt this internal shift as he stood there at the fitness center desk, glowering at the blubber-jiggling Fobbits on the bikes. He felt it when he sat in the dining facility, keeping his head down to avoid possible eye contact with members of his former company. He even felt it when he was floating in the middle of the Aussie pool, rubbing a cool can of beer across his neck and face and listening to the inane cheerfulness of the men and women playing water polo around him.

Once, one of the men, brick-red skin flaming around his sunglasses, had been reading a newspaper and called out to the rest of them, "Oy! Get a crack at this headline, mates: CHENEY ADMITS HE OVERESTIMATED IRAQIS' ABILITY TO RE-CLAIM THEIR NATION IN WAKE OF INVASION."

Shrinkle had rung out a laugh and said, "Yeah, no shit, Sherlock!"

The bloke had gone on to read more of the story but Abe had fallen into a self-contained silence after that, paddling around the pool on his inner tube and wondering why he felt such relief from jeering at the vice president, *his* vice president. Inside his British skin, Abe was filled with light and froth, as if he were made of spun sugar. He was free to do what he pleased, Richard Belmouth or no Richard Belmouth, and America be damned.

He had made his way to the shallow end, hoisted himself out of the water, then padded over to the soldier reading the newspaper. "I say, old chap, could I bother you for that section of newsprint?"

"Sure, here y' go, Dick."

Abe took the sheet, quickly folded it several times, then launched the paper airplane into the air to the cheers of all those around the pool. The plane caught a current of air, which it rode over the wall and, just like that, was gone forever.

Heart thudding on his tongue, Abe had announced, "And *that's* what I think of the bloody Yanks and their Limp-Dick Cheney!"

24

GOODING

In the dining facility, Chance Gooding stuffed himself with chili mac, mashed potatoes, a slice of pepperoni pizza, two bags of potato chips, four carrot sticks, and two desserts (strawberry shortcake and fudge brownie). He ate with aggressive determination, only glancing up at the TV once when he heard a reporter tell the camera, "Officials here say that, mission by mission, brick by brick, they are winning the hearts and minds of the people in a war that will prove to its doubters that it's possible to triumph through democracy."

"Bullshit," he muttered, though he'd meant to keep it in his head.

It had been a bad week of death and he was getting tired of typing the phrase, *Names of the deceased are being withheld until next of kin have been notified.* Whatever emotional impact these words might have once carried had gone fuzzy and numb by all the repetition. Dead soldiers were now little more than names and hometowns, corpses simply objects to be loaded onto the back of C-130s somewhere and delivered like pizzas to the United States.

This didn't sit well with Gooding but he didn't have much time to think about it because, like orders at a pizza joint, those bodies kept rolling in. All he could do to keep up with the demand was type the same press releases time after time until they became like words to a song he was memorizing.

Here at Division Public Affairs, Gooding never released the names; that was a task left to the Pentagon and usually came a week, maybe two, after the soldier had been delimbed by the bomb or barbecued in the driver's seat of the Humvee. By the time the wordsmiths at the Puzzle Palace had issued the terse, official announcement, the staff in Baghdad had long since moved on to another death, and another, and another after that.

This week, in particular, had been gruesome and full of sad gore.

The thuds striking the earth were barely noticeable to the cubicle mice in Division Headquarters, what with the constant murmur of voices punctuated by sporadic laughter, the stream of official radio chatter from the SMOG speakers overhead, the insectoid static drone of the air-conditioning, and the very thoughts inside the soldiers' heads that steadily cried out, "Home! Home! Home!"

No, the thuds were hardly audible—mere distant thumps, like a giant was walking over the crest of the horizon with hard, measured footsteps. The soldiers of Shamrock Division paid them no mind, like all the other daily thumps and thuds and thunder cracks of bombs.

But less than twenty minutes later, they snapped to attention because now those distant explosions were front and center in Shamrock Division operations and SMOG filled the air with its chatter of acronyms. Terrorists had fired mortars and rockets into a crowd of thousands who were congregating at a mosque in al-Kadhimiya in honor of an ancient imam's birth (or perhaps it was his death—either way, it was a religious celebration of his coming or going).

At least eight indirect fires were launched at the pilgrims from two different sectors of the city, one landing on the mosque, the others falling outside and along the miles-long stream of chanting Shi'as. The first reports estimated the civilian casualties in the hundreds; a few hours later, that would be downgraded to seven dead and a few dozen injured. Sham Div helicopter pilots floating in the sky nearby saw the rockets launched; they pinpointed the source, locked on target, and effectively wiped out the terrorists with one squeeze of one decisive finger, blasting them straight to whatever Allah they had been praising. Ground troops also quickly descended on the area and rounded up more than fifty people and pieces of evidence, including a metal tube that had most likely been used to launch the rockets.

Back in Cubicle Headquarters, Staff Sergeant Gooding's first instinct was to *not* issue a press release but, rather, to step back and allow the Ministry of Interior to handle the media (which it did in due time, with only minimal assistance from the U.S. Army, thankyouverymuch).

However, in the meantime, the Sham Div's chief of staff, noting the extreme gravity of the situation and how the tide of public opinion could quickly turn to a tsunami of unrest with little provocation, had descended from the upper floor of the palace, arriving at the Public Affairs cubicle with his bald pate already agleam with excited sweat.

"P-A-O!" Colonel Belcher barked, causing Chance Gooding to jump a good two inches off his chair and accidentally
type a word in his midday report that looked something like
terr33oris6&.

"Sir! Yes, sir!" Gooding barked back.

Major Filipovich poked his head over the top of his cubicle,
then quickly disappeared, as fast as a turtle sucking its head
back into its shell.

"We need to get something out there right now!"

"You mean the al-Kadhimiya mosque incident, sir?"

"No, the fact that there's now soft-serve ice cream at
the DFAC." Colonel Laser Beams sent two buzzing red lines
through the air, drilling holes into Gooding's forehead. "*Of course*
I mean the mosque bombing, PAO. For God's sake, Sergeant,
get with the game plan."

"Yes, sir," Gooding, chastened, sputtered. "I-I'll have something for you to look at in two minutes, sir." Without being too
obvious, he used the heel of his hand to wipe the sweat from
his forehead, then he did a little *tappity-tap-click* number on his
keyboard and pulled up a press release template labeled "Terrorist Atrocities." The laser beams still boring into the back of
his skull, Gooding knuckled down and started changing names
and dates.

"Very good, I'll wait." The chief rocked back and forth on
his heels. "By the way, where's your boss?"

Gooding didn't miss a beat in his keyboard tap dance.
"Lieutenant Colonel Harkleroad is in a meeting, sir."

"Yeah, I'll bet. Probably in close conference with a slice of
apple pie over at the DFAC, huh?"

Gooding half-turned in his chair and gave the chief what he hoped would be interpreted as a conspiratorial grin and not a sneer of insubordination. "No comment, sir."

(Eustace Harkleroad was, in fact, at that very moment in the Post Exchange buying the last two bags of Cheetos cheese puffs and a six-pack of Diet Coke. He would spend the rest of the day in his office scrolling through SMOG reports and nervously brushing cheese dust from his Desert Camouflage Uniform, where it fell on his lap and belly like an accusatory beacon.)

The chief snapped his fingers and pointed at Gooding's computer screen. "Back to work. We need to stay ahead of this one. Tempest fugit and all that shit."

Peck-peck-peckity-peck-peck.

The chief hovered over Chance's shoulder, jingling the loose change in his pocket and occasionally providing guidance on a word here and a word there, shaping, patting, and molding the press release so that Division Headquarters could eventually issue accurate information in coordination with the Ministry of Interior but keeping the words generic and hazy enough to allow for wiggle room when this all came boomeranging back to them.

When the chief had read the press release and declared it to be good and squared away according to his personal judgment, he stabbed a finger at Gooding's computer screen and barked like a city editor, "Send it!"

Chance sent the press release into cyberspace, feeling like he'd just released a dove into the air, his words now flapping and fluttering their way to newspaper editors' desks all across America. Really, though, the Division's little massaged, 150-word press release was a mere afterthought in the grand scheme of things because, by that point, the wire services had already filed their own stories with no help from Division Public Affairs. Nice try, though.

The chief, grunting and satisfied that he'd just single-handedly managed to turn the tide of public opinion, walked away without another word, fingers still jingling the coins in his pockets.

When he had disappeared up the stairs, Gooding said, "It's safe now, sir. He's gone."

Major Filipovich's cubicle puffed an audible sigh and said in its most contrite cubicle voice, "Okay to finish my game of solitaire now?"

"Have at it, sir."

And so they went about their daily routine. Gooding read e-mails, he saved photos to the archive, and he lingered long enough in the bathroom to read a chapter in his current novel (*Hard Times* by Charles Dickens). The Fobbits carried on, business as usual. They went to lunch and ate their celery sticks and parmesan chicken breast and blueberry cheesecake, they came back to their desks and fell into the torpid slumber of postlunch lethargy, they passed around e-mail jokes, they compiled reports, they copied, they collated, they stapled.

Then the Bad quickly morphed into Worse.

Back at the marketplace near the al-Kadhimiya mosque, teeming with one million devout pilgrims, in an already edgy crowd still cleaning up after the mortar attack, someone yelled, "He's got a bomb! Watch out! He's going to blow himself up!"— Arabic words to the effect of "Fire! Fire! Fire!" in the proverbial crowded theater. Only a few dozen pilgrims actually heard the warning, but that was enough.

Hours later, a grim-faced interior minister would step up to a porcupine bristle of microphones and issue a statement, saying one person had "pointed a finger at another person, claiming he was carrying explosives . . . and that led to the panic."

The beast with eight thousand feet had buzzed and murmured, started churning, then a wave of panic rippled outward from the ground zero of whoever had sounded the alarm (which, according to later reports, in all likelihood was a false alarm planted by a terrorist). The eight thousand feet pivoted on eight thousand heels and stampeded outward like a spreading stain. The huge mob of pilgrims pushed and screamed, shoved and ran, jostled and tripped, the fallen trying to rise but being kicked down by more and more feet fleeing the feared blast zone, those at the edge seeing the surging human tide and turning, walking rapidly at first, then, as they felt the hot breath on their necks, also starting to run and also tripping and falling and lying flat to be stomped and suffocated by all those sandaled feet, the eight thousand sandals now running, running, running with blind panic. Only to find Iraqi police had blocked off roads around the mosque, anticipating attacks on the hundreds of thousands of Shiites who were converging on the capital.

Dust clogged the air, swirled by screams and flailing limbs. The mob funneled onto the bridge, all of them squeezing toward the other end only to find their way choked by an impenetrable Iraqi police checkpoint. People were crushed, the breath pushed from their lungs, their ribs cracked, their organs compressed, the legs and arms and necks of young children snapped like thin, dry twigs.

Then, somewhere along the bridge, the pressure of human bodies grew too great and the railings broke and burst open, spilling body after body into the murky brown Tigris River forty feet below. Women covered in black from head to toe toppled over the edge and hit the water, their long abayas dragging them under with the sound of smacking lips. The current sucked and licked up the young children falling like little drops of flesh from the bridge overhead. And still the bodies pressed outward from the imaginary bomber, the pressure of the crowd at last finding an opening, a relief valve. Hundreds of bodies were jettisoned out of the break in the railing to the dirty, roiled water below.

Back among the palace's air-conditioned cubicles, all laughter came to an abrupt halt as the SMOG speakers delivered the grim news.

CNN started reporting wildly exaggerated figures of six hundred dead, then after just one commercial break, it climbed to 650 dead. Apparently, they'd heard from someone at the scene who said they heard someone had heard on *Al Jazeera* that Iraqi police were handing out those figures.

Other reports filtered in, saying fifty people eating at the mosque had been sickened and killed by rat poison. Gooding and Filipovich drifted over and watched al-Huriya television broadcasts. They were joined by Lieutenant Colonel Harkleroad, who had nervously emerged from hibernation, his fingertips glowing with neon-orange cheese dust. They pointedly ignored him as he stood behind them and coughed softly every time a new death tally scrolled across the screen.

One of the Iraqi generals came on and said not to believe any of the numbers that were being reported. However, no matter what anyone said, it was plain to see there were lots and lots of dead—too many corpses for such a non-IED incident. No one knew if there had even been a suicide bomber in the first place. At that point, it didn't matter.

An hour later, the number crunchers from G-2 came up on SMOG and announced that more people had died in the past half an hour than in all of the previous month.

It was the shout that killed, the words that devastated more than any shrapnel or flames could ever do.

The Fobbits, watching from their sterile distance, struggled to make sense of it. They tried to separate truth from fiction, rumor from confirmed reports. Sham Div sent teams of military police to neighborhood hospitals and the mosque to count bodies and report back as soon as possible.

Chance stared at the TV screens. *Al-Arabiya* TV was showing footage from the scene. Bodies were stacked like cordwood along the pavement. Some were covered with sheets, some were draped in tarps of gold foil (perhaps some building material dug out of the trash nearby). When they ran out of materials to use, mourners just pulled shirts up over the dead faces. Still, as the camera panned along the sidewalk morgue, the breeze lifted the corners of the blankets and the gold foil and the dead looked at Gooding through the camera—the open mouths with their teeth dirtied by river water, the rolled-back eyes, the knitted brows, the look of confusion. A young boy in a T-shirt, flies walking across his eyeballs, reached out his arms for his mother, her face up on the bridge rapidly receding from his field of vision. The camera panned. The buckled limbs, the splayed feet, the hundreds and hundreds of shapeless mounds beneath the sheets: it was almost too much for Gooding to bear.

He watched the still living walk among the newly dead, lifting the corners of blankets, taking a fast peek, then moving on to the next body. Every so often, a woman in black collapsed and started wailing, rocking back and forth over the news she didn't want confirmed—the "Yes, it's me" face of her sister, her mother, her husband, her child. One woman fainted completely away and several men rushed up to splash water on her face. The water was carried in plastic bags, as if they'd just come from a pet store with a few goldfish. They splashed the cold, clear water on the woman and picked her up by the still-limp arms and pulled her into the shade. One of the men yelled and waved to an ambulance crew. Two stretchers came—one for the woman, one for the dead body she'd just identified. They were both carried away, the stretcher bearers picking their way carefully through the miles of bodies that had been fished out of the Tigris and dumped along the road.

In time, the crowds dissipated, leaving the bridge to bear its sorrow alone—the span of pavement littered with trash, handbags, and the empty sandals of the dead.

Gooding went to his computer and typed his longest diary entry since he'd arrived in Iraq.

That night, when he returned to his hooch, he let his battle-rattle gear thump to the floor. He sat on his bed and stared at nothing for a full five minutes. Then, not knowing what else to do, he picked a DVD out of his collection and inserted it into his computer. *It's a Wonderful Life*.

2 5

SHRINKLE

Abe was in the PX trying to decide between Doritos and Funyuns when three of his former soldiers walked in, boasting loudly about how this was their first day off in three weeks and, *by fuck,* they were gonna get them some pogey bait before all the fuckin' Fobbits emptied the shelves. They smelled of sweat, unwashed uniforms, and, if one strained hard enough, the undermusk of blood that always reminded Abe of sniffing warm pennies.

He ducked to a crouch—down to the level of the Ruffles potato chips—so he wouldn't be seen by Lumley, Zeildorf, and Miller. Abe was wearing his now-standard work uniform: shorts and a T-shirt. He wasn't even wearing a helmet, let alone a hat. These days, he walked around the FOB as bare-headed as any KBR contractor. Rather than a 9mm pistol, he was now made to carry an M16 rifle like a lowly enlisted Fobbit. Shrinkle cowered in the aisle, his head crinkling against the Ruffles as he listened to the Bravo Company soldiers make their way through the PX, their smell and swagger clearing a path of Fobbits before them.

They were now two aisles away from Abe, browsing through the PX's pathetically small DVD section.

Miller—the die-hard movie geek of the platoon—was rhapsodizing about the History of Breasts in the Cinema. The PX was crowded with Fobbits taking a long lunch hour, but that didn't stop Miller from proclaiming, loud as a bullhorn, the merits of big-screen sweater meat: Jennifer Connelly in *The Hot Spot*. Demi Moore in *Striptease*. Julie Andrews in *S.O.B.* (now, *there* was a surprise! Mary Fucking Poppins ripping off her blouse and popping right out into your face, even if it *was* only for two seconds). Kim Basinger in *9½ Weeks*.

Zeildorf said, "What about Holly Wood Hills?"

"*Who?*" Miller asked.

"Holly Wood Hills. You know—*Sperms of Endearment, Glad He Ate Her, Lawrence of a Labia*. Any of those ring a bell?"

"I'm not talking porn here, Zeildorf. Porn is completely out of the question, off the table, man. This is strictly mainstream milk muffins." He paused and held up his counting fingers. "Now, where was I? Kim Basinger, *Nine and a Half Fucking Weeks* . . . Erika Eleniak popping out of the cake in *Under Siege* . . ."

Lumley piped up: "Don't forget about whatzername—Miss Tit-a-licious—Rosalee Somebody-or-Other—who was in *Up the Wazoo* and then the sequel, *Out the Wazoo*."

"Hell, *yeah*. Classic eighties teen sex comedy," Miller said. "My mother couldn't figure out why I was always washing my bedsheets after I saw that on HBO."

They fell silent as they browsed through the DVDs in the PX. Abe low-crawled through the aisles, trying to make it to the front entrance before they spotted him.

"Shit," he heard Zeildorf say. "Nothing but Disney and Adam Sandler."

"Well, what'd you expect?" Lumley said. "A boxed set of *Little Whorehouse on the Prairie?*"

"I still say we're wasting our time here," Miller said. "We should go to Hajji Mart for the bootlegs."

"All right, then," Lumley said. "Stop talking about it. Let's go do it."

They headed for the door but were stopped by the sight of their former commander crawling on his knees and elbows across the floor near the cash registers.

At that same moment, Abe Shrinkle also came up short as he ran into a pair of shoes, which were attached to a stout pair of legs in plaid-checked pants, above which were a pair of wide hips cinched with a belt, upon which were knuckled two fists on either side, all of which was topped by a swollen red face that loomed over Abe like a Macy's Thanksgiving Day Parade balloon. It was the PX store manager and he seemed a little pissed to find a customer low-crawling to the exit.

"Excuse me, sir," he said in a God-to-Moses voice, "but I'll take that from you now, if you don't mind."

Abe raised his head. "Huh?"

"The merchandise." The manager pointed at Abe's chest where he cradled a bag of potato chips in his arms. "Hand it over, sir."

What?! How did that *get there?* Abe got to his feet with a loud bag crinkle and a crunching-to-crumbs of the merchandise. "Allow me to explain . . ."

The store manager's face crimsoned like a thermometer.

"I'm sure there's a very good one and I'm sure the MPs will love to hear it."

"You see, I—" Abe faltered when he looked over at the front doors and saw Lumley, Zeildorf, and Miller watching him.

"C'mon guys," Lumley said. "Let's get out of here." They left, shaking their heads.

At that moment, Abe felt like someone had just taken a shit in his helmet.

Eight hours later—after convincing the manager, the two MPs, and, ultimately, the division Provost Marshal that he was not a common thief but, rather, an incompetent galoof who'd made an innocent goof—Abe sat on the bed in his hooch, the Greatest Hits of his care-package letters spread across his lap.

He'd just finished taking inventory of this week's care packages—macaroni and cheese (eleven boxes), *Hot Rod* magazine, ChapStick (five tubes), tuna fish (twenty-two cans), shampoo (six bottles—two for dry scalps), playing cards (four decks), a pair of slippers, newspapers from small towns in Indiana (seven issues, three missing the sports section), beef jerky, two packages of plaid boxers, Lifesavers (eighteen rolls), pencils (sixty-eight), pens (one hundred and twelve), a bottle of soap bubbles, nail clippers, ramen noodles, peanut butter, two dozen toothbrushes, toothpaste (one dozen tubes), crossword puzzles, a handheld fan, a box of Cheez-Its carefully blanketed in Bubble Wrap, a Three Stooges DVD, and a whoopee cushion.

Of the letters and postcards he'd received, there were messages from a fourth-grade class written in inch-high block letters ("I am studying to be a ninja when I grow up. As soon as I gradjuate from school, I will come over there and help you kick some Iraqi butt!"), a Sunday-service bulletin and a post-card from a church in Arizona ("We here at Wayfield Baptist appreciate your supreme sacrifice as you go about the business of ridding the world of evil"), and the latest in what had become a weekly correspondence from Mrs. Norma Tingledecker of Laramie, Wyoming:

My dearest Abe,

I pray this finds you alive and as happy as can be over there in the desert. I think of you often, especially when I gaze up into the cerulean blue sky, which arcs from horizon to horizon and I wonder if you, too, are looking up at that cerulean sky and thinking of me. Of course, in your case, there is most likely a terrorist rocket following the arc of the sky, carrying a payload of death for another group of soldiers. Am I right?

It's been a hectic close to summer here on the prairie, with the tragic crash of a tour bus of seniors on their way to Las Vegas, a hiker lost in the Snowy Range who was eventu-ally eaten by a grizzly, and the shocking revelation by one of our most long-standing school board members that he/she is a transvestite. On the home front, Ray insists on remaining married to me, which is a tragedy in and of itself. But none of this comes close to describing what you and your men are going through Over There [Abe hadn't had the heart to tell her of his demotion to towel duty].

You are doing the indescribable, the job no one else wants to do—leastwise men like Ray. The United States could learn a thing or three from what you are doing, my dear

Abe. Each year, we spiral ever downward into economic and moral decline. We're a ship without a rudder, an airplane without a compass. As a country, we need to rise to the occasion to get the job done at the level of soldiers like you who are getting it done in Iraq and Afghanistan. For this we can only thank you for setting the example, showing us the way to move forward to our goal of reclaiming our place as the #1 Nation.

Honor, fidelity, sacrifice.

As for Ray, the only sacrifice he'll ever know is having to settle for Schlitz when they run out of Coors at the Gas-n-Go. The no-good bastard. He's half the man you are. No, that's giving him too much credit. He's no better than the toenail on your left foot (no offense to your toenail). If only . . .

Ah, if only wishes were horses, you and I would have a herd of them. And, if my dreams ever came true, we'd be watching them graze at pasture as we sat on the front porch of our cabin in the Snowies, sipping Chablis and watching the blaze of sunset in our cerulean sky.

Ever yours,

Norma

P.S. I hope it doesn't shock or upset you to know that as I've been composing this letter I reached under the waistband of my sweatpants to touch myself.

After reading the letter, Abe had a bit of patriotic mist filming his eyes (and, truth be told, a bit of an erection tenting his khaki shorts), so he ended the day with a good cry and a repeat viewing of *Rambo III*. This helped erase the day's lousy turn of events.

His men may be ashamed of him, he may be temporarily barred from shopping at the PX, and he may even be a complete fuck-up at running a fitness center. But at least he had the camaraderie of the Aussie pool and the love of a distant, unmet woman, Mrs. Norma Tingledecker.

That night, Shrinkle dreamed of a pool, blue as the Caribbean, full of floating bare breasts. He also dreamed of wine and horses, wind-snapped flags and green parade fields, Rambo and Afghans. In his sleep thoughts, he was filled with might and power, bursting with muscles and rage. Sometime in the middle of the night, he slur-mumbled, "I'm your worst nightmare, Iraq."

26

GOODING

On the 283rd day of his deployment, Staff Sergeant Chance Gooding Jr. nearly bled to death. It came at the tail end of a chain of events that was invisible to the naked eye—it began with seasonal winds and finished with Gooding staring at a spreading crimson puddle beneath his feet, thinking to himself, "This is *not* how it was supposed to end."

For several days, all of FOB Triumph had suffered from a collective misery.

Most of the Americans had not read deep enough into their Iraq Orientation Welcome Packets—or, if they had, they hadn't retained it—to know there is a fifth season that hits the Middle East each summer with the kind of fury only a pissed-off Mother Nature can muster. The locals called the storms simoom, or "poison wind." When the wind reaches sustained speeds of fifteen knots, walls of dust five thousand feet high advance across the desert and dry lake beds, gathering microparticles of grit and silt as they boil across the landscape. The storms clog engines, cut visibility to a few feet, and line nostrils and lungs with something that feels like baby powder.

Chance Gooding Jr. was sitting on the edge of his bed reading *Don Quixote* when he felt the urge to start clearing his throat. Then he noticed it was getting harder to breathe, as if the air was thickening. He got up and opened his door. He was met with a wall of orange-brown air. It was a dust blizzard.

He couldn't see his neighbor's trailer fifteen feet away. At some point while he had been deep in Cervantes, the wind had kicked up, stirring all the talcum-powder dirt around Baghdad. Now it was filtering through the vents in Gooding's air-conditioning and laying a fine grit over everything in the room, starting with his respiratory system. He turned off his air conditioner and tried to go to sleep. But he woke two hours later, burning with the heavy air; each particle of dust was an ember, each breath was a suck of stifle. In the morning, his throat was raspy and there were mucus flakes in the hollows of his eyes.

He wasn't the only one to suffer through the simoom. Plenty of other Fobbits spent the day choking, complaining, and walking with an exaggerated forward hunch. By lunchtime, the air was hot and thick with turmoiled dust. The sky turned orange as cream of tomato soup.

Major Flip Filipovich had been in the fitness center when the simoom hit, the wind howling and scraping across the Quonset hut's metal curve. The guy who ran the fitness center —a real prick who hardly ever spoke to Filipovich—dashed around the room, stuffing towels into the gaps between walls and floor, saying in a contrived British accent, "Oh, bloody hell, bloody hell!"

When Flip emerged from the moist, stenchy interior, his skin slicked from fifty minutes of intense carb burning on the treadmill, he had a nasty surprise. He was instantly coated with the airborne dust, his chocolate skin turning orange in a matter of a minute. He wasn't wearing goggles so he was forced to put an arm in front of his face as he made his way back to his hooch, looking for all the world like goddamn Laura Ingalls Wilder in goddamn *Little House on the Fucking Prairie* during a blizzard. He was not happy, not in the least fucking little bit. Now he'd have to shower all over again before reporting for his shift at Headquarters. And no guarantee he wouldn't get caked with orange again during the short walk between his hooch and the palace.

Two days after the start of the simoom, Chance Gooding's sand-wracked throat and serial sneezes had turned to the flu and then one day he woke up with a cramped stomach and waves of nausea whirling through his body. He simultaneously gritted his teeth to keep the rising bile *down* and clenched his buttocks to keep the descending liquidity of his shit sucked *up*.

He knew exactly what had happened. The previous day, he'd come back from a morning run around Z Lake and, gasping strings of saliva, had headed straight for the water distribution point where the Twees handed out bottles of water from the depths of their chilled trailer, which was crusted with thick frost.

"You wanting water, yes?" asked the young brown man (Filipino? Pakistani?) standing in the frozen doorway.

"Yes," Gooding panted.

"You wait. I get."

Seconds later, the Twee came back out, holding a bottle by its screw cap between his begrimed fingers. Gooding was too winded and drained from the run and the flu to care about this lack of hygiene. As he grabbed the bottle and unscrewed the cap for a series of throat-pounding gulps, he was also too endorphin-delirious to realize the cap had not been sealed and was most likely a reused bottle that the pecan-colored Twee—another ambitious young entrepreneur forced to take cost-cutting measures where he could—had refilled with water from a garden hose.

Gooding hobbled back to his trailer, wrote a few lines in his diary concerning the mists rising off the lake "which dissipated like Saddam's regime itself," then showered and headed for the palace, where he faced another thirteen hours of keyboard banging and answering Lieutenant Colonel Harkleroad's beck and call.

He didn't make it through the entire thirteen hours, however. His bowels had been clenched by hot, scaly fingers shortly after the morning Battlefield Update Briefing. Gasping and groaning, he rushed down the hallway to the latrine, barely getting his drawers around his ankles and settling his ass on the seat before he released a tooth-grinding torrent of shit into the toilet bowl. For a few seconds, his head went dark and stars prickled his vision. He sat there moaning on the toilet seat for fifteen minutes before he thought it was safe to stand up and leave.

And so it had gone for the rest of the day until he'd been certain there was nothing left inside—but no, wait . . . here it came again!—and he'd walked back down the hall as fast as he could with a clenched asshole, which by now was thoroughly abraded and exhausted by the repeated wiping it had endured throughout the day.

Major Filipovich had been his usual cheery, concerned self: "Fucking A, Sergeant Gooding, you're about the greenest white guy I've ever seen. What's gotten into you? Or, should I say, what's gotten *out* of you?"

"Har, har, sir." Chance swallowed to suppress the bile rising in his throat like a hot thermometer. "Bad water is my guess."

"I told you to stay away from the Twees and their tap water, didn't I?"

"You did, sir."

"Well now you're finding out the hard way." Filipovich grinned and held up his lunch in the Styrofoam container he'd just brought back from the dining facility. "Hey, want a bite to eat?" The sausage link and boiled cabbage were still steaming and entered fully into Chance's nostrils as Filipovich held it out to him.

That's when Gooding completely lost it, grabbing for the garbage can and *hurking* a stringy yellow stream of bile onto a sheaf of discarded press releases and Sig Acts.

Harkleroad sent him home, saying they'd "get by somehow" until Specialist Carnicle came on shift in five hours, and insisted he go on sick call in the morning if he wasn't feeling better.

Fifteen hours later, he was *not* feeling better, no, not at all. His body brought him back awake at 4:30, a full two hours before the medics opened for sick-call patients.

Later, he would type these words into his diary:

> *To write about one's bowels is an embarrassing thing.*
> *But in this case it is necessary, in order to understand*

how I came to shed blood for the first—and hopefully
the last—time here in Iraq. I woke up at 4:30, my body
weakened from having continuously emptied itself for
the last twenty-one hours. At any minute, I expected to
start crapping out my stomach lining since there wasn't
so much as a crumb of food left inside me. Because the
medical aid station didn't open for another two hours, all
I could do was lay there, moaning and writhing. There
might have even been some gnashing of teeth. There was
certainly much cursing of Twees who fill water bottles
from garden hoses. Finally, when it was time, I got dressed
and walked down to the aid station, which was in a trailer
nine rows away. The wind was howling—okay, maybe not
quite howling, but certainly letting out a mournful moan
or two—and visibility was down to fifteen feet. We were
smack dab in the midst of the season of dust storms that
transform our little American enclave into a foreign land-
scape. There was so much dust (and particles of whatever
crap—literally—had been stirred up and carried here
from the city) that the morning sun burned everything a
bright salmon-orange. Baghdad was in full-on Mars mode.
I was forced to walk hunched over (which was okay by my
already sore abdomen) and hold my arm in front of my
face. I felt like an actor in an old MGM movie wander-
ing the desert in search of the Lost Platoon, or maybe he's
chasing some Arab marauders who have made off with
a distressed damsel, and for every two staggering steps
forward he is forced to take one back, and all the time
the actor is thinking to himself that if he can just make it
through this scene, then C. B. DeMille will yell "Cut!"

and the studio grips will turn off those giant fans and
the back lot will return to normal and they can all go to
the studio commissary and have midmorning martinis. I
struggled through the storm and finally made it to the aid
station, worried I might have contracted emphysema en
route.

Gooding, coughing simoom dust, mounted the wooden steps and opened the trailer door to an empty waiting room. This was his first time at the aid station—he prided himself on being the kind of Fobbit who worked so hard he didn't have time to worry about sniffles or coughs—and he was surprised by how cramped and threadbare the doctor's office seemed to be at first glance. A row of plastic orange chairs lined one wall, facing a small table with a computer and a vomit spill of papers and files. On the wall above, there was a dry-erase board that charted patient intake and time of release (blank at this point); in one corner, someone had drawn a daisy with a smiley face and written SHIQUANDA WAS HERE. The place smelled like dried blood on week-old bandages. Also, a little minty. A fluorescent light flickered and buzzed overhead. But that was it, nothing else in this room. Not even a pile of year-old magazines.

"What the hell kind of rinky-dink operation are they running here?" Gooding muttered. Then, overcome by a fresh wave of nausea, he slumped into a nearby seat. His M16 thumped to the ground and he held his head in his hands, waiting for the sickness to pass.

He heard someone come out of a room at the rear of the trailer and walk across the creaking floor.

"Help you, Sar'nt?"

Gooding looked up through the lace of his fingers. It was Specialist Blodgett, a guy he recognized from the support platoon, a medic who also happened to be one of the laziest, fattest slobs in the company. Gooding remembered seeing Blodgett on the monthly "esprit de corps" runs back at Fort Stewart (which he liked to call "spirit of the corpse" runs due to the lack of any real camaraderie generated by jogging six miles in the Georgia heat). Blodgett was always at the back of the pack, barely moving his feet above an Airborne shuffle as the other two hundred members of the company outpaced him down the road. It wasn't until they were back at the field outside company headquarters and the commander was wrapping up his falsely cheerful motivational speech that Blodgett would finally come into view, by this time walking across the field, blowing hard and shaking his thick, reddened head from side to side. He was a medic, for fuck's sake! He should have been one of the healthiest soldiers in the company. Physician, heal thyself!

"Help you?" he repeated, his sausage-y fingers poised with a pen over a clipboard.

"I'm sick," Gooding said.

"Yeah, no shit, Sar'nt. You and every other person who walks through that door."

"But I'm *really* sick."

"Yeah, okay," Blodgett admitted. "Your gills *do* look a little green. Here—" he held out the clipboard "—need you to fill out some basic information then we'll get you triaged, 'kay?"

Gooding nodded and took the clipboard. As he was filling out the intake form, the door banged open with a howl of wind and another soldier stumbled inside, crying out, "Fucking A!

Goddamned wind nearly ripped off my fucking face out there."
He slammed the door shut behind him and unwrapped the
scarf from around his mouth, then announced to the room,
"I'm sick!"

Blodgett called over his shoulder to someone in the back
room, "Hey, it looks like we got us an epidemic on our hands—
now there's *two* people out here who say they're sick. Oh, me,
oh, my! Whatever will we do?"

A voice sounding thick and sore from swallowing too much
windborne dust came from the back room: "Cut the comedy,
Blodgett. Just get them triaged and bring them back here."

"Roger, sir." Blodgett rolled his eyes and stage-whispered
to Gooding and the other soldier, "Doc's in a bad mood today.
I'd watch out if I were you."

Gooding returned the clipboard. "Here. This all you need?"

Blodgett glanced over the intake form. "Looks good enough
to me. We'll make up the rest as we go along." He turned to the
other soldier. "Have a seat and fill this out. We'll get to you when
we get to you, after we get through with Sarge here."

"Fine by me," the soldier said. "I got nothing to do and
plenty of time to do it in." He sat and started humming to
himself, tapping his fingers against the barrel of his M16,
which he still wore in a sling around his neck. His gills did
not look green and he seemed almost happy to be here at the
aid station. Fucking malingerer, Gooding thought, swallowing
another gob of bile.

"C'mon back, Sar'nt," Blodgett said, leading him to a larger
room at the back of the trailer. "Step into my laboratory—
mwuhahaha," the medic said in a lame attempt at a mad-scientist
imitation. His jowls quivered with laughter.

Blodgett sat at a computer and started copying the information off the clipboard, punctuating it every so often with *hmm* or *mm-hmmm*. Gooding took a seat next to the desk because his knees had turned to jelly. Blodgett told him to remove his DCU shirt, then wheeled over a blood-pressure machine on a long silver pole. A cuff went on Gooding's biceps and a thermometer was jabbed into his mouth. Blodgett watched the digital numbers on the machine, listening to the accelerating short blips, then frowned when they eventually settled and gave a long beep. "Hmmm. Okay, now I want you to stand up and we'll take your vitals from that position, too."

"Why?"

"We like to see how your blood migrates through your system. Systolic and asystolic, and so on, so forth."

It sounded like bullshit to Gooding but he stood anyway, trying his best to hide the tremble in his knees.

When the machine beeped again, Blodgett was still frowning. "Hmm. Okay, wait here and I'll go get Doc Claspill."

Apparently, Gooding's blood wasn't doing so well on its migration.

Blodgett returned, followed by Captain Claspill, a sleepy-looking man with a shock of tousled black hair sticking up off his head—as if the follicles themselves were still upset and angry at being pulled off the pillow an hour ago. When he spoke, there was sand in his voice. "Okay, let's see what we've got here." He took the clipboard from Blodgett, read what was on the computer screen, then went back and forth from clipboard to monitor for nearly a minute before he looked at Gooding sitting there with his drained face and throbbing stomach.

"All right," he croaked. "What I'm gonna need you to do now, Staff Sergeant Gooding, is remove your boots, loosen your belt, then hike yourself up onto this bed over here." He patted a cot—dust puffing up from beneath his fingers—and gave Gooding a wan smile. "You do that while I take a short break, then we'll see what's going on inside you, hmm?"

He left the room and Blodgett smirked at Gooding, holding two fingers to his lips then blowing out a puff of invisible cigarette smoke. "Doc's got his bad habits."

"I see."

"Says it opens up his blood vessels, helps him focus and concentrate."

"I'm not about to stop him." Gooding started unlacing his boots.

"Anyway," Blodgett said. "Just do what doc says and I'll be back after I go see what's ailing this other dude."

Gooding unbuckled his belt, then looked at the cot. It was covered with a stained wool blanket—Army-issue green—and sagged in the middle. At one end was a large, embroidered pillow with the silhouette of a grizzly walking across it—probably hand stitched by somebody's mother and sent over here to Iraq. Before he lowered himself into the sinkhole of the cot, Gooding wondered how many other unwashed heads had touched this grizzly pillow in the past week. Sterility appeared to be an afterthought here in the aid station.

He lay there for several minutes, eyes closed and hands folded across his chest like he was in a coffin, while the doctor sucked his way through a cigarette out back in the Iraqi wind and Blodgett interrogated the other sick-call patient in the outer room. Gooding closed his eyes, letting the rise and fall of voices match the rhythm of his lungs. First, he thought of his ex-wife, Yolanda, and wondered who might be screwing her even as he lay here dying in Baghdad. Then he thought about his desk in the palace and pictured a snowstorm of paperwork—Sig Acts and drafts of press releases—falling around his computer and burying it in deep white drifts. Then he thought about the disgraced captain Shrinkle and wondered what had happened to him. No doubt shipped home to a desk job back at Fort Stewart. Then, thinking about Shrinkle's hand grenade blowing up the truck drifted his thoughts to a suicide-bomb attack that had ripped through a bus terminal near the Green Zone last week. Gooding hadn't heard the blast from where he worked at his desk in the palace, but he'd read about it online like it was a dispatch from a war he was watching through opera glasses. One line in that news story, however, had brought it rushing close enough to punch him in the heart: *Ahmed Mahjoud returned to the blast site to search for his brother's head after identifying his headless body at a hospital morgue by the belt he was wearing.*

Gooding's bowels shifted and he clamped down. At the same time, a fresh wave of sour bile rolled through his stomach and threatened to blurp up his esophagus. He swallowed and pushed away the suicide bomber's head with its singed, bulging eyes.

The stink of cigarettes was sharp in his nostrils. Gooding opened his eyes to find Captain Claspill leaning over him, staring at him through those heavy-lidded eyes with what looked like boredom.

"You back with us now?"

"Yes, sir. Just closed my eyes for a second and I guess I drifted away."

"Hey, don't make me jealous. You don't want to know how long it'll be till I feel a pillow again. Damn double shifts." He blew out through his nose and the ghost of smoke was just as strong and sharp. He stood quickly, clapping his hands on his knees. "Well, okay. Let's see what's going on inside you."

Claspill pulled a stethoscope from his pocket, blew tar and nicotine on the metal disk for nearly a minute, and said, "Just one of the complimentary services we offer here at the aid station—no cold metal on skin."

"I appreciate that."

"Now just relax and give me three deep breaths and hold it on the third one." He lifted Gooding's T-shirt and placed the stethoscope in the center of his belly. Gooding breathed, breathed, breathed, held . . . and Claspill gasped as he listened to what was migrating through Gooding's innards. "Whoa!"

"What is it, doc?"

"I'm listening for normal digestive sounds but I'm not hearing any. The average person's guts are making noise all the time—little pings back and forth. Normally, it sounds like Rice Krispies. Yours, however, sounds like a NASCAR race in there. What've you been eating?"

Gooding gave him a rundown of the previous two days' menu, leaving out the episode of the tainted water bottle. He was too embarrassed to admit he'd almost been killed by a contract employee, a grinning little Pakistani/Filipino who, in the end, probably meant him no harm.

Claspill moved the stethoscope back and forth across Gooding's stomach, giving him breathing instructions, and continuing to frown. Eventually, he straightened, rubbed his eyes, and said, "Let's start you off with an IV. You're dehydrated, and we need to get fluids in you. Then I'm gonna prescribe some Imodium—just for shits and giggles. Pun intended."

Gooding thought, *Hardee-har-har. Excuse me if I don't laugh, doc, but I'm using all my muscles to keep my anus locked up tight.*

"You just wait here and I'll go tell Blodgett to start that IV. We'll get you fixed up and on your way in no time."

Gooding closed his eyes and thought about the drifts of paperwork and the headless bodies waiting for him back in the palace.

Blodgett was back with an armload of needles and clear plastic bags and a bedpan. "Doc says we gotta fill you with fluids, huh?"

Gooding shrugged weakly.

Blodgett organized his materials on a tray, put a paper pad under Gooding's arm, wrapped a tourniquet around his biceps, then held up a needle that glistened in the flickering fluorescent light. "Hope you aren't afraid of needles."

"I hate them, actually." Gooding turned his head away and put his mind on Pleasant Things: vanilla-scented candles, a Dickens novel, Vivaldi's concertos.

Blodgett smacked Gooding's forearm with two fingers, pulled the skin tight, then stabbed the needle into a vein. He held it there with one hand while he tore off a piece of tape with his teeth. Once the needle was secured in place, Blodgett reached for a rubber tube but had some trouble maneuvering it with his fat fingers. "I hate these damn screw-on caps," he grumbled. "They used to have 'em so they just slipped on." As he tried to attach the IV, Gooding could feel the needle move back and forth, carving out pieces of his vein beneath the skin.

Blodgett panted, sweated, and cursed the pharmaceutical makers of the IV tube. The needle sliced back and forth through Gooding's epidermis like a scythe harvesting a wheat field. For a minute, the new pain took his mind off his nausea and loosening bowels.

Gooding felt a gush of wet warmth across his forearm.

"Well, shit!" Blodgett cried.

Gooding didn't want to look. Feeling it was bad enough.

"Sorry about that, Sar'nt. Damn! Real sorry." Blodgett's breath whistled back and forth across his teeth. Then he grunted as the IV tube made a solid connection with the needle. "There. Success at last." He turned a little plastic wheel near the IV bag and Gooding felt something like cool spring water running uphill along his arm.

Still apologizing, Blodgett secured the needle with more tape, then wiped away the blood with gauze soaked in rubbing alcohol. "That oughta hold you for a while, Sar'nt. I gotta go man the front desk—it's almost rush hour here at the aid station—so I'll leave you to drink your IV cocktail in peace." He rose with a grunt, then left the room.

Gooding stared at the four walls. There were posters showing various views of the human body—both exterior and cutaway, exposing networks of veins and skeletal structures. They had titles like "What You Should Know About HIV and AIDS," "What You Should Know About Hypertension," "What You Should Know About Breast Cancer." He chose to stare at that last poster for quite some time.

Then his bladder started to throb.

"Hey, Blodgett!"

The medic poked his head into the room. "What's up, Sar'nt?"

"I gotta pee."

"Okay. Just gimme a minute."

"No, I mean I really gotta *pee!*"

"All right, all right. Hold your horses." He said something to the patients in the waiting room, then came and helped Gooding to stand and walked him by the elbow to the one-seater latrine. Inside with the door closed, Gooding groaned and sighed as he released an IV bag's worth of white piss.

Blodgett was waiting for him outside the latrine. "Talk about your racehorses."

They walked back to the cot, Gooding walking straighter now that his bladder had been unkinked.

"How you feeling, Sar'nt?"

"Better, actually. Doesn't feel like I have a nest of snakes in my guts anymore."

"Okay, whatever," Blodgett said. "I'll go get doc and see if we can unhook you."

He came back with Claspill, who then breath-warmed the stethoscope again and listened to Gooding's belly. Apparently, the NASCAR race had simmered down to a few low-speed laps around the track. "I'd say the IV's done its work." Captain Claspill started to yawn, then shrugged it off. He turned his sleepy gaze to Blodgett and ordered him to remove the IV, patch Gooding up, then send him on his way with two bottles of Imodium. "Remember," he said, placing his hand on Gooding's shoulder, "the word for the day is *water*. I'd recommend at least one bottle every three hours. Not enough to drown you but we've gotta keep you fluid-filled. Stop at the Twee trailer on your way back to your hooch and grab a few bottles."

Gooding nodded weakly, greenly, thinking to himself, *No fucking way*.

"If you still have the shits tomorrow, come back and see me. This isn't something to mess around with, okay?"

"Okay, sure, doc."

"Good enough, then." Claspill squeezed Gooding's shoulder, then left the room.

Blodgett shook his head as he bent to withdraw the needle. "I don't know how you did it, Sar'nt, but you got on the doc's good side this morning. Good thing, too. You should see him most days. Normally, he just prescribes Motrin and kicks them out the door, no matter what they come in here bitching about."

"That's comforting to know," Gooding said.

"Yeah, but that's really all most of these Fobbits need anyway. We never get any of the good stuff like shrapnel wounds or burns or shit like that. It's all 'Oh my, oh my, I've got a headache,' or guys who pig out at the DFAC then come in here complaining about how they can't stop shitting. And I have to tell them, 'Yeah, no shit, Sherlock!'" Blodgett released a few more jowl-quivering *har-har-hars*.

Gooding smiled to humor him.

Blodgett taped a cotton ball to Gooding's forearm, then told him he could put his DCU shirt back on. Blodgett went out to get the Imodium.

Gooding stood and reached for his shirt. He felt a liquid loosening in the crook of his arm, and then blood was flowing down to his wrist and spattering on the floor. He looked down and found himself in the middle of a Wes Craven movie.

"Blodgett! Help!"

The chubby medic rushed in, practically slipped in the blood, and said, "Oh, shit! Oh, fuck!" He stood there wobbling with nervous uncertainty while a thin stream of blood jetted in pulsing squirts from Gooding's arm. "Doc! Doc, *Doc*!"

Gooding slumped back onto the cot, woozy and tingling.

Claspill ran in, also squeak-slipping in the growing puddle of blood and shouted for Blodgett to get some gloves and clean up the goddamn mess. Claspill tiptoed through the blood, grabbed Gooding's arm, and centered a gauze pad over the hole that had been excavated by the IV needle. He held Gooding in that vise grip for about two minutes. His eyes were bright and shiny now. At last, he had a bona fide patient with bona fide blood in his aid station.

"You doing okay, Sar'nt?"

"I see a light at the end of a dark tunnel," Gooding moaned, his head starting to float away. "I'm heading for the light."

"Hey, we don't allow drama queens in here," Claspill said with a grim smile. "Snap out of it. You're gonna pull through this."

Gooding groaned again, licking his dry, suddenly cold lips.

Blodgett came back in and began splashing hydrogen peroxide on the floor at Gooding's feet. He grinned and said, "I like to watch it fizz."

The three of them looked at the blood turning orange and bubbling into a foam. Gooding had never seen so much of his blood in one place at one time. He felt himself drifting away into a faint.

"Come on, Sarge," Claspill said brusquely. "You're not gonna die. But I will tell you that this arm here is gonna bruise like hell." He pressed harder against the gauze. His fingers were wet and sticky with blood. With his other hand, he grabbed another gauze pad and did a quick exchange. This time, the blood was just a seep, like oil bubbling up from the ground, and not a full-blown geyser.

Gooding's head cleared and he started to breathe easier. Thoughts of having to get a prosthetic arm began to evaporate. The cold tingling remained in his fingers but now he was certain he was going to make it. He *was* going to pull through this okay.

Claspill lifted the gauze and took another look. Gooding's blood was still welling and running down his arm and there was a sizable hole in the skin. The blood, however, seemed to be slowing; certainly, it was no longer spurting like a faulty fountain.

"Looks like the clotting is taking effect," Claspill said. He put fresh gauze on the wound, then taped it securely around Gooding's elbow. "We can give you another IV—"

Gooding shook his head insistently.

"—or you could self-medicate with the Imodium and lots of water like I said before."

"I'll take option B," Gooding said.

"Okay, then," Captain Claspill said, wiping his fingers. "Too bad about the uniform, huh?"

Staff Sergeant Chance Gooding looked down and saw the dark-red stain that ran the entire length of his left thigh. Coin-sized drops of blood had also hit his boots.

But that was okay by Gooding. When he returned to Georgia, maybe he could wear the uniform into the local American Legion and it would get him a few free beers from all the old battle-scarred veterans sitting at the bar. "Hey, look who's here," they'd say. "Rambo from Iraq."

And that was the best a Fobbit could hope for, wasn't it?

27

SHRINKLE

Abe Shrinkle floated on his back in the Australian pool. The sun baked his skin but he couldn't feel a thing. He was splayed across a black inner tube given to him by Glennice, one of the busty, blonde Australian sergeants he'd come to know quite well over the past two months. Bo, the captain who'd first welcomed him to the Aussie side of the FOB, had been tossing Abe cold Foster's for the past hour and he'd been catching them one-handed, to the cheers and whistles of the others around the pool.

The Aussie pool had been put off-limits by the commanding general but that didn't stop Abe. All pools on FOB Triumph, in fact, were verboten, with the exception of an MWR-run "splash park" that consisted of an ankle-deep wading pool, a large red mushroom that gave off a shower of tepid mist, and a turtle that squirted water the color and warmth of urine from its mouth.

Thanks to the CG's edict (General Order Number Five), on this late September afternoon, there were no other Americans lounging on towels spread across the concrete or paddling laps in the minty-cool water. So Abe was safe. Of course, in the eyes of the Aussies, there were no Americans here at all—just the Down Unders and their friend from the British Museum, a likable enough bloke who liked to drone on ad nauseam about pottery shards.

Abe wondered how much longer he could keep it up. It wasn't the accent he was worried about—it was quavery and came and went at random, but he'd watched enough movies to get most of it right. It was all the talk of archaeology and preservation that had him concerned about his ruse. Since he'd started rolling down the tracks on this train with no brakes, he'd been reading as much as he could about ancient Mesopotamia, leafing through *Western Archaeology Quarterly* during the slow hours at the fitness center. He was now a semiexpert on the Hanging Gardens of Babylon, the forty-five-day reign of Xerxes II, and the proven success of capillary gas chromatography in dating jug fragments. Ah, if only Lieutenant Colonel Vic Duret could see him now! He'd shit his pants—first out of anger, then jealousy. Abe, who had downed too many cold Foster's on this particular hot autumn afternoon, could hear him now: "I didn't put my ass on the line for that goddamn twinkle toes, pull his bacon fat out of the fire, and cut deals all the way up to Corps only to have him flaunt it in my face with this unauthorized rest and relaxation."

Well, Abe was sorry, but Vic Duret and the rest of Task Force Baghdad didn't know what they were missing when they adhered to General Order Number Five—and Numbers One through Four, for that matter. War was hell, but that didn't mean it had to be a living hell for those who fought it. Abe was starting to rethink his views on good order and discipline.

He wasn't about to tell anyone about his secret oasis, though. This pool was his and his alone. Call it his just deserts for doing a Fred Astaire tap dance away from the firing squad. He deserved his goddamn R&R after the wringer the goddamn Army had tried to put him through. Maybe it was just the beer talking at this point but Abe was swollen with a feeling of entitlement.

He popped open another can of Foster's, reveling in the *sssnick* and that first cool-bitter slide of the beer across his tongue. *Real* beer, not the near-beer of FOB Triumph's dining facility. Oh, if his men could see him now—floating on the water and drifting away on sun-toasted inebriation! There were times he wondered if torching that Local National to death underneath the fuel truck might not have been the best thing to happen to him. "Him" meaning Abe, of course. Not the barbecued Iraqi.

Richard Belmouth, née Abe Shrinkle, took a fresh swig of Foster's and pushed himself away from the wreckage that lay behind him. Now was not the time to think of death and destruction. Now was not the time to dwell on mistakes and irrevocable errors—the fuckups that could not be unfucked. No, now it was his duty to concentrate on archaeology and excavating sites with a toothbrush and dental tools here in the "cradle of civilization."

I don't know, he thought, *maybe things just have a way of working themselves out. Maybe it was hajji's time to go and my time to realize I wasn't cut out for this Army life. Maybe I should think about going back to school for archaeology when I get back to the States. Jolly good notion that, eh, guv'nor?*

His head spun with ideas. His inner tube spun in the deep end of the pool.

One of the brunette Australian lieutenants sat up and waved at him. Then, because she was so top-loaded, one side of her bikini failed in its mission and a healthy one-eyed breast popped out to say hello. The lieutenant looked down, laughed, then just left it there for Abe and the others to enjoy. She, too, received a round of cheers and whistles.

Abe balanced the Foster's on his lap and forced himself to concentrate on words like "Ur," "Babylon," "Kabala," and "Nineveh."

The nipple was winking at him. "Hellooo, Abe!"

Cuneiform. Mosaics. Chromatography.

This was the life.

"Oy, Belmouth! Is that a Foster's in your lap or are you just happy to see us?" Gales of laughter cascaded as Abe paddled to the center of the pool.

"Jolly good!" he shouted back to Bo.

He was the only one floating out here now, lazily spinning on his inner tube. The others stood around the concrete walkway toweling off and gabbing about how a company of Yank engineers were taking their bloody sweet time finishing a school in Mosul. The brunette's boob was still bobbing out there for all to see.

Mesopotamia. Mes. O. Po. Tamia. Hanging Gardens of Babylon. Bab. Y. Lon.

The water was cool as mint underneath his ass and sloshed delicately up his swim trunks to his nether region.

The nipple-eye caught Abe's eye once more. *Wink-wink, nudge-nudge.*

Sure, Abe Shrinkle thought of his fellow Americans—the ones out there on patrol every day, encased in Kevlar, the weight

of the flak vests pulling down on their shoulders like a yoke;
the ones out there cocking back their leg and kicking down the
doors of suspected bomb makers only to find a mother and her
three children huddled in the corner, even the drapery of her
black abaya fluttery with fear; the ones riding dusty mile after
dusty mile down the Sadr City streets, scanning the rooftops,
the doorways, the heart-stopping piles of trash; the ones who
came back to Triumph each night, shucking their vests and
helmets and collapsing on their cots, too tired to even lift a
thumb for a quick round of Xbox. Yes, Abe still let them parade
through his conscience but he could do nothing more than let
them trudge along on their funereal march, bass drum beating a somber tempo and the trumpets and tuba bleating in a
minor key. He could do nothing more than that, could he? He'd
been fired—sacked, as Richard Belmouth would say—and he
was no longer part of this war. Duret had removed him from
the action, snatched him out of harm's way, and, though his
men—his *former* men—still chewed at Abe's guilty conscience,
he had to admit he was grateful. If for nothing else than to be
given the opportunity to come over here to the land of nipples
and Foster's. He would forever be in Vic Duret's debt for this
small, incidental favor. He was an officer stripped of rank and
responsibility and weapons. He could no longer order one man
to kill another, nor could he legally do the killing himself. He
was through with the war and he just needed to bide his time
for another—what was it? Three months? No, two and a *half*.
The beer was making his brain heavy and slow to process. Another two and a half months and he'd be home free, back to soil
where, he'd already decided, he would resign his commission,
shed his uniform, and grow a goatee. Yes, a goatee would be

nice. Maybe just a soul patch if the hair didn't come in as thick and full as he hoped. Something professorial, something hip and with-it, something completely unrelated to what he'd been through over here, something far removed from the person who had once flame-broiled an innocent man to death.

Abe leaned back in the inner tube, spread his arms and legs, and let the wintergreen pool water lick his fingers and toes. He was alive, goddamnit, he was alive and he would stay that way for the next two and a half months, even if that meant coming to float in this protective womb of a pool every day, then that's what he would do. Jolly good.

He stared at the sky and marveled at how empty, how blank it was at that moment. Not a cloud, not a helicopter whisking someone to a combat support hospital, not even a stray bird.

He brought the Foster's to his lips and heard someone in the poolside crowd whistling at him, making the cartoon sound of a falling bomb, and he saluted with the beer can and called out, "Cheers, mate!"

The mortar had a mind of its own. It knew what it wanted. Flesh, human flesh. And if it couldn't have that, if it had to settle for the cobblestone of the street or the moist cushion of a farmer's field, then it would concentrate all its effort into sending fragments into as wide a circumference as possible, the hot shards of shrapnel finding their own incidental stoppages of human flesh, chewing their way through epidermis, muscle, vein, viscera, and organ. The mortar still preferred a direct hit, and if it could start at the crown of a skull and bore down through brain, spine, heart, bowel, and leg, and finish with heel, then it could die knowing it had just eaten the perfect Last Supper. This is what the mortar lived for and, come to think of it, died for. This is why it concentrated so much thought and effort into the parabolas of trajectory and so carefully calculated rate, speed, wind resistance, and curvature of the earth: all for the direct hit. Taking into consideration launch velocity, inclination angle, horizontal distance, and maximum altitude, to hit a target at range x and altitude y when fired from (0,0) and with initial velocity v the required angle(s) of launch θ are:

$$\theta = \tan^{-1}\left(\frac{v^2 \pm \sqrt{v^4 - g(gx^2 + 2yv^2)}}{gx}\right)$$

Precise calculation of variables is necessary when attempting direct hits.

The men who launched the mortar couldn't have cared less about parabolas or direct hits, it didn't matter one way or another to them if the mortar struck cobblestone or skull, as long as the end result brought maximum death and damage and bought them another day's headline. The men with their goat-meat breath and tongue-tangling supplications to Allah cared only about quickly setting up the tripod and firing tube from the back of a Toyota pickup truck in some quiet out-of-the-way neighborhood and launching with hasty aim. They cared only about firing blindly, then making a clean getaway, and if the end result was severed limbs in the marketplace, all the better, praise Allah. If they missed—and the mortar landed in a canal or a remote cow pasture—then, oh, well, there was always another day.

But the mortar cared. It cared where it hit, who it struck, how it spent its final moments of life before the death that brought wholesale death to others. It cared about the final target, whether it was rock, soil, water, or flesh. This is all the mortar thought about on the upward flight, the peak of the arc, and the down tilt of final descent. Sometimes, the very thought of opening its maw and gobbling a bellyful of human flesh filled it with such anticipation that it started to whistle a happy tune in its final moments, keening a kind of joy unknown to man.

No one saw it coming, they would all testify later. They *heard* it, yes, but never saw it. They only witnessed the aftermath: the red jetted spurt erupting from the center of the water—the dead center, you might say—as if the mortar had struck from below, pushing up from the bottom of the pool instead of falling from the sky. By the time the whistle registered on their brains and they realized what that awful sound portended—*oh, bloody fuck!*—there was no time to react, nothing to shout, only enough time to throw an arm across their eyes, as if *that* would protect them. And when they finally lowered their arms, all of them in their bikinis and trunks and Speedos-with-a-bulge still standing intact and realizing how lucky they were the mortar had struck dead center in the pool which, thanks to all those gallons of water, had cushioned them from the impact, they could only stare with slow-gathering shock and sadness at the watery smoky hole that had once been their pool. At that point, they were only thinking of how rotten their afternoons would be now that they no longer had a pool. What now? Sit in their trailers and slow roast to death with warm Foster's?

It was only when Glennice, reclining in tan-collecting bliss only moments before, sat up and started screaming that they looked over and saw the arm in her lap, the fingers still gripping the can of beer. It was only then that it hit them with a punch of nausea: that poor bloke Belmouth was gone. He'd taken a direct hit from the mortar while the rest of them had survived—drenched with the pink rain from the pool, yes, and suffering the unforgivable horror of a severed arm in one's lap—but alive nonetheless. *Alive!*

And just as quickly, with just as much certainty, Belmouth was gone, evaporated in the afternoon heat. It was almost too much for their minds to take in. Blink, he's here, blink, he's gone. Only a smoking, half-empty pool and an arm in a lap remained as evidence that their newest friend—*such a likable chap*—had ever walked the earth.

Someone suggested calling the British embassy but none of them moved. In the blistering Baghdad heat, they were all frozen as they stared at Glennice's lap.

Poor bloody bloke.

28

LUMLEY

Lieutenant Fledger, clad in full battle armor as if he'd already been prepared for the onslaught of grief his men were about to feel, burst through the door of the shower trailer and announced, "Men! He's dead!"

And so that's how they heard—three short, barked words. In the hiss and humidity of the water, Lumley and his men looked at Lieutenant Fledger, barely comprehending what he'd said. All they knew was that the company commander stood in their midst and they were naked.

The narrow trailer had been reconfigured with two rows of ten shower stalls and a long wooden bench running down the length of the trailer in the middle. The stalls had no curtains, so one was forced to keep his back turned to the room if one was modest; if not, if one was unabashedly proud of his manhood's length and girth, then the soap down was done in full view for all to see. Those in the opposite stalls and those waiting their turn on the bench had nowhere else to put their eyes—especially those on the bench who were, unfortunately, dick-level to their comrades.

Because there were no shower curtains, water streamed freely out onto the floor, where it swirled in a grayish mix of shampoos, soaps, and body washes—not to mention the clots of pubic hair, urine (courtesy of those who thought of the shower stall as a free standing toilet), and snot-oysters (courtesy of those who thought of the shower stall as their personal Kleenex). The wicked-looking lake of shower water and detritus forced those soldiers waiting their turn to keep their change of clothes stacked in precarious piles along the bench. At any given time, upon entering the shower trailer, you'd see half a dozen half-naked soldiers perched on the bench, feet tucked under them like birds, anxiously keeping a mound of clothes in check, constantly patting and restacking the trousers and T-shirts. Waiting for the next stall to open up was always a tense game of balance and shepherding clothes. Pity the soldier whose fresh-laundered underwear took a tumble off the bench into the foul water below. They all wore flip-flops (dubbed "shower shoes" by the military) and no one but *no one* went barefoot in here—they sure as shit weren't going to put their feet down in *that,* oh, *hell* no!

Long-handled squeegees were supplied in each shower trailer and a soldier, upon finishing his shower, was expected to do his part by pushing the water to the drain in the center of the trailer. The drain grates clogged easily and remained that way until the Twee maintenance crew from Thailand came at lunchtime to hand scoop the American filth into a plastic bag. And so sweeping with the squeegee had little effect on the water other than to create a system of ripples and waves that sloshed from one end of the trailer to the other.

When Lieutenant Fledger walked through the door and announced the bad news to those seventeen naked men of his,

Specialist Zeildorf was in the midst of pushing a tide of water toward the drain. Gray soup splashed over Fledger's boots and left a few dark curlies as it receded. Hardly the reception he, an officer in the United States Army, had been expecting. He lifted first one foot, then the other. This was like something out of a cartoon, but he—a reasonable officer in the United States Army—would choose to ignore it . . . for the time being. There were other pressing matters at hand. As a company commander of two months, he was untested in the task of delivering death notices to his men. Since Captain Shrinkle's departure, Bravo Company had gone through a charmed period of zero KIAs.

Before coming to the shower trailer, Fledger had looked through his West Point textbooks and his class notes but there was nothing to properly prepare him for such heartrending moments as this. He was a Polar explorer, all alone on this ice cap of grief.

He cleared his throat and tried again. "Men! Listen up! I've got some bad news and I think you need to sit down for what I'm about to tell you."

"I think we'll stand, if it's all the same to you, sir," said Brock Lumley from over his shoulder. He'd already had his back turned and his hands cupped over his crotch before Fledger finished speaking.

"What's going on?" Jacovich shouted over the static of his shower. "Who is that out there? I can't see a fucking thing!" Jacovich, shampoo in his eyes, blindly groped for a towel.

"It's okay, men. I know you're upset. But trust me, time will heal all your wounds."

"What the fuck's he saying?" Harris whispered to Snelling, but none too softly.

"Beats me," said Snelling from his crouch on the bench, wishing Harris would step back into his shower stall and take his hairy dick with him.

As the highest-ranking enlisted soldier in the shower trailer, Lumley spoke for the group. "Sir, I don't mean to be disrespectful, but as you can see, we're a little preoccupied right now. Is there something you needed?"

"Men, I don't know how to break it to you any other way. He's dead."

"Who's dead, sir?" asked Lumley, still hoping this crotch-cupping nightmare would end soon.

"Ah! Ah! My eyes, my eyes!" screamed Jacovich, still unable to find his towel.

"Captain Shrinkle," said Lieutenant Fledger, barely controlling the tremor in his voice. "Your former company commander." (As if they'd forgotten already, as if they could *ever* forget Shrinkle and his Bad Night in Adhamiya.) "He's dead. Gone. Obliterated, actually. A terrible, terrible attack at the Australian pool."

As if on cue, the hot water supply to the trailer ran out and twelve men started gasping and cursing at the shock of icy showers. "OhGodohGodohGod!" This was more like it, Lieutenant Fledger thought to himself. This was the reaction he'd been expecting.

Twelve men immediately started grabbing at the faucet handles, yanking them counterclockwise. "Holy shit!" "God-*damn!*" "Ah! Ah! Aiieee!" "My eyes! My fucking eyes are burning!"

"I know, men, I know. I was devastated by the news, too."

Lumley, his nuts shriveled by frigid water, knew he still had to speak for the group because this dingleberry standing in the doorway just wasn't getting it. "Sir? If you could just give us a moment?"

"Certainly, Sergeant Lumley."

"A private moment, sir—if you know what I mean?"

"Of course, of course. You all knew Captain Shrinkle longer than I—heck, I don't even know the man, only his legend—and there are undoubtedly some strong feelings running through this company right now. I'll be at HQ. You know where to find me when you need me." He started backing out of the trailer as his soldiers reached for their towels.

"Oh, and men?"

"Yes, sir?"

"I've asked the chaplain to address the company this afternoon at the sixteen-hundred hours formation. I'm sure whatever he has to say will bring comfort to the group as a whole."

The trailer door pulled shut behind him and Lumley held up his hand. "Shh! Wait for it. Let him get out of hearing distance." They waited five, six beats. Lumley lowered his hand. "Okay, go ahead."

Their voices came in an overlapping chatter.

"What in fuckin' hell?!"

"Who does he think we are? 'Overcome by grief,' my *ass*!"

"Did I hear him say 'Australian pool'? I thought that place was off-limits."

"Shrinkle gone? Wow. Never thought I'd see the day."

"Hey, does anybody have any Visine? My fucking eyes are still burning!"

And so they blustered and bluffed their hidden grief with hard, impervious comments as they tiptoed through the murky water and dressed themselves for another day's patrol. They talked tough but there were, among those seventeen men, at least three or four who were genuinely shocked and saddened by the sudden loss of Captain Abe Shrinkle. They kept their heads down and contributed little to the macho talk pinballing around the shower trailer. These were the soldiers of the company who had once shared a kind moment with the late Captain Shrinkle—perhaps he gave them a smile and a thumbs-up when they were feeling down; or maybe there had been something about the way he handed their mail to them, treating the letters from home with the respect they deserved; or maybe he'd once sat down next to them, uninvited, at the dining facility and agreed, yes, the meatloaf here *was* pretty damn good. Yes, these few men in the shower trailer would miss their old commander. He may have been a doofus who made a lot of bad decisions but it still sucked that something like this had to happen to him. No one deserved to be "obliterated." Not even the worst officer in the United States Army.

29

GOODING

From the Diary of Chance Gooding Jr.

> *1,996.*
>
> *For those of you marking your scorecards at home, that's the tally of Operation Iraqi Freedom as of right now, this instant, this nanosecond before the next bomb is detonated, before the next grubby thumb presses the remote-controlled cell phone trigger or the next zealous Muslim chanting "Allahu Akbar!" steers his car bomb toward a U.S. convoy and some unlucky soldier bites the bullet, dubiously privileged with his fifteen minutes of fame as Number 2,000.*
>
> *But that's four bodies down the road.*
>
> *For now, the score hovers at 1,996.*
>
> *Better mark it in pencil, though. And have an eraser handy.*
>
> *The media are drawn like jackals to a watering hole by the number 2,000. These sharp-fanged saliva-lipped*

members of the Fourth Estate claim it's a milestone—one to be marked with a top-of-the-fold story. They love the sensuous curve of the two and the plump satisfaction of those triple zeroes, lined up like perfect bullet holes— BAM! BAM! BAM!

2,000 is a number most Americans can hold in their minds and use it to remember the awful waste of this war, this overlong field trip to the desert where we got ourselves tangled in a briar patch and stuck to the tar baby of terrorism.

30

HARKLEROAD

The number 2,000 had plagued Eustace Harkleroad for weeks. Each day brought a fresh round of tick marks, inching closer and closer to that grand total score of two thousand American bodies killed since 2003—bullet-riddled, beheaded, and bomb-blown to smithereens.

Months ago—what now seemed like years—he had opened the latest issue of *USA Today* to read that fifty-eight American troops had died in Iraq in February, the fewest fatalities since fifty-four had died the previous July, according to the Pentagon. Translating the death count into a daily rate, February's losses were down sharply from January and less than half those in November. The February figures now raised the total U.S. death toll in the war to 1,490.

Even as he had folded the newspaper, bent his head, and tucked into his sausage and eggs that long-ago February morning, the body-o-meter was clicking over to 1,500, thanks to a suicide bomber who rammed his truck into a U.S. checkpoint twenty miles south of Salman Pak.

When Harkleroad got to his office that day in February, booted up his computer, and read the e-mail from G-3 Ops, he stared at that figure—the one standing at attention, the slouching five, the zeros with their empty, shot-out innards. It was such a nice, perfectly shaped number—deceptively pretty, falsely clean. Then he thought about trying to count 1,500 people (heck, let's not even make it people—say, Popsicle sticks, instead) and he realized how hard it would be to count, how exhausting to tally that volume of Popsicle sticks. He was sure he'd lose track halfway through—distracted by the image of sitting on the back porch with his mother, slurping a Fudgsicle evaporating in the Tennessee heat—and he'd have to start over from the beginning. One thousand, five hundred. That was nearly half the number of soldiers in the entire division.

Now the figure seemed quaint, already antiquated.

An additional 496 bodies—plus another three unlucky souls this morning—had been added to the pile since February and this was rapidly becoming a problem, a whopper of a problem that lay across his shoulders like an iron harness.

For the last two weeks, the Public Affairs Office had been besieged by phone calls from reporters, begging to be embedded with task force units that had suffered an unusually high body count. This, the reporters said, would give them a greater chance of being on the scene when number 2,000 meets his (or her) fate.

The reporters are deplorable, yes, but who can blame them? Harkleroad thought. *They are merely fueled by ratings, which, in turn, are stoked by the American public, who, in turn, self-righteously lament the media's obsession with this grim milestone.*

When, during a recent staff meeting, Lieutenant Colonel
Harkleroad proposed embedding the Associated Press with a particularly unlucky battalion so the reporter would be there to capture
firsthand the two thousandth instance of death in theater, the chief
of staff went bright as a fire engine. "Not only *no,* but *HELL no!* I'm
not embedding those goddamn jackals just for that reason. That's
just sick, plain and simple!" Other officers looked at Harkleroad
and softly *tsk-tsk*ed. "Jesus, get your head out of your ass, PAO."

"Yes, sir." Meekly.

"And while we're on the subject, I'm still waiting on that
Comprehensive Analysis Report on how our press releases have
been faring in the Iraqi media."

"Yes, sir. You'll have it today, sir." Harkleroad slumped farther into his seat as the chief of staff moved on to his next
target, G-4 Logistics. The beans-and-bullets clowns had just
misdirected a shipment of MREs, supposedly bound for FOB
Weathervane but which ended up at a remote village of camel
herders who, reports claimed, had found the dried beef patty
with mushroom sauce surprisingly tasty.

Later, on the phone with the reporters, Harkleroad's voice
was as gentle as could be. He tried to let them down easy.
"Look—first of all, there's no guarantee you'll be with a unit
that will have a casualty, nor do we even know if the two thousandth casualty will come from our task force. It's not like we
can produce a death on demand. Second, we're not particularly
fond of the idea of the media making a big deal out of Number
Two Thousand. What about Number 556 or 1,998? Have you
stopped to think about them? They were just as significant to
us, *they* had fellow soldiers who agonized over their deaths, *they*

had families back home who will forever feel the gaping loss of their loved one. And now you tell me you want to put this family—the loved ones of Number Two Thousand—through even more pain and trauma by making a big deal out of it in front of the cameras for all of America to watch? I understand what this will mean to your ratings and, yes, I know the producers back in New York are breathing down your neck, and, trust me, I have taken your request under serious advisement. I have done due diligence and run it all the way to the top of the chain here at headquarters. But I'm afraid the answer is most definitely *No*."

Okay, he hadn't said exactly all *that*. Speeches like that never came easy for Eustace, he was a man of stutter and fumble. What he'd actually said was, "Hi, um, this is Lieutenant Colonel Harkleroad over at Task Force Baghdad and I, uh, have a bit of bad news to report. Remember that, uh, embed request you sent over our way? We-ell . . . I ran it up the flagpole here at headquarters, and . . ." Et cetera, et cetera.

When Eustace *did* run it up the flagpole all the way to the Old Man trimming his toenails in his penthouse office overlooking the SMOG floor, the chief of staff accompanied Harkleroad and did his talking for him.

General Bright's hunched back was to them; he was intent on making sure the nail slivers made it to the garbage can. They fell like white rice kernels and plinked against the metal.

"Sir, PAO here is asking for permission to put the *New York Times* with 4-23, to let the reporter spend a week with the unit, twenty-four/seven, get to know the soldiers, touchy-feely shit like that."

"Hmm." *Snick plink snick plink snick plink.* "Well, isn't

that what we pay PAO for—to engage the media in telling the Army story?"

"Yes, sir, sure. But this one has a little different spin on it."

"Oh?"

"PAO here says the *New York Times* is primarily interested in 4-23 because of their mortality rate."

"And?"

"And they want to be there on the scene when Number Two Thousand's luck runs out." Colonel Belcher grinned lopsidedly at the CG's back. "Apparently, these dickwad reporters have got a crystal ball and they know, without a doubt, that our two thousandth KIA will come from 4-23."

"Is that so?" *Snick plink snick plink.* The CG raised his head and half-turned toward his two officers.

"That's what PAO here says they say. I haven't personally seen any evidence of said crystal ball."

"Well, I'd sure as shit like to get my hands on their crystal balls," the CG said gruffly, catching and sharing the chief's grin.

"Squeeze 'em till they break, right, sir?"

"Pulverize 'em into little itty-bitty shards."

The two men laughed as Harkleroad stood there, hands clasped behind his back, endlessly wringing his fingers.

"So, sir," the chief said, bringing his laughter to a sudden halt. "About this request from the *New York Fucking Times* . . ."

The CG resumed his toenail clipping and stared at a blank spot of air, furrowing his brow and giving the matter his deepest attention. Colonel Belcher looked sideways at Harkleroad and couldn't stop grinning.

. . . *snick snick snick SNICK* (a particularly troublesome cuticle) . . .

The CG looked up, as if surprised to see the two men still standing in his office.

"Hm. Yes," he said. "Well . . ."

Harkleroad's fingers turned acrobatic flips as he leaned forward on his toes. He did *not* want to go back to the *Times* with bad news one more time.

The commanding general looked at the chief of staff and said, "You tell PAO I think it's a brilliant idea, putting a reporter with 4-23."

Belcher choked on a string of saliva. "Sir?"

"Sure," Bright said, "let the reporter have at it—full access, talk to anyone he wants, show him all the maps, get him involved in the whole planning process, throw our arms wide open, and give him an honorary Classified clearance."

Now the chief was starting to grin big time. His lips were loose rubber across his face.

"If he says Victim Number Two Thousand is gonna come from 4-23, then I think we should respect his powers of psychic observation," the CG continued. "While we're at it, have Harkleroad here personally escort the *New York Times* when they go out on patrol. I've even got a special flak vest he can wear."

"You do, sir?" The chief was barely keeping it in at this point.

"Sure, I do. It's got a big ole red bull's-eye painted on the back—makes it easier for Johnny Terrorist to see when he's aiming at Number Two Thousand. This way, we can be assured the reporter can be right there on the spot when the blessed event happens."

"Brilliant, sir! Brilly-fucking-int!"

Harkleroad's face throbbed with shame.

The general's face rippled downward, all humor gone from his eyes and mouth. "Now get the fuck out of my office, both of you!"

The chief herded Harkleroad ahead of him out the door, turning once to give the Old Man an unanswered wink before leaving.

When Lieutenant Colonel Harkleroad learned the identity of Soldier Number Two Thousand, his guts torqued and blood predictably seeped from his nostrils. This was not how he'd expected it to play out, not in the least little dilly-dink bit. From Number 1990 onward, he'd been keeping track with tick marks on the dry-erase board mounted on the wall next to his desk.

Private Ralph J. Egbert, KIA, Salman Pak. *Tick.*

Sergeant First Class Israel Munoz, KIA, Sadr City. *Tick.*

Specialist James D. Apgar, KIA, Sadr City. *Tick.*

Private Ellis Wheeler Jr., KIA, Mosul. *Tick.*

Private First Class Andrew C. Mount, KIA, Mosul. *Tick.*

Second Lieutenant Erika Sheridan, KIA, Adhamiya. *Tick.*

Specialist Isaiah D. Washington, KIA, Ramadi. *Tick.*

Specialist Aaron L. Karst, KIA, Ramadi. *Tick.*

Private Jamie Rosen, KIA, Ramadi. *Tick.*

For days, he'd stared at that next blank spot, playing guessing games with gender, rank, location. If he had his druthers, who would he, Eustace L. Harkleroad, prefer the two thousandth American casualty to be? A Hispanic sergeant who leaves behind a wife and eight children in El Paso when his too-fast Humvee hits a bad bump in the road and flips into a canal? A milk-fed Midwestern boy, so quickly promoted to captain, barely five years out of West Point, who burns to a crisp in the back of an armored personnel carrier? A black female medic stabbed to death by one of her patients, a crazed Local National whose bandages she'd been so lovingly, tenderly, *heroically* changing as he lay on a cot in the Combat Support Hospital when, with a sudden crescendoing growl, he reared up, whipped out a box cutter, and sliced her jugular (investigation still pending)? He prayed to God that Number Two Thousand wouldn't be just another bland, run-of-the-mill death—blah-blah patrol struck an IED in the neighborhood of blah-blah, killing Private Joe Blah-Blah. When it finally came, Harkleroad hoped the last tick mark would have the punch of patriotism, a heart-tugging story that would bring a misty tear to the eye of even the most callous, hard-drinking reporter in the Associated Press. America deserved a grand, glorious death to mark this most ignoble of occasions (he could never use that phrase, of course, but he sure liked the sound of it).

"Where are you?" he asked the blank spot on his dry-erase board. "*Who* are you?"

When he finally got his answer, late in the evening after the evening BUB and just before he was about to leave the palace for his hooch, he was stunned into disbelief. And nosebleeds.

"Are you sure?" he asked the major from G-1 who had just set the fresh-printed file on his desk. After reading the contents—three pieces of paper: a SMOG report and the personnel file—he closed the folder and asked again, "Are we absolutely certain he's the one?"

"Certain to the nth degree," the major said wearily. He'd just come on shift, but this already looked like it would be a long one. "He's the only U.S. casualty in all of Iraq today. Hard to believe, I know, but we've been on the phone with Basra and Taji for the last two hours and they've confirmed they have no kills in their sector, which *never* happens but apparently it did today. Blue moons are on the rise."

"But—"

"I'm afraid there are no *buts,* sir. We've done the arithmetic five times and this—" he craned his neck to read the file label "—Captain Shrinkle is the one. He's Number Two Thousand."

Harkleroad read the SMOG report again and shook his head. "Are we absolutely certain of the circumstances? We've confirmed it was the Australian pool and there were no other Americans present?"

"Check, check, and triple check."

"And this affadavit from the Australian officer about the alleged false identity. You've confirmed with the British em—"

"Ad nauseam, sir." The major sighed. "Like I said, we've done the math, we've made the calls, we've eliminated any doubt. Now, if you've got nothing more for me, sir, I need to get back—"

"Yes, yes, go ahead." Harkleroad leaned back in his chair and clutched the file folder to his chest. When the major had gone, whisking out with a grating officiousness, Eustace started muttering, "No, no, no, *NO!*"

After another five minutes of rocking and moaning, stanching his nostrils, and failing to deny the undeniable, he got himself together and climbed the stairs to the second floor. He knew what he had to do, where he had to go, who he had to face.

The chief of staff was sitting behind his desk, clicking his mouse and scowling at the screen. The overhead fluorescent lights winked off his polished head like a warning beacon. He'd been called back to the palace before he'd had a chance to finish his dinner. It was Italian night at the dining facility and there was a dime-sized spot of spaghetti sauce on his cheek, dried and forgotten.

"PAO!" he barked, not even looking up from the report scrolling across his screen. Somehow, he'd sensed Harkleroad was standing there in his doorway. Perhaps snuffling back the still-prickling nosebleed had given him away; or maybe he just oozed fear like a pheromone. Eustace advanced a few feet inside the carpeted room.

"Sir?"

"You've seen this shit-doggle I'm looking at right now?"

"The casualty report on Captain Shrinkle, sir?"

"Of *course* the casualty report on Shrinkle—what the fuck else would I be doing back here in my office at this hour? What I want to know is, what are we going to do about it? What plan have you come up with for addressing this little problem of ours in the media? I'm assuming you've got a plan and the reason it's not sitting at the top of my in-box right now is only because you haven't had time to print it out and carry it up to me." He pulled his eyes away from the computer screen and looked at Harkleroad's empty hands.

"Of course, sir. That's exactly it." Harkleroad had no plan. His mind had been stunned into temporary stasis and he had no clue what he would do about Shrinkle, the disgraced American officer (murderer! towel jockey!) who had been masquerad-ing (deception!) as a British national (international complica-tions!) while carousing (drinking! bikinis! swimming!) with the

Australians (polynational complications!). It was a scandal on so many levels he couldn't even begin to count. Oh, good gravy! Even if Shrinkle had not been Number Two Thousand, this would still be a problem, most certainly a whopping migraine for the PAO staff. But now that he'd drawn the winning lottery number—

"So . . . ?"

"Sir?"

"The plan, PAO, the plan! In less than ten minutes, I'll have the Old Man on the horn wanting to know how we're going to approach this in the media and I've got to have at least one little fucking bone I can throw his way. What have you got for me? Sum it up now and you can turn in the written report later tonight." The lights blinked cruelly off the chief's dome.

Think, think, *think*. Like a dog emerging from a frigid lake, Harkleroad shook off the paralysis. A plan. A bone. A doorway out of this mess. "What if . . ."

The chief cocked his head, light bouncing all about the room. "Ye-es . . . ?"

Just as certainly, light trickled into Lieutenant Colonel Eustace Harkleroad's mind. "What if, sir, what if this KIA *wasn't* one of ours?"

"Come again?" Colonel Belcher shoved a pinkie into his ear and comically wriggled it. "I think my hearing's gone on the fritz."

If that was a personal dig, Harkleroad chose to ignore it. He brazenly picked up the personnel file from the chief's desk. "This may be the worst idea in the history of man, but what if the deceased person in this SMOG report wasn't Captain Shrinkle? What if somebody got it wrong? What if the deceased really was a British national named—" he flipped open the folder "—Richard Belmouth and we incorrectly identified him as our Captain Shrinkle?"

"PAO, it seems to me you're still suffering from cranial-anal dislodgement." He looked back at his computer screen. "The report I'm looking at here says it was Shrinkle—"

"According to whom, sir?" His voice was winding up to a higher pitch as the plan flooded every crevice of his brain. "According to the Australians at the pool? According to the ones who knew him as a Brit named Belmouth? According to a bunch of beer-swilling Aussies who never met our Captain Abe Shrinkle?" He was on a roll now. His mother would be so proud if she were standing here watching his mind unfolding like a flower. "I say we stick with the fiction that the deceased is an unfortunate British archaeologist. We'll figure out what to do with Captain Shrinkle later."

The chief's jaw had long ago dropped open and stayed there. "Ho-ly shit, PAO. When you come up with a whopper, you really deliver a big one, don't you?"

Harkleroad couldn't stop himself—he was rolling uphill at full speed now. "As for forensics, sir—well, from what I've been able to gather, nothing remained of *Richard Belmouth* other than an arm. No dental, no dog tags, not even any swim trunks. He was completely and totally vaporized by the mortar."

"That arm have any fingerprints?"

"Sir, if you look at the report, you'll see the fingers were burned down to nothing but nubs, every last one of them. You couldn't really call it an arm anymore, for all intents and purposes." He sniffed and swallowed a snot-gob of blood. "Lucky for us, if I do say so myself."

The chief sat back in his chair and jiggled his mouse a few times. "You're right . . . obliterated. Wiped off the face of the earth. Well, I'll be fucked . . ." The chief of staff sank into deep, troubled thought. Then he started to growl. "That's all well and good but the fact remains we still have Shrinkle to deal with. The gym will be calling before long, wanting to know why he's not there to hand out towels."

"Oh. Errr . . . ummm . . ." Harkleroad's brain clicked and whirred.

"We can call him whoever we want, but he'll still be a hot poker up our ass."

"That's true, sir, and to be honest . . ." His nose started to retingle. "To be honest, I haven't thought it all the way through. That—that aspect. But, um, I have faith a solution will eventually come along and we'll know how to handle Captain Shrinkle." He pressed forward valiantly. (Good gravy, his mother would be proud!) "The most important thing at the moment is denial of identification. If we say the body isn't ours, then it isn't, is it, sir?"

The chief was still growling but the growls were starting to die down to mere grunts. "Denial of identification, huh? I don't know if the Old Man will buy off on it."

"He doesn't have to, sir. In fact, he shouldn't. What he doesn't know won't hurt him, et cetera. In fact," here he allowed himself a small smile, "in fact, I'm starting to believe in Richard Belmouth myself, sir. I don't know why we're even bringing Captain Shrinkle into the conversation."

The chief glared at him. "Don't get cheeky, PAO."

"Yes, sir." Meekly, but still thumping with excitement. "Let me also respectfully remind you, sir, we're talking about Number

Two Thousand here. Do we really want the media to grab hold of this scandal-plagued officer who died in an equally horrific-but-scandalous manner and blow it all out of portion, like we know they will? If we don't deny this body was ours, then we'll be spinning until we're dizzy, sir. I suggest we wait for the next casualty to come along—hopefully, a more noble death, sir—and make that soldier America's two thousandth. Take the spotlight shine off Captain Shrinkle."

"Let me think about this." The chief swiveled around and looked out on the SMOG floor. Only the peak of his polished skull could be seen over the back of the chair. The seconds passed like metronome clicks. Harkleroad's heart skipped and tripped, caught itself, then came back thudding harder than before. It had been years since he'd put his mind to such compressed, tremendous exertion and now he was feeling a little faint. Plus, he had to pee.

At last, the chief swung back around, gave his PAO a significant look, and said, "You're right."

"I-I am, sir?" *Snuffle.*

"Yes, you are. One hundred percent Grade-A undeniably right."

"Thank you, sir."

"IT'S THE WORST IDEA IN THE HISTORY OF MAN!"

"Sir—?"

"Now get the fuck out of my office and don't let me see you again unless your fat fingers are holding a file folder containing a plan that doesn't include global scandal on an idiotic level. You come up here and your hands are empty, I'll chop 'em the fuck off." He opened his desk drawer and pulled out a Swiss Army penknife his father had given him on his fourteenth birthday—the blades now rusty and dull—as proof that he'd carry out his threat to Harkleroad.

"Sir, if I may—"

"ABOUT FACE . . . FORWARD, MARCH!"

Eustace did as ordered and promptly marched into the wall next to the chief's door. He recovered with a bounce and, cupping his hand over his nose, marched at a good clip down the marbled hallway. He left a trail of nose blood that a Twee contractor named Majid would mop up later that night, wondering what in Allah's name had taken place here in the former dictator's palace, what terrible violence had erupted amid the gold water fountains and taxidermied water buffalos to take the life of another man? Majid would cluck his tongue, worried not for the first time about the safety and sanity of his American protectors.

From: eustace.harkleroad@us.army.mil
To: eulalie1935@gmail.com
Subject: Dispatch from a War Zone, Day 291

Mother,

I've been missing you powerfully hard lately. (And Pap-Pap, too, of course.) Most nights I sit on my cot, mortars screaming overhead, the occasional AK-47 round pinging off the reinforced walls of my trailer, and I swear on all that's holy I can smell your sweet potato casserole baking in the oven all the way over here in Saddam's former kingdom. I don't mind telling you, it brings a tear to my eye—and a flood of saliva to my mouth.

Speaking of which, thank you a thousandfold for your latest care package and all those Moon Pies. I immediately put
them to good use. And thank the First Redemption ladies
for their little treats as well. I am already using their "Jesus
Saves" coasters and they look very nice underneath the
bottles of Gatorade.

Speaking of which, Gatorade has become my drink of choice
over here—especially the Glacier Freeze flavor, which just by
its very name does wonders for transporting me away from
this crushing heat. I often joke with my subordinates that if
I could carry around an IV drip bag full of Glacier Freeze, I
would. They all laugh appropriately. I've become something
of the comedian among my staff since coming over here. I
often catch them laughing at something I said when they
don't think I'm looking. It does my heart good to know I have
built that kind of rapport with my fellow staff officers.

I guess I owe you an explanation for not writing to you more
frequently as of late. The truth is, I'm so terribly, terribly
busy, dear Mother. Demands come at me from left, right,
north, and south. My schedule is filling up faster than a cop's
belly in a donut shop! This explains, in part, my lack of correspondence with you as of late. That and the fact we are being
shelled every other day. But NOT TO WORRY, Mother! I am
fine!

I have been spending far more time here at Headquarters
than I would have liked. You know me, I'd much rather be
out in the thick of things, bullets whizzing past my earlobes,

pulling my men through the hot zone with courage and fortitude. But alas, the CG demands I stay put here at the palace
where, as he says, my "services" are "vitally needed." It pains
me to surrender all I could be doing out on the battlefield for
another round of long, dry, boring, insufferable staff meetings. But, if the Old Man says it must be so, then I have no
choice other than to dutifully comply. I don't want to burden
you with too much in the way of fret and ulcers, Mother,
but rest assured I am performing up to the very limits of my
capabilities here in Baghdad. I long to be out on the streets,
pounding the pavement on patrol, but Duty calls and I must
answer by remaining at my desk for more hours than I'd like.
Fluorescent lights are my trial, cubicles are my tribulation.

Invariably, this means a good deal of staff meetings. Some
days, it feels like all we do is talk our way through this war. If
only words were bullets, we would have slaughtered the "hajji
bastards" (their words, not mine) a thousand times over. This
morning, for instance, we sat around the table—me literally at the CG's right hand—and talked for hours and hours
about the "Shrinkle Situation." Have I mentioned this particular gnat-in-a-sow's-ear before? If not, it's only because it's
been one of those Super-Secret HUSH-HUSH sticky wickets that should go no further than the front entrance of the
palace. Even now, my telling you about it is, I am guessing, a
breach of some international-level security classification. But
not to worry, Mother! I've been personally assured by a Major
Leipley over in G-6 that personal e-mails are NOT monitored
(not like the old days when they used to black out entire
sentences with Magic Markers and families on the receiving

end couldn't make heads or tails of what their soldiers were writing to them about). There is no Big Brother here at Headquarters, Major L. tells me. Even so, it would be best to delete this e-mail after reading it. If you have printed it out to read—as I know is your habit—then I suggest you tear it into tiny pieces and eat it. All in the name of National Security, Mother!

Back to Shrinkle: that's the name of a very unfortunate captain in one of our brigades, a poor fellow who happened to be in the wrong place at the wrong time. If I tell you that it was the aforementioned Australian pool, then I'm sure you can guess the magnitude of this tragedy. By dipping in the Aussie waters, Captain Shrinkle made this an Incident of Global Proportions.

And that is what we were arm wrestling about at today's staff meeting, which had been called by a very apoplectic commanding general. I was able to calm him down by reassuring him that word of the incident had not yet reached the media and that I had managed to contain any and all leaks. This calmed the CG down. He even clapped his hand on my shoulder (right there in front of everyone!), called me his hero, and compared me to the Hoover Dam in holding back all the waters of misinformation and gossip. I assured him this was one dam that was never going to crack.

The rest of the meeting proceeded apace for hours on end as we "cussed and discussed" the Shrinkle Incident. G-1 talked about their role in the whole situation, the poor major stumbling and bumbling through his apologies about initial misidentification (they thought our American KIA was a British National!!) and then trying to save himself by reading a three-page report on how they had immediately corrected and un-notified the British parents of a certain Richard Bel-mouth (a nice, doddering couple from Liverpool who had no idea their son was in a war zone) and how strategic guardrails were being put in place in G-1's daily operations to ensure this kind of thing would never happen again. G-1 even had a PowerPoint that charted what he called the New and Im-proved Personnel Notification Process. Snoozeville! Though I did my very best to stifle my yawns in front of the Old Man. A hero never yawns, after all.

After G-1, we went around the table and G-2, G-3, and G-5 all had their chance to chime in. If the poor Captain S. had not already been blown to bits, we would have talked him to death in that room.

I'm sure by now you're probably wondering what in the glory blazes this "Shrinkle Incident" is all about, aren't you, dear Mother? Well, as they say in the movies, I could tell you, but then I'd have to kill you.

—that was a joke, Mother. Ha ha ha! Of course, I would never DREAM of harming a tender hair on your beautiful head.

But seriously, I really am not at liberty to tell you all the details. Suffice it to say there was a man (Capt. S.) who

was fond of engaging in unauthorized activity (swimming)
at an off-limits location (the Australian pool), until one day
his nefarious habits caught up with him and he fell victim
to enemy action (ka-BOOM! ker-SPLAT!). The fallout has
been potentially disastrous but, as I told the Old Man in the
meeting today, I have managed to avoid and avert (that's my
new motto: Avoid and Avert) any mention of this in the press.
That's why you won't be reading or hearing about this particular black eye any time soon (or EVER, if I have my way).
Captain Shrinkle is being laid to rest in two days and so, too,
I hope, will the rumors surrounding his demise.

I'm sorry to be so obscure about this, Mother. Rest assured, I
will tell all when I return, cupping my hand and whispering in
your ear. Until then, please NOT A WORD of this to Jim Powers
at the *Murfreesboro Free Press* or the ladies at First Church of
Redemption. This is just our little globally proportionate secret.

Your ever-loving son,
Stacie

31

GOODING

From the Diary of Chance Gooding Jr.

When it happens, I'm in my hooch, lying on my bed in my underwear. I've fully recovered from the Great Blood-letting Incident of 2005 but in some respects I still feel drained. Lethargic, depressed, sparked out. We're so close to going home—the word "redeployment!" tolls like a bell, distant but clear—that the thought of it binds me with fear. I'm certain I won't make it to the end, but that the end will come for me instead.

Redeployment is like the slip of paper in a fortune cookie. What are the chances of "You are about to stumble into great wealth" happening? Slim to none. The chances of you walking out of the Snapdragon Chinese Restaurant and stumbling off the curb into oncoming traffic? Confucius say, "Chances are good."

These days, I'm trying not to think of Captain Shrinkle and his sad demise but it's impossible. He keeps coming

*back to me again and again. I only met the guy once, but
now all I can think about is him floating in that Qatar
pool on R&R. I want to go back in time, throw down my
book, jump in that pool, grab his hand, and pull him
out of there, out of Qatar, out of the war zone entirely. It
would be like a Medal of Honor heroism nobody knew
about. Saving one man's life from the death that waited
for him to step off the curb.*

But I didn't. I just sat there with Catch-22 *in my
hands, watching him float on the water, his hands fluttering at his sides, swimming toward his future.*

*So anyway, today I'm here in my hooch, partaking of
my daily half hour of reading before I go to breakfast, then
on to the fourteen-hour shift at the grist mill of Army Public Affairs. This time,* Don Quixote *is in my hands.*

*I'm in the midst of highlighting a passage with a
neon-yellow pen*—Fictional tales are better and more
enjoyable the nearer they approach the truth or the
semblance of the truth—*when it happens. The sky splits
with a scream and a bone-buzzing explosion shakes my
trailer. The cheap wood-grain paneling creaks and cracks
from the concussion and the sound is so loud and startling
it's like someone punched my heart.*

I toss Don Quixote *aside and sit up, completely uncertain what I should do. I'm in my underwear and slippers.
Should I get fully dressed in battle rattle, grab my M16,
and run outside to see what happened? Or should I just
throw on my T-shirt and shorts and poke my head out the
door to, as LTC Harkleroad is fond of saying, get "situ-
ational awareness"?*

I opt for the latter.

I look up and down the gravel lane running through our trailer city, fully expecting to see the headquarters building smoking from where a mortar punched through the roof. Several other half-dressed soldiers have also stepped out onto their porches, blinking in the early-morning light. We scan the sky for black smears of smoke. When we don't see anything, we look at each other, shrug, and go back into our rooms.

I pick up Cervantes and start reading again. Less than thirty seconds later, another sharp boom shakes Trailer City, and another one forty-five seconds after that.

Okay, that's it, I'm getting dressed and getting the hell out of the room—though if I think walking around outside, or even running to the office, is going to make me any less vulnerable to being hit by a rocket, then I'm as stupid as a man who enters a rainstorm without an umbrella.

I go to the chow hall, seeking safety in numbers and comfort in eggs and bacon.

When I get to work, the first thing I ask Specialist Carnicle is, "Just what the hell was that?"

"I know! Did you hear it, too?" She's all eyeballs and slack mouth. Apparently her cage was rattled, too. "I mean, Double-U, Tee, Eff, Sar'nt?"

"How could I not hear it, Carnicle? What was it? A mortar? A car bomb just outside the wire?"

Carnicle shakes her head. "They were chattering over SMOG a few minutes ago. They said it was a little wake-up barrage from our terrorist friends in Sadr City: Goooood Morning, FOB Triumph!"

"Jesus, they're getting bold."

"It's like they can see our Deployment Clock ticking down. Bastards are going whole hog before we leave."

"Any damage?" I ask.

"Yeah, I guess a mortar landed at the Fitness Center. Punched a hole clean through the roof." She makes a whistling sound that ends with a saliva-burred explosion in her mouth. "SMOG guys say no casualties. Unless you count the deaths of a treadmill and two exercise bikes. Which, come to think of it, is no great loss for the lard-asses around the palace here. They'll probably think it's a good thing. One more excuse for them not to exercise."

The fitness center? Isn't that where—? Ho-ly fuck! *My blood turns to ice. The fitness center, the place where Captain Shrinkle worked, was just bombed.*

So that's it. Fate being what it is, he would have been killed anyway, no matter how many times I pulled him out of that pool in my dreams. Death is relentless and unswerving.

Carnicle starts grabbing her things. "Can I go now? I wanna get to the chow hall before the terrorists turn it into a pile of smoking rubble."

"Sure, go ahead, Carnicle," I say, but I'm not paying attention to her anymore. I'm thinking about the way those booms rattled my teeth. I'm thinking about a swimming pool full of blood, bone, gore. I'm thinking about mortar trajectories and how thankful I am that hajji's numbers were off by .001, sparing me and the rest of Trailer City. I'm thinking about the minute hand on the Deployment Clock freezing at five till midnight, never to click forward again.

Then tonight, as I'm walking back to my hooch after work, I hear the war. I mean, really hear *it.*

Up ahead of me, somewhere just outside the wire, there's a crescendo-ing boom. It's a flower of sound opening its petals.

Five seconds later, a red tracer round shoots up in the air—a signal of some kind.

Then comes the gunfire. It's Our rifles and Their rifles talking back and forth. For nearly three minutes, there's a steady vomit of M4 and M240 gunfire: Brrrrappp! Tut-tut-tut-tut-tut! Brrrrappp! Brrrrappp! Chug-chug-chug-chug-chug-chug-chug-chug-chug! Tut-tut-tut-tut! Brrrrappp!

The war is Out There; but on nights like tonight, it sounds like it's In Here.

The longer I'm in Baghdad, the more I'm convinced I'll be leaving in a pine box.

In fact, the closer we get to redeployment, the faster the attacks seem to come—a horse increasing its gallop as it sees the finish line. It's as if Death has a quota that must be fulfilled before the Seventh Armored Division leaves Iraq. I don't know how the door kickers do it out there. Don't they feel Death's cold scythe grazing their shoulders every day?

I may be a mere Fobbit, but I feel it—that blade against my neck. Honestly, I don't know how much more of this I can take.

32

DURET

How much more were they expected to take? First, Jerry the XO who got his legs cut off at the knees, then those three (what were their names, dammit?) eating burgers at the food court when the mortar struck, then that unforgivable rash of suicides (two in First Brigade, one in Third, and then another in HQ Company), then Major Woody with the sore groin that had turned out to be a problem with his prostate that turned out to be cancer and he was whisked off to Walter Reed, then the staff sergeant (name? . . . again, it was a blur) in Second Brigade who'd taken a sniper bullet in the neck, and now *this*—the gruesome death of Abe Shrinkle, parts scattered everyfuckingwhere.

Lieutenant Colonel Vic Duret leaned over the toilet and puked again—this made three times since breakfast—and saw, with some small measure of relief, it had finally turned to bile. His stomach had nothing left to bring up. He flushed the toilet and, for a moment, stood watching his sour yellow anger swirl down and disappear.

He went to the sink and rinsed his mouth. There was no one else in the latrine, a small mercy of privacy. But, unbidden, the image and smell of what had been left of Shrinkle coming from the unzipped body bag—a solitary arm, rigor mortis fingers still clutching a can of beer—as the doc asked him, "Was he yours?" rushed back to Duret and he started gagging all over again. He spit one last bitter wad into the sink and willed himself to stop it, *just stop it*.

Ross was there again—his flaming body careening through the offices of Cantor Fitzgerald, his screams choking off into a harsh, staticky crackle—but Duret pushed his brother-in-law away as well, putting all his concentration on something, *anything* else—how his wife's nipple puckered beneath his tongue, for instance.

That's better. Focus on the Real World. Grab what scraps you can and call them your own.

Duret's wife was back there in Hinesville waiting for him and she was expecting him to get through this. She *demanded* he pull through in one piece. She didn't care about whether or not he brought all of his men home (though *he* cared, oh, yes, he cared), but he damned well better return to her none the worse for wear. She told him this in so many words on the phone every week and, like it was one of their marriage vows, he would do his best to please her. For his efforts, he would be rewarded with her breasts at the finish line.

That's how he thought of her: there at the end for him, whooping and smiling. Not how she really was—moody, glazed with Prozac, listless—but how he wanted her to be. How he *needed* her to be. His bouncy cheerleader.

Duret wiped his mouth again, steadied himself against the

sink, then picked up his helmet and left the latrine. He had a memorial service to lead.

Vic Duret sat in the front row, his battalion arrayed in solemn rows behind him. The sun oven-baked his bare head but, inside his uniform, forks of cooling sweat ran down his shoulder blades, through the forest of his chest hair, along his inner arm, into the canyon of his ass crack.

In front of them, under the speckled shade of camo netting, on a raised platform of nailed plywood and two-by-fours: Abe Shrinkle's combat boots—all that remained of the man (unless you count the care-package bounty of his trailer which, according to the Brigade Ops S-3 who'd spent the afternoon inventorying the contents, included thirty-five rolls of toilet paper, eighteen packages of teriyaki beef jerky, a complete set of Louis L'Amour westerns [unread], two Harlequin Silhouette romances [read], eleven tubes of ChapStick, a bag of dried prunes, two jigsaw puzzles [kittens, a snow-covered barn in Vermont], two dozen cans of unsalted peanuts ["enough to choke a fucking elephant"—S-3], a whoopee cushion, assorted crayon self-portraits from third graders at George Washington Elementary in Des Moines, Laffy Taffy, Altoids, Certs, Starbursts, Sprees, fifty-three bars of individually wrapped soap from a Holiday Inn, an equal number bottles of shampoo, six toothbrushes, two tins of boot polish, and a series of letters from a Mrs. Norma Tingledecker ["contents of which were being analyzed by DIV G-2"—S-3]).

But they were here to mourn Abe Shrinkle, not praise the contents of his trailer. The man and his boots deserved a few words in his honor—even if he *had* come close to ruining the brigade's legacy with his clownish command and general idiocy.

Duret shook his head. No, he'd vowed not to go there. Nitwit or no nitwit, Shrinkle was still an officer in the U.S. Army—*had* been an officer until Duret had demoted him to Towel Wrangler—and he deserved the standard Army farewell due to all those who lost their lives over here in battle.

But what to say, what to say?

Duret thought back to his regular Barbecue Mondays at Fort Stewart and the staff officers and company commanders who stood around his backyard, sweaty PBRs in one hand, waving away grill smoke with the other. Had Shrinkle been there with them? Duret had thought so, but now he couldn't be sure. His least-trusted company commander had a way of melting into the background, rarely contributing anything to conversations about the Falcons or the Braves. Not that there was much to say about anything. These Monday night get-togethers were an attempt on Duret's part to "bond" with his officers—something his West Point textbooks had once suggested—but when they were all there in the backyard swatting smoke and staring at the burned patches of lawn, what did they have to talk about? Work? Training schedules? Mutual acquaintances they'd heard were killed near Bagram? Duret had kept himself busy rotating the spitting brats and burgers, letting his men fend for themselves in awkward knots of twos and threes around the lawn. He closed his eyes and pictured the backyard but he'd be damned if he could see Shrinkle there nervously sipping a beer.

Under the sun dapple of the camo net, the chaplain was winding up his Scripture verse ("though our outward man perish, yet the inward man is renewed day by day") and throwing in a Bach reference ("sheep may now safely graze in Captain Shrinkle's pasture") then turning it over to Colonel Quinner who took the podium with an electric squeal from the microphone and started in on a too-long sermonette of his own ("At times like this, I'm reminded of what the great war journalist Ernie Pyle once wrote on the occasion of the death of a certain Captain Waskow: 'He carried in him a sincerity and gentleness that made people want to be guided by him'"), which had nothing to do with Abe Shrinkle.

Soon, it would be Duret's turn to step up and face the rows of his soldiers. What he would say about the dead officer (*dead meat*) still remained a mystery. He'd spent the last two days agonizing over the eulogy (in between parlaying with an al-Dora sheikh and monitoring an especially tense situation in New Baghdad), the words somersaulting in his head. He eventually pulled a few choice clichés out of his ass for this memorial service. He'd gone around all day scribbling a line or two at a time in his notebook, trying to come up with the best way to describe Shrinkle that didn't involve the words "reckless," "lily-livered," or "wishy-washy." What could he possibly say about incompetence that didn't sound too harsh at a funeral? What were the good, decent qualities of Abe Shrinkle? What was the best that could be said of a man who was known more for his inaction and indecision than he was for unflinching leadership? How do you analyze the content of a man's character by the way he invisibly sips his beer?

Maybe he'd start by talking about Abe's care packages.

Quinner wrapped up with a Thought for the Day ("*Gather ye rosebuds while ye may*") then sat down. There was a prolonged silence as they all stared at the boots. The rows of soldiers rustled. Someone farted softly and off-key.

With a start, Duret brought himself out of his reverie, shook off the torpor of heat and lack of sleep, then rose and stepped to the front. He looked at the blurry rows of beige uniforms, the red pulsing faces, the winking sheen of sweat-dewed buzz cuts. They were waiting for him to open his mouth and get this over with so they could all return to their hooches, their motor pools, their dining facilities. Duret clenched his jaw. *Say something, say anything.* Jungle drums and boot stomps and falling mortars pounded in his head.

He swallowed bile, then began: "Abraham Lincoln Shrinkle was born on July 3, 1979, to . . ."

33

HARKLEROAD

From: eustace.harkleroad@us.army.mil
To: eulalie1935@gmail.com
Subject: Dispatch from a War Zone, Day 294

Mother,

Brace yourself. What I am about to tell you will cause you no end of consternation and palpitations. This news will undoubtedly bring you to your knees in despair, wailing and begging God to shed mercy on Eustace L. Harkleroad, your one and only son.

This will, in fact, probably be worse than the time you burst into my bedroom thirty-five years ago to discover me touching myself in inappropriate ways (as I beclaimed at the time and still do today, it was a one-time-only weakness— I was unable to resist the charms and attractions of Ms. Raquel Welch in that month's *Playboy*—so please give it a rest, Mother!).

Yes, it's worse than that. Worse even than the time I voted for Jimmy Carter.

It gives me no pleasure to deliver this news and I don't know quite how to do it, so I will just plunge in feet-first.

I have been fired. Let go, down-sized, stripped of my rank, pilloried, lashed to the mast, whipped, and thrown overboard.

Are you still there, Mother? I do hope Pap-Pap was taking a break from pruning the magnolias and was present when you clicked open this e-mail and that he was quick with the smelling salts. I know how you get in moments like this, Mother.

Believe me, I would much rather have told you this in person, looking you straight in the eye, catching you when you fainted, etc. But circumstances prevent me from doing so. No, Mother, I have *not* been clapped in leg irons and thrown into Abu Ghraib! (Though, truth be told, that would probably be preferable to what I'm now going through.) By "circumstances," I mean I am about to be embroiled in an international incident and the news media will soon plaster my name and face all over the airwaves, slandering me at every turn, smearing the good reputation of Eulalie Harkleroad's only son. Out of courtesy, I wanted to give you advance warning of the coming storm. It is a *hurricane*, dear Mother. A hurricane of global proportions that could very well leave the Army in shambles. Though I am only peripherally involved, I have no doubt "Eustace Harkleroad" will soon be dripping with scorn from Tom Brokaw's lips and it will not sound pleasant to your ears, dear lady.

What, you ask, has brought about this calamity to the Harkleroad dynasty?

Unfortunately, I am not at liberty to fully discuss the details at this time. Suffice it to say that whatever you hear about me has only about a teaspoon of truth to it. I have been caught in a net that's been cast wide here at Headquarters. There are forces at work against me even as I type this. Men walk the very halls of this palace intent on doing me no good, thinking up ways to slander my name and crucify me on the cross called Scapegoat.

A man—a certain rogue Captain S. whom I've mentioned before—a lousy leader of men, a ne'er-do-well who done wrong—was the catalyst for an international scandal and I, for some reason, have gotten myself tangled in the bear trap. Even now, I can feel the jaws biting my ankles and, try as I might, I just cannot shake myself loose.

All will be revealed in good time, Mother. But for now, rest assured I am doing all right. In fact, things have actually gotten a little better in the short time I have been stripped of rank and responsibility. For one thing, I have a lot more time to spend sitting in my trailer, catching up on all those Find-a-Word books you sent, as well as taking leisurely strolls through the Forward Operating Base, feeding the geese, and generally getting a new lease on life.

I am down, but I am not out. Not just yet.

As such, if you could see fit to send a case of Moon Pies to me as soon as you can, I am sure that would go a long way in easing my distress.

I remain your ever-loving son,
Stacie

Harkleroad's finger hovered over the SEND button as he hesitated over this particular e-mail. Did he dare send such a whopping fabrication to his mother, only to possibly bring on conniptions of such magnitude that they could eventually lead to her actual demise? Was it not completely un-Christian of him to put her through such agony?

Yes, of course it was.

His finger curled back away from the keyboard and he set his hand on the desk, staring at the lies he'd just typed.

Because the truth was, he had *not* been pilloried, he had *not* been stripped of rank and responsibility. Not even the slightest clank of leg irons reached his one good ear. He was still Lieutenant Colonel Eustace L. Harkleroad, Seventh Armored Division Public Affairs Officer, leader of men and dictator of media relations.

The truth was, he was still standing on the periphery of the scandal that was sure to break over his head at any given minute. Though a week had passed, the news media had not yet sniffed the wind and gotten a whiff of the stink issuing from the Australian pool. Harkleroad was still in reprieve mode.

But not for long.

There were rumors whispering through the marbled halls of the palace. Even now, he could hear the bloodhounds baying and the wolves scratching at his door. Soon, he had no doubt, they would burst in—tar bucket in one hand, sack of feathers in the other—and his career would be over. It was only a matter of hours. Maybe minutes. He would have to—

At his office door, a cough.

Harkleroad looked up and saw the chief of staff standing there, hands on hips, laser eyes boring through the air in his direction.

"P. A. O." The chief said it just like that—turning three letters into three curse words. "What are we going to do, PAO?"

"Sir?" Harkleroad snuck a glance at the unsent e-mail on his computer screen. A trickle of tears stole into the space behind his sinuses as he thought of his mother crumpling to the floor.

"What. The fuck. Are we. Going. To do."

"With Captain Shrinkle, sir?"

"No, with Fred Flintstone screwing Betty Rubble. Of goddamn course with Captain Shrinkle!" Colonel Belcher's cheeks billowed and he did not look well, not well at all. "This is a shit sandwich someone is going to eat, and the command group has unanimously decided that someone will be you, PAO."

Harkleroad gulped. "Well, sir, uh, for one thing, I have my staff working on a series of press releases focusing on plausible deniability."

"I don't give a gnat's fart about your little press releases. They're the least of our concerns right now. Small potatoes next to the *New York Fucking Times*. THAT'S what I'm talking about, Harkleroad. What do you plan to do with them? THAT'S what we want to know."

"Sir?"

The chief's mouth dropped open. "Don't tell me you don't know we've had a reporter from the *Times* calling us every fifteen minutes for the past hour, asking all sorts of questions about rumors they've heard concerning an American officer and pool parties and sex orgies here on FOB Triumph. Do NOT sit there and tell me you haven't already started to take counteraction on this."

"Sex orgies, sir?" It issued from Harkleroad's lips like the aforementioned gnat's fart.

The chief clapped a hand to his forehead. "Oh, good *Lord*! Are you even in touch with your own staff, Harkleroad? Have they not been feeding you intel on this for the past hour?"

Now Harkleroad could see Staff Sergeant Gooding standing unseen behind Colonel Belcher's sweat-gleamed head. He'd slipped quietly into view and was gesturing wildly for Harkleroad's attention. When he got it—Harkleroad's glance flicking over the chief's left shoulder—Gooding pantomimed cocking a revolver, putting it to his head, then pulling the trigger. Then he mouthed something Harkleroad couldn't quite make out—possibly, "I just came on shift and found out about it this very minute, but not in time to stop the chief of staff from coming over here and reaming you a new butt hole." Gooding shrugged and softly retreated to his cubicle.

"Well, PAO?"

Harkleroad coughed. "Sir, I, uh . . . I *am* on top of it. You just threw me for a momentary loop, that's all. The *New York Times*. Yes, yes, I'm taking care of them even as we speak. I have my staff on top of it like white on rice—" he prayed to God that Staff Sergeant Gooding had the good sense to be sitting at his desk, at least *pantomiming* a telephone call and the composition of a release "—and, and, I'll, uh . . . have something to you within the hour."

"You'd better, PAO. You'd better." Belcher took two steps into Harkleroad's office, leaned forward, then growled. "Because if you don't, the Old Man will be shitting bricks sideways tonight."

"Roger that, sir. No worries, no worries. I'm all over this one. In fact," Harkleroad said, taking it one step further, "I've already given this whole mess it's own special name."

"Say what?" The chief's eyebrows crossed like swords.

"I don't know what the CG will think of this, but in order to stay one step ahead of the press, I'm christening it—" his mind whirred and clicked "—Operation Veiled Mongoose."

"*What?!*"

"I'm—I'm still working on it, sir. If the CG doesn't like that, how does 'Stealth Rabbit' sound?"

The chief choked and sputtered and most likely would have taken another three steps forward, planted his knuckles on Harkleroad's desk, and given him a what-for if a junior G-3 officer, a weaselly captain with florid patches of acne down one side of his throat, hadn't entered the office, cupped his hand to the chief's ear, and delivered urgent news about another power plant sabotaged by Sunnis in Sadr City. The chief's attention was diverted and Harkleroad was spared. Colonel Belcher and the acne-riddled captain turned on their heels in unison and left the office, the chief tossing over his shoulder, "Shit sandwich, PAO! Shit sandwich!"

When they'd gone, Harkleroad's bowels went all loose and watery and he seriously thought about punching the SEND button on that e-mail to his mother, but decided to hold off for at least another hour. Right now, he needed to perform damage control with Staff Sergeant Gooding. Dead Soldier Number Two Thousand had become a monkey on his back, an albatross around his neck, a squirrel up his ass.

Thirty-three minutes later, Eustace Harkleroad stood in the middle of the Public Affairs cubicle, holding the third draft of a press release, which—he hoped—dexterously glossed over the events of the preceding week. Sweat sprang from his scalp and the meat of his index finger stung with a paper cut from when he'd grabbed the release too quickly off the printer. Overhead, the air-conditioning rattled and hummed but did nothing to cool his overheating body.

Staff Sergeant Gooding watched him. Major Filipovich watched him. From her porch swing in Tennessee, his mother watched him.

With this one thin sheet of paper as his sole defense, Harkleroad stood at the center of a growing inquisition.

The chief was back and—arms crossed, eyebrows raised—he was waiting for an answer. Had he come up with anything better than "Stealth Rabbit," or whatever the fuck it was? And what about the *New York Times*? Had Harkleroad thrown them a bone, as ordered? Well, PAO? What about it?

Harkleroad's throat had long since seized up, choking off the breathy croak of an answer.

The air-conditioning wheezed and banged. Outside, the war boomed and whistled with a rising fury.

Inside the palace, officers, NCOs, and privates from other staff sections popped their heads up and down over the cubicles to stare at Harkleroad, looking like faces bobbing on a gray ocean.

And now—*Oh, my gravy!*—here came the commanding general! He *never* ventured down here to Cubicle Land. Eustace Harkleroad knew this could only portend the beginning of the end. The CG threaded his way through the cubicles, his jaw chomping on something unseen—gum? a cigar? Harkleroad's liver, which the CG himself was about to eviscerate? The CG was growling. That, too, was not a good sign.

The chief still stood there, arms crossed, skull gleaming, eyes blazing bright, burning lasers in Harkleroad's direction.

What would it be? Stealth Rabbit? Burping Walrus? Whisper Snake? This scandalous mess needed a label, a name to make it all sound hunky-dory. The CG would expect an answer in exactly nine seconds and Harkleroad had no idea what it would be. The light winked off the chief's skull as he, too, turned to watch General Bright storm through the maze of cubicles, bound like a missile straight for Harkleroad.

At Harkleroad's elbow, the printer belched Significant Activity reports, none of them sounding good. No, not good at all.

Staff Sergeant Gooding pointed at the paper trembling between Harkleroad's fingers. "Sir? Are we good to go? Can I send it to the media?"

"I—" Harkleroad whispered, "I—it's—"

The telephone rang again. Gooding reached over, picked up the receiver, and listened for several seconds, then said, "Hold on just one moment, please." He looked at Harkleroad with eyes beat brown with fatigue. "It's them again, sir. The *Times*."

Something slithered loose from Harkleroad's bowels and squished into his underwear.

Overhead, the voice of SMOG talked to him, repeating the same thing over and over, but Eustace couldn't make it out, it was all vowels and those vowels echoed in round circles throughout Saddam's marbled palace until they collected, gathered in a swirl, and rose in one tornado of sound that funneled into his ear, his good ear. It was nonsense to him, the nonsense of the war, now scattering debris inside his head. It went on, and on, and on . . .

As anxiety funneled its way to Harkleroad—the CG, the chief, the soldiers patrolling the streets, the no-good so-and-sos at the *New York Tiddleywink Times,* and, who knows, maybe even armies of once-defeated terrorists rising from the dead, all converging on him like ants swarming a lump of sugar—he felt himself shrink from a decision. All these things tussled in his mind, along with the worry of displeasing his mother. If he said anything—"Yes," "No," or "Maybe"—it could prove to be the wrong thing, and *then* how would Eulalie Harkleroad hold up her head at Wednesday Night Bible Study?

Staff Sergeant Gooding's hand was cupped over the receiver. "Sir? What should we say?"

Harkleroad struggled to shake off his anxiety. "Tell them . . ." He faltered, not for the first or the last time, at a loss for words. "Tell them . . ."

In the back of his nose, he felt the first prickling tingle of descending blood.

34

GOODING

Tell them what, sir? Tell them we're all doomed? Tell them we've reached the end of the symphony and all that remains is the timpani roll and the cymbal crash? Tell them no matter how many words we put on pieces of paper, it's all useless in the end because those press releases just wind up as some editor's paper basketball arcing through the air into a wastebasket in a newsroom somewhere in South Dakota? Tell them that?

Chance Gooding Jr. felt part of himself break away, like a chunk of glacier calving, a slow-motion slip and slide into arctic waters. Something inside fled, never to return. He was in the war, but he was not of the war.

In his hand, he could feel the buzz of voices on the other end of the phone connection. They came through the holes of the receiver like ants and started biting his skin.

His skull swelled with blood, a gnat cloud of stars swept across his vision, and his head snapped free to rise like a balloon. He bobbed against the ceiling over his desk and watched it all unspool across Cubicle Land:

The reams of Significant Activity reports,
self-replenished every hour.
The impatient cursor blinking on his computer screen, waiting
for the approval of the press release.
The tip of Harkleroad's nose, the nervous blood that would soon
grow to a red mustache on his upper lip.
The CG threading his way through the cubicles, a missile aimed
at the trembling target: P-A-Fucking-O.
The clack and clatter rising from a hundred
keyboards in the palace.
The voice of SMOG reeling off another casualty:
arm broken, foot missing.
Someone across the room whooping at a
computer solitaire victory.
Someone else brewing a cappuccino with a boiling hiss.
And, outside the palace on the other side of the FOB, Gooding could see an American sergeant at an M16 firing range
teaching an Iraqi sergeant—for the twenty-eighth time—about
breath control and trigger squeeze. The nod of the Iraqi, the
raise of the weapon, the jerk of the
trigger, and the wild shot that went high and brought
down a goose that, until that moment, had been
enjoying a peaceful migration south. And farther
beyond the protective ring of security around the American
base, the scream of a Local National being tortured by Sunni
interrogators. The cold, precise snip of pruning shears remov-
ing a set of toes one at a time. The laughter, the scream, the
"*Allahu Akbar!*" And farthest away of all,
the intangible thud of a mortar striking the earth
followed by the mewl of sirens.

Gooding's head floated back down, returning to his neck with a crisp snap. He blinked and he was himself again.

That is why he can be so certain of what happened next. For the first time since entering this combat zone, he was himself and he knew exactly what he was doing.

He hung up the phone with a loud *clunk,* cutting off the *New York Times* in mid-antcrawl. His breath coming fast and hard, he logged off his computer, rose from his desk, and announced in a trumpet-clear voice to the cubicles at large: "I've had enough."

Then, before he could change his mind, Chance Gooding Jr. sprinted from the Seventh Armored Division Headquarters. As he exited the palace, vaulting down the marble steps two at a time, he left behind his M16, his battle gear, a slack-jawed Harkleroad, and a still-growling commanding general.

He shot past the guards at the checkpoint, past the rows of trailer hooches, past the shores of Saddam's Z Lake, past the fitness center with the new hole punched in its roof, past the Australian pool, past the motor pool, the dining facility, the chapel, the What-the-Cluck Chicken Shack, and the phone center with its spring-slap door—past the whole fucking lot of it, this temporary, soon-to-be-abandoned-and-razed American city called FOB Triumph.

He ran without cease. His legs were hot iron bands and his lungs were breath-harshed sacs near collapse, but still he ran.

It was only when he was within sight of the Main Gate, the dark mystery of Baghdad lurking just beyond the bristle of concertina wire, that Chance Gooding realized he had no helmet, no flak vest, no weapon. He hesitated for a second but then tucked his bare head to his chest and continued to sprint toward the guards at the checkpoint who were even now bringing up their rifles and shouting for him to "Stop!"

Somewhere to the north, a mortar shrieked across the sky, coming closer, ever closer.

ACKNOWLEDGMENTS

My thanks to:

- Dan Wickett,who posted some of my journal entries from Iraq to his Emerging Writers Network blog in early 2005. The result was an outpouring of encouragement and care packages full of *not* baby wipes or foot powder, but the finest kind of surprise a soldier like me could have found after he ripped away the packing tape: books. The EWN members kept me well-supplied with enough reading material for five deployments. Thank God it never came to that.

- Nat Sobel, agent extraordinaire, who read Dan's EWN blog and tracked me down while I was still in Iraq wondering what to do with all the notebooks full of journal entries. Nat changed my life when he wrote: "I've come to believe that only in fiction will this insane war finally reach an American reading public." *Fobbit* had its true birth in that e-mail. Thank you Nat for your unswerving faith in me for the next seven years.

- Norman Mailer, Joseph Heller, Richard Hooker, Tim O'Brien, and Karl Marlantes, for paving the road and lighting the streetlamps.

- The men and women of the 3rd Infantry Division with whom I served and who may find bits and pieces of themselves strewn throughout the novel like confetti.
- Early readers Aaron Gwyn, Kerri Arsenault, and Thom Mills who all saved me from embarrassing myself on more than one occasion. Any mistakes I've made writing passive sentences or loading weapons with the wrong ammo are entirely mine, not theirs.
- Peter Blackstock, Morgan Entrekin, and the entire Grove/Atlantic family, for taking me in and making me feel less like a fobbit and more like a literary warrior.
- Deighton, Schuyler, and Kylie who are the smartest, most resilient, and bravest brats I've ever known. During their most malleable years, they endured six upheavals, six moves to a new Army post, six traumatic interruptions in stability (again, for the hundredth time, I apologize about the gerbils who didn't survive the trip from Fairbanks to El Paso). They are better than the best children I could have ever hoped for.
- Jean, but especially for three moments: August 1983 when she turned to me and said, "You're a better writer than you are an actor;" December 18, 2005, when she stood at the end of a long walk across a Fort Stewart parade field and her arms and lips said "Welcome Home;" and December 2, 2010, when she turned to me in the parking lot after the first public reading of *Fobbit* at the University of Montana Western and, tears in her eyes, said, "Wow. Just *wow*." She is better than the best wife I could ever dream of having.